DESTINED TO THE LYCAN

The Shadow Realms

REGINE ABEL

COVER DESIGN BY
Regine Abel

ILLUSTRATIONS BY
Tommy
Atenebris
Niklas Cloister
Vvevelur
Lau_Isa_Sen
Hojolabor
Pleko

Copyright © 2025

CONTENTS

DESTINED TO THE LYCAN

She trusts him with her life.

Terminally ill, and with no possible medical or magical cure in sight, Amara turns in desperation to the Weaver. To her dismay, the solution she offers sends Amara on a mission even deadlier than the illness slowly killing her. She enlists Remus, the only Lycan guide who consents to take her on this perilous journey. Although afflicted by his own curse, Remus is strong, fearless, and the fiercest protector Amara could have hoped for. The gentle soul behind his intimidating exterior touches her deeply and gives her an even greater reason to want to live.

He would gladly die to save her.

Cursed from birth and treated as a pariah by his pack, Remus is resigned to live as a lone wolf. When Amara comes seeking aid, his joy at realizing that she's his Twin Flame is quickly crushed. Amara is dying and the only cure is pure insanity. Against all logic, Remus pledges to save the sweet and courageous female who looks at him like a worthy male, not a feral beast to be banished.

After a lifetime of misery, Remus will fight the Gods themselves to protect the one good thing Fate has ever given him... or die trying.

DEDICATION

To those who never give up, no matter how many curve balls life throws their way. Even when the deck is stacked against you, even when you seem to constantly weather one storm after another, remember that the sun always eventually shines. And when it inevitably does, its light will shine all the brighter for you who have fought your way out of darkness.

To those who show empathy for its own sake, not for praises, not for profit, and not in exchange for some kind of benefit. The kindness you show today will be repaid to you often in unexpected ways and at the time you need it the most.

To those who choose not to be monsters, especially when it's the path of least resistance.

CHAPTER 1
AMARA

The soothing sound of the bells dangling overhead resonated through Ronika's shop as I pushed the door open. It served as both an apothecary and medical clinic. Before moving to Willow Grove, I heard wonders about the rather average hedge witch who suddenly acquired tremendous powers and became the most renowned healer in the region. That she was also the only known person to have won a battle against the infamous necromancer Cornelius further increased the mystique surrounding her.

After the foul male's demise a few months ago, many wondered if she had a hand in it. But the type of dark magic used to trap him in an endless torment couldn't have come from her. Only a demigod—or maybe even one of the Ancients themselves —gave him that well-deserved comeuppance for all the pain and harm he inflicted upon others for generations.

Ronika waved me in from behind the counter where she was filling some small jars with a variety of healing herbs. The smile that lit up her beautiful face warmed me from the inside out. From the first time I met her, I remembered thinking that she could be an angel walking among mortals. Although I knew better, there was no question that something happened when she gained that sudden wave of greater power, and that she was now more than a standard human.

There was nothing odd about it, to the extent that humans increasingly embraced arcane practices. The question always revolved around whether they dabbled in the light or dark side. Ronika radiated light and compassion.

I returned her smile, inhaling deeply the pleasant fragrance that always swirled around the front half of the shop. It was light and floral, with a hint of spice and sweetness. Above all, it stirred an instant sense of peace and well-being. Considering the back of the store had a consultation and healing room, it only made sense that she would use the perfect blend of healing runes and incense to set the appropriate atmosphere for her patients and clients.

"Hello, Amara! Do come in," Ronika said warmly while flicking a strand of her long hair over her shoulder.

It boasted an unusual color, a stunning midnight blue which gradually turned into a lighter purple towards the tips. It looked beautiful against her lightly tanned skin, a pale shade of brown. Where I loved to dress in the bright colors of my Beninese heritage—in stark contrast to the majority of the residents of Willow Grove—Ronika usually wore muted shades, in this instance a forest green dress.

She extended her hands towards me. "I see you're quite burdened. What goodies do you have for me today?"

I closed the distance between us, my medium heels clicking on the dark hardwood floors of the shop.

"It's a brand-new set of twenty candles created with you specifically in mind," I replied enthusiastically as I handed the basket to her.

"Me?" Ronika echoed, her eyebrows raised with curiosity as she peered into the basket.

I nodded. "Mmhmm. They're made with soy wax and Caladrius feathers."

Ronika's jaw dropped, and excitement lit up her beautiful face. She waved a hand above one of the candles, and a powerful magic swirled around her. I couldn't help the surge of envy that coursed through me. Although born from a long line of talented Mambos—Vodou priestesses—my mother made sure not to allow me to develop my powers. Tragic events made her turn her back on what had previously been a heritage my family took great pride in.

"That's fantastic! You truly are the best in your field!" Ronika exclaimed. "Do you know how long I've been looking for someone to be able to harness the healing powers of the Caladrius into arcane paraphernalia? Even without lighting it, I can feel its potency. It will do wonders when treating my patients. But I can see that it would also do a lot of good to the common folk by simply using it at home. You should sell them in your own store."

I smiled and nodded. "I intend to. But as you are my favorite and most valued customer, I wanted to bring them to you first."

Her face melted in an affectionate expression that once again moved me deeply. She was barely ten years older than I was, and yet the way she looked at me reminded me of my mother. Not for the first time, I wished she would have followed me here when I moved to Willow Grove a couple of months ago.

"Just like you are one of my favorite business partners and customers," she replied gently, before taking on a concerned expression. "How are you feeling lately?"

My shoulders slouched, and a familiar sense of despair and defeat swelled within me.

"Not too great, I'm afraid," I replied dejectedly.

"It came back?!" Ronika asked with a crestfallen expression.

I nodded. "I've started feeling unwell again. Eating is a struggle, and I constantly feel weak and dizzy. At completely random moments, I'll break into a sweat, and my vision will blur."

Ronika frowned with an air of genuine confusion. "It doesn't make sense. Have you coughed blood again?"

I shook my head. "No. However, the same symptoms I felt the first time around are coming back, but even faster than before. At least, so it seems..."

This entire situation made even less sense because I always enjoyed perfect health. When I moved to Willow Grove two months ago, all had been well. The first symptoms appeared at the end of the fourth week. Initially, I thought the stress and exhaustion of relocating to a different State and starting a new business were finally catching up to me. But once I started coughing blood, I could no longer deny that something far more serious was happening.

"My mother thinks I'm cursed," I said with derision.

Ronika firmly shook her head, clearly rejecting that possibility. "I do not see any curse on you. Whatever is ailing you is not of a magical nature, of this I could almost swear. Come, let's go to my examination room."

Although she gestured for me to head towards the room, she marched to the front door to put up the sign that she was giving a consultation so that any new customer would know to be patient.

As I made my way into the room, I couldn't help a glance towards the door to the left. Ronika always kept it closed. I suspected she had an altar or shrine there. The rumor said she performed a few exorcisms, which would require a much different setup than the traditional medical room we were now entering. The entire shop was actually an extension of her home, which also housed a powerful Warden Tree in the garden.

"Why does your mother believe you're cursed?" Ronika asked with genuine curiosity as she closed the door behind her.

Simultaneously, she gestured for me to sit on the examination table in the middle of the room. To my pleasant surprise, I noticed she actually brought one of my Caladrius candles with her. The mythical bird whose feathers I had used to make them was a powerful healer. If blessed enough to meet one, a sick patient would only have to remain still while the snow-white bird stared at him. It would absorb the sickness out of the patient and then fly towards the sun so it would burn it out of him. But if the bird did not make eye contact, it either meant it could not take your sickness away, or that it chose not to do so because you did not deserve it.

I had been so blessed as to meet a Caladrius, but it would not make eye contact with me.

"She actually doesn't know that I'm sick," I confessed sheepishly. "It would devastate her."

"I'm confused," Ronika said carefully.

"I'm displaying the same symptoms as with the mysterious illness that killed my father when I was still a toddler," I explained grimly. "When the doctors and healers failed to identify the cause or to cure him, Mother turned to the Houngans and Mambos, hoping that the spirits would help. After all, my family faithfully served the loas for generations. But they also didn't have answers for us. Mom was devastated and left Benin shortly thereafter to start over here. And although she taught me about our culture, she's been adamant about having no magic in our lives at all. She barely tolerates the fact that I create witch candles. But they put food on the table."

"I can see why she would feel that way," Ronika replied with compassion. "Is that why you left your State to move here in Willow Grove?"

I shook my head. "My uncle—Mom's older brother—passed away recently. In his will, he bequeathed his mansion to me. He only has one daughter who stayed in the old country and has no desire to move here."

Ronika's brow creased. "I'm sorry for your loss. Did he fall to the same illness?"

"No," I said firmly. "It was a stupid horse accident. Something spooked his mount. My uncle got knocked off the saddle and fell at a bad angle, breaking his neck. I was just shocked both to discover I had blood relatives here, and above all that he would put me in his will as I had no recollection of him. I was too young when we left."

"Did your mother know?" Ronika asked.

I nodded. "We had a big falling out over it. For the longest time, I told my mother that I wanted to go back home for a visit and to reconnect with our family. But she always had some excuse to put it off. Truth be told, she kept us pretty isolated. If not for my candle business, I would hardly ever meet anyone. Needless to say that she lost it when I told her that I wanted to accept my uncle's gift. She swore up and down that it was cursed, and that if I went there, I would meet a terrible death."

The shocked expression on the healer's face reflected the distress I felt when I first realized that the symptoms manifesting themselves shortly after my arrival seemed to confirm my mother's dire prediction.

"Is it?" Ronika asked carefully. "Is the house cursed?"

I shook my head. "Sadly, it isn't. It would have been too easy had that been the case. Willow Grove is home to some of the most powerful sorcerers and exorcists. I brought three different ones to try and determine if some evil force within was slowly killing me. But they detected no evil spells or malevolent presence."

Ronika pursed her lips, her beautiful dark brown eyes going out of focus as she reflected on my words.

"I recall you mentioning that you first became sick approximately one month after arriving here," she mused aloud. "If the house isn't making you sick, can you think of any unusual places you might have visited in search of ingredients for your candles, or merely while exploring the region?"

"Believe me, I wondered about that as well. But I have not

gone to any of the cursed places everyone warns us about, least of all a freaky place like Hemdell. As for my ingredients, I have only bought them right here in Charmers District, aside from what I already had and brought here with me. However, I have acquired some exotic reagents from the artifact traders in town. I first thought that maybe I was having an adverse reaction to one of them. But they are not anything no one else has used before. Had they been the cause, surely someone would have recognized the symptoms."

Ronika nodded slowly, her expression troubled. She gestured for me to lie down on the table. I promptly complied. Despite the fear discussing my health issues always brought forth, I couldn't help a proud smile when she shortened the wick off my Caladrius candle before lighting it up. She then began passing it slowly a few inches above me, as one would to examine something with a magnifying glass.

In many ways, it acted exactly like that for someone with her arcane powers. For commoners, using this candle would only suck out some minor illness or injuries, like quieting a particularly unpleasant headache, dimming some seriously sore or achy muscles and joints, mending a cold, or dousing a fever. But in the hands of a master healer like Ronika, it would give her an open window into what was ailing me.

Lying down as I was, all I could see was the air blurring around the candle. Its flame changed colors and intensity depending on where Ronika was moving the candle above me. She would be seeing a clear vision, almost like an X-ray. I didn't have the magic to do the same, but the colors of the flame indicated undeniably that something was truly wrong with me.

"By the Gods," Ronika whispered under her breath, with an air of disbelief.

"That bad?" I asked with a nervous laugh to hide how distraught I felt.

"The disease has indeed returned. But this time, it is

spreading much faster than before. This looks like a case of frequent exposure to some sort of toxin or poison. Except I've never seen anything like it before. I don't know what could attack your body in this fashion. Are you sure you're not exposed to anything?"

"I genuinely cannot think of anything," I replied, defeated. "The arcanists and I have scoured the entire house and found nothing. And I've only gone to places that other people also visit regularly. I have no clue what this is."

Ronika gave me a sad look. "I won't lie to you, Amara. Your illness is beyond me."

"You can't be serious!" I exclaimed in a crestfallen whisper. "You're my only hope. Dr. Osborne also gave up on me. And none of the witches could assist me. You were able to take the illness away last time. Can't you do it again?"

She gave me an apologetic look. "I cannot cure you, Amara. I should be able to remove some of the infection and mend the damage to your organs. But it is not a cure. Whatever is ailing you is still there and will grow again. Sadly, it now knows how to attack you and will continue to spread faster each time."

"So I'm doomed?" I asked, crushed.

A sliver of hope sparked deep within me when she hesitated. That she didn't flat out say no meant an option remained.

"I have no clue where to begin to investigate your case. Right now, this toxin inside you is bound to kill you sooner than later. All I can do is to delay it," Ronika said carefully. "You need someone with greater power."

"Someone like who?" I asked, as if she had made a ridiculous statement.

"Cliona Nox, the Weaver," she said in an almost solemn tone.

I recoiled and stared at her in shock. "The Weaver?!" I exclaimed. "She rejects everyone who comes knocking at her door. As I understand it, unless you have something of extreme value to her, she will not give you the time of day. What could I possibly have that she might want? I'm just a candle maker."

"I won't lie and pretend that she has an open-door policy. No one truly knows why she grants her assistance to some and not to others. You would be surprised by what she may deem valuable. Anyway, what have you got to lose? If her gates open, then you're in luck. If they don't, then we will continue to look for other alternatives. But at least, we'll know for sure that we explored every option."

The urge to argue burned my tongue. I heard so many things about the Weaver, most of them scary. No one knew exactly what she was. While the common folk often referred to her as the Hag, rumor had it that she was in fact one of the Ancients, and maybe even a goddess descended amongst mortals to entertain herself.

The problem was that the lucky few who benefited from her assistance never spoke about what had transpired between them or what the cost of her services had been. Naturally, that led people to spread all kinds of outlandish statements implying that one had to sell their soul to her, sacrifice someone dear to them —especially a child—or to subject themselves to some sort of unholy ritual in exchange for her aid.

Ronika never implied—let alone hinted at the fact—that she personally benefited from the Weaver's assistance. That didn't stop everyone in Willow Grove—me included—from thinking her newfound impressive healing powers had been a gift from the Weaver. But what had been the price for it?

"Very well," I conceded at last. "Like you said, at this point, I've got nothing to lose. The worst thing that could happen will be for me to be turned around."

Ronika smiled then proceeded to heal me the best she could with a mix of magic and potions. By the time she finished, the lancing pain I hadn't fully realized was eating me alive completely faded. It had grown so gradually and in such a subtle fashion that I became used to it and pushed it to the back of my mind. But now, I could see the difference as the sudden feeling of being free, healthy, and full of energy surged through me. It was merely a reprieve, but one I intended to use to the best of my ability to seek a cure before it came back with a vengeance.

Before releasing me, the healer handed me multiple vials containing a potent tonic to help give me a boost whenever my energy level crashed. It felt odd to have her pay me for the candles when I felt like I owed her even more for the treatment. But she charged ridiculously low prices, nominal at best. She truly was a healer at heart, in the profession for the sake of improving the lives of her patients, and not as a scheme to enrich herself.

The entire journey to my new home, I debated when to head over to the Weaver's house, and above all, what I could offer her as compensation should she bless me with opening her gates. What could a goddess possibly need from someone like me?

I crossed the small bridge over the moat leading to the entrance and stopped my carriage right in front of my mansion. I'd inherited a well-maintained gothic house on a large private land. Four towers rose above the three-story home. Black gables adorned the witch's caps topping them. The decorative shingles, columns, and railings around the balconies on each of the upper floors as well as on the front porch presented the same dark color. Thankfully, the paler sandstone hue of the stone walls brightened the otherwise slightly ominous style of the house.

A flock of birds took flight in the distance, soaring over the tall trees of the peaceful forest surrounding the estate. One could hunt some small game within it, mostly rabbits, deer, and the occasional pheasant.

Sighing, I climbed the short flights of stairs, accompanied by the soothing sound of the water flowing below, and the singing of the windchimes dangling over the porch. I made a beeline for my workshop to put away the supplies I purchased in Charmers District. The prospect of working at long last with a centaur's hoof dust and a chimera's venom thrilled me beyond words. I never would have been able to get my hands on such reagents in the small town of Harmstead, where I grew up. I eyed my cauldron, itching to get to work. But I needed to go to stable my horse first.

No, you need to go see the Weaver first.

My shoulders drooped, and my stomach knotted with apprehension. It didn't take a genius to know I was procrastinating. The prospect of meeting the Weaver scared me. I honestly couldn't say if it was the woman herself or what she potentially would tell me that I feared the most. My gut screamed that her verdict—assuming she even received me—would be a devastating blow.

Delaying won't make it go away.

In fact, delaying only enabled the disease to progress further. Every minute wasted could be another nail in my coffin.

Groaning inwardly, I exited my workshop and headed back to my carriage. As excited as I felt about experimenting with new candle recipes, I wouldn't live long enough to see how well people would receive them if I keeled over.

For a split second, I debated whether to simply ride on horseback or once again use my carriage. In the end, I settled for the latter. It shamed me to admit that the fact the carriage would go slower played a big part in that choice.

The one-hour journey to the Weaver's home both took forever and flew by too quickly. It gave me far too much time to imagine the worst possible scenarios as to what she might want as payment for her assistance. How far was I willing to go? What would I deem too steep a price in exchange for saving my life? The part of me that couldn't wait to be there and to get this whole ordeal done and over with battled with the part that dreaded what was about to happen. I almost hoped that the gates wouldn't open.

The silhouette of the gates appeared in the distance, flanked by tall pillars atop which gargoyle-looking creatures stood watch. From all accounts, one shouldn't be fooled by their stony appearance. They weren't statues but powerful guardians that could tear any would-be trespassers to shreds if they didn't heed their warning to turn back.

To my shock, long before I even came within range, the doors quietly parted open as if pushed by an invisible hand. My heart leapt, my conflicted emotions going into overdrive as fear and hope warred within me in equal measure. I softly gasped when the eyes of both creatures lit up with a yellow glow. They didn't emit a single sound but turned their heads to stare at me as I passed through the gate. The only thing that kept me from peeing myself was the complete absence of any threatening demeanor on their part.

Eyes wide, I crossed the two-hundred-meter path up to the house, framed by the most exotic forest I ever beheld. While I recognized some of the plants and trees, others were completely foreign to me. One thing was for certain, very few people could boast having access to what had to be an immense fortune in greenery. Even from here, I could feel the potent magic contained within them. What I wouldn't give for only a few leaves, petals, or sap from this treasure trove.

I frowned in confusion as I closed in on the humble, cliché witch hut that greeted me at the end of the path. There was no way so powerful a being would live in such a house. Surely, this was some sort of illusion. But the door opening with a will of its own before I even stopped my carriage knocked all those wandering thoughts right out of my mind.

I swallowed hard as another wave of worry twisted my insides. But cowering stopped being an option the moment I crossed the gates. Come what may, I was committed. I stepped down from my carriage, absent-mindedly patted my horse's neck in a soothing fashion, and made my way towards the house.

Despite the soft light emanating from the open door, it still resembled a gaping maw eager to swallow me whole.

With an assurance I certainly didn't feel, I stepped inside the house to find the Weaver sitting behind a table facing the entrance. If not for her somewhat otherworldly appearance and the undeniable power radiating from her, one might have believed her to be a receptionist manning the front desk.

She was beautiful, her age undefinable in light of the smoothness of her lightly tanned skin, and yet undoubtedly ancient. Her pupils narrowed into vertical slits in the purple sea of her irises as she watched me approach. She tilted her head to the side and distractedly ran a hand along the endless length of her silver white-hair plaited in a single braid that pooled to the floor.

"Greetings, Amara Sanni. I was expecting you," the Weaver said in a throaty and slightly seductive voice that sent a shiver down my spine.

Too stunned that she already knew my full name, I stopped dead in my tracks and gaped at her while my mind struggled to catch up. This fumbling behavior made no sense coming from me. I wasn't the type to just freeze or panic in the face of adversity. Whatever inner turmoil I felt, I normally shoved it down and rose to the moment until the situation was resolved.

But then, I'd never stood in the presence of a goddess before.

A taunting smirk stretched her lips. With a conviction I couldn't explain, I realized she knew exactly what thoughts were currently crossing my mind.

"Have a seat," she said, waving slightly to my left.

Before I could ask where, a grinding sound from behind startled me. My jaw dropped when I glanced over my shoulder to see a chair I hadn't noticed by the door gliding over the wooden floor and stop in front of the table. Although I'd seen mages and conjurers use telekinetic abilities, it had never been so effortless.

Swallowing hard, I complied.

"Thank you, Weaver," I said, finding my voice at last. "And thank you for agreeing to see me. As you know my name, it appears that the rumors are true when they claim that you know everything."

She snorted, an amused glimmer flicking through her purple eyes as her pupils dilated again into a rounder shape—which honestly made her come across as less intimidating.

"Everything, no. I wish that were the case. But most things, yes. For example, I do not know your ultimate fate, only potential outcomes," she replied.

I instantly perked up. "Any positive ones?" I asked, slightly embarrassed by the excessive eagerness in my voice.

She pursed her lips and gave me an assessing look. "Yes," the Weaver said at last.

"So you know the cause of my illness, or whatever it is?" I asked, leaning forward.

"It is not an illness but poison slowly killing you," she stated matter-of-factly.

I recoiled. "Poison?! Which one? Where and how did I get infected?"

A speculative expression fleeted over her face before it returned to a neutral state. "That's for you to figure out."

I blinked and stared at her in confusion. "What? If you know what it is, why not just tell me?"

"I cannot solve things for you," she replied carefully, her face taking on an air of intensity that almost had me squirming in my chair. "You need a cure, and I can tell you where to find it. But securing it is your burden to bear. While I'm allowed to tell you that you're poisoned, you must find the source and eliminate it."

I took a moment to digest her words. Whatever doubts might have lingered in my mind as to the fact that she was a goddess or one of the Ancients totally faded. Only gods and demigods were bound by Covenants. Some demons and familiars could also fall under such restrictions, but she was neither of those lesser beings.

"Very well," I replied hesitantly, my mind still racing. "I have tried in vain to find the source of my illness. But what happens if I acquire the cure first without finding the source?"

She waved a dismissive hand. "You will be fine. If you manage to get the cure, then you will be immune forever."

"Is it the same thing that killed my father?" I asked, tension seeping into my voice.

"Yes," she replied factually.

My chest constricted as the unpleasant thought that had plagued me since the first symptoms manifested themselves reared its ugly head again.

"You said it is a poison killing me. So this is not genetics, right? It is not some hereditary illness passed down to me?"

"It is not."

I clenched my teeth as anger surged through me. "That means someone is after us."

"It is a fair assumption," she responded in a noncommittal fashion.

That, too, angered me. I wanted to snap at her and demand that she give me proper answers. She held the information I needed. I didn't doubt for a moment that she knew the exact identity of the person who had taken my father's life and who was now after me. But who were they and why? Above all, why now?

As far as I knew, my uncle had no other children or significant other who lived here in the Americas. No one contested his will or even expressed the slightest interest in moving here or claiming the house. Therefore, it made no sense that this inheritance could be the motive for the attack. But if it wasn't, why wait until I came here instead of many years ago while I still lived in Harmstead?

I almost questioned her about all of this before catching

myself. She couldn't answer any of these questions. Pressing her about them would not only be pointless but also risk alienating her. As I desperately needed her assistance, I carefully worded my following requests.

"Will I find the culprit?"

"It is a potential path," she conceded, a glimmer of approval flashing through her unusual eyes.

This only seemed to further support my suspicions that she could read my mind. As I was an emotional wreck right now, it wasn't ideal. I could simply take comfort in the fact that she didn't seem displeased with how I was handling things so far.

"And if I fail to catch them, how bad will things be for me?"

She hesitated for a long time. For a split second, I wondered if she had not heard the question. Then I realized her eyes had slightly gone out of focus. The Weaver was undoubtedly prodding the complex network of the future before answering.

"There are too many potential outcomes from one extreme to the next. The choices you make while you attempt to find the cure will help narrow down the likely outcomes," she finally said in a non-committal fashion.

I opened my mouth to prod further, but the look on her face made it clear she considered the topic settled, and that it was time for me to move on.

I cleared my throat and shifted uneasily on the wooden chair.

"So what must I do to acquire that cure?" I asked in a subdued tone.

Once again, a strange expression flashed over her features. For a reason I couldn't explain, my back instantly stiffened. I would hate her answer.

"You must receive an even greater poison to kill the one spreading inside of you."

I nearly jumped out of my seat, my entire body jerking as if under the impact of a physical blow.

"WHAT?! A greater poison will kill me even faster!" I exclaimed in a self-evident tone.

"Not exactly," she said calmly. "What you need is to be bitten by the snake tail of the Cursed Demon Wolf."

I gaped at her as if she had lost her mind.

Seemingly unfazed by my horrified expression, the Weaver continued explaining in a conversational tone. "The venom will first attack the poison that's eating you from within. Only once it has been eradicated will the venom start harming you. When it does, you will need a second bite from the fangs of the sick wolf. This time, the saliva will neutralize the venom."

"That's suicide!" I exclaimed. "The Cursed Demon Wolf is rabid! By all accounts, he kills on sight anything foolish enough to come within range. And you expect me to voluntarily subject myself to his bite, not once but twice?!"

She bowed her head in concession. "Ranael is indeed rabid because of the curse. But he's also Marchosias' son. Demon wolves are protectors. It is in their DNA. In Ranael's case, you are correct that he will attack anyone he randomly encounters because his madness rules him. However, if he is summoned, his protective instincts will take over."

I blinked while struggling to accept her words.

"Do I understand correctly that summoning him will nullify his curse?" I asked disbelievingly.

She shook her head, confusing me even more. "It will not *nullify* it, only temporarily pause his feral side. You must invoke his protection while summoning him. He will be bound by it. But once he comes, you must hurry. The protective bond will only last so long before madness takes him again."

I nodded slowly, realizing that he would effectively be subjected to the same constraints as any other summoned demon. And then, my eyes suddenly widened as a thought struck me.

"Wait, aren't demon wolves also bound by truth?" I asked.

A discreet smile stretched her lips. "Yes. Demon wolves will always answer any question truthfully. But remember, you have little time. Do not waste it on futilities. Secure a safe bite from Ranael quickly."

"But how do I even summon him? I only have a very basic knowledge of the arcane," I said sheepishly. "Anything related to candle magic I master, but summoning is definitely not one of them."

"Fear not, child. I will show you the ritual," she replied with a dismissive gesture.

I licked my lips nervously. "All right, thank you. How do I find him? I've heard of the legend of the Cursed Demon Wolf, but not much else."

"Retain the services of a guide in Wolfmoon Mountain," Cliona said firmly. "The Howl Inn is an excellent place to find one. But be warned that the journey is perilous. So pick your guide wisely. Once you've been bitten by the snake tail, you will need your guide to take you back to safety."

I swallowed hard and nodded slowly. "How will I know when I'm ready for the second bite?"

"The capillaries under your skin will start turning black," the Weaver said with an almost malicious glimmer in her purple eyes.

A part of me realized that she was deliberately trying to freak me out as it seemed to amuse her.

I swallowed hard again, refusing to show how well she was succeeding in that endeavor.

"That sounds rather painful," I said carefully. "Will I be in any condition to go back to Ranael for the second bite?"

The strangest expression fleeted over her features. She didn't respond right away. While her face betrayed nothing of what thoughts were crossing her mind, I understood at a visceral level that this would be a key part of the trial that awaited me.

"Pick a guide you literally trust with your life, and all will be well," she replied in a mysterious tone.

"Trust with my life?" I echoed with disbelief. "How am I supposed to do that with someone I will have just met?"

She shrugged with a taunting expression. "That's for you to figure out. But do so swiftly. Time isn't on your side. Just so you know, Ronika cannot help you again."

My stomach dropped, and a sense of dread and borderline despair washed over me. That she knew of this when I had not even remotely hinted at the help the healer had given me truly messed with my head. But this confirmation that I no longer had this safety net wrecked me.

"How much time do I have?" I whispered, my voice slightly shaky.

To my surprise, the Weaver didn't answer right away. She glanced instead at the wall behind her to her left. I couldn't see anything there but an empty wall. The way she examined it, there was something beyond my capacity to perceive. Only then did I take a moment to look around the large room I had just spent the past twenty minutes in.

It looked more spacious inside than one would expect from the outside. This further supported my theory that the exterior was an illusion. The left side of the room had a multitude of scrolls, grimoires, and various parchments that undoubtedly contained the type of advanced magic most spellcasters, conjurers, and arcanists would sell their souls for. The opposite side of the room had countless vials containing potions and liquids. I couldn't even begin to imagine what purpose they served. It also boasted an impressive collection of herbs and reagents that would likely be worth an insane amount of money on the free market.

But it was the spinning wheel next to the wall that retained my attention. Only then did I finally notice that a golden thread from the wheel pointed towards the wall before fading away. This could only mean that whatever she was spinning was displayed on that wall but invisible to my layman's eyes.

Before I could dwell further on the matter, the Weaver turned her attention back to me.

"If you go on this mission to seek out Ranael, your fate will be decided in the next six weeks. But if you don't go, you will die in less than two months," she said in a factual manner.

This struck me like a boulder to the chest. I clasped my hands in my lap, squeezing them tightly to keep them from shaking. I took a deep breath, not even realizing that I was slowly nodding as if in acknowledgement of the inevitable.

"I see. Is there no other way than exposing myself to the bite of the Cursed Demon Wolf?" I asked, hating the pleadingly hopeful tone in my voice.

"There is. But do not get your hopes up. You would never live long enough to see the alternative paths through. Had you come to me a month ago when you first noticed the symptoms, you would have had other options. That window has closed. However, even if you had come then, I would have strongly suggested you go to Ranael instead. This path is the one that ensures the greatest possible outcome for you."

My shoulders drooped, and I nodded again, this time with resignation. "Should I leave now then?"

She shook her head and took on a serious expression. "Not today, but in three days time. Only go to the Howl Inn on the day after the full moon."

"*After* the full moon?" I repeated suspiciously.

"It's called Wolfmoon Mountain for a reason," the Weaver replied as if I'd said something stupid. "Various Lycan packs share the territory."

"Yes, I'd heard as much. But I thought the full moon business was just legends and folk tales parents tell their children when they misbehaved, like some kind of boogeyman?"

She gave me an indulgent and slightly mocking smile. "All legends and folktales are rooted in reality. Lycans are indeed not affected by the werewolf curse. The full moon doesn't affect them. But there *are* werewolves. You don't want to be caught by one of them on the full moon. Get to the inn the day after."

"Understood," I said before clearing my throat and giving her a wary glance. "So... What is your fee for your assistance? I doubt my rarest witch candles will entice you."

Her disdainful snort stung.

"I have a respectable amount of savings, and I could sell—"

"Your blood," the Weaver said, interrupting me.

"Excuse me?" I asked, stunned.

"Once cured, you will give me a phial of your blood," the Weaver said firmly.

I recoiled and stared at her in outrage. "What? That's out of the question!"

"Relax, foolish girl!" she said sternly. "I will not use it to harm, control, or bind you. If you survive this ordeal, your blood will have the serum to the most virulent poison in existence. I want it."

The tension knotting my back instantly loosened, but only partially. "What if I don't survive?" I challenged.

She shrugged. "Then I will have failed to help you, which will void your debt."

"So my surviving family wouldn't be held accountable?" I insisted.

"No," she said in a tone that brooked no argument. "The contract is between you and me. If you are cured, you'll owe me a phial of your blood. If you die, then we both lose, and the contract is voided."

I pursed my lips, my mind still racing about all the ways this could go wrong.

To my surprise, the Weaver rolled her eyes with an air of exasperation. "I pledge that your blood will be used solely to derive a healing serum. In no way, shape, or form will it be used to harm you or anyone else."

My jaw dropped. You didn't play with a pledge. It acted like a blood oath. Breaking your word had grievous consequences that no one wanted to face. You just had to be careful with the terms of the pledge. A clever play on words would suffice to fool you into thinking the pledge granted you far more protection than it truly did.

But in this instance, I could find no fault or loophole within it.

"Very well. Then we have a deal," I said softly.

The triumphant smile that stretched the Weaver's sensuous lips threw me. It was so brief and quickly hidden that I wondered if I'd imagined it. As I doubted saving my life ranked high in her priorities, I could only assume that the serum in my blood truly held a great value to her.

She spent the next twenty minutes teaching me how to summon Ranael. By the time I left her house, a light shone over me, pushing away the crushing despair that had been engulfing me.

However impossible the odds, I now had hope.

CHAPTER 2
AMARA

I set off right before noon on the morning after the full moon. My initial plan had been to leave at sunrise, but a nasty storm delayed my departure. Once more, I debated whether to simply ride my horse or use a carriage. In the end, my phaeton made the most sense as the hood would provide some protection if the weather acted up again, on top of providing more room to bring additional clothes, basic hiking equipment, and the paraphernalia that would assist me in the summoning ritual.

The journey to Kairn—the small tourist village at the entrance of Wolfmoon Mountain—stretched indefinitely. On top of giving me far too much time to think of all the ways in which things could go wrong, seeing the sun steadily dip to the horizon further increased my wariness. Thankfully, my trip proved uneventful as the road there was quite safe. Crossing paths with a growing number of other tourists and travelers in both directions the closer I got to my destination helped tremendously. I finally reached the inn a little before 9:00 PM.

The three-story hostel made of dark wood and beige bricks dominated the other, much smaller buildings of the village. At a glance, I counted about twenty establishments, most of them reminding me of tourist traps, aside from the convenience store and blacksmith. Based on the research I performed over the past three days while waiting for the full moon to end, only a handful of families actually lived in Kairn. Namely the innkeeper Misty Starlight and her family, as well as the sheriff Darion Lovell. Everyone else lived with one of the Lycan packs who owned their individual section of the surrounding territory.

The large doors of the inn parted open, giving me a glimpse into the busy dining area. The delicious scent of roasted meat wafted to me, accompanied by the sound of music and the undefined noise of animated conversations. A large male immediately made a beeline for me and waved a huge hand in greeting.

I did a double take once I realized that he was just a teenager. The unusual silver color of his eyes, and the furry tip of a pointy ear peeking through his luscious black hair gave away the fact that he wasn't human. I had never met a Lycan before. But it didn't take a genius to recognize this boy as one.

"Greetings, Madam. Will you be staying the night?" he asked, his slightly higher-pitched voice further confirming his youth.

"Yes. It's getting much too late to venture into the wild," I said with a nervous laugh.

"Wise decision," he concurred, his smile broadening.

Although he didn't have fangs, his pristine white canines were clearly sharper and more prominent than with a regular human's. I gladly accepted the hand he extended to help me down my carriage. His nostrils flared, and a troubled expression quickly hidden flashed over his boyish features, dimming the happy warmth he'd initially displayed. I almost asked him what was wrong, but he swiftly turned away from me to pick up my belongings and carry them inside.

I patted my horse on the neck then followed the young man inside. Although conversations didn't stop when I entered, quite a few of them slowed down as many of the patrons eyed me with undisguised curiosity. Most of them were males, with less than a quarter of them being females. To my surprise, only a handful of humans mingled amongst the guests. It suddenly struck me that the Lycans used this place as their usual hang out. This boded well as it was always a good sign when the locals regularly frequented an establishment. It meant good service and quality.

Being somewhat of an introvert, so much attention focused on me made me self-conscious. At least, none of the stares were intimidating. While curiosity dominated, a few of the males eyed me with blatant admiration devoid of the lurid edge that would have made it vulgar or disrespectful.

For a reason I couldn't explain, instead of making my way to the counter and addressing the innkeeper, I just stopped a few steps inside the room, facing the crowd.

I cleared my throat, and all the conversations ended, even the couple of musicians providing entertainment stopped. With every eye locked on me, I swallowed hard and summoned all my courage before projecting loudly so all could hear.

"I'm sorry to interrupt your evening, but I'm looking for a guide to take me on a hazardous mission. I will pay well," I said.

Many people perked up, interested eyebrows raising as they gave me an assessing look.

"How hazardous?" a male called out, drawing my attention.

He was sitting behind the largest table in the inn, surrounded by eight other people, two of them females. Even sitting down, I could tell he was extremely tall. His broad shoulders and ropey muscles screamed of tremendous strength. While all the other Lycan males would put most human men to shame with their impressive physiques, this one stood out from the rest. I suspected he was the alpha of his pack.

"Very hazardous," I replied.

He gave me a slow once over and gestured for me to approach. Once again, there was nothing inappropriate in the way his silver eyes glided over me. I would describe it as clinical, as if he was attempting to gather information about me that would give him a better sense of who he was dealing with.

As a merchant, I often did the same with customers, especially those who asked me for the type of candles used for advanced arcane rituals. While being a strong proponent of minding my own business, I would not sell a product to someone I believed intended to use it for evil or harmful purposes. Dark mages often wore some form of symbols of power or artifacts to enhance their magic. It gave a good sense of what type of practices they were into. Similarly, you had the penny pinchers who were dressed in fancy garb but always tried to haggle for a cheaper price.

However, as I wove my way through the busy tables, a few of the Lycan patrons stiffened, some even recoiling as they crinkled their noses or scrunched their faces. Before I could question that odd reaction, one of them addressed me in a shocked voice, making my steps falter.

"You're sick!" the male exclaimed. "The stench of death is all over you."

I flinched, my chest constricting that the poison should have progressed so much inside me that it was so easily detectable already to beings with highly sensitive noses. Refusing to give in to despair, I lifted my chin defiantly as I stared at the younger male. He seemed to be about my age, late twenties or early thirties. Although a little less imposing than the one who I suspected to be their Alpha, this man was still sturdily built. His dirty blonde hair curled gloriously around his handsome face. He also had the silver eyes of a wolf, but with a longer, more oval-shaped face instead of the squarer jaw of his counterpart.

"Yes, I am dying. Thus, the urgent need for this mission. I need the counter poison to the one that's killing me."

"And what counter poison would that be?" the first, older male asked, reclaiming my attention.

I closed the remaining distance to him and nervously ran my

fingers through my curly hair. His nostrils flared as he inhaled my scent, imitated by the other people around him, the ones farther away leaning in to get a better whiff. The air of pity that descended over many faces had my innards twisting even more.

"Are you after the Orestan flowers from the Dark Vale?" he asked when I didn't answer right away.

I shook my head and licked my lips, bracing for how they would respond to my answer.

"No, it's something far more challenging to acquire. I need to be bitten by the snake tail of the Cursed Demon Wolf Ranael," I said as firmly as I could.

A deafening silence settled over the room while everyone stared at me in disbelief. I couldn't tell whether seconds or minutes went by. It just felt like an eternity to me. And then the booming sound of a male voice laughing behind me triggered a domino effect with everyone else swiftly joining in.

"You're insane!" the younger male exclaimed behind me. "The current poison clearly broke your brain, woman!"

"Enough, Ulric," the older male said sternly, silencing everyone else.

"I mean no disrespect, Rolf," Ulric said in a somewhat conciliatory tone. "But this poor woman is obviously not thinking clearly. Who in their right mind would deliberately seek out Ranael?"

"I'm not insane," I countered forcefully before shifting my attention back to the older male who he had called Rolf. "His venom is the only cure for what ails me. I got the confirmation from the Weaver herself."

A general gasp rose in the room followed by some incredulous whispers amongst the patrons. Rolf narrowed his eyes at me, his face displaying a mix of suspicion and curiosity.

"The Weaver granted you an audience?" he asked in a dubious tone.

"Yes, she did," I replied, holding his gaze unwaveringly.

"How the fuck did you pull that off?" he challenged, apparently still unsure if he was impressed or still doubtful of the truthfulness of my statement. "And at what cost? The Weaver doesn't help anyone unless they have something of great value for her."

"Indeed," Ulric interjected. "What could she possibly want from a dying girl, pretty though you are? Did she ask for your soul?"

Biting my tongue not to tell him to piss off, I gave him an irritated look. "The compensation for her assistance is between me and her. It's no one else's business. All I want to know is whether someone among you will be my guide."

As one, everyone turned to look at Rolf, confirming my suspicion that he was one of their alphas. My heart sank when he shook his head with a commiserating expression.

"I'm afraid that will not be possible," he said in a soft, almost paternal tone. "Taking you to him would be a murder-suicide. Ranael will eat you as an appetizer and your guide as his main course. Only a fool would go on such a mission. I'm sorry. I can set up a meeting for you to speak with one of our shamans. Maybe they can offer you an alternative cure that we will be glad to help you with. But not this."

"*This* is my only hope," I said in a pleading tone.

The way his face closed as he held my gaze without flinching crushed me. I knew that look. Rolf would not be swayed. Desperate, I glanced around the room, attempting to make eye contact with anyone present. But every single person averted their eyes.

"Won't anyone else help me?" I asked around.

"Do not waste your time," Ulric said in a gentle but firm voice. "We do sympathize with your plight, but none of the packs will partake in this madness. The best we can offer you is to take you to a shaman."

I opened my mouth to argue but closed it, defeated. There

would be no changing their minds, at least not right this instant. I needed to regroup, gather my thoughts, and come up with an alternative that might sway them. The Weaver would not have sent me here in vain. There was a solution, and I would find it.

Despite the non-negligible crowd, I spotted a few free tables still available. Clenching my teeth, I gave the two men a stiff nod then made my way to a booth at the far back of the large room. Before I even settled on the wooden bench, the musicians started playing seemingly right where they left off when I barged in, and conversation resumed as if I'd never interrupted their evening.

It made me feel even more abandoned and unimportant. Who cared about some random human? My passing would make no difference in their lives. And my customers would soon find a competitor to replace me. In a few months, I'd become one of those 'funny' anecdotes that guides would share with their clients regarding the weirdest request they ever received. With time, the story would get embellished. They would probably describe me as crazed, my clothes torn half to shreds, foaming at the mouth, walking down the streets made of packed dirt, shouting at the top of my lungs for Ranael to come take me.

Tears pricked my eyes, and my throat constricted. I couldn't decide if I wanted to wallow in self-pity more than I wanted to yell at everyone here, to call them out for their cowardice and heartlessness. And yet, the rational part of me couldn't blame them. In their shoes, I'd likely have turned me down as well. But what was I supposed to do?

The Weaver told me to come here. So what am I missing?

Movement at the edge of my vision startled me. I'd been so lost in my grim thoughts that I didn't notice an elderly woman approaching. She was an Asian woman with electric blue eyes. I vaguely recalled seeing her standing behind the counter when I entered. To my shock, she was holding a tray with a huge bread bowl. She set it in front of me, and the delicious aroma of the thick stew filling it wafted to me.

My stomach instantly growled its approval. I hadn't realized just how famished I was.

"Thank you," I whispered, giving her a sad but grateful smile.

"You're welcome, honey," she said in a motherly tone that had my chest tightening. "The name's Misty. I'm the owner of this place. May I sit with you?"

Surprised and slightly confused, I nodded and gestured for her to proceed. She smiled and complied. Despite her slender, almost delicate constitution, Misty wasn't frail. An undeniable strength lurked behind her wizened appearance. Aside from the unusual color of her eyes, her pointy wolf ears, and her slightly prominent canines gave her away as a Lycan as well. The contrary would have been shocking, considering it seemed to be the main hang out for her species.

"My name is Amara," I replied as she settled on the bench across the table from me.

"A lovely name for a lovely young lady," she said gently.

I caught myself smiling. There was something incredibly soothing about the female. To my shock, a powerful desire to have her hug and console me hit me like a ton of bricks. While I undeniably was a cuddler, I didn't have random urges to hug and be hugged by strangers.

"I'm sorry to hear about your plight," she said carefully. "As you likely realized, there is no point debating the matter further with the people here. None will take you. But there is another who might."

I froze, halfway through bringing a spoonful of meaty stew to my mouth. "Another?! Who?"

"His name is Remus," she said in a conspiratorial tone.

"Misty! Don't drag the Cursed One into this!" Rolf shouted.

The elder woman jerked her head towards the alpha to glare at him. "He's not cursed. He's merely a sick wolf."

I froze, my eyes widening upon hearing those words.

"A sick wolf?" I echoed, tension audible in my voice.

She nodded with a grim expression. "Remus was born 'sick' although even that isn't quite accurate. During her pregnancy, his mother was infected by Ranael, the true Cursed Wolf. She died from the venom, which she sadly passed on to Remus. He was born with that same poison coursing through his veins, but it doesn't affect him. You would never know that his blood is toxic if you saw him walking around."

"So he's not actually sick," I countered carefully. "He just has venomous blood, right?"

She hesitated. "That's correct 99% of the time. But the poison only grows more toxic when the full moon rises, which also affects his... mind."

My jaw dropped in sudden understanding. "He becomes rabid on the full moon?!"

She pinched her lips and reluctantly nodded. "Yes. But it's only that one night. Otherwise, he's the sweetest male you'll ever meet," she added quickly in a reassuring tone. "Remus actually specializes in the type of hard and dangerous missions others won't take. I have no doubt he will be open to assisting you."

I frowned, baffled by her obvious eagerness to convince me but also by the apparent flaws in her logic.

"Why does he specialize in dangerous missions? Is he suicidal?" I challenged.

To my surprise, rather than being taken aback or fumbling to find an answer, Misty smiled with approval, as if she'd hoped I would ask that specific question.

"He's not suicidal at all, quite the opposite. His plight has helped him appreciate life and the hardships people face even more acutely. Remus knows what it's like to be desperate for a solution to a problem that appears unsolvable. His condition has made him bold, determined, and undaunted," Misty said with conviction.

"Why the fuck would Remus accept this? Ranael cursed him

and killed his parents! Why in the world would he want to partake in a mission that would take him right back to the creature who caused his condition to begin with? He's the last creature Remus would ever want to come close to! You're giving this poor girl false hope," Rolf interjected.

Misty huffed and made a dismissive gesture.

"I'm not! Remus was infected by the demon wolf. Their bloods have similarities. Ranael sees Remus like a member of his pack... almost as kin. He will not attack him."

My eyes widened in understanding.

"If that assessment is accurate, then this Remus sounds indeed like the ideal guide to take me there," I mused aloud.

"He absolutely is!" Misty replied enthusiastically.

"He's cursed!" Ulric objected. "Don't—"

"Enough!" Misty snapped. "None of you will help this girl, and now you're trying to spread lies about the one person who just might? Is your hatred for the poor boy so deep you will condemn her to a certain death?!"

The two men recoiled, visibly hurt by her words.

"We do not hate him," Rolf countered, offended. "And we definitely do not wish this woman any harm. But this mission—"

"*You* may not hate him, but your words are just as damaging," Misty said sternly, interrupting him as well.

"*I* do not *hate* him either," Ulric protested. "But I've experienced first-hand how lethal trusting him can be."

"You're conflating completely different situations, conveniently ignoring your own responsibility in that unfortunate mishap, and clinging to something that happened decades ago. Let it go, you foolish boy!" Misty snarled.

Despite their obvious desire to continue arguing, both men kept their peace, the hard glint in the older woman's eyes daring them to challenge her further. Seeming satisfied when the two men begrudgingly averted their eyes, she returned her attention to me.

"Where is this Remus?" I asked. "In the end, he's the one who can confirm whether he'll do it or not."

"He's gone hunting," she replied in a softer tone, her friendly demeanor returning. "He should be here in the morning or the day after tomorrow to sell his catches and see if there are any customers in need of a guide."

"Perfect," I said, a sliver of hope seeping into my voice. "I will need a room for a few days then, and I also have a phaeton that your stable hand took care of."

"Of course, sweetheart. We'll make sure you're comfortable while you wait. Remus is a good man," she repeated.

The affection in her voice raised a million questions in my mind. Were they related somehow? She wasn't his mother, but the protectiveness and the way she praised him hinted at a deep bond.

For some reason, it reassured me. I didn't know that woman and had no particular reason to trust her. And yet, I did. At a visceral level, I believed her to be honorable.

Reaching across the table, Misty squeezed my hand in an almost maternal fashion, then rose to her feet, and went back to her duties behind the counter. However uncertain things remained, I once more had hope.

CHAPTER 3
REMUS

G ently tugging on my horse's reins, I stopped my carriage in front of the inn. A proud smile stretched my lips as I glanced at the impressive haul I was bringing to Misty. While meat supplies were never an issue in Wolfmoon Mountain, the rare meats I'd managed to procure were in high demand and hard to come by. You needed to hunt in the type of dangerous territories wise people avoided.

It wasn't arrogance, stupidity, or greed that drove me to venture into those perilous areas to hunt. But monsters recognized each other. They feared me more than I feared them. Or rather, they dreaded my tainted blood. Biting me would cause more harm to them than to me, giving me a free pass pretty much anywhere I went.

It was the only blessing of the curse that plagued my entire existence.

I deftly hopped down my carriage and pulled two of the large beasts from the wagon, plopping one over each of my shoulders. I grabbed two smaller beasts—though still the size of a big dog—and carried them in my hands. For a reason I couldn't explain, it wasn't so much to reduce the number of trips it would take to bring everything inside. I just wanted to make an impressive entrance. It made no sense as I'd never been the braggart type.

As this haul would bring me a pretty penny, I could take an extensive break if no interesting hunting or guided escort contracts came my way. I'd never been particularly hungry for money. With my skills, I could rake in massive wealth. However, a comfortable roof over my head, a full belly, and the ability to pay all my bills without worry were more than enough for me.

But my heart sank as soon as I approached the large doors of the inn. Judging by the sound of multiple voices inside—too many of which I recognized—the place was packed. I'd hoped most of them would be off hunting or guiding customers through the mountain or neighboring forests. I truly wasn't in the mood for the passive-aggressive remarks and semi-veiled bullying from my detractors.

Over the years, it had gotten better, with a majority of the packs leaving me alone. Even the most obnoxious haters weren't as aggressive and relentless as when I'd been younger. The massive size and strength I'd developed growing up undoubtedly played a significant part in their newfound restraint. Still, silent but hostile looks often stung as much—if not more—than openly snide and derogatory comments.

Despite being heavily burdened, I effortlessly opened the inn's heavy doors. The loud sound of conversations shrunk by half. It shouldn't have shocked me. While my presence often caused that type of reaction, it was never to this extent. A few conversations would pause or slow as they watched me enter before dismissing me from their thoughts and resuming right where they left off.

This time, it was almost a deafening silence that hailed my entrance, and it had nothing to do with the impressive catch I was carrying. But my brain couldn't focus on this odd behavior.

As soon as the doors parted, the most enticing scent slapped my nose. My mouth watered, my skin heated as my blood boiled, and my steps faltered as a wave of dizziness washed over me.

Impossible!

And yet, this physiological response couldn't be denied. Something—or rather someone—had whipped my mating heat into a frenzy.

My Twin Flame was here.

My nostrils flared as I inhaled deeply, my head jerking this way and that as I sought the source of this divine aroma. It took half a second that felt like an eternity before my gaze zeroed in on the beautiful stranger sitting in the far corner of the dining hall of the inn.

By Ferazan, she was breathtaking!

The tight, black curls of her lustrous mane framed her stunning face, with obsidian eyes, a noble nose, and generous lips that beckoned me. She was lost in thought, her slightly pointy chin resting in her palm. My mouth watered further as my gaze roamed over her flawless skin, the dark color of kalena stones when they granted a wish.

Is she my impossible wish come true?

In the split second it took me to register all these details about the enthralling stranger, the silence around me had grown even more deafening. Tearing my gaze away from her, I forced myself to head towards the counter where Misty was busy pouring some drinks. But the pristine sleeveless top of my Twin Flame and her long, fiery orange skirt shouted at me to reclaim my attention.

Although the conversations gradually resumed, countless stares weighed heavily on me.

"Remus! There you are, love!" Misty exclaimed, her face taking on that maternal expression that always made me melt from the inside out.

"I am!" I replied with sincere enthusiasm despite still being utterly distracted by the stranger. "And I come bearing gifts!"

"So I see! Although gifts are normally free," she added teasingly. "These ones will ravage my purse, but it's an expense I'll gladly make. You couldn't have brought me this abundance of dusk boars at a better time!"

"Oh? Something big is happening?" I asked as I circled around the counter and plopped the two river goats on a large cart Misty pointed to.

She nodded with a broad grin. "I have a big group of human hunters coming this week from overseas. They want to sample some of the more exotic game and fish to be found in the region," she explained.

"Please tell me they're not planning on hunting dusk boars themselves?" I asked, horrified.

She chuckled. "Relax, son. They're not that insane. They just want to sample what is too dangerous for them to catch themselves. But they will want to hunt."

"Good," I said, tension bleeding out of my shoulders. "Any other interesting customers looking for a guide?"

Although I spoke the words nonchalantly, the look Misty gave me hinted she wasn't fooled in the least. The glances I kept stealing in the direction of the beautiful stranger didn't help my cause.

"There's been quite a few visitors over the past couple of days. All of them have secured a guide, except for one. A very special case," she added in a strange tone as she took the dusk boar off my left shoulder.

"A special case?" I repeated, curious.

She nodded. However, the way her happy demeanor dimmed set all my senses on high alert.

"Yes. She's a client specifically for you."

My brow shot up. "For me? Why?"

Although I instinctively knew she was speaking of the beautiful stranger, that she would say she was specifically for me made no sense. Unless you were a Seer, you couldn't guess that a person was someone else's Twin Flame. Sure, witnessing their physiological responses in that person's presence would give it away. But Misty had not seen me near that woman yet. So what could prompt such a statement?

"Nobody else will take it," Misty said, matter-of-factly. "Her mission is not just a tough one, it could qualify as suicidal."

I stiffened, a sense of dread washing over me. Of course, the day I find my Twin Flame, there would be some kind of drama pushing her to self-harm. To my dismay, despite the worry settling in the pit of my stomach, my mouth watered some more, and the fire burning in my veins cranked up another notch. I swallowed hard and willed my gaze back onto Misty.

My cheeks heated with embarrassment when I found the elder woman staring at me in shock, her nostrils flaring.

"By Ferazan! Remus, you're in heat?!"

I flinched and averted my eyes, feeling mortified. There was no reason for me to feel ashamed that I should have found my Twin Flame. And yet, a lifetime of being told I was an abomination that should have been put down at birth left indelible scars. The packs always made it clear I had to stay away from our females not to harm or taint them. To this day, any involvement I ever got with a woman—or even merely considering it—had me feeling like a criminal.

"I'm not in heat," I muttered, wishing I could disappear.

"So why are you...?"

Misty's voice trailed off as understanding slowly dawned on her. A flurry of emotions flitted over her wizened features: shock, disbelief, and finally elation. In that final instant, I realized I'd been holding my breath, bracing for the inevitable air of disgust and outrage that one such as I would dare think I could possibly be someone's fated mate. My heart filled with love for the older woman when her face lit up with pure joy for me.

"Your Twin Flame! That sweet child is your soulmate!" she whispered with a thrill in her voice. Before I could answer, her eyes flicked from side to side as she seemed lost in intense reflections. "How the stars align. It all makes sense now. It was fated."

"What? What do you mean?" I asked, confused.

She frowned, gave me a critical once over then, visibly displeased with my appearance, the innkeeper dragged me into the back kitchen.

"Misty, what are you doing?!" I exclaimed when she grabbed a clean cloth, wet it, and started scrubbing me as a mother would clean a rambunctious child who had smeared dirt all over himself from playing too roughly outside.

"You have to speak to your mate. But I must prepare you first," Misty replied absentmindedly while still scrubbing me.

I couldn't decide whether to laugh or be outraged. She didn't even seem to realize what she was doing. I wasn't actually *dirty*. At best, I had maybe a tiny streak of dried blood and the random strands of fur from carrying the beasts over my shoulders.

"Her name is Amara, and she's dying," Misty brutally dropped.

I froze, all fussing forgotten as my blood turned to ice. "What?" I breathed out.

"She's poisoned and requires a rare antidote that can only be found in these mountains," she said grimly.

"I'll get it for her," I said without hesitation. "What does she need?"

The sad look she gave me had my innards twisting. Misty threw the—essentially still clean—cloth into the sink and took both of my hands in hers. When she locked eyes with me, I braced for what would be terrible news.

"You must be strong, Son. The cure… It involves Ranael," she said in an apologetic tone.

I took a step back, her words striking me like a physical blow. Shaking my head, I tried to pull away from her, but she tightened her grip on my hands and closed the distance between us.

"Hear her out, Remus. Amara isn't foolish or some crazy lunatic pursuing a far-fetched charlatan cure," she quickly added in a pleading tone. "You're her only hope. I just warned you so that you would be prepared. But please, listen to her with an open mind."

"That's insanity, Misty! Ranael destroys anything he touches. He's taken my parents from me, and now you want me to deliver my mate to him to be butchered?!" I snapped, yanking my hands out of hers.

"Of course not, silly boy. I want you to be happy, Remus," Misty said in a reasonable but firm tone. "You may not be my blood, but I've always loved you as if you were the fruit of my body. The moment I saw this girl, I knew she was a beautiful, special soul. Now, I understand why. Fate sent Amara to you. Whatever challenges lie ahead, who better than you to see her through it? Listen to what she has to say. And if you still disagree, then you can plead your case with her as to why a different course of action might be better."

I stared intently at her, torn by conflicting emotions. My every instinct screamed that she was completely out of her mind to even suggest I should entertain such a mission, let alone that my Twin Flame should pursue an obviously suicidal endeavor.

Voss timidly approaching with a large bowl of steamy spiced wine interrupted us. At seventeen, the youngling was already a mountain of a male. I couldn't wait to see what a magnificent beast he would turn into once he reached full maturity. Too bad he had too sweet and gentle a disposition. He would have made a formidable alpha.

"Thank you, darling," Misty said warmly to her grandson, sounding relieved for the timely distraction.

She hastened to the boy and took the bowl with both hands before bringing it to me.

"Here, bring this to your mate. She ordered it while waiting for you to arrive. Go on, Son. And please, keep an open mind," Misty urged while gently pushing me out of the back kitchen.

I almost resisted in order to argue some more, but she wasn't the customer who needed convincing. And this gave me the excuse I needed to approach my Twin Flame without giving away the fact that my interest in her went well-beyond any business transaction.

To my shock, as soon as I exited the kitchen, I found Amara staring in my general direction, a hopeful expression on her stunning face. The disappointment that immediately took over the moment she spotted the bowl in my hands almost made me smile. Under different circumstances, I would have been amused by her mistaking me for a server. But Misty's revelations were messing with my head.

I didn't know this woman, but she was my life mate. I'd be damned if some poison took away the one good thing to have happened to me in decades.

A polite smile settled on Amara's sensuous lips as I stopped in front of her table. She extended a delicate pair of hands towards me to take the bowl. My eyes flicked to her long and slender fingers as they closed around the cup, and I couldn't help an appreciative smile upon seeing the pearl-colored nail polish which adorned her well-manicured nails. I always had this inexplicable obsession with nice hands, especially with well-groomed nails or claws.

Sadly, my fellow Lycans often proved to be rather neglectful on that front. They justified it by saying the minute they shifted into their wolf form to run or hunt, dirt or blood inevitably found their way underneath their claws. True though that was, it took seconds to clean.

"Thank you," Amara said in a friendly manner.

Nine Hells! The sound of her voice sent the most delicious shiver down my spine. It was soft and a little throaty as it glided over my skin like a warm summer breeze. She was even more breathtaking up close. My fingers twitched again with the need to sink into the lustrous curls of her puffy hair. I wanted to dive deep into the fathomless depths of her obsidian eyes and explore the most intimate corners of her psyche and discover all the hidden beauties of the goddess fated to me.

"My pleasure," I replied in a gentle tone, surprised I was even able to speak, then gestured at the bench across the table from her. "May I sit?"

She slightly recoiled and stared at me with a reserved look laced with confusion.

"My name is Remus Beltaine. Misty told me you needed a guide?" I said.

Her face lighting up with both understanding and elation did the strangest thing to me. I could count on one hand the number of people who had ever displayed such happiness at finding out my identity.

"Oh, Remus! Yes! Yes, please do have a seat!" she exclaimed with a thrill in her voice. "My name is Amara... Amara Sanni. And I'm indeed desperately looking for a guide for a challenging mission. Misty had nothing but praise for you. So I'm hoping you will be willing to escort me to my destination."

She spoke that last sentence with a slightly nervous laugh. The vulnerability with which she stared at me, and the almost pleading glimmer in her eyes had me aching to simply say yes to anything she desired.

But that would be pure madness.

As I settled down on the long bench of the booth, I discreetly inhaled her intoxicating scent. It made me dizzy, and my skin heated a bit more. However, the underlying sickly-sweet stench of impending death clawed at my heart, confirming Misty's ominous words. As shocking as her brutal admission had been, I was grateful for the warning which now enabled me to more stoically handle whatever Amara would throw my way.

"I will do everything in my power to help you achieve your goal," I replied cautiously. "However, I need to hear more about that mission before I can commit to anything. Misty hinted that it is quite dangerous."

A sliver of fear flitted over her features. I instinctively knew that it wasn't the mission itself that scared her, but the potential that I might refuse to take her when she revealed it to me. Once again, the irrational need to simply give her whatever she wanted burned deep in my gut. But as much as my protective instincts demanded I reassure and appease her, keeping her safe—even against her better judgment—was my new priority.

Amara nodded and ran a nervous hand over her hair.

"It is," she conceded. "I'm sick. Or rather, I've somehow become infected by a lethal poison that is slowly killing me. The cure can only be found in these mountains."

"I'm sorry to hear of your condition. But why do you need a guide to take you to the cure? Wouldn't it be safer for you to remain here and hire someone like me to go fetch it for you?" I asked, pretending like Misty hadn't already dropped that bomb on me.

The same hint of fear sparked in Amara's eyes, quickly hidden. She licked her lips and squared her shoulders before launching into the detailed retelling of the circumstances that led her to leave her peaceful life in Harmstead and settle in Willow Grove. How the symptoms manifested a month after her arrival, and how they matched the mysterious illness that had claimed her father's life when she was but an infant.

"Let me get this straight," I challenged, a hint of disbelief in my voice. "You are infected by a poison, but don't know which. You also don't know who poisoned you or how they did it. But you *know* what antidote you need and where to find it?!"

Seeing Amara flinch, because of my tone as I spoke those words, the incredulous expression on my face, or a mix of both utterly shamed me. I hadn't meant to give her the impression that

I thought her stupid or reckless. But you couldn't cure something if you didn't know what you were fighting.

I opened my mouth to apologize, but she didn't give me the opportunity to do so.

"I know how it sounds," she replied in a defensive tone while lifting her chin defiantly. "But I'm not some airhead on a fool's errand. A few days ago, I consulted Ronika, the best healer in the region—if not the country. She recommended I seek out the help of the Weaver, and I did. It is Cliona Nox herself who told me what the cure was and where to get it."

My back stiffened as I stared at her in shock and disbelief.

"The Weaver granted you an audience?!" I exclaimed.

She nodded. "Truth be told, it blew me away. I never expected her gates to open for me. But I had nothing to lose in at least trying…"

I continued to stare at her, robbed of words, and my mind reeling. So many times over the years I sought the Weaver's assistance, but to no avail. Did that mean that I couldn't be helped or simply that I had nothing to offer worth her while?

"But… what did she ask in exchange for her counsel?" I asked, shamed by the envy twisting my gut.

"Some of my blood, once I'm cured. She will be able to derive a potent antidote from it," Amara explained, then swiftly raised her palms in an appeasing gesture upon seeing my scandalized expression. "Don't worry. I'm well-aware of the fact that my blood in her hands could be used in extremely harmful ways against me. But she pledged not to wrong me and to exclusively use my blood to extract a serum, which will also only be used for good."

"A pledge?!" I exclaimed, flabbergasted. "You extracted a pledge from the Weaver?!"

Amara shook her head. "I didn't *extract* anything, she *volunteered* it. My reaction to her request made it clear I wasn't comfortable with giving an ingredient against me to an arcanist

DESTINED TO THE LYCAN

of her caliber. Whoever she intends to cure with that serum must be of great importance to her," she added pensively.

"Hmmm," I responded in a non-committal fashion. "And what is the antidote you seek in the mountains?"

My Twin Flame shifted uneasily in her seat. She absentmindedly reached for the medallion of her necklace. I didn't know the tear-shaped, amber-colored stone in it, but watching her dainty fingers fiddle with it hypnotized me.

"I must receive two different poisons to counter the one currently killing me. The first is a bite from the Cursed Demon Wolf's snake tail to destroy the poison in my veins. And once it's done, I need him to bite me with his fangs. His saliva will neutralize his venom. And then I'll be cured."

Despite Misty's warning, I gaped at Amara, gob smacked. This was not only worse than what I expected, it was beyond insane.

"I know how crazy it sounds," Amara added when I just continued to stare at her as if she'd lost her mind—which I was starting to believe might be the case. "But the Weaver taught me a summoning ritual that will temporarily bind Ranael as my protector. During that short window, he won't be able to do anything that would harm me."

"Injecting you with his snake's venom *is* going to harm you!" I countered in a self-evident manner.

She gave me an indulgent smile and replied in a reasonable tone. "Technically, that's true for anyone else. But in my case, it will actually do me good as it will eliminate the poison harming me."

"Fine," I conceded with reluctance. "Demon wolves are indeed protectors. But Ranael is rabid. He cannot be expected to respond normally to a protection summons."

Without missing a beat, Amara relayed to me everything the Weaver told her on that front. By the time she stopped, I felt beyond torn as to how I should respond. This entire plan screamed of pure madness. Like my peers, my instinctive reaction was to reject her request to assist her in this endeavor. It genuinely struck me as murder-suicide. However, she wasn't just some random potential client. Amara was my Twin Flame. For that alone, I had a duty to stand by her, come Hell or high water.

As much as I didn't believe this mission had the slightest hope of success, I couldn't dismiss the fact that the Weaver set her on this path. Cliona Nox *never* got involved unless she truly believed the task could be achieved. She also only ever helped if there was something in it for her, something unique that she fiercely coveted. She *wanted* my woman to succeed.

And this can save Amara's life...

I ran nervous fingers through my hair as I continued to stare at her, deeply divided. And yet, something on my face must have given away the fact that my heart had already caved even if my brain continued to grapple to come to terms with the inevitable. The timid smile that settled on her lips, and the hopeful glimmer that lit up her beautiful eyes gave it away.

"I went to the Weaver four times, but her gates never opened for me," I mused aloud with a hint of self-derision.

Amara looked at me with a curiosity laced with compassion. "May I ask why you went to her?" she asked in a soft voice.

I gave her an assessing look. "You have likely heard that I have certain... issues?"

To my relief, she didn't play dumb or seem uncomfortable about it. She merely nodded, her expression still welcoming and attentive.

"Some people say you're cursed, but Misty says you're sick."

It was my turn to nod. "Honestly, I think it's a bit of both. Thirty-three years ago, my parents went hunting but ran into Ranael. That never should have happened as the demon wolf was lurking way outside of his usual roaming area. He attacked them, and although my parents both managed to escape, my father was badly scratched. They conceived me in the couple of days that followed the attack. And then my father's health suddenly started declining."

"Oh no," Amara whispered with compassion.

"The first three days after the attack, he only thought that he was feeling unwell due to being bruised and battered. But on the fourth day, he declined at an exponential rate. Death claimed him on the twelfth day."

"Your poor mother must have been devastated."

"By all accounts, she was crushed. She had not been scratched, but her own health started declining in the weeks that followed. People initially assumed that it was depression and juggling a difficult pregnancy at the same time. But then, by the fifth month, they could smell Ranael on her—or rather around her womb."

"Ranael's venom had also infected your father's seed!" Amara whispered in horrified understanding.

I nodded, my teeth clenched with the old anger that always resurfaced every time I thought of how that single dreadful encounter shattered our lives.

"They sought the help of every healer and shaman possible, but to no avail. My mother died at the beginning of the eighth month of her pregnancy. They had to cut me out of her body. Lycan usually come out of the womb in our human form. I came out in my wolf form, reeking of Ranael. In a nearly unanimous decision, the pack decided to cast me out and left me in the woods to either die of exposure or be eaten."

"WHAT?! But you were an innocent child!" Amara exclaimed, outraged.

"I was," I replied in a conciliatory tone. "But I understand their fear. I was a danger that would likely bring death and destruction to the pack. To many, I was an abomination, the unholy offspring of the Cursed Wolf."

Amara shook her head, clearly disgusted. "Yet, despite their cruelty, you survived," she added with awe.

That did something funny to me. People usually viewed my survival as further proof that I was some kind of unnatural creature that shouldn't exist. They believed I enjoyed the protection of some unmentionable entity intent on unleashing me onto the world at the right time.

"Indeed, against all odds. A wildcat took me in. I never understood why she did it. After all, it's not like she couldn't smell Ranael on me, too. And yet she raised me alongside her cubs as if I was her own," I said, the old affection resurfacing for the wild beast who had shown me more compassion than my own people.

"That's amazing!" Amara said with wonder. "I guess nothing beats a mother's instinct to protect and nurture a youngling in need. But how did you reconnect with the pack?"

"A little after I turned two years old, the pack came hunting on her territory. Mama tried to protect me and my siblings, but I ended up being the one protecting all of them," I said wistfully, then chuckled at her bemused expression. "Even though we're not the same species, I will always think of her and her cubs as my family, since they technically were in the first crucial years of my life."

"I can see that," Amara replied with approval, which touched me further. "But how did you protect them? Did you attack the pack?"

I shook my head. "I just took a menacing stance in front of them, and the pack kind of freaked out when they saw me. As I had never learned how to speak, I had no idea what they were saying. But I found out later that they thought I was a demon or a revenant. They just hightailed it out of there. As one of the Wise of the pack, Misty came to investigate. It took many days of her carefully approaching and enticing me to earn my trust."

"Wow! So your relationship goes a long way back!"

I nodded. "If not for her, I would have remained a feral beast. After a couple of months, she finally convinced me to come with her," I said, my heart filling with love for the elderly woman. "I don't think I could have done so without Mama's blessing. But a part of her understood that I needed to go to my people to reach my full potential. I continued to visit her until her passing a few years ago."

"Do you still see your siblings?" she asked gently.

"No. Most of them moved on as soon as they reached maturity. They were also growing uncomfortable with me the more 'human' I became," I explained pensively. "To better fit in, I was now almost always in my human form, whereas I had spent the first couple of years exclusively in my wolf form. It wasn't easy learning to speak, walk on two legs, use my hands and utensils, cook food and all that other weird stuff people do. Wearing clothes was definitely the most annoying part."

Amara snorted, and her eyes slightly went out of focus as she was likely trying to picture the younger version of myself throwing a tantrum at being asked to put clothes on.

"But how was life for you here after the pack accepted you?" she asked carefully.

I snorted with self-derision. "To this day, none of the packs have fully accepted me. They mostly tolerate me because of Misty. Now, things are better than back in the day, but I'm still somewhat of an outcast. They're afraid of me."

"Why is that?" she asked in the same soft voice thankfully devoid of any condemnation or suspicion.

"My blood and all my bodily fluids contain a low concentration of the demon wolf's venom. It is the weakest in my urine and saliva, meaning that neither could cause harm to anyone exposed to them. But frequent exposure to any of my other fluids would result in death."

"Hmmm... I can see why that would worry people, but

unless you're planning on bleeding or sweating all over them, their fear seems a little excessive," Amara mused aloud.

The way I shifted uneasily didn't go unnoticed. My Twin Flame immediately gave me an intense gaze as she waited for me to continue.

"Over the years, they had in fact gradually relaxed around me until I hit puberty. From that moment forward, I became negatively affected by the full moon. I kind of... become rabid until sunrise."

My chest constricted, and I swallowed hard when Amara slightly recoiled, a shocked expression descending over her features. Although she didn't display the horror such a confession usually triggered in others, my words clearly struck her hard. I just couldn't interpret what emotions were coursing through her. But a lifetime of rejection made me fear hers came from a similar place.

"The full moon?" she echoed, her wheels spinning. "I wonder if that's why the Weaver told me to wait until after the full moon to come. What happens to you then? What do you do?"

That also hit a nerve. Had the Weaver foreseen that no one else but me would consider taking her on that mission? Had she specifically requested Amara delay her arrival until it was safe to be around me?

"Nothing," I replied forcefully. "I have many safe places that I lock myself in until the sun rises. While enraged, I'm too mindless to unlock the door of my cage. And as a second safety measure, there is a magic circle surrounding each of them that will not let me out until my mind is at peace again. So no one has to worry about me ever causing harm during that night."

My heart soared when her shoulders relaxed almost imperceptibly with relief.

"That's good then. It sounds like you have it all under control." She hesitated, licked her lips nervously before carefully asking the question I expected. "Have there ever been incidents?"

I shook my head. "Never, not even the first time it happened. There are sufficient signs that the change is upon me hours prior, which allows me to go into a safe place first. Anyway, the pack would have taken me out a long time ago if my rage ever harmed anyone."

The glowing smile she bestowed upon me had me melting from the inside out.

"Then that's all good enough for me. The question is whether you consent to be my guide. I'm not above begging. I desperately need your help," she said, her eyes flicking between mine.

I heaved a sigh.

"Every fiber of my being is shouting for me to shut down such an insane request. Logic demands I say no," I replied gently.

"But?" she insisted with a voice filled with hope.

I hesitated and gave her an assessing look. "Can you even make it there? Ranael dwells in a plateau beyond the Dark Woods. It is a hard road, and we can only ride so far before we have to set out on foot. This involves a long and difficult climb. No flying mounts will take us there. With your current health, you might not be able to handle it. The weather can be very temperamental in these areas. And sometimes, we may not even find a cave to shelter in."

"I will keep going even if I have to crawl," she stated with determination. "I'm dying, Remus. The Weaver said I must reach the Cursed Wolf at least one week before the full moon. Whatever it takes, even if I have to set off on my own, I will get there. I refuse to just sit idly while my life is fading away."

Her words made me frown. "Why one week before the full moon?"

"Until now, I wondered about that. I believe she always meant for *you* to be my guide. Which explains why she wanted me to come after the full moon, and why we must complete the mission at least a week prior to the next one. Ranael must bite me twice, the second bite a few days after the first one."

"Leaving us with a couple more days for me to take you back to safety before locking myself up," I whispered with sudden understanding.

She nodded firmly while holding my gaze unwaveringly. "Yes. This cannot be a coincidence. The Weaver always meant for it to be you."

I didn't know how I felt about that. A part of me rejoiced. Surely, this was another sign from Fate. But what if I failed her?

"Very well," I conceded at last. "But I will need a bit of time to prepare. We shall leave the day after tomorrow."

"Thank you!" Amara exclaimed.

In her enthusiasm, she unconsciously reached for my right hand and clasped it between both of hers. The fire in my blood— which had cooled during our conversation—flared again, setting my skin ablaze. I swallowed hard and gently squeezed her hand back in a reassuring fashion.

In that instant, I knew that nothing and no one would stop me from helping her achieve her goal. We would get her the cure she needed, even at the cost of my own life.

CHAPTER 4
AMARA

After a restless first night, the following day dragged endlessly with not a single sign of Remus. More than once, I forced myself to silence the panicked little voice screaming that he had vanished on me and would be a no-show in the morning. And yet, another much louder voice told me to stop being silly.

That total stranger awakened in me a bone deep trust that I couldn't explain. Granted, Remus was insanely handsome, tall and muscular in a way that almost made me feel fragile. The beastly aura that emanated from him was both intimidating and enticing. A truly feral creature lurked within him, contained by a sweet and highly protective male.

The fact that he went rabid during the full moon should terrify me and automatically eliminate him as a potential candidate. However, although I didn't know her either, I also implicitly trusted Misty. Her vouching for him, and the Weaver's words about finding someone I trusted with my life on the day after the full moon reinforced my belief that he was the one.

To my chagrin, I didn't really take the time to visit the village or even hang out in the common room. The visiting packs made me uncomfortable. The pity and disapproval in their eyes rubbed me the wrong way. As much as I appreciated that they stemmed from a wish to protect me from the male they perceived as a threat—not to say an abomination—it pissed me off how they treated him.

Throughout our conversation that first night, their gazes never strayed from us, all of them condemning, many visibly fighting the urge to intervene. I almost wished one of them actually did so when Remus finally consented to be my guide. As much as I disliked confrontations, I would have gladly ripped them a new one for refusing to help me and yet attempting to prevent the one who would from doing so.

Considering the long journey that awaited us, I rested as much as possible in the comfortable bed that Misty had put at my disposal and had most of my meals in my room.

On the second day, I made my way down to the dining room, my stomach fluttering with nerves and excitement. Remus stated we would head out around 8:00 in the morning. I wanted a solid breakfast before hitting the road and to grab a few snacks to bring with us.

Halfway down the stairs, the sound of a heated conversation reached me. I almost stomped my feet to make my approach clear so that they would be warned should this be a private matter. However, I immediately recognized Ulric's voice angrily addressing Misty. That single sentence made it clear they were talking about me.

"He can't take her!" Ulric hissed. "You know as well as I do that this whole thing is suicidal!"

"Leave it be, Ulric," Misty said sternly. "The decision is made."

"You know that he only wants to fuck her!" Ulric snapped.

I barely repressed a gasp, feeling outraged on Remus's behalf.

"Stop it!" Misty snarled.

"It's true!" Ulric insisted stubbornly.

"It's not. And even if it was true, what does it matter? Remus would never force himself on a woman. Or are you insinuating the contrary?"

"Of course not," he said angrily, which both surprised and reassured me. "But his seed is foul. He should have been put down decades ago."

"By Ferazan, why can't you just leave him alone?!" Misty exclaimed, discouraged.

The same thought crossed my mind as a protective anger surged within me. Such vitriol against Remus felt personal. What had transpired between the two men to stir such hatred?

"Remus will ruin her," Ulric said forcefully, as if that was all the justification he needed.

"Have you forgotten the part where she's dying?" Misty challenged with annoyance. "What if he manages to save her? Wouldn't that be a good thing? At least he gives her a chance."

"No, he will only delay the inevitable as he will kill her with his seed," Ulric argued stubbornly. "And even if she survives—which I highly doubt—she will bear him cursed pups. Do you really want more of *him* running around?"

Another wave of anger welled within me upon hearing the contempt with which he said the word 'him.' Just as I was wondering why he felt so adamant that there would be some sort of romantic involvement between the two of us, Misty provided the answer.

"First of all, I love this boy. Having more of him around would be a blessing, not a curse," Misty said with a conviction that had my heart filling with affection for her and gratitude on behalf of Remus. "Second, you and everyone else know that she is his Twin Flame. You've seen the symptoms the moment he walked into the room. The mate bond is sacred. We have a duty to honor it."

"That demon shouldn't have a Twin Flame!" Ulric hissed.

"Enough!" Misty snapped in a hushed tone, while casting a nervous glance towards the staircase.

My stomach knotted. I hadn't meant to eavesdrop. Considering how long I had been standing there, I could only presume I unconsciously reacted in a way that gave away my presence. Then again, maybe my scent finally wafted to them. Either way, there was no point attempting to further hide my presence.

Shrugging dismissively, Ulric turned to boldly face the staircase, a determined look on his face.

"Don't shush me. She deserves to know the truth!"

"And what truth is that?" I challenged as I climbed down the remaining stairs, all thoughts of apologies for listening in fading away.

"Remus is dangerous!"

"Dangerous how? By helping me when no one else will?!" I said defiantly.

"By lusting for you when he is sick!" Ulric exclaimed as if it was self-evident.

I shrugged while stopping at a respectable distance in front of him. "Assuming you are correct, neither of these things are a crime. At least, he's willing to help me when the rest of you would leave me to die."

"Only so he can bed you!"

I rolled my eyes. "So what? Whatever his motives, he's the only one who stepped up in my time of need. The question is why do you care so much? Why are you so determined to get in the way?"

"Remus thinks you are Twin Flames," Ulric articulated slowly as if he was starting to think I was too dense to understand what should otherwise be obvious. "He will therefore try to seduce and claim you."

"Again, why is that bad? He's handsome, skilled, respectful, and has come highly recommended," I added, casting a meaningful glance at Misty. "I could think of far worse men to be paired with, assuming he and I even are soulmates. And you can spare me the comment about him being sick. I am too, remember?"

"You don't understand," Ulric sighed, frustrated.

"*You* are the one who doesn't understand," I interjected with aggravation. "If he and I truly are Twin Flames, then Fate will see to it that things work out for us. If we're not, then we'll just part ways. If this mission results in my death, then so be it. I'm already dying. I have nothing to lose, but much to gain. So unless you know someone else who will take me all the way to the end, then I really don't want to hear anything you have to say. Just stay out of my business."

Ulric stood there fuming, his fingers twitching as if he was fighting the urge to grab me by the shoulders and give me a good shake to knock some sense into me. After a few moments, he growled in frustration then uttered a string of swear words as he stormed out of the otherwise empty inn.

I stared at his receding back in confusion before a soft chuckle from Misty reclaimed my attention. She was smiling at me with a tender expression that instantly made me ache for a hug from my mother. It was strange what a strong connection I had developed with this woman in such a short time.

"What's his deal?" I asked the older woman, genuinely baffled.

"It's a long story," she replied with a discouraged sigh. "Ask Remus about him. It is *his* story to tell."

I opened and closed my mouth a couple of times, hesitating as to how I wanted to word my question before blurting it out.

"Is Remus safe?" I asked sheepishly.

"Yes," Misty replied with a conviction and firmness that wiped out any lingering doubt I might have had. "You will never find a more noble and trustworthy male than my Remus."

The maternal possessiveness with which she spoke that last

sentence made me smile. However unusual their relationship had come to be, that female truly loved him like her own.

"Is it true what he claimed?" I caught myself asking again. "Does Remus think we're Twin Flames?"

Misty's face softened, although I didn't miss the sliver of worry in her silver eyes. I couldn't explain why, but I believed concern over how I might react to her response triggered that reaction.

"It is true," she confirmed carefully. "There are clear signs when Lycans meet their other half."

"You mean fever, dry mouth, high pulse rate, dilated pupils, and a darker sclera," I asked.

Misty's eyes widened in surprise. "That's correct. Although you missed the aching fangs and change of scent. Still, you know a lot about my people."

I shrugged to hide how flattered I felt by her impressed expression. "I had a couple of days before I set off on my journey here. So I read everything I could about Lycans to have a better idea of what I would be dealing with."

"Smart girl," Misty said approvingly. "But cast away any fears you may feel. Remus is a good male. He truly is like a son to me. You couldn't have hoped for a better guide to take you on this perilous journey. There is no doubt for any of us that you are Twin Flames. He wouldn't have brought it up to you until the mission was over. He will not pressure you in any way. Just follow your heart and your instincts. Fate will sort the rest. None of this is a coincidence."

"Thank you," I said, genuinely grateful.

"Now enough chit chatting. Have a seat so that I can properly feed you before you set off," Misty said in a tone that brooked no argument.

I chuckled as she shooed me towards one of the stools at the bar before vanishing inside the kitchen. She returned moments later with a mountain of food. I shamelessly dug in, chowing down far more than I thought myself capable of. The greedy side of me wanted to keep going but making myself sick from gorging too much would be counterproductive.

Just as I was pushing back my plate, the front door's discreet whine claimed my attention. My heart skipped a beat upon seeing Remus walk in. By the gods, he looked good enough to eat. I had been too distraught the first time we met to fully appreciate his beauty, but that man was truly stunning.

He had to be at least 6'5, and 230 lbs. of pure muscle. The silky, dark brown hair that cascaded in soft waves down below his shoulders had my fingers itching with the need to sink into it. The possessive yet protective glimmer in his golden eyes as they glided over me had my toes instantly curling. Seeing his white sclera steadily darken as he approached me messed with my head. This physiological response confirmed beyond any doubt that we were indeed matched. Lycans had no control over this.

Instead of freaking me out, it sent a pleasant heat spreading through my chest. I hadn't been looking for love, and I couldn't deny that my desperate circumstances likely influenced my positive response to this situation. But this only gave me something more to live and fight for. I didn't know this man, but I was happy and willing to explore what could possibly be.

He made a beeline for me, a gentle smile stretching his generous lips. I had never been much into hairy men. While he had a nicely trimmed mustache and beard gracing his square jaw, there were only some patches of fur on the outer edges of his shoulders and arms and a few strands of hair peeking through the loosely laced collar of his sleeveless shirt. My shameless mind immediately wondered if it continued down into a happy trail under his garment.

Yes, Remus is truly a delicious-looking male. And he's mine…?!

I nervously slipped down my stool to stand before Remus as he was closing the distance between us.

"Good morning, Amara," Remus said as he stopped in front of me.

"Good morning, Remus," I replied, feeling stupid as I tried to repress an inexplicable urge to giggle like a schoolgirl.

"I'm glad to see that you've already eaten," he said, apparently unaware of my inner turmoil. "I hope you are well rested as I would like us to set off immediately. Ideally, we will ride hard and fast today as the weather forecasts are iffy at best, and I can smell storm rain in the air. If we make good time, we should be able to reach the Hunters Lodge before nightfall, and hopefully before the storm begins."

I nodded and cast a furtive glance outside through one of the large windows before returning my attention to him.

"Sounds like a plan. But what if we don't make it?"

"There are caves along the way that we can shelter in. It won't be as comfortable, but it will keep us dry and warm," he explained in a gentle tone.

"Perfect," I replied, relieved.

Obviously, I would sleep wherever we needed to, but I'd never been too keen on roughing it outside. Creepy crawlers and I didn't really get along.

Misty walked out of the kitchen with a couple of leather bags, which she extended to Remus.

"Here is some food to hold you over for the first leg of your journey," she said in that maternal tone I was growing used to. "It's nothing fancy, just some breads, dried meats, nuts, and fruits."

"Thank you, Misty," Remus said before kissing her forehead.

I smiled, moved to see her ruffle his long hair as if he was but a young boy. It was all the more endearing that she looked so petite and fragile compared to his impressive height and mass.

"Take good care of my girl, out there," Misty told him with false severity. "I'll have a feast waiting to celebrate your return."

My throat constricted as I smiled back at the elder woman.

She caressed my cheek and ushered us out of the inn. To my surprise, only two horses awaited us outside. I glanced towards the stables, expecting Voss to bring out my carriage only for Remus to give me an apologetic look.

"We cannot use your carriage. Not only will it be too slow, but we will also leave the horses at the inn once we reach it in four days. We must travel light. I've already packed everything we need," Remus explained in a gentle voice.

Although I should have expected it, I still felt a little distraught to have so few things with me. Aside from the candles and reagents for the summons and a few changes of clothes, I couldn't bring any of the other creature comforts I had hoped to carry with me, including a rolled sleeping mat.

As we bid our farewells, the first few familiar faces started making their way towards the inn. I lifted my chin defiantly at their disapproving glances and followed Remus as we made our way out of the small village. To my chagrin, he immediately set a fast pace not too conducive of conversing as we headed north towards destiny.

CHAPTER 5
REMUS

For the thousandth time, I cast a guilty glance towards Amara. We'd been riding for hours, only slowing down for our mounts to rest a little, as well as very brief stops for food and drink. Despite her obvious discomfort at times, my woman displayed an impressive resilience without a single complaint. I hated that her first experience exploring Wolfmoon Mountains should be under such dire circumstances, and that it should occur in such a strenuous fashion.

However, peering up at the darkening skies reinforced the validity of the punishing pace I had set. The gathering clouds upset me more than words could express. I'd hoped we would have traveled much farther before the storm came upon us. Normally, I would have delayed our departure until the weather cooperated better. But my woman was on borrowed time.

In that single day separated from her, the scent of death that clung to her had noticeably increased, despite its subtlety. The need to protect and save Amara burned in my gut. I just wished I had wings to fly her directly to our destination and get all of this over with for her sake.

When I veered off the packed dirt road we'd been following

since exiting the village, my mate gave me an inquisitive look. I slowed down my horse to a slow trot, and she immediately adjusted her mount's speed to mine.

"The storm will begin soon," I explained, gesturing with my chin at the dark clouds hanging menacingly overhead. "We must find shelter before it does."

"Okay," Amara replied in a soft voice that failed to hide the obvious relief she felt.

Another wave of guilt swept through me. I couldn't tell if the fear of being caught outside in the elements or exhaustion from our rough journey so far prompted that reaction. Then again, it could very well be a mix of both.

"There's a cave located less than a mile from here. If we hurry, we'll be there shortly," I said, pointing in its general direction.

"Lead the way," she replied with a grateful smile.

I picked up the pace, cutting through the woods until we reached our destination. This area was safe, the local wildlife mostly made of herbivores and small mammals more likely to run from us than to attack.

Seeing Amara's face light up as the trees parted to reveal a tall rock outcropping brought a smile to my face. Although this place was anything but fancy or comfortable, I loved how I felt as if I was caring for my mate.

I stopped the horses outside the entrance of the natural cave. Over the years, my peers modified the opening to form a sheltering wall that kept strong winds or rain from getting inside whenever we needed to seek refuge within. They carved an additional section to act as a temporary stable for our mounts.

I hopped off my horse and hastened to Amara's side to help her down. The way she beamed at me made me feel dizzy. How could anyone pack so much kindness, gratitude, and warmth in a single smile? But it was the feel of her slender waist beneath my palms as I lifted her off her ride that messed with my head. The memory of her hands holding mine came flooding back. I didn't want to release her after setting her down on her feet. I just wanted to draw her into my embrace and bury my face in the puffy curls of her hair.

My skin heated, and my vision brightened as I forced myself to release her. To my shock, an almost shy expression fleeted over my mate's beautiful face. But it was the pleased—almost smug—edge to her smile that retained my attention.

Does she know what is happening with me?

Judging by my physiological responses, I didn't doubt my sclera had darkened. Did she know what it meant? Did she notice how much warmer my skin got whenever I was in close proximity with her? If so, would it be too bold of me to assume this satisfied smile meant she wouldn't be opposed to a relationship with the likes of me?

But now wasn't the time to speculate. A loud rumbling in the distance indicated the storm would begin any minute now. I quickly secured our horses in the nook connecting to the main area through a doorway on the left side, and relieved them of their burden while Amara fed them.

She joined me shortly thereafter in the main room. Its organic shape vaguely resembled an oval, with a high ceiling in the center which slanted down towards the edges. The packs had smoothed down the stalactites and sharper edges that made staying here slightly hazardous. Five sconces illuminated the room with purple magical flames, creating an intimate and soothing ambiance. Although mostly barren, the cave offered a makeshift table and benches, which had been carved directly out of the stone.

"Have a seat and eat," I offered in a friendly manner as I pulled out some of the food Misty provided. "Tomorrow, I will hunt for us and serve you a freshly cooked meal once we reach the lodge."

"Don't worry about such things," Amara said. "This isn't a

guided tour for leisure. I don't expect gourmet meals and fancy accommodations. So long as I go to bed with something in my belly, and we're not getting rained on, I'm happy."

"Those two things I can definitely promise," I said teasingly. "But a bit of extra comfort is always welcome."

"Agreed," Amara replied. "But I don't want you fretting over it or going out of your way to make it happen. I'm just grateful you agreed to take me on this journey."

"You're kind, but I will always fret over the welfare of the people in my charge," I replied, keeping it neutral when I really wanted to say that I would do anything for the comfort of my mate.

"So I see," she replied, waving at the cave. "This isn't a random formation. This table and benches are clearly manmade, even though they are still rough."

I nodded. "Hunters frequently use this place, as well as hikers. Normally, they will put a sleeping mat on this slab for the night."

She frowned while glancing at the large section of stone I was pointing at. Two more similar slabs had been roughly carved into the rectangular shape of a single bed.

"If people regularly use them here, why didn't you let me bring my own mat on this journey?" she asked, confused. "Sleeping directly on the rock or on the ground will be rather uncomfortable tonight."

"Because the mat will become too cumbersome later on in our journey," I explained in an apologetic tone. "I really hoped we would reach the lodge tonight so you would be more comfortable. As I previously mentioned, the path we must travel will grow increasingly rough. In fact, I will carry you for the last leg of the trip."

Her eyes widened in shock. "Carry me?!"

I nodded with a teasing expression. "Technically, you will actually ride my wolf."

Shoving the piece of dried meat I was holding into my mouth to free my hand, I leaned down to retrieve the harness from one of my bags propped up against the side of the bench. Amara stared in disbelief as I unfolded it to show her.

"This was one of the reasons I needed an extra day before our departure," I explained smugly, although a sliver of nervousness reared its head at her potential reaction. "I made this harness for you yesterday."

Robbed of words, Amara's gaze flicked incredulously between the harness and my face.

"Ride you like a horse?" she asked in a hesitant voice.

"Yes," I replied, suddenly feeling self-conscious.

She stared at me a second longer, seeming unsure as to how she felt about it. "Do you do that often for people?"

I recoiled and looked at her as if she said something outrageous. Although that question was fair under the circumstances, it still rubbed me the wrong way.

"Never! This will be my first time doing this," I said, sounding a little offended.

"But you will do it for me?" she insisted, a strange expression fleeting over her features.

I responded with a grunt and a stiff nod.

"Why?" Amara asked with sincere confusion.

"Because you are sick, and you will absolutely need it if we are to reach our destination. The journey will put far too great a strain on you without my assistance. I pledged to take you to the cure, and I'm a man of my word," I said.

That same strange expression flashed over her face. She chewed her bottom lip as if pondering whether to ask the question that clearly burned her tongue.

"Would you do this for another sick customer?" she asked at last.

"No."

Her brows shot up at the swift and definitive way I responded.

"Would you take another dying person to Ranael, if they asked?" Amara insisted when I didn't expand further.

I hesitated. "Probably not."

She scrunched her face when I reached for another piece of dried meat and started chewing instead of providing additional explanation for my stance.

"Is it for the reasons Ulric claimed?"

I froze, stopped mid-chew, and studied her face as if it would reveal what she meant. My mind raced as I speculated about what horror he might have said about me.

"What did he say?" I asked cautiously.

She held my gaze unwaveringly, her face unreadable.

"He said a lot of wild things," she replied in a non-committal fashion.

"Like what?" I insisted, annoyed to have her give me a taste of my own medicine.

"He claims that you are dangerous, and that you're only taking me so that you can bed me."

I jumped to my feet, anger and outrage swelling within me. "I'm not a rapist! I would never trap a woman or lure her into the woods just to have my way with her!"

Amara raised her palm in an appeasing gesture and indicated for me to resume my seat.

"I know. Ulric confirmed as much. Please, sit down," she said in a soothing voice.

My jaw dropped, and I remained still, my mind reeling until she once more gestured for me to sit.

"He did?" I asked, confused as I settled back down on the bench.

She nodded. "He claims that you believe we're soulmates."

A wave of heat rushed to my cheeks, which felt on the verge

of bursting into flames. I squirmed on my seat, and scratched my nape, feeling mortified.

"That idiot speaks out of turn," I grumbled. "He needs to learn to mind his own business."

"Are you saying that he lied?" she pressed, clearly unwilling to let it go.

I wanted to drop the topic, especially since her face was impossible to read. What if I gave the wrong answer? What if I confessed and it turned her off?

"I'm just saying that it's not important," I replied evasively.

"It is important to *me*," Amara said, her voice hardening slightly.

I inwardly cursed Ulric to the darkest pit of the Nine Hells as my mind raced to find a suitable answer.

"Amara, I will do everything in my power to get you to the cure and to protect you from any harm, including from myself," I said, choosing my words carefully.

My stomach dropped at the way her face closed off, her air of disappointment cutting me deeper than the sharpest knife. I heaved a sigh, and my shoulders slouched in defeat. This was not how I wanted to broach the topic of the bond that united us.

"My physiological reactions in your presence say that you are indeed my Twin Flame," I mumbled, my eyes lowered in shame.

I braced for an outraged outburst that never came. My whole life, I'd been told that it would be blasphemy and even criminal for one such as I to take a mate, and worse still, to reproduce.

"See? It wasn't that hard," Amara said in a soft voice.

Stunned, I flicked my gaze up to lock eyes with her. My jaw dropped at finding her smiling almost timidly at me.

"Is that why you agreed to help me?" she prodded further, tilting her head to the side.

Still flabbergasted by her reaction, I nodded absent-mindedly. "Mostly, yes. Although I would have likely tried to convince you to go a different route had you not been set on this mission by the Weaver."

"So without those two factors, you would have turned me down like the others?" she insisted.

In that instant, I realized this line of questioning went beyond merely confirming a rumor she heard. My mate was assessing the type of male I was. I quelled my instinctive reaction to try and guess what answer she wanted from me. If Fate meant for us to be together, we would fall in love with who we were, and not who we pretended to be.

"Your being my Twin Flame means I would do anything in my power for you. But had you not been, I would have still tried to help you. I probably wouldn't go to the same extremes that I'm willing to go to for you. But I honestly cannot say for certain what I would have done. What I *can* say without a doubt is that, without the Weaver's involvement, I don't think I would have agreed to go all the way. Even now it feels like an insane undertaking," I admitted.

Amara pursed her lips and slowly nodded as she weighed my words. "I understand. Truth be told, I came here believing no one would agree. So I'm glad you did."

I gave her a timid smile, and a somewhat awkward silence settled between us. By the way she was looking at me, my mate seemed to expect me to say something more. I cleared my throat and went for it.

"Does it bother you that we are… fated?" I asked carefully, bracing for her response.

To my shock, Amara smiled, that same air of adorable shyness creeping back onto her beautiful face. She shook her head.

"Not at all. In truth, I find it very flattering," she said sheepishly. "You're a very handsome male. And by all accounts, wolf flames are extremely loyal and very protective of their mates. What woman wouldn't want that for herself?"

"I am sick," I challenged.

She shrugged. "So am I."

"But you won't be once we heal you," I argued.

"*If* we heal me," she countered.

"*When* we heal you," I said sternly while giving her a disapproving stare.

She chuckled and bowed her head in concession. "*When* we've healed me, we'll figure out a way to heal *you*."

I gave her a sad smile. "Unfortunately, there doesn't appear to be a cure for me. The Weaver wouldn't even see me."

Amara waved a dismissive hand. "Because it wasn't the right time. After all, she sent me to you. It cannot be a coincidence."

As much as I didn't want to allow myself false hope, I couldn't help it taking root deep in my heart.

"Ultimately, Fate will decide," I replied in a non-committal fashion.

She nodded, her gaze going out of focus as she reflected on something before returning her attention to me with a speculative glimmer in her dark eyes.

"Assuming that our mission succeeds, and that we do like each other, would we be able to lead a normal life together?"

My heart leapt, and a powerful emotion nearly choked me that she seemed so open to a possible future with me.

"I'm normal in most ways," I replied a little too eagerly. "If we built a life together, I would only be away on the night of the full moon, and we also couldn't have pups."

My mate pensively chewed her bottom lip and slowly nodded again. "I remember you mentioning something about your seed, as did Ulric."

My anger flared at the wretched male's interference in my personal affairs. But I silenced it. Now wasn't the time to let him ruin what could potentially be the beginning of the rest of my life.

"Correct. Exposure to my seed and my blood would be dangerous. But everything else is safe," I confirmed.

"Then we'll just be a normal couple who uses protection," Amara said matter-of-factly.

I stared at her in awe, too many emotions clashing within me. She looked so reserved and demure that I never expected she would so openly discuss such matters with me. But once again, it was the ease with which she seemed to accept that we were indeed meant for each other that took my breath away. Obviously, she was no more in love with me than I was with her as we'd just met. And yet, she was acknowledging our bond like any other Lycan would, even though she couldn't feel the same physiological responses I did.

Whatever the reason, I welcomed it.

"Yes, we will be," I said, embarrassed by the emotion audible in my voice.

She smiled again, but it quickly faded as a frown creased her forehead. "I'm curious though as to why Ulric hates you so much."

I flinched, the sorrow I had pushed back down years ago rearing its head again.

"It's a long story," I said dismissively.

She raised an eyebrow, giving me that look I was starting to recognize, which meant she wouldn't let me dodge the question.

"We've got time," she deadpanned.

I snorted and nodded in defeat.

She tore another piece of bread with some cheese and began to chew as I gathered my thoughts.

"This whole mess dates back too many years. It started before my birth. Ulric is actually my cousin. You met his father, Rolf, who is the current leader of our pack. Only the Apex Alpha can occupy that role. My mother was Rolf's sister. He blames my father for killing her, and me as well."

"You?! But it was the poison that killed her, not the pregnancy!" Amara exclaimed.

"Yes, but that poison was transferred to her through my father's seed. And as I grew, the fluid exchange between a mother and her child poisoned her further. So he's not entirely wrong, although I was as much a victim in all of this as she and my father were. For all that, he's never been mean to me. But he cannot silence the resentment he felt about it."

"I can see that."

"But he also disliked my father. You see, it isn't uncommon for the leadership of the pack to pass from father to son. A competition is held whenever it is time for leadership to change, or if one of the members wants to challenge the Alpha for the position. My father won against Uncle Rolf. He was our pack leader until his untimely death, which allowed my uncle to ascend."

"Which means you would have been the Alpha had your father lived!" Amara said with sudden understanding.

"I would have been first in line for the role and been raised accordingly," I gently corrected. "I still would have needed to defeat challengers for it, and I actually did. Except, I didn't want to be the Alpha because of my sickness. So I forfeited that honor."

"If not for your illness, would you *want* to lead the pack?" my mate asked with genuine curiosity.

I shook my head without hesitation. "Back then, I would have said yes. But not anymore. Too many people would resent following me. And truth be told, I have grown fond of my freedom and of being a lone wolf."

"So does Ulric resent that you are shunning the role that will likely be his? It must be embarrassing for him to know that a better wolf exists out there?"

I gave her a sad smile. "No. It's not uncommon for some powerful alphas not to wish to take on that mantle. Not everyone is made to lead people. The problem occurred when we were young pups. After Misty brought me back to the pack, my cousin was my only friend. In fact, he treated me like a blood brother. Unfortunately, pups tend to play rough. People warned him not to play with me, and especially not to bite me. But he did... All pups do."

"Oh no!" Amara whispered, pressing a palm to her chest. "He got sick?"

I nodded, my chest constricting as the memory of those dark days came flooding back.

"He'd done it countless times before, but he'd broken skin for the first time that day. It was only a couple of drops of my blood, but it was enough that it almost killed him. For years, Ulrich was lame. His lungs were too weak for him to be able to run or perform any type of exertion. He had no balance, suffered from impaired vision, and had a faulty nose. He went from being a promising hunter to a complete burden... or at least so he perceived himself. And he was only eight years old."

"By the gods... it must have been horrible, especially at such a young age," Amara said, her voice filled with compassion. "But that wasn't your fault. You didn't deliberately set out to harm him."

"I didn't. But as a pup, Ulric believed that no harm would ever come to him from me because we were brothers. And brothers didn't hurt each other."

"But you had no power over your blood sickness!" Amara exclaimed in a self-evident tone.

"I know. But he was just a child. He felt betrayed. And as the adults banned me from seeing him, I never got a chance to explain to him how sorry I was, that I had no control over it, and that I loved him. Instead, he believed that I had poisoned and then abandoned him."

"No one explained the truth to him!" Amara said, her outrage audible.

I clenched my teeth and shook my head as the old resentment resurfaced. "Not only did they not explain to him, but they also fueled his anger. They never approved of our friendship. This was their opportunity to put an end to it once and for all. The fact that the other pups bullied him over the following years for being weak and useless to the pack only fanned his rage against me. Seeing me thrive and excel in all things physical while he wasted away made him hate me more."

"But he looks totally fine now and strong," Amara argued.

I nodded. "He is indeed fine now, the gods be praised. His mother took him to every witch, healer, and shaman she could find. They eventually fixed him, but it was a long and painful journey. He only survived because he had been healthy and just swallowed a couple of drops. Had he received more, he would have perished."

Amara frowned, seeming to struggle with something.

"I can understand why he might have resented you as a child. But I'm confused as to why he still hates you so much today. Are you sure he doesn't resent you for being stronger still?"

I pursed my lips and carefully gave the matter a second thought. "Honestly, I don't know. People have taunted him about the fact that the 'cursed wolf' is better than him, and how they will have to settle for the lesser Alpha. But this type of mockery isn't uncommon. Lycans can be total jerks in the way we jest with each other. He did get mad about it once and challenged me to a duel, which I won."

"Thus proving the rumors right," my mate said softly.

I sighed heavily, feeling defeated. "Maybe I should have let him win."

"No," Amara said forcefully, taking me aback. "Had you done that, and anyone had noticed, it would have been even more humiliating for him. It's better that Ulric faces the truth. In the end, he remains stronger than everyone else, including the idiots who try to rile him up. Any way you cut it, there's always someone better than we are out there. I just find his resentment of you to be petty."

"Do not think too ill of him," I said softly, then smiled at her stunned expression. "As aggravated as I am at times by his behavior towards me, I do not hate him. Ulric is a good man in spite of it all. He's just deeply hurt and feels betrayed because of the poison everyone fed him during the hardest time of his life. He was my friend when I had none. In my heart, he will always be my brother. I still miss him."

"You have a good heart," Amara said pensively with an odd glimmer in her eyes. "Do you think your relationship can ever be mended?"

I shrugged while putting away the remaining food. "No clue. But the door remains open as far as I'm concerned. That said, we should probably turn in for the night. I want us to head out at first light."

My mate nodded. She rose to her feet and headed for one of her bags, which sat on the left platform used as a makeshift bed. She rummaged through it and retrieved an off-white, thick candle with dark specks. To my surprise, she placed it on the stone table. I eyed her with curiosity, confused by her actions. As we were preparing to sleep, it struck me as strange to add more lighting sources when I'd been about to snuff the torches.

Amara traced the runic pattern carved on the candle with her index finger while whispering an incantation. She then waved her hand above it, the wick instantly catching fire. She uttered another incantation before turning back to me with a satisfied smile.

"You're a witch?" I asked, surprised.

She gave me a stunned look, then shook her head with an amused expression. "Not at all. I'm just a chandler and perfumer."

"Okay, that was also my understanding. Seeing you casting a spell threw me," I said, still confused.

"That's because, over the years, the demand for witch candles has grown exponentially. So I learned candle magic and some basic spells to imbue my candles with unique properties. My mother disapproves," she added, scrunching her face. "She's very reluctant about anything to do with the arcane. But that's a story for another time."

"What does this candle do?" I asked, my curiosity piqued.

"It's a Wayfarer's Candle made of beeswax and a centaur's hoof dust," she explained. "It helps with walking, running, healing leg injuries, and restoring weary travelers. We'll feel a bit more refreshed in the morning."

"That's excellent," I said approvingly.

"We'll need it," she added while casting a less-than-impressed look at the rock slabs that served as beds.

I mentally berated myself again for not bringing the mat regardless. We could have left it at the inn. But we were already overly burdened.

Shifting uneasily on my feet, I scratched my nape.

"The rocks are indeed quite hard and uncomfortable for humans to sleep on," I said carefully. "I could offer you an alternative, but I don't want you to think me too bold."

"Oh?" she said, perking up. "What alternative would that be?"

I cleared my throat, feeling ridiculously self-conscious. "Normally, when Lycans sleep in the wild, we do so in our wolf form. We're quite massive and furry. It would be a lot more comfortable and warmer for you than that stone slab," I said, my cheeks burning with embarrassment.

Amara's eyes widened. "Are you offering for me to use you as a mattress?"

"Only if you wish," I said quickly. "I'm not trying to be weird or anything."

Seeing her chuckle immediately quelled the panic that wanted to rear its head.

"It's okay. I don't think you're being weird. But now I'm curious as I have indeed heard that your wolves are huge. Can I see?"

The eagerness in her voice sent a warm feeling spreading through my chest.

"Gladly. But I must strip out of my clothes first so as not to ruin them," I added sheepishly.

"Right, that makes sense. I'll just turn around while you do," she said enthusiastically before spinning around.

A part of me regretted that she did. Lycans had no problem with nudity. We regularly stripped in front of each other before shifting and strutted about naked after reverting to our human form following a hunt. Another part was just grateful that she seemed so comfortable around me when people usually feared us because of all the rumors about us being feral.

I swiftly stripped out of my clothes. Before I even finished, my blood stirred again, my skin heating as my woman's scent shifted ever so slightly. It wasn't full on arousal, but the thought of me naked behind her excited my female.

This was a good sign for the future.

"Just so you know," I added quickly before initiating the shift, "once in my wolf form, I can't speak. I'll understand everything you say, and I remain fully sentient. I just won't be able to form human words."

"Understood," Amara said, stopping herself in extremis from glancing at me over her shoulder.

I almost said that wolves could communicate telepathically with each other, and that the day we bonded, she would gain the ability to hear me as a wolf. But this would be a conversation for a later time.

The familiar pain of the shift washed over me. A soft gasp escaped my woman when the sound of my bones cracking and rearranging themselves reached her ears. I'd grown so used to it that I no longer paid attention to it. But now, I realized how scary and ominous it likely sounded to a human, especially isolated as we were, and with her not seeing the transformation that was causing it. She shuddered, and hugged her waist, but remained still, looking away from me.

The transformation only took a few seconds, but I didn't doubt it felt like an eternity to her. I emitted a soft growl followed by a whine to let her know I was ready. Amara started turning around, her slow movement clearly designed to give me a chance to balk if I needed more time.

Her jaw dropped, and her mesmerized look as she took in my wolf form turned me upside down.

"By the gods!" she whispered. "You're magnificent!"

Pride swelled within me, and I puffed out my chest as I carefully approached her. She met me halfway without hesitation. No words could describe how it felt for her to fully accept me in both forms.

My throat constricted when she instinctively raised her right hand to caress this side of my neck. She no sooner started touching me than she yanked her hand back, a mix of shock and guilt on her face.

I emitted a growling purr and stretched my neck in a way that made it clear she could go right ahead and pet me. There was something magical about our wolf form. People either feared us or immediately melted with the need to hug and pet us like they would with a dog. Even though their minds understood that we were still a person, the natural restraint one showed another individual just vanished.

Amara giggled and reached out for my neck again. Nine Hells, I could have died right there and then when the softness of her hand stroked my dark fur with a reverence that wrecked me. I wanted to feel her hands all over me, to be claimed as her mate.

My purring growl grew louder, making her bolder in the way she petted me. To my dismay, she pulled away too soon.

"Now I see why you offered for me to ride you. You're as big as a pony, but prettier and definitely fluffier," she said in an amused tone.

I made a chuffing sound in lieu of laughter. I rubbed the side of my snout against the back of her hand then jumped on top of one of the slabs used as beds. I settled down sideways. Amara smiled, then walked around the room, waving her hand in front of the runes below each sconce to snuff the magic fire.

The room fell into nearly complete darkness, aside from the flickering flame of the Wayfarer's Candle in the middle of the table. Heart pounding, I watched my female come to me. Without hesitation, she climbed onto the slab and snuggled deeply against me. My chest constricted as a wave of affection and almost rabid possessiveness crashed over me. I wrapped my paws around her, drawing her more tightly against me, my fluffy tail settling over her like a blanket.

A loud purr vibrated in my mate's throat.

"Oh yeah, you're far more comfortable than that slab of rock. I can get used to this," she whispered.

Fate willing, she would.

CHAPTER 6
AMARA

Wrapped in a divine cocoon, I grumbled in displeasure at the annoying motion trying to pull me out of the best dream I've had in far too long to remember. I snuggle more deeply into the softest pillow. The heat emanating from it warmed me to the bone.

Heat from a pillow?!

Even as that thought snapped me out of my slumber, a chuffing sound followed by a slow growl had me wide awake in a blink. Wide-eyed, I stared at the face of a giant wolf half a second before his massive tongue licked my entire face.

"Hey! You're going to make me sticky!" I exclaimed while pulling my face away from him.

Remus emitted that chuffing sound again that I believed was his way of laughing in his wolf form then rubbed his temple against mine before releasing me. He deftly hopped down the stone slab that we had slept on. I instantly felt cold and bereft, not only to be deprived of his embrace, but also because his body literally radiated heat like a bonfire. The thought that proximity to me might be the cause had a swarm of butterflies fluttering in my belly.

By the gods, he was truly magnificent in his beast form. He stood well over five feet from the bottom of his paws to the tip of his ears, his snout at a height with my face standing up. His lustrous fur was a darker shade of his dark brown hair. His golden eyes starkly contrasted with it, giving him an almost supernatural edge. The fur around his neck was surprisingly thick. It didn't compare to that of a lion but vaguely reminded me of the one from the Maine Coon cats.

My fingers itched with the urge to sink through it and to caress him all over. I nearly whimpered with need just at the memory of how soft it felt against my face as I slept snuggling with him. Had he been an actual pet, I'd be all over him right now. It kind of messed with my head that a man hid behind that beast form.

A man who believed me to be his soulmate...

He gestured with his head for me to follow before heading towards the exit of the cave. Intrigued, I tagged along, the bright light of the early morning sun blinding me as we stepped outside. He circled around a small outcropping of rocks, revealing a recessed nook where a couple of water barrels had gathered rainwater.

"Thank you!" I exclaimed.

He bumped the back of my hand with his snout then turned around and headed back inside the cave. I splashed some water on my face and performed some quick ablutions before rejoining him. To my chagrin, in that short time, Remus had reverted to his human form and donned his pants.

My ears burned with embarrassment at the naughty thoughts that crossed my mind as to what he might be packing inside his pants. Did he have a knot like canines or the standard equipment in his human form?

My gaze roamed back up his bare chest, appreciating the view. His body was sheer perfection. I didn't fight the wave of possessiveness that swept through me. After all, *he* was the one who claimed we were fated.

To my dismay, I looked up at his face to find him staring at me with a discreet smile laced with undeniable smugness. I averted my eyes, mortified to have been caught ogling him.

"I hope you rested well?" he said with a hint of amusement while putting his shirt on.

"Fantastically well, thank you. You're the best pillow and mattress in the world," I deadpanned.

He snorted. "That's one title I never expected to earn, but I welcome it."

We settled at the table and quickly ate more bread and dried meats with some fruits. We washed down our meal with some cider from a canteen, packed our stuff, and resumed our journey.

I would lie by saying it wasn't arduous. Being mostly sedentary, I wasn't used to such long rides on horseback, and especially at such a fast and hard pace. Frankly, our mounts' endurance blew my mind.

For all that, I loved how Remus constantly checked up on me, assessing my current state, and ensuring my welfare. We only stopped long enough to stretch our legs, rest the horses, eat, or answer the call of nature.

Saying I was relieved when we finally reached the Hunters Lodge would be the understatement of the century. Every muscle in my body whined and complained. My back and legs felt incredibly stiff. I probably looked like a waddling duck as I took a couple of steps towards the large two-story wooden building.

To my surprise, it appeared totally vacant. Not a single light illuminated the countless windows. I cast an inquisitive look towards my companion, who effortlessly grabbed all our bags off our horses.

"Just like the cave that we slept in last night, the lodge is a public location that everyone may use freely," Remus explained when he noticed my confused expression. "There are three other similar lodges in the area. All the guides like me pitch in a fixed amount every month to maintain them. Some basic supplies are always available and regularly replenished by the caretakers. But some of the things we have to replace before we leave, like fire logs if we use them."

"Oh! That's pretty neat then. But what if there already were other people here," I asked. "Would they have turned us away?"

He smiled and shook his head while making his way to the front stairs. "There are eight bedrooms in the lodge, and a few couches in the living area that can also be used as beds. Multiple parties can share the place. However, it rarely occurs as guides normally communicate with each other where they intend to go to avoid overlaps whenever possible."

"Fair," I replied, shadowing him as he reached for the door handle. "But what if some random interloper decided to drop by? We're in the middle of the woods. Some psychopath could sneak in on us during the night, pretending to seek shelter, and then slaughter us in our sleep."

Just as I spoke those words, my skin tingled. I jerked my head up to look at the sudden lights that appeared above me as I crossed the threshold of the house.

"Protection wards," I whispered with sudden understanding as he waved his palm in front of an arcane symbol by the door.

Remus nodded then walked further inside the lodge. "This is but one of many. You didn't feel them, but we crossed quite a few protective wards on our way here. Our shamans have scattered them on a one-kilometer radius around the building. No dangerous animal can approach, and any person with evil intent will be immediately repelled. There's a reason why Wolfmoon Mountain is deemed one of the safest and most sought-after hunting and hiking destinations. No danger can come to you here, my mate."

I bit the inside of my cheeks not to chuckle when Remus

visibly flinched at subconsciously using that term of endearment. He was so incredibly cute.

Obviously, it was much too early for us to refer to each other in such a manner. And yet, I liked it coming from him. I didn't want anyone to think they could own or control me. But there was something incredibly flattering and comforting in the underlying possessiveness with which he claimed me.

"I'm glad to hear it," I said with a smile. "I might be a little skittish when it comes to random strangers showing up at my front door."

"Understandable," he replied, relieved that I didn't seem offended by his slip up. "But now that we have entered the house, and I claimed it, it will warn us if anyone approaches during our stay, not that there should be any visitors until two days from now. But we'll be long gone by then."

"I like the sound of that," I replied enthusiastically.

He obviously assumed I meant the fact that we would get warned if an intruder showed up. Although that was true, it was mostly the fact that we would have the house to just the two of us that pleased me. As an introvert, I wasn't too keen on hanging out with big crowds. But more importantly, I wanted to get to know this fascinating man with whom I could possibly spend the rest of my life. We'd been together for two days now, which we mostly spent racing through the woods. That had not been too conducive of any type of bonding time.

"There are two bedrooms on this floor," Remus said, waving towards the back of a large corridor on the opposite side of the open living and dining area at the entrance of the lodge. "The other six rooms are upstairs and are accessible through the staircase over there. You will find two hygienic toilets—one on each floor—and there is an outhouse in the garden. Unfortunately, there are no baths or showers. We normally bathe in the river at the back."

"I don't mind a midnight bath," I said in a reassuring tone, even though it was still early evening.

"Excellent!"

He glanced out one of the many tall windows before casting a speculative look my way.

"I would like to go hunt for our meal tonight to spare our food reserves from Misty. Would you feel comfortable remaining here in my absence?" he asked carefully.

"You said it's safe, and that the wards will keep any one with hostile intentions at bay. Therefore, I don't mind staying here alone for a little bit," I replied in a friendly tone.

He beamed at me. "It certainly is. I would not consider it otherwise. It shouldn't take me long. There's plenty of small game in the area."

"Take your time. I'll look around and pick a room in your absence."

"See you soon," he said before heading out.

I watched him through the window as he first secured the horses and fed them. Guilt surged through me that I didn't even think of doing it or even offering to do so. To my surprise, he didn't strip and shift into his wolf form but simply broke into a run at dizzying speed with no apparent weapon on him.

I shrugged and started exploring the place. It held an undeniable masculine edge, the typical hunting lodge all made of wood, with some animal skull decorations, carpets made of fur, and sturdy furniture more focused on functionality than fashion.

Three couches, four chairs, and a handful of cushiony stools provided ample seating in the living area which faced a large fireplace. At the other end of the room, four round tables, each with enough chairs to seat ten people filled the large space across from the kitchen area. To my pleasant surprise, it had a gas stove. The cupboards offered all the necessities, including dishes, pots and utensils, and basic spices.

As I headed down the corridor, my confusion at seeing five

doors when Remus stated there were only two bedrooms on this floor was quickly dissipated. One of them acted as an armory with a variety of hunting paraphernalia, including bows, arrows, traps, daggers, fishing equipment, and even some camping gear. The next room appeared to serve as a processing room for butchering meat and cleaning or treating the hides. The third was a fairly small water closet, which I swiftly made use of.

My instinctive desire to replace the unscented soap with one of the fragrant ones I made faded as swiftly as it popped into my head. Hunters would never want to add unnatural scents to them that might reveal their presence to their prey.

The unremarkable bedrooms were clean and on the small side. Rather, the massive bed eating up most of the space made them look smaller than they actually were. The only other furniture in the room was a set of nightstands, a chair in the corner, and a small console on top of which to put one's belongings. None of the rooms contained a closet or chest of drawers.

After some deliberation, I chose one of the upstairs bedrooms at the back of the house which had a stunning view of the backyard and the luminous trail that led to the river a short distance away.

Not knowing how long Remus would be gone, I sauntered back downstairs and started a fire in the hearth. I lit the stove and heated some of Misty's cider with cloves, cinnamon, nutmeg, and brown sugar. Too bad I didn't find any allspice, but this would do.

I was just finishing that task when the front door opened. Startled, I spun around to see Remus walk in proudly holding up two sizable rabbits.

"I'm back," he said with a grin.

"Wow! That was fast!" I exclaimed, a strange warmth spreading in my chest at his mere presence.

The rational part of me wanted to believe that relief at no longer being alone in this strange place prompted it. But another part of me acknowledged that there was more to it. I just liked being around him. Remus had a way of making me feel safe even without doing anything. And the way he looked at me when he thought I wasn't paying attention had my stomach fluttering in the most pleasant way.

"There's a reason why I'm our pack's best hunter," he replied, puffing out his chest while approaching me. "But something smells wonderful."

"I made some hot spiced cider for us," I said timidly. "If you'd like, I'll pour your cup while you unload your catch."

The powerful emotion that fleeted over his features had my stomach do a couple of backflips. I realized then that people didn't normally do sweet things for him. The urge to spoil him instantly surged deep within.

"I would love a cup," he said almost timidly.

"Perfect! Mulled cider coming right up!" I replied in a semi theatrical manner that had him chuckling.

I loved how it softened his face and gave him an almost boyish edge. As he turned towards the corridor to head to the processing room, he glanced at the hearth before looking back at me with an impressed expression.

"And you also got a nice fire going!"

It was my turn to puff out my chest smugly. "I may not be much of a fighter or a hunter, but you'll soon discover that I have many other talents."

"I do not doubt it, my... Amara."

I almost chuckled at his embarrassed look when he caught himself right before he would call me his mate again. It was so damn adorable. Nothing could describe how endearing it was to see the sweet and vulnerable side of such a strong and otherwise intimidating man.

He cleared his throat and mumbled something unintelligible while gesturing clumsily towards the processing room. I watched him almost escape, a silly grin stretching my lips. As I began to fill two cups with the cider, a wave of dizziness crashed over me.

I promptly put down the pot, some of the hot beverage splashing over the counter. Both palms resting over the cool wooden surface, I took in a couple of deep breaths. My throat constricted, and my chest felt as if a heavy weight had settled on top of it, making it nearly impossible for me to breathe. My innards twisted as what felt like a sharp dagger repeatedly stabbed them. My pained gasp was no more than a whisper, a hiccup at best.

Then in an instant, all the symptoms disappeared as quickly as they had manifested themselves.

I knew the poison coursing through me had not vanished. And yet, the absence of blatant symptoms other than the constant tiredness had almost lulled me into thinking I would be relatively normal until I received the cure. But the reality was that my health would steadily decline with each passing day. Remus's harness no longer felt like a somewhat excessive kind gesture.

Will I even be healthy enough to perform the ritual?

The reality of my grim situation struck me hard. I was indeed living on borrowed time.

Taking a deep breath, I took a few steps in front of the counter to make sure that crisis had fully passed. I finished filling the cups then gingerly made my way to the processing room. I found Remus making quick work of cleaning the rabbits.

Unaware of what had transpired, he beamed at me, his golden gaze softening as he watched me approach. He put down his knife and reached for a cloth to wipe his hands.

"No!" I exclaimed, stopping him before he could pick it up. "I got it."

Surprised, he observed me with undisguised curiosity. I put my cup down at the corner of the table and wrapped both of my hands around his cup. Stopping in front of him, I lifted the tin mug to his lips.

Once again, the powerful emotion that had wrecked me earlier descended over his handsome features. It was a potent mix of wonder, affection, and gratitude laced with a hint of possessiveness and disbelief. He leaned forward and took a few sips. The whole time, his gaze never strayed from mine.

A purr vibrated through his broad chest.

"Delicious," he said, his voice a little deeper than normal as he licked his lips.

"Glad you like it," I said, a whirlwind of emotions raging through me.

I really liked Remus. Why had I just met him now? What if the next few days were all that we would ever have? The connection between us couldn't be denied. I wanted to explore it all, not rush through it or be cheated of what might have been. But this brief episode in the kitchen was a stark reminder that life was fleeting and to never take anything for granted.

"More?" I asked.

He nodded. I lifted the cup to his lips so he could drink some more. This time, a few drops trickled at the corner of his mouth. Without thinking, I wiped it with my thumb, then licked it off my finger. I froze for a split second once I realized what I had done. Seeing the white of his eyes darken, as if storm clouds had rushed in, lit a flame in the pit of my stomach.

Despite my embarrassment, I didn't avert my eyes as his gaze bore into mine. A silent communication passed between us. Neither of us commented about what I had done, but something undeniably shifted between us.

And that was fine by me.

I smiled. Remus glanced at my lips, his desire to kiss me almost palpable. I silently encouraged him to proceed, but he simply reciprocated the smile then resumed cleaning the meat.

That, too, was fine by me.

Many other men would have jumped at the first opportunity to get frisky. His restraint spoke volumes about the type of male he was, making me feel even safer with him. A healthy dose of sexual tension also had its perks.

Remus paused every so often so that I could give him another sip. We talked amiably as he completed his work. Although the cider had a low alcoholic concentration, it still helped me relax and loosen up a little. I loved the keen interest he displayed as I told him about my chandler and perfumer business.

"You know, mages often come in the mountains seeking some rare reagents for their rituals," Remus said pensively as we returned to the kitchen. "We have several plants and creatures that are highly coveted. Once everything is settled, I'll be happy to bring you the ones that could benefit your business. We even have a phoenix that drops by from time to time."

"That would be amazing!"

He grinned, pleased by my reaction.

"I should do the cooking since you hunted and cleaned the rabbits," I offered, pointing at his catches as he laid them on the counter.

He firmly shook his head. "It's my duty to provide and care for you. And you made us mulled cider and started the fire."

I snorted. "That's hardly comparable! It took little effort!"

"As does hunting for me. You even noted how quickly I did it."

He chuckled when I scrunched my face, failing to find a counterargument.

"Now stop fretting and rest," he said in a falsely severe tone as he gestured at one of the tall stools by the counter for me to sit on. "How do you like your meat?"

Defeated, I complied and hoisted myself onto one of the benches. I'd never been too fond of those raised seats. I liked sitting at the standard height of a chair, with my feet firmly resting on the floor. The footrests on the high stools never did it for me.

"Fine, you bully," I grumbled with false displeasure. "For rabbit, well-done, please. For red meat, I usually go with medium. But let me guess, you eat yours rare?"

He chuckled. "In my human form, yes, usually rare. Though I can enjoy fully cooked meat, especially in a stew. But as a wolf, I eat raw," he replied while taking out some spice.

I tilted my head to the side, my curiosity piqued. "Do you have a preference between human and wolf form?"

"Wolf form," he said without hesitation. He gave me a sheepish smile in response to my stunned reaction. "I spent the first two years of my life entirely as a wolf. It took me a while to come to terms with being a man instead. As people didn't like me, I often found peace and escape while roaming as a wolf. It stayed with me. Life is simpler in the wild. That I'm faster, stronger, with more acute senses as a wolf certainly plays an additional part in it."

I nodded slowly. "That makes sense. I envy you, and all shifters for that matter. It must be amazing exploring the world in a completely different form."

"It is," he concurred. "Do you wish for accompaniment for the meal? There's a small garden outside from which I can fetch some tomatoes and—"

"That's not necessary," I said gently, interrupting him. "Meat will be enough for tonight. And what you're cooking smells really good. Once we're done, I wouldn't mind taking a dip in that river out back."

"You got it."

Remus cut up one of the two rabbits so that each part would cook faster. The second rabbit hardly saw any heat. Calling it rare wouldn't even begin to qualify. Had it not been skinned and gutted, that rabbit would have hopped right off his plate and back into the wild. At least, it wasn't bleeding.

We settled at one of the four tables with another cup of mulled cider to eat. Remus devoured his whole rabbit like a starving man. I didn't miss how his canines lengthened as he dug in. He even ate most of the smaller bones, leaving the skull and other bigger ones. I ate less than a quarter of mine. Beyond the fact that it was far too much food for me, the poison killing me affected my appetite. I increasingly struggled with various foods, my stomach rebelling far too often.

"Here, have the rest," I said, pushing the meat towards him.

"You don't like it?" he asked, his crestfallen expression making me want to smoosh his face.

"No, silly," I said with a chuckle. "It's really good. But I'm full. I never ate much, and my si…"

My voice trailed off as I stopped myself, not wanting to dampen the mood. But the damage was done.

"Your what?" he asked softly. "Your sickness? It's affecting your appetite?"

I nodded with an apologetic look. To my shock, he reached across the table to grab my hand and gave it a gentle squeeze.

"Then don't force yourself. Once you're cured, I intend to feed you with all kinds of wondrous delicacies I've grown quite expert at preparing, even meat cooked to medium," he added, making a face as if it were blasphemy to prepare meat that way.

I immediately melted, squeezed his hand back, and gave him a grateful smile. Remus was truly growing on me.

"But I will not eat all of it. Let's keep a similar portion as to what you just ate for you to have for breakfast," he said in a tone that brooked no argument. "The rest, I'm happy to relieve you of."

I chuckled watching him nearly gulp down the remaining half of the rabbit at lightning speed.

"By the gods!" I whispered, flabbergasted. "You're a bottom-less pit. I bet you're still hungry!"

He snorted and shook his head. "I'm not. Granted, I could eat more. But I'm not actually hungry. I'm comfortably sated. Now come. Time to put this away before giving you that dip in the river."

We cleaned everything up, and I wiped the dishes as he washed them. There was something heartwarmingly domestic about it all. I could picture this becoming a routine I would greatly enjoy with this man.

Once done, I hurried to the room I had picked to retrieve my nightgown and met Remus back in the living area. He had already removed his shirt and shoes and was holding a set of towels and a bar of soap. We exited the house through the back door, down the hallway, past the armory and the two ground floor bedrooms.

Although the view had been stunning from the upstairs bedroom, walking out of the lodge and into the courtyard almost felt like stepping inside a fairy tale. The wall over the door frame glowed. At first, I thought that protection wards had lit up. But it was a different set of runes that our presence activated. Simultaneously, two rows of glowstones stirred to life, illuminating a wide path leading to the river.

On the right side of the path, a generous garden offered a variety of fruits and vegetables. Considering the total absence of weeds and how healthy each plant looked, the caretakers had to frequently drop by to maintain them. However, I suspected that a green witch also had a hand in it. On the left side of the path, a beautiful gazebo adorned with a few vines and surrounded by fragrant flowers provided an inviting place to relax and enjoy a pleasant conversation while sipping a refreshing drink.

Countless fireflies danced around in a mesmerizing and luminous choreography to the sound of the crickets chirping. I realized I had slipped my hand into Remus's when his thumb gently glided over its back. His tender smile felt like the sweetest caress.

The clearest water sang happily as it trickled down the semi wide river. Although I would have loved for there to be a waterfall, I couldn't complain about the enchanting tableau it presented. Multiple tall decorative rocks and a few sculpted stone benches provided strategically placed seating for people to enjoy the view.

"You can strip in here," Remus said, pointing to a rectangular building at the right of the path, which I initially thought to be an oddly located outhouse. "The area is safe. You can just go directly into the river when ready. I will go over there, on the other side of that tall tree. Don't worry, I'll be within hearing distance."

I frowned. "You don't have to go," I blurted out, surprising myself. "I'm not prudish, and I would feel safer with you here, even though I know the wards protect us."

"Uh…"

He stared at me, looking uncertain. I couldn't say if it was discomfort at the thought of us bathing together, or if he wasn't sure this was a good idea.

"But don't worry, I will manage, if it makes you uncomfortable," I added, suddenly feeling self-conscious for being so forward.

"It doesn't!" he replied quickly, as if fearing he had offended me. "I'm a Lycan. Nudity means nothing to us. It is *you* I'm concerned about. If it's just that you would prefer I stay in your line of sight, I can sit on one of these benches while you bathe, and—"

"No," I once again interrupted in a soft voice. "I genuinely mean that I don't mind you bathing with me. So long as you're not uncomfortable, then neither am I."

"Then together it is," he said with a tender smile.

My stomach fluttered as I watched him carefully place the towels on one of the benches and proceed to detach his pants. Not wanting to be caught ogling him, I forced myself to avert my eyes, placed my nightgown on the large rock next to me, and proceeded to strip out of my clothes. Despite the hour, the early summer night air was comfortably warm with only the slightest breeze.

I removed my pants first, then my shirt. As I'd been spared from overly generous breasts, I avoided the uncomfortable corsets like the plague and usually stuck to a stay or chemise. For convenience during our trip, I had opted for a stay and short drawers. My eyes still averted, I removed my undergarments and neatly folded them on top of my other clothes before finally turning to face Remus.

He was standing in his glorious nudity a couple of meters away from me. Unlike me, he appeared to have no qualms examining me. Although his sclera had once more darkened, and despite the obvious glimmer of desire in his golden eyes, there was nothing lurid or vulgar in the way he observed me.

Obviously, I did the same. The thought that he had surprisingly very little body hair fleeted through my mind. Aside from his neatly trimmed beard and mustache, Remus only had a sexy patch of hair on his chest which narrowed into a happy trail down his chiseled abs and then blossomed into thin curls below the pelvis. The outer edges of his shoulders and arms also had a soft trail of fur that demanded to be petted.

To my dismay, I couldn't boast about displaying the same restraint he did. With a will of its own, my gaze zeroed in on his manhood. My toes curled at finding it partially erect. It was long and thick, with bulging veins along the shaft, and a pair of testicles. Although generally shaped like the penis of a man, it possessed a narrower head. However, it was the rounded bulge close to the base of the shaft that retained my attention.

"So you do have a knot!" I blurted out.

The words no sooner crossed my lips than I visibly flinched, mortified.

"Nine Hells! I'm so sorry!" I quickly added.

To my utter relief, Remus burst out laughing. He glanced at

his shaft, totally unfazed, before peering back up at me, a mischievous glimmer in his golden eyes.

"I do. All Lycan's do. But there's no need to apologize. Your curiosity about me is rather flattering. I can only hope you're not disappointed."

Despite the teasing way in which he spoke those words, I didn't miss the underlying sliver of worry.

"Disappointed?" I echoed, incredulous. "You're stunning."

Once again, I couldn't believe how my mouth just kept running away with me, even though I meant every word. However, the way he lowered his eyes and smiled shyly crushed any mortification I felt. By the gods! I would never tire of seeing this vulnerable and insecure side of him that made me want to give him a bone-crushing hug.

"Thank you, Amara. You're breathtaking as well."

"Thank you," I replied with an exaggerated curtsy.

He burst out laughing again. And just like that, the awkwardness between us faded. He smiled and extended a hand towards me. Without hesitation, I placed mine in his. He gave it a gentle squeeze and led me towards the water at a slow run.

A gasp escaped me as we entered the river. For some reason, my brain irrationally expected it to be lukewarm. It wasn't freezing but a lot colder than I'd been ready for. Before I could give in to shock, Remus released my hand and then splashed some water my way. I gaped at him in outrage, to which he responded with a shit-eating grin before quickly hastening away from me.

That obviously triggered the instinctive need to retaliate. I gave chase, wading through the shallow part of the river while trying to splash some water on him. As soon as I succeeded, he turned around, his yellow eyes glowing, and his fangs descending. This should have freaked the living daylights right out of me. Instead, my stomach did the most delicious backflip, and I squealed before attempting to flee.

He gave chase, pretending like I was being lucky in escaping him a split second before he would have caught me. I was screaming and laughing until he finally grabbed me by the waist, tossed me in the air like I weighed nothing, and then caught me right back as I entered the water.

"Now I feast!" he said in a menacing fashion before snapping his teeth at me, a hair's breadth from my skin, pretending to take bites out of me.

Still laughing, I playfully feigned being in agony while begging for mercy. When he relented, I was hiccupping with laughter. It took my brain a moment to realize how tightly he held me in his embrace, and how I hung onto his shoulders with both hands. Simultaneously, it also dawned on me that this little play aimed at distracting me from the discomfort of the cold water. And it beautifully succeeded.

Our gazes locked, we remained still as our pulses settled. Being pressed against each other fully naked should have been awkward. And yet, this didn't just feel natural, it seemed preordained. Our bodies fit perfectly together.

I couldn't tell who moved first. One moment we were lost in each other's eyes, and the next, the plush cushion of his lips was claiming my mouth. I melted against him, and his arms tightened around me. His right hand glided in a gentle caress down my back before settling on my behind. I vaguely wondered why his left hand was fisted against my upper back. But to my dismay, rather than deepening the kiss, Remus ended it. He pulled back, gave me a possessive look that turned me upside down, then leaned forward to place a soft kiss on my forehead.

Without a word, he released me and extended something my way. Only then did I realize he'd been holding the bar of soap in his left hand the whole time.

"Thank you," I whispered, overwhelmed by conflicting emotions.

He smiled, his gaze intense, yet unreadable. He caressed my

lips with the back of two fingers in a way that screamed that he wanted to kiss me again. I wished he would. Sadly, Remus turned around and swam away.

Feeling bereft, I began washing myself while watching him doing a few laps around me. It almost felt like watching a shark circling its prey, waiting for the right time to strike.

And that, too, turned me on.

As I finished soaping my body, I extended the soap towards Remus. The swiftness with which he approached confirmed he'd been keeping an eye on me the whole time. That should have creeped me out. Instead, I silently berated myself for not making more of a show of it so that he would kick himself for cutting things short earlier.

Remus emerged from the water like a sea god. His sclera was pitch black as he closed the distance between us. My breath caught in my throat when thin plumes of smoke started swirling around him.

His heat!

His skin had gotten so hot from being in my mere presence that the water was evaporating right off him. Cue exploding ovaries. My inner walls contracted, and a dull throbbing pulsed between my thighs.

To my shock, instead of beginning to wash himself, Remus grabbed my shoulder and turned me around.

"What are—?"

The question died on my tongue when he began washing my back for me. I leaned into his touch and bent my head down to give him better access to my nape. By the gods! His hands were so hot, the heat seeped deep into me, all the way down to my bones. I couldn't decide if I felt more languid or aroused.

Too soon, he stopped. I glanced over my shoulder to find him slowly using the soap on himself.

That annoyed me.

A part of me wondered if all of this was truly as innocent as it seemed, with him simply being attentive to my needs, or if he was deliberately teasing me. Whatever the answer, I didn't care. Without thinking, I nabbed the soap from his hand. His frown of confusion turned to surprise when I worked up a lather then started rubbing the soap all over his chest.

Remus clenched his teeth, and the right corner of his upper lip quirked into a semi-snarl. The throbbing in my nether region increased at the sight of his fangs peeking through his partially parted lips. He wasn't attempting to intimidate me. I doubted he was even aware of his current expression. The way his abdominal muscles contracted beneath my palms further seemed to confirm my assumption that an effort to suppress his sexual urges caused that snarl.

He swallowed hard, a mix of tension and disappointment gleaming in his golden eyes when I rubbed my palms over his pelvis before circling around to his back instead of pursuing my journey south. Remus leaned into my touch as I washed his back. His muscles appeared to bulge and gain even more mass, coaxing me into giving him an impromptu semi-massage.

Nine Hells! No male should be so perfect. I wanted to rub myself all over him. Instead, I caressed a path down his spine, enticed by the lure of his perky behind, which begged to be grabbed. His breath hitched when I ran my hands over both perfectly round globes and gave them a proper squeeze.

A low growl rose from his throat. It sent the most delicious shiver coursing through me. My stomach did a backflip when Remus turned his head to look at me over his shoulder, his fangs bared, and his sclera the darkest Obsidian. He looked as if he wanted to ravage me right there and then.

Truth be told, I wanted him to.

I wasn't the type to kiss on the first date. And yet here I was, ready to go all the way with a Lycan I met only a handful of days ago. The depth of trust he stirred within me defied any logic. When the Weaver told me I needed to find a guide I would trust with my life, I had believed her to be insane. But here we were, naked in a river, and me already visualizing a future with this male.

Eyes locked with his, I slipped my hand to his front in a bold caress. He hissed when my fingers closed around his length. The twin bulges of his knot pressed against my palm. I lowered my eyes to peer at my prize as I launched into a journey of discovery. But it was thwarted before it even fully began.

A startled yelp escaped me when Remus suddenly spun around, placed both of his hands on my behind, and lifted me in a powerful movement. For a split second, I feared he was just going to impale me on his thick cock in a single savage thrust. But he simply slammed me against his body before claiming my mouth in a brutal and hungry kiss. On instinct, I wrapped my arms and my legs around him.

Effortlessly holding me with one hand below my butt, Remus fisted my hair on my nape then tilted his head to the side to deepen the kiss. A bolt of lust exploded in my nether region as our tongues mingled. The sweet taste of the mulled cider I prepared for us earlier lingered on his breath. However, it was the unusually rough texture of his tongue that retained all my attention. Each caress resonated directly in my clit. My wild imagination immediately started picturing what it would feel like between my thighs.

As we continued to kiss, the sharp tips of his fangs grazing my tongue or bottom lip whipped my blood into a frenzy. I'd never pictured myself as an adrenaline fiend. And yet, this sliver of danger turned me on beyond words. The cool water around us clashed in the strangest way with his increasingly feverish skin. That my presence put my man in heat could no longer be denied.

Water sloshed around us as Remus waded to the shore, our lips still locked. Contrary to my expectations, he didn't head back to the lodge but stopped barely a few meters from the edge of the river and lay me down on what I initially mistook for a bench. Too distracted by the searing heat of his body against mine, and his callused hands roaming all over me, it took me a moment to realize that the uneven shape beneath me belonged to a large rock covered in moss.

My mate broke the kiss, making me whimper in protest. But his mouth venturing along my jaw line down to my neck quickly silenced any disapproval I might have contemplated. He kissed and nipped his way down to my breasts while his hands traced a burning trail on my skin, over my stomach, and down my pelvic area.

The twin sensual assault of his hand slipping between my thighs and of his mouth closing over my left nipple sent my mind for a loop. I didn't know which sensation to focus on between the rough texture of his tongue licking and laving my nipple and his thick fingers teasing my slit before drawing circles around my engorged little nub.

My breath hitched, and I dug my fingers into the lustrous strands of his thick mane. Unable to decide whether to press my chest to his mouth to increase the sensation of his ministrations or lifting my pelvis for greater contact with my nether region, I ended up alternating. In no time, my hips were gyrating while pleading words trickled urgently out of my mouth. I wanted more...

No. I *needed* more.

As if he sensed my unspoken desires, Remus carefully inserted what I presumed to be his index finger inside me while his thumb continued to massage my clit. He gradually picked up the pace as I began to crest. My legs shook, and the burning fire swelling deep within threatened to consume me.

My climax slammed into me with a suddenness that left me reeling. I cried out, and my back arched over the moss-covered rock. I was flying high, waves of bliss still sweeping through me from the intense pleasure he had given me. My eyelids felt heavy, and my limbs too weak to move as I struggled to get back to reality.

Remus pushed himself up on his forearms and kissed a path up my still trembling body. However, instead of lying on top of me to take things to the next level, he gave me a long and passionate kiss, then straightened.

My vision still blurred, I gave him a questioning look. The possessive tenderness with which he gazed upon me had my toes instantly curling. My inner walls contracted with anticipation as I tightened my embrace around him in a clear signal that I was ready and willing to proceed.

To my dismay, Remus picked me up and carried me like a bride. I was about to argue when it suddenly struck me that he probably wanted us to do the deed for the first time in the comfort of a proper bed.

For the briefest instant, I considered reminding him of our clothes neatly folded on a rock by the river. Not wanting to interrupt the moment, I dismissed that thought and covered his muscular chest with kisses and caresses as he made his way into the lodge. Anyway, the weather was fantastic, and there were no signs of rain any time soon.

The deep growl that vibrated through his chest had me throbbing in all the right places. I almost urged him to move faster as he climbed the stairs to the second floor at a leisurely pace. But I kept silent, content to tweak and nip at his perky nipples. I could feel the steely rod of his shaft pressing against my side with each step.

Too focused on groping my man, I barely paid attention to our surroundings. It was only when he lowered me onto the mattress that I realized we had entered the bedroom. A thrill coursed through me as I crawled back further onto the bed and extended a hand towards him in a beckoning fashion.

A searing flame was burning low in my belly, its intensity further fanned by the predatory look on Remus's gorgeous face.

His sclera having turned pitch-black with desire, the call of his Twin Flame made his golden eyes glow with an otherworldly light that was both terrifying and thrilling.

Once again, my mate took me aback by not lying on top of me. Although he joined me on the bed, he spent the next eternity kissing and caressing every inch of my body, worshipping me with his hands, mouth, and tongue. Every time I attempted to reciprocate, he would pin my wrists to the mattress or flip me onto my stomach to pursue his ministrations. He would only turn me onto my back once I yielded to his will.

But when the rough texture of his tongue found its way to my engorged nub again, my mind all but fractured. Each flick of his tongue felt like lightning bolts struck my clit and radiated its blissful tendrils throughout my body.

Remus's smug and approving growls resonated directly in my clit as I shouted his name in ecstasy. His thick fingers slipped inside me, moving at a frenzied pace as they made love to me. My head rolled from side to side as an endless stream of throaty moans tumbled out of me. Before I could recover from this latest orgasm, a blinding light exploded before my eyes when he crooked two fingers inside me, grazing my sweet spot just the right way for me to shatter.

My head spun, my skin tingled, and a raging inferno set my veins ablaze. My lover continued to devour me while fucking me with his fingers until I lay limp like a broken doll. Only then did he relent.

At long last, Remus climbed over me. Even in my daze, I could feel the massive club pressing against my stomach. A tiny voice at the back of my head, mostly drowned by bliss, wanted to panic at the prospect of me trying to receive his massive girth. But I squashed it.

We were soulmates, which meant our bodies were perfect for each other.

To my shock, Remus didn't settle between my thighs. He

flipped us around so that he would lie on his back and me on top of him.

I groggily lifted my head to look at him questioningly.

"Rest, my mate," he said in a gentle voice, made deeper and more gravelly by what had to be unsated desire. "An arduous journey awaits us in the morning."

"But... What about you?"

He smiled tenderly, caressed my cheek, and then kissed the tip of my nose. "I'm fine, Amara. You have no idea how much pleasure I derive just from your responses to me. Seeing you climax has undoubtedly become my new drug."

My cheeks heated, and the oddest mix of arousal and embarrassment coursed through me at the thought of how I had responded to his touch. Prim and proper definitely didn't apply.

Still, I frowned in response. "Be that as it may, you didn't find your own release. I can still feel how hard your 'third leg' is against my stomach."

He burst out laughing. "My Flame, my 'third leg' as you so eloquently put it is constantly hard in your presence. Do not fret about that."

Although he had meant for this to lighten the mood, I continued to stare at him intently.

Remus sobered and then heaved a sigh. "I'm genuinely happy and satisfied with our encounter."

Despite the sincerity in his voice, I didn't need to read mind to know he was holding himself back.

"Is it your illness?" I asked in a gentle voice.

To my surprise, he didn't flinch or avert his eyes. For a few seconds, he held my gaze unwaveringly, his expression serious as he carefully chose his response.

"I will not risk exposing you to my seed in any way. It is dangerous for anyone, but even more so for you in your current weakened state," Remus said calmly, but firmly. "Once you are cured, we can consider using condoms woven in protection spells commonly used with demons and other nether creatures. But not before then."

I wanted to argue, feeling like I was cheating him out of a more-than-well-deserved reciprocity. But after my flare up earlier, I couldn't risk anything that would further jeopardize my faltering health.

I pinched my lips, my displeasure obvious as I reluctantly nodded in concession.

"Do not pout, my mate," Remus said gently. "You have no idea what you have already given me. I've dreamt of being touched and held the way you have by someone who knows exactly what I am and accepts me as Fate made me. You have given me more joy in the few days we've known each other than in any other time I can think of in my entire messed up life."

My chest constricted for him upon hearing the depth of sincerity and emotion in his voice. However, on top of the potent wave of sympathy it triggered, a powerful sense of protective-ness surged within me for him. I didn't know when or how, but I would find a way to bring him the peace and happiness he deserved.

"Fine," I grumbled with a playful poutiness. "We'll do it your way *for now*. But once I'm cured, I will stop at nothing to make sure you are as well."

Despite the indulgent smile he gave me, I didn't miss the glimmer of sadness and resignation that flashed through his golden eyes.

"Believe me, Amara, I have sought the assistance of every healer, shaman, or arcanist possible. I am beyond help."

"You haven't spoken to the Weaver," I argued stubbornly.

"She won't open her gates for me," Remus reminded me in a slightly chastising tone.

I shrugged and gave him a mischievous look. "She didn't before. But I have an in with her now. She wants my blood once I'm cured. I'll sweettalk my way into convincing her to see you."

He snorted, and caressed my cheek, his eyes glowing with infinite tenderness.

"We'll see," he replied in a non-committal fashion. "But whatever the future holds, the Weaver already blessed me by sending you to me. I am happy."

I melted as I snuggled deeper into him. "So am I."

"Sleep, my mate. We have a tough journey ahead."

CHAPTER 7
REMUS

It took every ounce of my willpower to pull myself away from my mate's embrace as she continued to sleep soundly. We still had a couple of hours left before we would need to start moving. I felt chilled to the bone without the warmth of her body wrapped around mine.

But that same thought squashed the wondrous memories of our intimacy. Throughout the night, Amara's body had gotten unnaturally hot, and not in the way mine did when being in the presence of my Twin Flame triggered my heat. Once or twice, my female had winced and even moaned in pain. Thankfully, it hadn't awakened her.

Those undeniable signs of her illness progressing had me on the verge of panic.

We were still very far from our destination. I suspected Amara was hiding just how unwell she actually felt. I would push hard for us to make even better time, but I didn't know that it would suffice. Worse still, what if that hastened her decline?

I couldn't lose her.

Forcing myself to cast out those grim musings, I headed outside to gather our discarded clothes by the river, then vented my frustration and sense of helplessness by chopping wood to replace the logs we used last night. I caught and prepared another rabbit for breakfast and added a few berries and vegetables from the garden before returning to our room.

With an hour left, I climbed back into bed with my mate. The way she instinctively wrapped herself around me, even in her sleep, brought a smile to my face. By Ferazan, how did she manage to make me feel so loved and wanted with every slightest gesture?

I had just begun dozing off when Amara stirred against me. Not wanting to rob her of the short rest time we had left, I remained still. But she didn't. What I first assumed to be her right hand absent-mindedly caressing my chest in her half-slumber quickly proved to be deliberate and calculated. My stomach did a backflip when my mate gently rubbed her cheek against my chest, then turned her face to cover it with soft kisses.

My breath hitched when her lips closed over my right nipple. I sank my fingers into the tight curls of her puffy hair, their softness like a cloud under my palm. A growly moan vibrated through my chest as the burning heat of her tongue began to tease my nub. I should stop her, but every fiber of my being hungered for her attentions.

The guilt and shame of a lifetime of being reminded daily that an abomination such as I was forbidden this type of intimacy shouted for me to push her away. I fisted my hand in her hair, intent on tugging her head back. Her teeth grazing against my nipple then nipping it made my mind go blank.

Her right hand greedily roamed over my body as Amara moved her head to cater to my other nipple. A powerful shiver coursed through me when she raked her nails down my abdominal muscles. A bolt of lust exploded in the pit of my stomach, and my fingertips ached with the need to extrude my claws.

My pulse picked up, and my skin heated as her wandering hand ventured further south. A strangled growl escaped me as her dainty fingers wrapped around my quickly hardening length. I fisted the blanket with my free hand, my claws shooting out and digging into the fabric when she began to stroke me.

Every single one of my senses shouted for me to stop her. But it was so damn good! Technically, this was still safe. So long as I didn't release my seed, no harm could come to her. But even if it did, so long as she didn't ingest it, or that it didn't enter her in any way, be it vaginally or through some open cut, she would be safe. So long as...

I cried out as the inferno of her mouth closed over the head of my cock. Between the overwhelming pleasure of her touch, and my desperate efforts at rationalizing why it was okay to indulge a little longer in her ministrations, I hadn't realized that her mouth had been trailing a path down my pelvis.

Amara bobbed over me three or four times before I recovered enough from the shock and blissful sensation to yank her head back and away from me.

"No, Amara!" I exclaimed, my voice pained from the burning need to beg her to continue instead.

"I'll be careful," she said, her tone almost pleading. "I won't swallow."

"It's too risky! What if a drop seeps out?" I argued, trying to pull away from her.

"Then I'll steer clear of the head," she countered stubbornly. "You're mine, Remus. I won't be denied what's mine."

Without waiting for my response, Amara dove right back down, sliding her tongue from the junction of my testicles up the base of my shaft, before teasing the seam of my knot. My legs jerked, and my stomach contracted painfully as she resumed stroking me in earnest. As promised, my mate's mouth never ventured higher than the halfway point of my length. The way she squeezed my knot, twisting her wrist just perfectly with each upward motion had liquid fire coursing through my veins.

My testicles felt heavy and on the verge of bursting when she sucked one of them into her mouth, her tongue swirling around it while she fondled the other one with her free hand. Tension quickly built as I tumbled down a vortex of endless pleasure. I wouldn't last long yet didn't want her to stop.

Without thinking, I yanked the corner of the blanket and slapped it on the tip of my cock, partially covering it. Heedless of the fabric impeding her movements, Amara pursued her ministration at an even more frenzied pace, having no doubt realized that my climax was imminent.

I sensed it half a second before it struck me like lightning at the base of my spine. I shoved my mate away with a bit more force than intended, but nowhere near enough to be harmful. Having visibly expected it, Amara flowed with the movement, rolling to the side. Even as I spun to a sitting position at the edge of the bed, I clasped my hand with bruising force around my cock still partially covered by the blanket. With a savage roar, I shot my seed in blissful spurts that left me disoriented. With a will of its own, my hand stroked me brutally, squeezing my knot which was pointlessly swelling.

As I filled the blanket, Amara knelt behind me, the warm skin of her chest pressing against my back. She wrapped her arms around my chest, caressing me and kissing my nape until I was fully spent.

When I finally stopped stroking myself, I felt weak and dizzy. But above all, I felt cherished as I leaned back against my Twin Flame, who tightened her embrace around me.

"You reckless female," I growled disapprovingly. "You said you'd do things *my* way."

Far from being repentant, Amara chuckled smugly. "Yes, *last night*. Today is a different day. And I was careful."

"Not enough!" I grumbled.

"Fine, then we'll work *together* on finding ways that you are comfortable with. But you will not deny me your pleasure."

I muttered something under my breath, which only made her

giggle some more. The rational part of me wanted to be mad—and likely should be. But the needy part of me was utterly grateful for this wondrous woman.

"Well, I need to go dispose of this biohazard," I said begrudgingly, pointing with my chin at the soiled blanket, even as I wiped myself clean. "You should get dressed and come down to have breakfast. It is nearly time for us to head out."

"Okay," she said in a docile voice before giving me another bone crushing hug.

I melted from a powerful emotion swelling within me. Turning my head to the side, I glanced at her beautiful face over my shoulder. She smiled affectionately at me, then brushed aside a rebellious lock of hair from my forehead.

"Thank you, my Flame," I said softly.

"Any time," she whispered before leaning forward.

Our lips met in a deep and passionate kiss. Something settled inside me. I didn't need my physiological responses to tell me this woman was my Twin Flame. Even without that trait, I would be falling hard for Amara. As the Gods were my witnesses, I would do everything in my power to save her and keep her forever.

We parted with much reluctance, then set about our respective tasks. After burning the blanket—as washing it with regular soap and water couldn't guarantee my toxins were neutralized—I warmed up our meal, and we ate quickly.

Once the lodge was back in order, with clean new sheets on the bed, we set off on our journey. My chest constricted as the silhouette of the building rapidly vanished behind the thick foliage of the trees.

"We will reach the Haunted Woods in about ten minutes," I said in a serious tone as we reached the packed dirt road that crossed most of the region. "Under different circumstances, I would take another route, but this will save us at least two days."

"With that name, it doesn't sound particularly safe," she said warily.

"It's fairly safe, so long as we remain on the path," I said reassuringly. "Various wards and protection magic keeps most foul creatures from stepping onto the road."

"*Most* but not *all?*" Amara insisted.

I smiled approvingly. "Nice catch. Most low-level fiends, revenants, and abominations will be repelled by the wards. A high-level demon or mythical creature *might* be able to ignore them. But they never come here. The people who travel this road have nothing that they want. However, there is some wildlife that occasionally shows up while hunting. I will have no problem dispatching them."

"Okay," Amara said, still looking uneasy.

"Here, wear this amulet," I said, bringing my horse a little closer to hers so that I could hand her the necklace. "It will block the abilities of the majority of mystifiers in the forest, if it ever came to that."

"Mystifiers?" Amara echoed, while taking the pendant.

"They're animals, plants, or sentient creatures with the power of illusion," I explained. "If you enter the forest, they could make you believe that you're following the road when you're in fact heading deeper into the woods, where they will ambush and devour you."

I hated the fear that fleeted over Amara's face as a shiver coursed through her. My words and actions should bring her peace, confidence, and make her feel safe.

"So long as you wear the amulet and stay close to your horse, it will also remain calm and be immune to the lure of the mystifiers," I added. "Just focus on the road ahead and ignore anything or anyone that tries to lure you into the woods."

"Understood."

With that established, I set a fast but sustainable pace for our horses. Although no physical sign or marker indicated the beginning of the Haunted Woods, an undeniable shift occurred the moment we crossed its invisible border. The air felt thick, damp, and almost slimy. It took on a sickly-sweet scent that revolted my sensitive nose.

Amara shuddered, and her deliciously dark skin erupted in goosebumps. The tension emanating from her was almost palpable. Pride filled my heart watching her staunchly move forward despite her misgivings. Externally, my mate could fool people who mistook her demure demeanor for a meek and submissive personality. But my female was no pushover. She held a quiet strength that surged forward when needed, destabilizing those who stupidly underestimated her.

Remembering the assertive way in which she had claimed me as hers and stating imperiously that I wouldn't deny her what was rightfully hers still had me tingling in all the right places.

Too soon, the malevolence of this wretched place became even stronger. Most people would be unable to say what was amiss, but an undeniable sense of unease would overtake them. Although still green, the grass had taken a dull hue. The tree branches laden with lush leaves seemed deceptively normal. However, upon further inspection, one could see how twisted and deformed they truly were.

A discreet but alluring melody tickled my sensitive ears. I glanced at my woman. Her human ears couldn't perceive it. And yet, a shiver coursed through her as she peered uneasily towards the dense woods. Amara was unnerved and subconsciously distressed. Not for the first time, I'd noticed her ability to perceive things with far more accuracy than the common mortal. I suspected she might be an empath.

I launched into a casual conversation to help distract her from our cursed surroundings while also affording a reprieve to our horses by slowing our pace.

"What are your plans once you are healed?" I asked with feigned nonchalance.

Amara chewed her bottom lip, her eyes going out of focus for a brief instant as she reflected on her answer. I felt stupid for feeling hurt that she didn't immediately answer that she would settle down with me. Before I could even squash that thought, my mate refocused on me so suddenly, I almost felt as if I'd gotten caught red handed doing something I shouldn't. The strangest expression flitted over her features. Once more, I wondered if she had perceived my emotions or if I was over-thinking things.

"I inherited a very nice house in Willow Grove. In truth, it is quite the gothic mansion," my mate replied pensively. "It would be perfect for me to run my candles business, especially with so many witches and arcanists in the area. Since my arrival, I've gotten many new customers interested in enchanted candles as well as summoning ones."

"I see," I said in a non-committal fashion, my mind racing. "Your craft should indeed be very popular with the merchants in Charmers District."

Willow Grove was a short distance away. If Amara welcomed me into her home, I could easily travel back to the mountain to hunt and perform my guide work.

She nodded even as she eyed me with an unreadable expression that seemed laced with a hint of taunting. Did she know what thoughts were crossing my mind?

"But I could live elsewhere as well," she added with a shrug. "I would be fine going back to the house or the shop I want to set up once a week or so. I don't need such a fancy home. Thankfully, I make a comfortable enough living with my craft. As I love being free to go where I want and to be able to unleash my creativity untethered, I'm open to go wherever the wind blows or Fate leads me."

Each of her words had the most wondrous heat spreading through my chest. You didn't have to be a genius to understand her underlying meaning. The intensity in her gaze when she spoke of Fate confirmed that she would be willing to follow me in my more nomadic life. What she failed to understand was that, as much as I also loved the freedom of roaming free in the wilderness, my circumstances forced me into that hermit life. I wanted to lay down my roots somewhere with someone who would love me as unconditionally as I would love them and raise together however many offspring we might be blessed with.

I was opening my mouth to respond when Amara jerked her head to the right, her eyes flicking this way and that. She appeared to look for someone while straining her ears to better listen to something.

She had finally heard the siren calls.

"Are you hearing this?" Amara asked, an air of uncertainty on her beautiful face.

I nodded with a serious but calm expression. "It is the alluring whispers of the evil spirits of the woods."

Her eyes widened, and she gaped at me while further trying to discern the sounds that were still a bit too subtle for her human ears.

"Wow. How can such a pretty melody come from something evil? It really makes you want to get closer to better listen," my mate said with a frown.

"That's the whole purpose. You *must* resist," I warned sternly.

The indulgent smile she gave me instantly silenced the fear blossoming within me.

"Don't worry, Remus. I have no intention of becoming wood demon food," she said teasingly. "It is definitely enticing. Had you not warned me, I very likely would have gone to investigate. But your words have not fallen on deaf ears. I didn't embark on this crazy journey to be healed by a demon wolf only to hand myself over to be devoured by some mystifier."

"Good girl," I said approvingly.

I tried to resume our small talk, namely prying about her life with her mother in their old town, but my woman became increasingly distracted. It wasn't the enticing melody that had her on edge, but the growing intensity of the dark magic permeating the area. It clung to us like dirt on sweaty skin. Even the air seemed too thick to easily breathe it in.

Amara gasped and pulled on her horse's reins so suddenly it reared back. For half a beat, I feared it was going to knock her off. Thankfully, I had chosen for her one of the most experienced and best trained horses from the stables. It had ventured often enough in similar areas not to be easily spooked or angered.

My mate pointed a finger towards something ahead to the left side of the road. I glanced in that direction, and anger instantly surged within me upon seeing a beautiful little boy sitting on a large rock only centimeters away from the road. His fancy clothes were torn as if he had run through a forest of thorns. Hugging his knees to his chest, he was rocking back and forth, weeping discreetly.

"Do not be fooled, my mate," I said in an imperious tone. "This is not a real boy, but a dark forest spirit. This is an illusion meant to lure you into the woods. A clear giveaway is the fact that none of their limbs or any part of them actually touches the road. The mystifier who created this illusion is only projecting the appearance of one of its former victims."

My woman gasped. "A doppelganger?!"

I shook my head. "No. Doppelgangers rarely venture in these parts. They stick closer to inns and populated areas. Prey is a lot more abundant there. As they take the appearance of their victims, on top of acquiring all of their knowledge, doppelgangers prefer to feed on people."

"Right. There isn't much to gain from devouring a mindless monster that people would avoid on sight," Amara replied with a shudder. "Whereas a human, especially an attractive one, will make it easier for them to attract another victim."

I nodded, glad that she understood so well, even as I hated

that she should be exposed to this disturbing side of the otherwise wondrous mountains that I called home since birth.

As we rode past the evil spirit, his weeping turned into a heart wrenching wailing that almost even had me wanting to go to the "boy" and console him. But I picked up the pace, my mate gladly following with an air of relief. Seconds later, the sound stopped abruptly. I glanced over my shoulder to find the spot where the illusion had been sitting now completely empty.

Over the next hour, nearly two dozen such spirits manifested themselves. The weeping child, pregnant woman, confused elderly, and even wounded pet each made an appearance in various forms. Some of them followed us, running alongside us in the forest while calling out for help. Instead of breaking my female, each appearance only seemed to reinforce her resolve and even immunity to their allure.

"Seriously?!" Amara exclaimed with an air of disgusted disbelief.

I burst out laughing, both because of how unimpressed she was and by the stunned expression of the latest illusion. It was a man in his late twenties with common clothes clearly too big for him. He was kneeling in the grass where he had been frantically trying to pick up gold coins and precious gems that had spilled out of a large pouch. He had been a petty thief who struck a big win by robbing a rich jewelry merchant only to meet his demise in the Haunted Woods. Many fools met a similar fate in their ill-advised attempts at recovering his loot.

Truth be told, I actually considered going after it myself. Because of my sickness, most wild beasts and demonic creatures gave me a wide berth. My blood was poison to them, so they didn't bother with me. In the end, I chose not to as I had no need for wealth. What was the point without anyone to share it with?

According to the rumors, a powerful sorcerer successfully retrieved it a few years later.

"You'd be surprised, my mate, by how many fools would

have fallen for this trick. Greed is a powerful thing," I said teasingly even as pride filled my heart.

The haunting melody was now playing full force. By rights, my woman should be all but fighting a losing battle against its enticement. Granted, the amulet I gave her was working overtime in shielding her from its appeal. But it still should have been difficult for her. And yet, she seemed unfazed aside from her natural discomfort to be surrounded by so much evil magic.

A mother carrying an infant was approaching the edge of the road but suddenly froze. Then, to my shock, she vanished into thin air, and the haunting melody stopped abruptly. My spine stiffened, the tension I felt reflected on my woman's face.

Ears perked, nostrils flaring, I tried to detect what could have possibly frightened the spirits away. Unfortunately, we were downwind, which prevented me from smelling whatever lurked ahead, while they would get a good whiff of our scents.

I removed my shirt and extruded my claws, ready to jump into action if needed. And then I saw them. Three Aegarims leapt out of the forest and onto the road. Amara gasped, the scent of her fear slapping my nose even as I cursed aloud. Those wretched things were fast and hunted in groups of three or four.

"That's not an illusion, right?" Amara asked, her voice thick with fear.

I stopped my horse and jumped down. "No, those are wild beasts, and they're coming for you."

Calling them 'wild beasts' was quite an understatement. Aegarims were abominations. They had once been proud Lycans like the rest of our clans. But hunger for greater strength and power sent them down a dangerous path. They consorted with evil forces and performed unholy experiments on themselves. Bit by bit, they lost their sentience to feral urges, reflected by their shifting appearance.

Gone were their lustrous fur and muscular bodies. Instead they now resembled the twisted offspring of a rat with a scrawny

Lycan covered in dark green scales. The five golden horns jutting from their rat-like, impish faces and the golden spikes lining their spine were the remnants of their fornication with demons. They ran on all fours like in the olden days of their former glory, but their front legs were anatomically closer to a human's but with oversized hands that only possessed two long fingers tipped by vicious claws.

As unholy creatures themselves, the Aegarims didn't fear the spirits in the woods and were immune to their illusions. They regularly fed off mystifiers, which explained why they all fled the minute the beasts showed up. But Aegarims craved human flesh, and especially the brains of sentient beings.

"They can smell my blood is bad, so they won't attack me. They will be relentless unless I get to their leader in the woods."

Even as I spoke, I stripped out of my pants. There was no time for me to fully undress as the creatures were racing at dizzying speed towards us.

"In the woods?!" Amara exclaimed as if I had lost my mind.

"I'll be fine, my mate. Nothing will attack me here. I'm cursed. Once I kill their leader, they will scatter. Stay on the path and keep moving. I will catch up to you," I said in a commanding tone.

"But what if there are more beasts ahead?!" my mate exclaimed, while pulling a dagger out from its sheath on her belt.

"No others will wander on their territory. I care for you, Amara. Promise you will stay on the path. I can't lose you!"

"I promise!" she replied in a trembling voice.

Lifting myself on my tiptoes, I crushed her lips in a far-too-brief desperate kiss, then ran towards the incoming beasts, who were now barely twenty meters away. I shifted even as I ran, my underwear tearing as my body expanded. I should have sliced them off first to spare myself the pain of the fabric digging into my flesh before it finally snapped. But my anger at the incoming creatures who would dare threaten my mate reclaimed all of my attention.

I charged the male in the middle, slamming into him with enough force to send him crashing into a nearby tree. The second one attempted to run past me, but I grabbed it by its back leg, my claws digging into its flesh as I held on to it before spinning around and flinging him with all my strength towards the third one who was barreling down towards Amara. He struck his companion with massive force. Even from where I stood, I heard at least a couple of their limbs breaking from the force of the impact.

They lay stunned, their limbs tangled as they struggled to get back up. I ran to them as my mate galloped past us. With a vicious swipe, I raked my claws along the flank of the third Aegarim, all but eviscerating him. The second one, which I had used as a projectile to knock off his companion, opened its massive jaw in an attempt to bite my face off. I grabbed his mouth with both hands, carefully avoiding the countless dagger teeth and spread it impossibly wide open until the lower half broke right off. I slammed the beast's destroyed face onto the ground, and stomped my foot on its neck, crushing it. The creature emitted a gurgling whimper, and a violent spasm shook its body before it went still.

But I was already on the move.

Amara was racing ahead with my horse following her. But the first beast I had sent crashing into the tree had recovered enough to give her chase. I raced after them, fury giving me wings as I quickly caught up to my prey. With a powerful leap, I landed on the creature's back, flattening it to the ground. It emitted a guttural sound as air rushed out of him. My heavy weight crushing the creature kept its lungs from expanding enough to breathe. It thrashed beneath me in a vain attempt to knock me off. I savagely sank my fangs on each side of its nape and snapped its spine. After a brief, high-pitched, whimper, the creature went limp.

Movement in the forest caught my eye. At least two more Aegarims were racing in the cover of the woods towards my mate. For a split second, I considered going after them, but it would only encourage more of them to follow suit. Instead, I ran into the forest, howling loudly to make sure they heard me. Their steps faltered as they glanced in my direction and realized where I was headed. As expected, they gave up chasing after my mate and darted after me.

To my shock, only a few meters into the woods, I spotted nearly a dozen more beasts scattered nearby. It was extremely unusual. Aegarims usually lived in small packs of six, and rarely more than ten. This one easily had more than double. A single whiff of me sufficed for them to scatter. I didn't chase them but followed my nose to the matriarch. I made a beeline for her.

Realizing what my intentions were, the pack rallied, throwing themselves in my path to protect her while she attempted to flee. Like us wolves, Aegarims had a fairly complex language based on howling. In this instance, she was sounding the retreat. My bloodlust demanded that I decimate her entire pack before her very eyes and then tear her to shreds. Had we been closer to the full moon, I likely would have done so in my mindless rage. But my mate was alone on the road in the Haunted Woods. My need to protect her superseded any primal urges to shed blood.

With one final warning growl, I gave up pursuit and raced back to my mate, my bloodlust unsated.

CHAPTER 8
AMARA

Heart pounding, I galloped hard along the road. A part of me wanted to push harder, but the other feared going too far. I kept glancing over my shoulder for any sign of Remus trying to catch up with me.

No words could express just how terrified I felt for my man. The lizard-rat-dogs that attacked us would haunt me for a long time. Although Remus made mincemeat out of them without breaking a sweat, I suspected many more lurked in the woods. What if their greater number overwhelmed him? What if he was, right at this moment, lying in a pool of his own blood while I selfishly fled?

The alluring song returned with a vengeance the moment my man vanished inside the woods. It didn't entice me in the least now that I knew what it was. Instead, it was giving me a splitting headache.

The spirits knew I was alone.

The urge to turn around and go get him clawed at me relentlessly. Obviously, it was stupid and even suicidal to even consider it. I cast out that foul temptation and plowed forward.

Just as I was considering slowing down the pace to spare the horses, a deafening silence suddenly descended over the forest.

Panicked, I jerked my head around in every direction to see what could have scared the spirits this time. Was the threat ahead or sneaking up from behind? I slowed down the horses, fearing I might be running into a trap, but also dreading to backtrack.

"Stay on the path," I whispered to myself, echoing Remus's words.

I hated that he left me to run into the woods. There was no question he did what he believed would keep me safe, but I felt abandoned. And right now, fear twisted my insides. I didn't know how to fight, and what little magic I possessed only allowed me to enchant objects with light magic and beneficial spells.

The distant sound of breaking branches and heavy steps had me do a half turn on my horse to look at the east side of the forest. My heart nearly leapt out of my chest when a massive dark shadow raced through the trees.

And then, a beloved howling broke the frightening silence.

"Remus!" I breathed out, joy and relief crashing over me.

I stopped the horses completely and partially turned my mount to face the forest. The giant wolf continued to approach only to disappear behind a gigantic tree. Seconds later, Remus reappeared on the other side in this human form. I jumped off the horse, tears of joy rolling down my cheeks as he nonchalantly half-walked, half-jogged towards me.

He beamed at me and opened his arms wide. A nervous laugh escaped me as I returned his smile. I took two steps towards him before stopping dead in my tracks. My blood turned to ice as I glanced down at his feet.

He was still inside the forest.

I peered back at his face to find him frowning in confusion at me. I didn't need a mirror to know what suspicious expression I displayed.

"Come out of the woods," I ordered while taking an involuntary step back.

Remus snorted. To my shock, rather than trying to convince me to come to him instead, he gave me an approving smile before resolutely walking out of the woods. A wave of relief washed over me when he calmly stepped onto the path.

"Good girl," Remus said as he slowly closed the distance between us. "For a moment, I feared you would fall for it."

"You wretched male!" I said, half-joking and half genuinely disapproving. "It was mean to test me under such serious circumstances."

"There could never be a better time than now when facing true danger," he countered before once more opening his arms wide.

This time, I didn't hesitate and threw myself into his embrace. Even as I did so, I caught myself glancing into the woods for any sign of the wild beasts. I nearly melted when his strong arms closed around me, holding me tightly. By the gods, how I had missed him even though we'd only parted for a few minutes.

"Are you okay?" I asked, reluctantly pulling away to have a look at him.

"Of course," he said smugly. "Aegarims are no challenge for me."

He leaned forward to kiss me, but just as our lips were about to meet, I instinctively averted my face. Something was off. It was him, and yet not. His kiss landed on my cheek instead, and I felt him stiffen in my arms. Obviously, he knew I had deliberately avoided his kiss. Our eyes met, and all my senses went into full alert.

It's not him!

The certainty with which that thought fired off in my mind left me reeling. His face hardened at the same time as I tried to push him away. He tightened his hold around me as an evil smile stretched his lips.

And then it finally struck me.

He's fully dressed! Remus stripped out of his clothes before running into the woods.

I tried to fight him off, but I might as well have tried to push a brick wall. He chuckled maliciously before fisting my hair with one hand and yanking it down to expose my neck. His golden eyes took on a reddish hue, the pupils narrowing into a vertical slit while his fangs descended.

"Let me go!" I shouted while fighting in vain to free myself.

"Never, my sweet. Nothing, and no one—especially not those pathetic runes—can protect you from me," he whispered in a voice full of threats and promises.

I screamed as his fangs sank into my neck. Liquid ice flooded my veins. Half a beat later, a veil of darkness descended before my eyes, and I went limp.

My skin tingled in that odd way it often did as you slowly emerged from a deep slumber. It took me a moment to realize that a threatening sound nearby had stirred me awake. My eyes snapped open, and I inspected my surroundings. To my shock, I was lying on a stone plateau by a cliff, surrounded by a dark forest a short distance away.

I couldn't detect a single soul nearby, and yet the powerful sense of being observed by a predator gnawed at me. My head jerked up at a sudden flapping sound. My blood drained from my face when I finally spotted the massive silhouette of a demon wolf circling overhead.

I glanced back at the ground beneath me, and I nearly fainted upon finding it bare, without the protective circle I should have drawn before facing Ranael. A savage growl overhead reclaimed my attention. My eyes locked with his, and I felt paralyzed when he dove towards me.

On instinct, I shot to my feet and attempted to flee. But I couldn't outrun him, and there was nowhere to hide. The bare plateau extended for at least two hundred meters before the tree line began on the south edge. A steep rock wall bordered the eastern edge, and a deadly cliff ended the remaining sides. I couldn't even attempt to draw a circle, not that I had anything to do it with.

Despite that, even as I ran, I tried to invoke his protection just like the Weaver taught me. But the demon wolf was too enraged. The shadow of his massive wingspan blocked the sun over me seconds before he would reach me. I dodged left. Although Ranael flew past me, he still managed to rake his vicious claws up my back.

A burning pain exploded between my shoulder blades, and I stumbled to the ground, screaming. Despite the excruciating pain, I pushed myself up and got on my knees. With powerful flaps of his wings, the demon wolf flew in a wide circle before heading back towards me. I tried to block him out of my mind. Gritting my teeth through the pain, I swiped my fingers over my wounds to gather my blood freely trickling out to draw a circle on the ground.

My heart was trying to pound its way out of my chest as I began reciting the protection circle spell. But the wretched beast dove again, interrupting me. I rolled to the side to avoid him, which took me partially out of the circle. Once more, Ranael inflicted another wound on me by raking my calf with his talons. I cried out and nearly fainted. He'd sliced me so deep I could see the bone through the cut.

Feeling faint and in agony, I once more knelt inside the circle and used more of my blood to repair the part of the circle I damaged while rolling out of the way. Feeling lightheaded, I rushed through the incantation. Without candles or all the proper reagents, I didn't know how well the protection would hold, but it was all I had.

Or at least, all that I might have had if given a chance to complete it.

I barely had two words left to complete the incantation when the demon wolf slammed into me. It felt as if a ram struck me. I flew back a few meters and landed hard on the stony ground. The brutal impact on my lacerated back would have wrested another scream of agony from me had I not been winded from the force of the blow.

I never had a chance to release another scream. The demon wolf pinned my shoulders to the ground with both his massive front paws, then his snake tail repeatedly bit my neck and face. An atrocious burning sensation set my entire face and neck ablaze. My throat immediately shut down. I couldn't breathe or emit any sound.

Ranael leaned forward and growled menacingly in my face before swiping his claws over my neck, slicing my throat open. Choking on my own blood, I watched him flap his wings. He ascended maybe three or four meters above me before opening his mouth wide. As a stream of fire rushed towards me, my last thought was for Remus.

We should have had more time together.

CHAPTER 9
AMARA

I startled awake, confused to find myself in a warm and comfortable woodhouse. Despite the horrible injuries I vividly recalled sustaining, I couldn't feel any pain or discomfort anywhere in my body.

The joyous flames of a fire danced in the hearth. Gas lamps illuminated the room, giving it an almost dreamy halo. The pleasant scent of roasted nuts and hot cocoa tickled my nose. How my brain managed to register that this stove to my left was empty made no sense as my focus laid squarely on the other-worldly creature in front of me.

He slouched in an empire chair near the fireplace. He was beautiful in a terrifying way. His eyes—a deep and unsettling shade of red with the vertical pupils of a snake—stared at me with an intensity that made me want to squirm. Underneath his grayish blue skin, lightning-shaped stripes appeared to pulsate with a soft glow. Whitish-blue hair tumbled down to his clavicles in soft waves. It framed a haunting face, very human in appearance—like his body—with a square jaw, plush lips stretched in a taunting smirk, and a proud nose.

He narrowed his eyes at me. His exquisitely long lashes cast a shadow, making him harder to read.

"Welcome back, Amara Sanni," the stranger said in a purring voice.

It was just as haunting as his face, with an accent that didn't quite qualify as British, but definitely not American. He straightened in his seat, his impressive abdominal muscles tightening for a split second. He was naked except for a white, Grecian skirt which fell to his knees, a golden belt, and Roman sandals laced up to the middle of his calves. If not for his unusual skin, he could have been one of the gods of the Olympus.

"Who are you? Why did you take me? How do you know my name? And where are we?" I asked in rapid fire, as I glanced around the room with that last question.

I hadn't meant to respond that way, but my mouth just ran away with me.

Instead of snapping back at me, the stranger chuckled.

"So many questions," he said tauntingly. "I am Lyall. A little bird told me about you. And this is my temporary home," he added, waving at the house.

That he hadn't answered why he took me didn't go unnoticed. Although I intended to press him on that matter, I rejoiced that he was at least communicating in an unthreatening fashion. Forcing myself to speak in a non-belligerent or accusatory tone, I calmly pried further about recent events.

"You pretended to be Remus and then created that horrible illusion where I died, didn't you?" I asked softly.

"I did," he replied with a shrug.

"Why would you do that?" I asked, genuinely baffled.

"For fun? To see your reaction? To test your skills? Or maybe just because I can..." he said in an almost pensive fashion.

He was obviously baiting me, likely wanting to stir an

outraged reaction from me. But this male was an apex predator. I wouldn't give him any reason to get worked up and lash out at me. Although I wasn't physically restrained in any way, my body felt unnaturally weighed down, as if an invisible force was shackling me to the comfortable padded chair he had settled me in.

Is any of this even real? Am I trapped in another illusion? Is he still testing me?

Too many questions were firing off in my mind. For now, I could only play along and hope to come out on the winning side. Above all, I needed to understand what his intentions were.

"Okay. But that still doesn't tell me why you took me against my will," I said carefully. "If you just wanted to test my reactions to your illusions, you could have asked."

"I will let you take a wild guess as to why I took you," he replied in a dangerously sweet voice filled with a dare.

I frowned, unsure as to what kind of answer he expected. By the way he had phrased his sentence, he seemed to imply that the answer should be obvious.

"Honestly, I cannot think of any reason why you would," I said in all sincerity. "I suspect that you already know that I'm sick. My blood is poisoned. If you planned on eating me, it would almost certainly kill you. That could explain why you haven't bothered—assuming that was your intention to begin with."

He burst out laughing, the sound full and throaty in a way that I found quite pleasant. If he wasn't so deliberately intimidating, he would be an extremely attractive male.

"Yes, it is a very nasty poison that courses through you," he conceded with almost malicious glee. "But it's no threat to me. I could devour every single morsel of your tender flesh and remain unscathed."

My jaw dropped as I stared at him.

"I'm what you could call a doppelganger. I absorb the

appearance, knowledge, powers, and skills of anything I eat," Lyall said smugly.

"Permanently?!" I exclaimed.

He chuckled and shook his head. "Some things, yes. But other things, no. However, I'm immune to all poisons. So eating you won't hurt me."

He stated that last sentence with an undeniable threat. But my mind went back to the beginning of his previous description of his abilities. If he absorbed the appearance of anything he ate, did that mean…?

"Where's Remus?! Please tell me you haven't hurt him!" I pleaded, fear twisting my insides.

His gaze darkened, and his face took on a hungry, almost sensuous expression. The sharp tips of his fangs peaked between his parted lips, and he placed his right hand over his crotch, as if to adjust himself.

"Fuck, the scent of your fear is divine," he hissed as if he was fighting to keep control over some primal urges. "It was to be expected as your natural scent is also delicious. Even the stench of death clinging to you fails to ruin it. No wonder the pup wants you."

"Please, tell me he's alive!" I begged. "Please tell me you haven't hurt him."

He tilted his head to the side and studied my face as one would a strange creature that defied logic.

"I haven't… yet," he said at last.

A choked sound of relief escaped me. "Then I beg you to leave him be. You already have me. If it's food you want, then eat me and let him go."

To my surprise, my offer appeared to anger him.

"Why would I?" he asked in a harsh tone.

"Remus is a good man!" I exclaimed.

Lyall huffed with disdain and waved a hand. "He's cursed

and an outcast. The pup is a danger to others. Even his blood could kill."

"He's sick!" I countered, outrage audible in my voice. "It's not his fault that he was born this way. Despite all the hardships he faced, he still turned into a good man. From the moment we met, he's been kind, protective, and honorable towards me."

My jaw dropped, and I recoiled when Lyall slammed both his hands on the arms of his chair, his face twisted with fury.

"You don't know him!" he spat angrily. "You're vulnerable and desperate, easily manipulated by anyone who could give you an ounce of hope. For all you know, he's just playing you."

I shook my head firmly. "Even though he and I just met, I trust him with my life. We're Twin Flames."

Lyall snorted, his anger seeming to fade as quickly as it flared, and a disdainful expression settled on his features.

"Are you?" he asked mockingly. "He could just be saying that to get you to blindly follow him."

Once more, I firmly shook my head. "His physiological responses to me are undeniable. Others of his pack also noticed. In fact, it was one of them who pointed it out to me, and I was the one who forced Remus to confess."

Lyall clenched his teeth and stared at me quietly for a few seconds that felt like an eternity. Why was he so displeased about the connection between Remus and me?

"And so now you're in love?" he finally asked, his voice dripping with contempt.

I gave him an unimpressed look before replying. "Of course not. As you said so well, I don't know him as we've only recently met. But I love how I feel around him and the wonderful way he treats me. If I survive this sickness, there's no doubt I will fall madly in love with him."

He snorted again, looking at me as if I was stupid. "How idealistic. Except that your perfect Twin Flame utterly sucks at protecting you. He abandoned you in the middle of the Haunted Woods, and I only had to stroll in and nab you."

Although I had indeed hated that he left me on the road, he had not *abandoned* me. Remus did what he believed was the safest approach at the time. This blatant attack against my man only whipped my need to defend him.

"Remus didn't abandon me. He made a difficult choice under dire circumstances. He had no reason to think you would be lurking nearby. In fact, he said that no beings like you ever wandered in that area. So what were you doing in the Haunted Woods?" I challenged.

"I will grant that his assessment was fair," Lyall conceded with a taunting smirk. "I shouldn't have been there, but I was curious about you."

My eyes widened. "About me?" I echoed, confused. "Why? How did you even know of my existence? I'm nobody, just a chandler from a small town."

"I wanted to know who was so bold and arrogant to want to kill Ranael," he said, his voice and expression hardening. "My little test proved you completely unsuited to face the demon wolf. And you think you can just show up and subdue him?"

"What?! No! I don't want to kill him!" I exclaimed, stunned. "I don't know who told you that, but it's completely false. I'm going there seeking his protection. Did you not see me recite that incantation in your illusion?"

"His protection?" Lyall asked, taken aback. "For what?"

"So that he will bite me with his snake tail to counter the poison that's killing me, without inflicting me any other harm," I replied in a factual manner.

Of all the reactions he could have had, sitting there, gaping at me as if I had grown an extra limb on my forehead was the last thing I expected.

"You're insane!" Lyall whispered before seeming to recover

from his shock. "His venom will kill you, silly female. No one survives the venom from Ranael's tail!"

"It won't kill me if I get the second bite after his venom neutralizes my poison," I said with confidence. "I know how crazy this sounds. Truth be told, I thought the same thing the first time I heard about the nature of the only cure I could hope for in the time I have remaining. But the Weaver sent me. She taught me how to invoke Ranael's protection and the steps to follow to achieve my goal."

His face completely shut down. He leaned back in his chair, almost as if he needed to put distance between us. His eyes went out of focus, and he appeared lost in deep reflection as if trying to solve an impossible riddle. My tongue burned with the urge to ask him what was going through his mind, but I held my peace.

After a few moments, he refocused on me. "Why would the Weaver send you on this impossible mission?" he whispered.

Although he addressed the question to me, it seemed to be more of him musing aloud a question to himself.

"You will not survive it," Lyall said in a factual manner devoid of his previous taunting or malice. "In fact, you will likely die before you even reach the plateau. And assuming you make it, Ranael will kill you, or you will die of his venom. The poison ailing you is spreading extremely fast. Even from where I sit, I can literally see it multiplying inside of you. There are still ten days left in your journey. But there are barely seven or eight days left in you. At this point, eating you would be showing you mercy."

"You lie!" I shouted, even as despair surged within me.

Where he'd previously been deliberately needling and provoking me, this time, I sensed no deception from him.

"I *never* lie," he said matter-of-factly. "You can feel it, too. The clock is ticking, and you're running out of time."

My shoulders drooped, and I blinked back the tears pricking my eyes. I wasn't ready to die. Beyond the fact that I was too young to already leave this world, I had just met my soulmate. I hadn't come this far only to fail now. And why would the Weaver have seen me if I was a lost cause? She sent me off on that mission because a path to success existed, however slim it might be.

And then it struck me.

I jerked my head up to look at him, an impossible hope blossoming in my heart.

"You... you could help me! You're good with poison!" I swiftly added when he stared at me in confusion.

He recoiled and looked at me as if I was insane. "Why the fuck would I help you?"

"Because you can! Because it's the right thing to do!" I replied as if it was self-evident.

"I'm a monster," he countered in a tone that implied it should be obvious. "I don't help people. I play with them until they go insane, or until I tire of the game. And then usually eat them."

I held his gaze for a few seconds, and then the oddest sense of peace washed over me.

"No, Lyall," I said in a calm but confident voice. "What you are is a doppelganger. Being a monster is a choice. You can choose to be good."

He huffed, his expression making no doubt he thought my sickness affected my reasoning.

"Why would I? There's no fun in that. Fear and pain taste like the nectar of the Gods."

"So does happiness," I challenged.

He made a disdainful gesture. "Happiness is too hard to elicit. Mortals are masochists. Even when an idyllic life is handed to them, they will turn away from it and seek the path of sorrow and hardship."

"People make poor choices, it doesn't mean that they crave pain," I argued. "The harder something is to attain, and the more rewarding it is. Where's the fun in just settling for the lowest hanging fruit all the time?"

"Because chasing after the fruit out of reach means that there's a chance you will never claim it," Lyall countered. "And assuming you finally do, it will either have gone too ripe or fallen on its own to rot at your feet. But right now, I really want to hurt you while you're still just perfect to be harvested."

I didn't know how to react or respond to those words. He meant them. The dark side of him hungered to unleash the violence that dwelled inside. And yet, I wasn't afraid. At least, not that *he* would cause me harm. The same way an almost immediate connection had formed with Remus briefly after we met, I felt something similar—although different—with Lyall.

It made no sense.

Before I could come up with an answer, Lyall suddenly stiffened. He slightly turned his face to the right, and his eyes went out of focus. At first, I thought he was trying to listen to something beyond my human hearing. Then his vertical pupils dilated, and I realized he was visualizing something in his mind's eye. Moments later, he refocused on me, his expression mostly unreadable, and yet a hint of anger had seeped back in. His pupils narrowed back to a slit, and the redness of his eyes— which engulfed his entire sclera—appeared to take on a darker, more ominous hue.

"Your pet is looking for you," he said in a neutral tone.

I perked up and would have leaned forward if the magical force pinning me to my chair hadn't restrained me.

"Remus is near?!"

"Mmhmm," he replied, his face initially unreadable before a malicious smile stretched his lips. "The pup is playing my game. Search as he may, he will never find you without my consent. In fact, I think I'll feast on him first."

"No! Let him go! He's no threat to you," I exclaimed.

"I'm well aware of that," he said disdainfully. "But I'm hungry."

"Then eat *me*! Like you said, I won't make it anyway. But he has his entire life in front of him. Please, leave him be."

Once again, my words infuriated him. Even though the little voice at the back of my head shouted that I had nothing to fear from Lyall, I plastered myself against the backrest of my chair when he lunged forward. Both his hands resting on the arms of my chair, his nails extruding in terrifyingly long claws, he stopped with his face inches from mine.

"You don't fucking know him, and yet you would die for him?!" he hissed.

I swallowed hard but lifted my chin defiantly.

"Yes, I would," I replied, holding his gaze unwaveringly. "He took a major risk for me when no one else would. My survival was always a long shot. But at least he tried, and for a while he gave me hope when there was none to be found. So if I must die, I will gladly do it for him. But I refuse to be the cause of his death."

The right corner of his upper lip quirked up in a snarl. A million different thoughts fleeted over his otherworldly features as he stared angrily at me.

"You assume it's either him *or* you," he said in a sickly-sweet voice.

"You can't eat both of us!" I exclaimed, flabbergasted.

"Says who?" he challenged mockingly.

"Please, Lyall, just let him go," I pleaded.

To my shock, the red hue of his eyes shifted, taking on a slightly bluish-red tinge. A drawn-out purr vibrated from his throat. A sensuous expression descended on his face, and his eyes flicked to my lips.

"I love the way you beg. Beg me again, Amara," he whispered.

I opened my mouth to tell him to fuck off, but instead, I caught myself complying.

"Please, Lyall. I beg you," I whispered.

His purr resonated even more loudly. His upper lip quivered, as if he was fighting the urge to bare his fangs. It struck me that he couldn't decide whether he wanted to kiss me or sink his fangs into me.

"I should just keep you," he mused aloud.

Although I didn't believe he had spoken those words for me, I still responded.

"You can't keep me. I'm dying, remember?"

His eyes flicked to mine, and he stared at me with an intensity that left me feeling naked and exposed.

"I *can* keep you alive," he said in a factual manner.

My heart skipped a beat. "You can cure me!"

He shook his head. "I did not say that. Only that I can keep you alive. I can counter the poison in you when it spreads."

"Nine Hells! Why didn't you say that sooner? I will buy that medicine from you!"

He snorted and shook his head. "No, silly female. It's not something that can be sold," he said before exposing his sharp fangs and slowly running his tongue over the right one. "I must bite you, likely once or twice a week."

My shoulders slumped as the spark of hope fizzled. An angry growl vibrated through Lyall's chest, startling me.

"Why are you sad? Don't you want to live? I'm offering you a solution," he hissed.

"But that's not living," I argued in a soft voice. "If I agreed, I would in fact be living in limbo and fully at your mercy. You could withhold your bite to punish me whenever I displease you or to coerce me into complying with whatever demands you make of me."

"I may be a monster, but not *that* kind of monster," he snarled. "I could make you happy, Amara. I can be anything you want, whenever you want. Even that pup you're so fond of."

Speechless, I stared in disbelief as his features appeared to melt like wax under intense heat. Simultaneously, the lightning-shaped stripes under his skin glowed with great intensity, blinding me for the briefest second. I blinked twice and then gasped when I found myself staring into Remus's beloved golden eyes.

"Remus," I whispered.

My mind knew better, but my eyes desperately wanted to believe the illusion. He leaned forward to kiss me. Every fiber of my being screamed for me to meet him halfway, but seconds before our lips would meet, I managed to avert my face. He stopped a breadth's hair from my cheeks.

"Please don't," I whispered.

He hissed angrily and bared his teeth at me.

"What the fuck does he have that I don't?" Lyall snapped. "I'd be a better healer and protector than that sick pup can ever be!"

"He's my Twin Flame!" I exclaimed as if it was self-evident. "I'm not the female meant for you. Your soulmate is out there somewhere."

He snorted with disgust and pushed away from me, straightening as he shifted back to his natural form.

"I'm a monster," he said with self-deprecation.

"By choice, not by nature," I countered. "There's something beautiful in you. It shines through every time you cast aside your anger."

"Flattery won't work on me, human," he said sternly.

"I never lie," I replied, echoing his own words.

"Is that so?"

To my shock he grabbed my wrist angrily and sank his fangs in the inner side. I cried out at the sharp sting. Then liquid bliss flooded my veins as he began to drink from me. He wasn't gorging but taking small sips. Through the haze of euphoria provided by whatever he had injected me with, I stared in wonder at his divine beauty. His eyes had completely lost their red color and were now the most beautiful shade of purple. A mesmerizing light emanated from the lightning under his skin. They seemed to slightly undulate, bathing him in a soothing halo. Behind him, two beams of light protruded from his back vaguely forming the shape of a massive pair of ethereal wings.

He's not a doppelganger.

Whatever he was, he undoubtedly possessed divine blood. Was he the offspring of a Fallen? Or the hybrid child of a doppelganger and an angel? But even as those thoughts fired off in my mind, I realized that he wasn't actually feeding by drinking my blood. Lyall was plundering my memories.

I couldn't tell how much time passed. It could have been seconds or hours. I'd been floating in too deep a state of well-being to keep track of such a menial concept. Lyall pulled his fangs out of my wrist and licked the puncture wounds. Fascinated, I watched them seal shut in a blink.

Lyall straightened and stood towering over me. My chest constricted upon seeing the air of deep sadness and resignation on his beautiful face as the angelic glow dimmed around him. What had he seen that left him this defeated?

"Two bites..." he muttered to himself. "The Weaver and her damn mind games..."

"What?" I asked, confused.

"Think carefully on her words," Lyall said in a mysterious fashion. "They do not mean what you think."

"What do you mean?" I insisted.

He stared at me quietly for a moment as if pondering how he would answer before shaking his head.

"It is time for me to go see your pup," he said at last.

"Please, don't hurt him!"

His anger flared again. To my shock, he fisted my hair on my nape and crushed my lips in a brutal kiss. It lasted less than a second and felt more like punishment than an attempt at seduction. His face an inch from mine, he locked eyes with me, their angry red hue making no mystery as to his current state of mind.

"What fate befalls the pup is up to him," he snarled. "Pray that he makes the right choice."

"What does that mean?"

He didn't answer. He released my hair then marched resolutely out of the house, leaving me alone, confused, and distraught.

CHAPTER 10
REMUS

As I ran back to the road, I used all the calming techniques I had developed over the years to help rein in my feral side when the full moon approached. My blood still boiled with the lust to kill. While I didn't fear harming my mate in any way, I didn't want her seeing this unbridled side of me. At least, not so early in our relationship.

She trusted me, of this I had no doubt. She also felt a great deal of affection for me. I wanted it to blossom into a deep and undying love. With all the challenges facing us right now, making her feel unsafe in my presence was the last thing we needed.

I sprang out of the woods onto the path, running on all fours in my wolf form. I would have preferred coming to her as a human, but I didn't run as fast that way. Strangely enough, I also felt self-conscious at the thought of running buck naked in front of her. That made absolutely no sense considering nudity was normal among Lycans. Furthermore, I could honestly say that I had a very nice body. So this sudden shyness was completely irrational.

But as I raced down the path, those wandering thoughts

quickly faded from my mind. By now, I should either be hearing the sound of our horses galloping in the distance or at least get a glimpse of her silhouette ahead. Granted, I chased the Aegarims fairly deep into the woods. Still, I hadn't been gone so long that my mate could have traveled that far, even pushing the horses to their maximum.

My stomach twisted with a sense of unease, and I redoubled the speed at which I ran. The complete silence further fueled my growing panic. The mystifiers and evil spirits wouldn't sing for me as my blood was poison to them. But I should hear their whispers to my woman had she been in range.

My gorge rose at the thought that another pack of Aegarims might have been lurking even farther ahead. It shouldn't be the case as those beasts hunted over a large territory that they fiercely defended against other packs.

But this pack counted far more members than they normally do.

I shouldn't have left her. It had been reckless and arrogant of me to think she would be fine because I could easily dispatch the threat. If anything happened because of my negligence...

My blood turned into ice in my veins, and I howled in despair as I finally noticed Amara's footprints on the packed dirt where she dismounted her horse. But it was the presence of a second set of footsteps that truly destroyed me. Something—or rather *someone*—had walked out of the woods onto the path.

Nothing good could safely travel the Haunted Woods.

Worse still, I couldn't pick any scent that might identify the interloper. All I perceived was Amara's scent and the one from our horses. My mind raced as I mentally reviewed the limited number of creatures I knew that either possessed no scent or excelled at masking it enough to make it nearly impossible to detect. All of them were dreadful.

I rushed into the forest, following what lingered of my woman's distinct aroma. Traipsing through these cursed woods always felt like diving into a concentrated pool of evil. To my dismay, I couldn't see any sign on the ground of the horses' hooves or of my mate's footsteps. A part of me began to wonder if I was under the effect of an illusion making me think I was actually following her scent. But I didn't feel any magic directly affecting me.

Could the creature who took her be winged and flew a short distance above ground?

Without slowing down, I glanced up at the trees overhead. There were no signs of any broken or disturbed branches that might indicate something big had flown through them. Each branch was so thick and long they almost created a dome over-head. Only smaller creatures could fly by without the risk of crashing into one of them.

And then her scent vanished altogether.

I stopped dead in my tracks and sniffed the air in vain. Heart pounding, I backtracked until I picked up the scent again. To my dismay, it was now leading me in a completely different direction than the one I had been following. Five or ten minutes later —I couldn't tell anymore as time seemed to have lost all meaning—the same thing happened again. Rage, confusion, and growing despair had my chest so constricted I could barely breathe as I retraced my steps until I picked up her trail again heading in yet another direction.

By then, I no longer doubted that I was trapped in some sort of illusion. The question was which type. As I still couldn't feel any magic being used on me, I could only speculate that I was either being physically controlled by a creature or a plant, or that a powerful mystifier had taken control of me.

Was I even moving in the real world or just standing still like a statue? Was I being wrapped inside the cocoon of a fiendish creature? Was a beast eating me alive even as I wandered aimlessly in this nightmare?

Whatever the case might be, I had to keep moving forward.

Giving into despair would guarantee my demise, and with it my mate's as well. If only for her, I couldn't fail.

I shifted back into my human form before climbing on one of the trees to get a better long-range view of my surroundings. To my shock, I spotted what looked like a cozy wooden house in the distance. The light smoke rising from the chimney indicated that a fire was burning inside.

This house shouldn't exist.

My every instinct told me it was a bait to lure me into a trap. But I had nothing else to go on. I jumped down from the branch I had been perched on, intent on turning back into my wolf form to race towards my new destination. However as soon as I hit the ground, an acute pain stung the back of my leg. I stumbled forward. Just as I was about to regain my balance, thorny vines wrapped around my leg yanking it backwards. The ground rushed towards me, and I barely managed to throw my hands in front of me to avoid face planting.

Sharp cutting pain stabbed every inch of my body as the vines continued to wrap around me like a boa constrictor, with countless sharp needles stinging me with their numbing venom.

I couldn't believe an Arraphilon would attack me. Those wretched creatures looked like a four-meter-long centipede whose cylindrical body resembled a thorny branch covered with leaves. Its upper body had a few extra limbs that could almost pass for two sets of arms without hands. It had no eyes to speak of or even anything that could be deemed a face. If not for the series of horns around its head, the latter could have belonged to a lamprey with its circular mouth filled with needle teeth.

Most people would be oblivious to the creature's presence as it usually lay flat on the ground, often around the base of a tree. It would lie in wait, wrapped in a way to look like a pile of fallen leaves or just random greenery in the underbrush. In my desperation to get to my woman, I'd neglected to pay better attention to my surroundings.

Still, that creature never should have attacked me. It could smell the toxin in me. And yet, it continued to sting me with its thorns and even gave me a couple of bites in its impatience to feed. I didn't waste time and energy trying to fight it in my human form. Although the Arraphilon and I possessed comparable strength—mine likely a bit greater—I would sustain far too many wounds from its thorns and be slowed down by its numbing venom if I tried to pursue this fight like this.

Instead, I immediately shifted into my wolf form. Not only would my fur provide non negligible protection from the thorns, but I also regenerated faster as a wolf. Furthermore, my bigger size in that form made it harder for that creature to constrain or crush me. As expected, the Arraphilon soon loosened its grip to avoid being ripped apart by my significantly wider girth.

I swiped my claws at it, splitting it in half. The creature's shrill screech had my ears painfully ringing. From the pain and shock, the Arraphilon released me for barely a couple of seconds, which sufficed for me to escape its clutch. However, the creature would never be defeated so easily. Both halves thrashed on the ground for another beat before chasing after me.

My skin tingled from the numbing effect of my attacker's paralytic toxins. Thankfully, they weren't strong enough to truly impede or incapacitate me. But sustained exposure to a greater amount would eventually leave me in a vulnerable position.

To my dismay, the ground started moving all around me with many more Arraphilons coming out of hiding and springing into action. I cursed inwardly that I should find myself in such a trap. Granted, even with my heightened sense of smell, detecting their presence was extremely difficult as their scent matched too closely that of other plants and vegetation in the forest. The fact that most creatures never bothered with me due to my condition had also made me a little careless and overconfident when it came to my own safety while wandering in dangerous places.

Two of the wretched fiends leapt at me, one of them landing

on my back. I jumped, contorting midair while swiping my paws at it to keep it from successfully wrapping itself around me. Although I didn't split that one in half, I managed to inflict a long gash one-third of its body, which was enough to make it fall and writhe in pain. With a few leaps and evasive maneuvers, I dodged the other assailants. However, that wouldn't work for much longer. With so many of them chasing after me, the combined effect of their paralytic venom would guarantee my demise.

I hacked and slashed at them, clenching my teeth through the pain of the successful bites they managed to sneak in. Although their attack made no sense, they would need to ingest too much of my blood or flesh before my toxins kill them. By then, it would be too late for me. I would need fire to eradicate them all in one fell swoop.

Even as I began to weaken, a thought suddenly sparked in my mind. I veered east, running as fast as I could while fighting off my pursuers. While searching for my mate, I remembered seeing a patch of bitter morels. Less than thirty meters from my salvation, a sharp pain in my right leg made me lose my footing. An Arraphilon had savagely bitten my Achilles tendon, and it felt as if lighting had struck me there. I crashed hard on the ground, even as my assailant used its frontal limbs to climb on me.

Leveraging my momentum, I rolled with the fall to get back onto my paws. My right leg wasn't fully responding, but I ignored it. I reached for the creature crawling over me with my front paw and viciously stabbed my claws into it. This time, I didn't attempt to cut it in half but tore it right off me. I cried out in pain as its thorns ripped me to shreds and tossed the creature with all my strength into the patch of bitter morels. It landed with such force in their midst that it crushed a few of them. The morels spit out their toxic spores, and the Arraphilon screeched in agony. It tried to slither away but barely moved more than a few centimeters before it began writhing, its thorns falling to the ground, and its leaves darkening and withering.

A second Arraphilon lunged for my throat, but I caught it with my maw and flung it in the same general direction as its fallen companion. Within seconds, it met the same horrendous demise. I half-ran, half-limped closer to the patch of morels, but not so much their spores would affect me, and turned to the other creatures that had been chasing me. To my shock, they were all gone.

And so was my pain.

Instead, I stared at a handsome doppelganger standing less than ten meters away from me. He was leaning on his forearms against the doorframe of a charming wood and brick cabin. Intricate wards, the like I'd never seen before, adorned the entrance of the dwelling. I didn't need to be an arcanist to know they were powerful enough to keep at bay the foul creatures that haunted these woods.

It shouldn't be here. When I surveyed the woods from the tree branch, the cabin had been located in a different direction and at a much greater distance than the one I covered while escaping the creatures hunting me.

"Not bad, pup," the doppelganger said in a mocking tone. "You can think creatively and have decent situational awareness."

I straightened as I shifted back into my human form.

"Where is she?" I asked in lieu of a response, unfazed by my nudity. "If you hurt her—"

"Then what?" he interrupted in a provocative fashion. "What will you do? Or rather what *can* you do against one such as I?"

I glared at him, searching for an appropriate response, but failing miserably. Lycans were naturally immune to many forms of mind control, even more so when benefiting from the protection of a talisman like the one I wore. The ease with which he had engulfed me in that illusion without me ever even realizing the moment I entered it blew my mind.

While the lightning streaks beneath his skin clearly gave him away as a doppelganger, he didn't resemble any of the ones I had seen or heard of before. They normally had a very pale, grayish or off-white skin complexion. The streaks were also thinner and more discreet. From a distance, they could be mistaken for old scars. His skin was a fascinating shade of dusky blue. His streaks were far more prominent and seemed to pulse with an inner light. Unlike others of his species, he didn't have stormy gray eyes. His were entirely red—sclera included—with vertical pupils like a reptile.

Even from where I stood, I could feel the potent magic swirling around him. He wasn't a mere doppelganger, but something far more powerful and lethal.

"It's funny that you should care now about her welfare when you callously abandoned her," he mused aloud before I could come up with a proper repartee—not that I had one to begin with.

But those words felt like a slap in the face. They stung all the more that I had been berating myself for that very reason.

"I didn't abandon her," I snapped. "I was protecting her from a pack of Aegarims. Remaining on the path would keep her safe while I lured them away."

"Clearly, remaining on the path did not," he countered tauntingly.

"You shouldn't have been there!" I spat angrily. "Your kind doesn't wander in these parts."

"And yet, here I am," he replied, spreading his arms wide as he took a few steps towards me, his face hardening. "You had one task, and you utterly failed. What good are you?"

I flinched, the words cutting me deep. It took every ounce of my willpower not to respond to his provocation. He was clearly trying to rile me up, likely to push me into attacking him so that he could kill me. Granted, his kind didn't need an excuse to take a life, but they loved to play games and fuck with their prey's heads before feasting on them.

"Where is she?" I repeated in a controlled voice, despite the anger and worry knotting my insides. "I can't smell her."

He shrugged. "Not too far."

"Take me to her," I demanded.

He raised an eyebrow, the same whitish-blue tinge as his long, wavy hair, in a way that hinted I was being a little too cocky.

"No," he simply replied.

I tried to dash forward to enter the cabin in search of Amara, but I was completely frozen in place.

"What the fuck?!" I muttered under my breath.

He snorted and shook his head at me. "Seriously?" he asked, as if he was disappointed by my stupidity.

"Who are you? And what are you?" I asked, hating how helpless I felt.

"My name is Lyall, and I'm a doppelganger," he replied in a factual manner.

I shook my head, the only thing I apparently still had control over.

"You're way more than that. Doppelgangers do not have the type of abilities you're currently displaying and are certainly not this powerful. This is another illusion isn't it?"

He merely smiled but didn't answer. His species didn't lie. Any word they spoke was either the truth or what they genuinely believed to be the truth. If they didn't want to reveal something, they would dance around it or play word games to fuck with you. They particularly liked wording things in a way that would deliberately mislead you if misinterpreted—which was likely to be the case.

"I want to see Amara," I said at last, annoyed when the silence stretched.

"What you want is irrelevant," Lyall said with contempt. "You lost all rights the moment you allowed her to be captured."

"I didn't *allow* her to be captured. One such as you never should have been here," I repeated.

"You're correct. And I wouldn't have been had you not allowed the word to spread about your mission. You technically lured me here."

"What?! Lured you here how?" I asked, flabbergasted. "Amara and I are both poisoned. Sentient predators steer clear of us because eating us would cause them great harm if not flat out kill them. So why come specifically for us?"

"Because she's special, and so is her blood," Lyall deadpanned.

I felt myself blanch, and my blood turned to ice. "What have you done to her? Please tell me you haven't harmed her?"

He snorted. "I haven't done anything to her… yet."

"Please, let her go. There is much better prey out there."

"There is, but I don't want them," Lyall replied in a mysterious tone.

"Then what *do* you want? Name your price."

He tilted his head to the side and examined me as if I was some kind of oddity. "What makes you think I don't already have what I want? You're both here at my mercy."

I shook my head. "You don't need both of us," I said with conviction. "Your breed doesn't gorge or waste food. My blood is rarer than hers. Feeding from me will make you more powerful. If you must have one of us, then take me and set her free."

He narrowed his eyes at me, the redness taking on a brighter shade that made him even more frightening.

"Take *you* instead?" he asked menacingly.

"Yes. But *after* I have completed my mission," I added.

By the way he gaped at me, my words truly shocked him. I could understand why. He burst out laughing, the full, throaty sound resonating loudly in the otherwise unnaturally quiet forest surrounding us.

He shook his head at me with an air of utter disbelief. "You're either extraordinarily stupid or seriously mentally impaired if you think I or anyone else holding you at their mercy would consent to such a thing."

"I will take a blood oath swearing to return once the mission is completed, whatever the final outcome. Amara's days are numbered. I must take her to the plateau while there's still time. It's only a few more days. I pledge to return."

To my surprise, my words seemed to infuriate him.

"You would give your life for a dying female you barely even know? Do you think yourself so fucking special that you could survive such a journey? Do you really think *you* are the one meant to protect her?"

"I do not think myself particularly special," I replied carefully, baffled by his irrational anger. "But I'm definitely determined to see this through. Amara is my Twin Flame. I'll do anything to save her."

"You don't even love her!" he snarled, further increasing my confusion at his odd reaction.

"You're correct. I'm not in love with her... yet. But I care deeply about Amara. My physiological responses to her may have been the initial draw, but the past few days in her company were enough for me to know that we're indeed fated, and that I will fall madly in love with her. I've never met such an amazing soul in my life or one whose mere presence makes me happier."

To my dismay, his fangs descended, and the longest, most vicious claws I had ever seen extruded from the tips of his fingers. By the furious way Lyall was staring at me, I believed he was fighting the urge to lunge and tear me to shreds.

What the fuck is going on?

After what felt like far-too-many seconds, Lyall appeared to get his emotions back under control. Although his fangs remained visible, his claws receded back to a more normal nail length. They remained still a little pointy but not dagger-sharp as they had previously been.

"If you truly care about her, then you will leave her to me," he said in a mysterious tone, his gaze intense.

I recoiled, my movements restricted by the paralysis he still had imposed on me.

"What?!"

"I can keep her alive," he continued, eyes locked with me.

My heart leapt. Doppelgangers didn't lie. Could he possibly help save her?

"You can cure her?" I asked, the hope audible in my voice.

It faded almost instantly when Lyall hesitated before shaking his head.

"I cannot cure her," he said carefully. "But I can neutralize the poison whenever it resurfaces. Amara could lead a long and safe life. You cannot make the same boast. Unlike you, nothing in these woods or throughout these mountains can harm me, and therefore anyone under my protection."

"Not even Ranael?" I challenged.

Once again, he hesitated. He lowered his gaze as he reflected on his response before locking eyes with me again.

"Ranael could never get to me unless I allowed it," he finally replied.

I wanted to pry further, but the expression on his face made it clear I wouldn't get any more information as to the potential outcome of a confrontation between him and the demon wolf. Anyway, that was the least of my concerns. All that mattered was my mate.

"You say you could neutralize the poison killing Amara. And after that? Will she be able to go back to her old life?" I asked.

"No. She will have to stay with me," Lyall said, lifting his chin with a subtle hint of defiance.

A powerful wave of jealousy crashed over me, and all of a

sudden, everything became clear. It explained his anger whenever I professed my devotion to saving her and how we were Twin Flames. The almost evil smirk that stretched his lips once he noticed I finally understood his intention to keep my woman for himself angered me.

"You can't have her!" I snarled. "You may covet her, but Amara is mine! She's *my* Twin Flame not *yours*."

"A Twin Flame that you are allowing to die," he spat back while taking two angry steps towards me. "Amara has seven days left to live, eight at the most. You will never get to Ranael in time!"

"You imply that you care for her and yet you detain us here, delaying us further? How about you help us instead?" I shouted back.

"And deliver her to you?" he replied in a disdainful tone.

It was my turn to look at him with contempt. "Based on your previous comment, I assume that you've tasted her blood, which allowed you to experience the wonder that she is, all her memories, and all her past experiences. And yet, you will let her die if you can't have her?"

"*I* am the better choice!" he shouted, slapping his hand on his bare chest. "I can be everything that she wants or needs."

"You can be an *illusion* of what she wants!" I countered. "Fate chose *me* for Amara. Your soulmate is another that you shall meet in time."

Lyall huffed, but I didn't miss the glimmer of pain that flashed through his eyes. In that instant, a part of my anger towards him gave way to a sliver of sympathy. I didn't know what he was, but I suspected that, like me, he was an outcast among his peers. Loneliness cut deeper than the sharpest tongue from those who belittled us.

"If you love her, you will put her welfare before yours," I said in a gentle tone. "If Amara was not my Twin Flame, I would reluctantly step aside and let you look after her. But Fate paired us. No one can ever love her more than I will, and vice versa."

"Like hell you would!" Lyall hissed. "You would cling to her even at the cost of her life, just like you are right now!"

I shook my head. "Like you, I do not lie. I will always put my mate's happiness before my own. In fact, I suspect that you've already made that same offer to Amara, and she declined. Just so you know, had she accepted, I would have honored her wishes, wrong though they might be."

"And you expect me to believe that drivel?!" Lyall challenged.

"The Weaver is never wrong, Lyall," I said calmly. "If you were the solution, she would have sent Amara to you, not me."

To my shock, Lyall released a savage growl and lunged for me. Paralyzed, I stood helpless while he painfully fisted my hair on my nape, yanked my head back, and buried his fangs in my exposed neck. I gasped at the sharp pain. I knew his people possessed a venom that numbed the point of puncture and could even put their victim in a state of euphoria that encouraged them to submit while having their deepest thoughts and memories plundered.

He afforded me no such courtesy.

He *wanted* to hurt me and was doing a great job of it. But I couldn't hate him for it. A doppelganger's bite allowed them to know a person even more intimately than they knew themselves. It was like having spent a lifetime with that person. His feelings for her weren't superficial. If I was already this crazy for my woman by just spending a few days by her side, I could only imagine how much more potent his affection for Amara had to be after he shared such a deep connection with her.

I hissed when he brutally pulled his fangs out of my neck tearing some of my skin in the process. He took a few steps back, staring at me with an anger that bordered on hatred. And yet, I didn't miss the hurt, sadness, and even resignation in his eyes. Once again, he appeared to be battling with himself not to give in to his primal and violent urges.

"I could kill you, right here and now, and make this entire discussion moot," he said in a dangerously low voice.

I swallowed hard, the movement making my puncture wound sting in my neck. I ignored the sliver of blood that trickled from it as I slowly nodded.

"You could, and there's obviously nothing I could do to stop it. But if you do, Amara will know, and she will never forgive you for it," I said in a reasonable tone. "You could choose to help us instead. And she will be forever grateful to you."

"I don't want her gratitude," Lyall spat. "I have no use for it."

"But you also don't want her to die," I replied matter-of-factly. "Her happiness is in your hands. It's up to you what happens next. Your choice to make."

That last sentence appeared to strike a nerve. I wondered if my mate had made a similar comment to him.

His shoulders slouched, and he appeared defeated. That took me for a loop. This vulnerable reaction from such an intimidating, powerful, apex predator seemed impossible. He turned to look at the open door of the cabin behind him. Bitterness, anger, and sorrow flashed in quick succession over his otherworldly features.

He glanced back at the ground then appeared lost in thought. I bit back the urge to try to further convince him. My gut told me that he had already come to a conclusion—and a positive one for us—but needed a bit more time to make his peace with it.

"You must counter the poison killing her," he said at last in an almost emotionless voice, his eyes still lowered. "In many ways, you are Ranael's son. A tamer version of his snake's venom runs in your veins. You're letting her die by denying it to her. It is too weak to cure her but concentrated enough to extend her life for a few more days."

I froze, my mind reeling. Obviously, I had always known that my blood, seed, and other bodily fluids contained some form of poison due to Ranael. But never once did it cross my mind that it could be the same as one of his two venoms. If the bite of the Cursed Demon Wolf's snake tail could neutralize the poison currently coursing inside Amara's veins, then I could potentially do the same for her.

"Are you telling me to give her my seed?" I exclaimed, still stunned.

To my shock, Lyall bared his teeth at me, every single one of them lengthening into sharp daggers while his features twisted into a terrifying demon, ready to kill. In that instant, I genuinely believed he was going to tear me to pieces.

He was truly in love with Amara and couldn't stand the thought of another's hands on her.

Time stood still while Lyall battled his inner demon. I lowered my gaze so as not to provoke him further. He was breathing heavily, his fingers twitching with the urge to stab me with their vicious claws. Although he didn't retract them, the doppelganger finally took a couple of steps back, his features still twisted with fury.

"Fail her again, and there will be no end to the torment I'll inflict upon you, pup," Lyall hissed, his voice sounding almost doubled. "Do not travel the woods tonight. Sleep here and leave at first light. Follow the blue trail to the path."

"What blue trail?" I asked.

He stared at me with something akin to hatred but didn't respond. The lightning stripes under his skin began to glow, and he shifted into a giant bird I had never seen before and took flight. Moments later, the illusion faded.

Gone was the lush forest all but hugging the cabin. Instead, I was standing in front of a cave in a clearing. Our two horses idled nonchalantly outside. But the scent of Amara hitting me hard was all that retained my attention.

I shouted her name and ran into the cave.

CHAPTER 11
AMARA

After what felt like an eternity of deafening silence, the cozy woodhouse suddenly faded around me, as did the invisible force keeping me shackled in my seat. Except, gone was the comfortable chair I had been trapped in. Instead, I found myself sitting on the large rock, surrounded by a cave. It shared many similarities to the one Remus took us to on the first night of our journey.

But before I could dwell further on whether this was a new illusion or a return to reality, Remus's voice calling out my name startled me. I jumped to my feet only to see him barge in. His face lit up as intense relief descended over his handsome features.

"My mate!" he exclaimed, his voice filled with joy.

Arms spread wide, he took a couple of steps towards me only to stop dead in his tracks with an air of confusion and hurt when I backed away from him. I didn't need a mirror to know what kind of suspicious expression was plastered all over my face. Understanding suddenly dawned on him, and he took on an air of sympathy as he smiled at me.

"All is well, Amara. It's me, your Remus."

My reaction had obviously been instinctive. But even before he spoke, I realized it was indeed him. I ran towards him as he finished his sentence and all but crashed into him as I threw myself into his arms. Stunned, he caught me effortlessly and didn't resist when I crushed his lips in an almost desperate kiss. He responded in kind, his strong arms holding me tightly as if he feared I would disappear.

The kiss ended at last, and he kept my face between both his hands, studying my features as if to make sure it truly was me and that all was well.

"Are you okay, my Flame?" he asked, his voice laced with worry.

I smiled and nodded. "Yes, I'm fine. What about you?"

"I'm alright," he replied, before frowning. "But how do you know it is truly me and not him?"

My smile broadened, and I caressed his cheek. "Your scent and the fact that you're naked confirmed your identity."

He blinked, baffled by that response, which made me chuckle.

"By the road, when Lyall first approached me, I realized that he wasn't you because he was dressed. You removed all your clothes, except your underwear, before you shifted when the beasts attacked. He walked out of the woods fully clothed."

He nodded slowly, a glimmer of admiration in his eyes.

"I can see that. He either didn't think of it or deliberately chose to take that risk as he likely has never seen me naked before and therefore wouldn't be able to replicate me in the nude, especially my groin or any scar I may have," Remus said pensively.

"Fair point," I concurred. "He also doesn't smell like you. In fact, I didn't really notice any scent from him. And he also doesn't feel like you or look at me like you do. His speech is different. It's subtle but he doesn't quite roll his Rs the way you do. And he doesn't have those cute orange specks in your

159

right eye," I added tracing his right eyebrow with my index finger.

"Someone has truly been paying attention to me," Remus said, his face melting with tenderness.

"I most certainly have," I replied, puffing out my chest. "But how do you know I'm not him?"

He burst out laughing. "Not a chance. No one possesses as intoxicating a scent as you do. No one else in this world sets my blood ablaze and whips my heat into a frenzy like merely being in your present does," he replied, tapping the tip of my nose with a finger.

I beamed at him. Then he took on a mischievous expression.

"Anyway, Lyall wouldn't have thrown himself into my arms. He wants to eat me, not kiss me."

My smile faded upon hearing those words, as the stark reality of our situation cast aside the joy of our reunion.

"Where is he?" I asked, glancing over his shoulder to peer at the cave's entrance.

"He left, and the illusion faded," Remus replied in a grim tone. "I had been frantically looking for you, but he had me trapped in some kind of a nightmare."

"We should leave in case he decides to return," I said with a shudder.

To my surprise, Remus firmly shook his head. "No. Night is already upon us. We will stay here and leave in the morning."

"Here?" I echoed, casting a wary look at our surroundings before locking eyes with him again. "Is it safe? Aren't we in the middle of the Haunted Woods?"

"As odd as this will sound, yes, but I believe we're safe."

He took my hand and led me to the large rock I had been sitting on. He settled down and drew me into his lap. Remus then proceeded to recount his search, the fight against the Arraphilons, followed by his conversation with Lyall.

Once he finished, I recounted my own encounter with the

doppelganger, the terrifying test he subjected me to against Ranael, and then my conversation here with him. I had to calm him down during the part with Ranael and remind him it had only been an illusion. Still, he hated that I endured any kind of pain, fake though it had been.

"You know, Lyall is in love with you," Remus said at last, his gaze boring into mine as he studied my response to his words.

I burst out laughing. "No he's not. He met me barely an hour ago. I can't tell if he's just infatuated or the type to covet what he can't have, but I wouldn't call it love," I said with an indulgent smile.

To my surprise, Remus shook his head firmly. "You're wrong. It is not an infatuation," he countered with the conviction that took me aback. "Lyall drank your blood. Through it, he has read every single moment of your past. He knows you more intimately than you know yourself, and probably better than I ever will even if we spend the rest of our lives together. He has absorbed a lifetime of memories and emotions that you've experienced, even those that you have repressed or aren't conscious of. And whatever he saw entranced him."

I frowned, feeling conflicted by his words. A part of me understood how exploring someone's psyche at such an intimate level could create a powerful bond. In which case, I empathized with the fact that he might now feel these emotions and likely also understand I couldn't reciprocate them. That would explain the defeated expression he showed in the end. But another part of me felt violated that he plundered what should be the most private thing anyone possessed.

"He wanted me to surrender you to him," Remus added softly. "Naturally, I refused."

My brow creased as I digested his words.

"How did you convince him to leave?"

"I cannot say that *I* convinced him per se. Ultimately, he

made that decision on his own. I didn't exactly refuse to give you up, but I also didn't consent."

"What? What does that even mean?" I asked, confused.

"I asked him to tag along and help keep you alive until we reached Ranael." He smiled at my flabbergasted expression and gently caressed my hair. "Your survival is all that matters, Amara. I cannot decide for you whether you should stay with him and benefit from the healing he could offer without putting your life at risk by facing the demon wolf. Whether you stay with him or continue the journey with me has to be your choice."

"My choice is to continue the journey with you," I said in a tone that brooked no argument.

He smiled and kissed my forehead. "The fact that he tried to convince me to release you told me that you had already turned him down. What he offers is not a solution. It would simply make you forever dependent on him. We must try for the *real* cure so that you can live freely according to your own terms, and not at the mercy and by the grace of someone else."

"Those were my thoughts exactly," I replied. "But thank you for not trying to decide for me or take away my freedom of choice."

"I respect you too much for that, my Flame."

"And I love you for it. However, I can't help but wonder if he's right."

"About you not making it to the plateau?" he asked softly.

I nodded grimly. "He said I only have seven or eight days left. As far as I know, doppelgangers cannot lie. Can we reach our destination before then?"

My heart sank when he shook his head.

"It will take us at least ten days even if we push as hard as we can. But Lyall said that I can slow down your sickness."

I perked up. "What? How?"

"Ranael's snake tail venom courses through me. It is a weaker version, which makes me toxic to others."

"But it's what I need to fight my poison!" I exclaimed, hope exploding inside me. "So you can cure me?!"

"No my mate, I cannot cure you. I can only slow its progress, not stop or reverse it," he replied apologetically.

I pinched my lips, slightly disappointed. But then nothing was ever this easy. Still, it was hope that we didn't have before. Then an unpleasant thought popped into my head.

"Are you sure that was what he said? Do you believe him?" I asked carefully.

He nodded with conviction. "Lyall wants you to live. He told me in no uncertain terms that if I fail you, he will hunt me down and make me wish for death. He truly fell in love with whatever he saw in you."

I squirmed in his lap, my face heating from embarrassment. Although I considered myself a good person—I certainly always strived to be—I didn't think myself particularly exceptional in any way. At least not so much that anyone would fall head over heels in love with me just for taking a peek at my mostly unre-markable life.

"You tamed a monster," Remus said teasingly.

I stiffened and frowned at him, which took him aback.

"He's not a monster," I said with a fervor I couldn't explain. I glanced away, staring at the ground without seeing it as I reflected on my interactions with the doppelganger. "Lyall truly believes he is, but I don't. A monster is mindless, controlled by their basest instincts. He just has a very strong feral nature. But deep down, I believe there is a truly kind man who is just very lonely. You should have seen the way he glowed when he was drinking my blood. It felt like being surrounded by divine light. I pray that he finds his soulmate one day."

"She's not you," Remus replied sternly.

I snorted as my gaze flicked back to him. "No, She's defi-nitely not me," I said teasingly, amused by this display of jealousy. "But going back to your venom, how do I get that from you?"

To my shock, Remus suddenly blushed and lowered his eyes in embarrassment. There was something so incredibly adorable, almost boyish in his timidity. The fact that he was so big, muscular, and intimidating when he wanted made it all the more shocking to see.

And then, I understood.

"Oh, I see!" I said, before giggling nervously.

The flame of arousal sparked low in my belly.

"Well, we should eat something and rest for the night," Remus grumbled to hide his embarrassment. "We rise at dawn and ride hard to reach the inn before the sun fully sets."

"Wow, someone's eager!" I said teasingly.

"Amara!" Remus exclaimed, which made me burst out laughing.

Considering the naughty games we played the previous night, I found it hilarious that he should be so prudish.

Still, he was right. I needed food and rest. The stress of the day, and my growing sickness were taking a toll. I felt guilty watching Remus taking care of everything while forbidding me from making any effort. He wisely chose not to go hunting for fresh food tonight in the woods, and we ate some of the rations we still had in our bags instead.

After taking care of the horses, he shifted into his wolf form, and I snuggled against him for the night. I couldn't believe how easily sleep claimed me. Considering we were in the heart of the Haunted Woods and only sheltered by a cave without doors, I should have been terrified. But the powerful wards that protected the cave and my man's warm body around me made me feel safe.

The next morning, we didn't dally. There was no nearby river to take a dip in, not that I would have risked venturing in any body of water within a cursed forest. We ate some dry bread and cured meats with the last of the cider Misty had given us. Remus donned his clothes, which he had wisely left with his horse before chasing after the Aegarims, and we set off.

Mesmerized, I stared at the strangest trail of mist that seemed to form in our path the minute we got on our horses. It had a bluish tinge, as if some tiny spirits or magical fireflies flew within it. Whatever it was, it didn't qualify as a random occurrence. It turned and circled around certain areas as we followed it and acted as a magical guide who took us back safely to the road. Not once during that trek did the alluring songs that plagued me the previous day manifest themselves.

Before his departure, Lyall instructed Remus to follow the blue trail. Was it an automatic phenomenon that appeared whenever someone sought refuge in the cave, or had Lyall personally set it up for us? I would probably never have the answer to that question, but my chest warmed for the doppelganger. If I managed to survive this ordeal, I would find a way to thank him.

As soon as we reached the road, we set a hard pace. We barely spoke at all, only indulging in brief chats whenever we would slow down to let the horses rest. None of the spirits pestered us for the remainder of the journey through the haunted woods. Once more, I couldn't help but wonder if it was due to some form of intervention on Lyall's part, or if he was following us, lurking in the shadows. I didn't doubt that his mere presence sufficed to send all the lesser creatures running for cover.

Just like when we entered the Haunted Woods, no clear sign indicated the moment we exited it. And yet an undeniable shift occurred. The air felt cleaner and lighter, as if a boulder had been lifted off my shoulders. The colors looked brighter, and even the exhaustion I felt significantly dampened. I realized then how that accursed place had weighed on me both physically and mentally.

We finally reached the inn an hour after sundown. The place was packed. It felt awkward walking in with so many eyes studying us as if we were some sort of anomaly. In that instant, I realized that word of our mission had spread here as well. No wonder Lyall heard about it. I still didn't understand why it drove him to seek us out. Even if we had meant to kill Ranael, why would he care?

Ignoring the borderline rude stares of the customers, Remus made a beeline for the counter manned by a portly innkeeper. As much as I enjoyed my privacy, having so much attention on me left me mostly indifferent. So long as no one directly pestered me, they were free to ogle all they wanted. But the less-than-friendly glances leveled at my mate angered me. It whipped the protective mama bear I didn't know lurked deep within me into a frenzy. It took every ounce of my willpower not to give them a tongue lashing.

At least, Remus seemed totally unfazed, having likely grown used to it after a lifetime of such treatment. I leaned against the counter as he began to speak to the innkeeper. The man in his early fifties had a jovial demeanor and appeared to frequently indulge in his own famous warm mead. He invited us to sit at one of the few remaining free tables while he had our room prepared as well as a hot bath drawn for us.

After a hearty meal—that my man all but inhaled—we headed upstairs to our room. The soundproofing was extremely good. Considering the substantial crowd loudly chatting and the small band playing live music, I expected the noise to make it difficult for anyone to enjoy some peace and quiet. The innkeeper probably had some witch or sorcerer cast a silence spell on the rooms.

It was pleasantly spacious. Inns tended to have smaller rooms to maximize the number of guests they could accommodate at any given time. This one had a massive bed and a small nook with a clawfoot tub. A dresser sat on the left side, across from a seating area consisting of two cushioned chairs and a coffee table next to a large window that gave a pleasant view onto the silhouette of the highest peaks of the mountain in the distance.

A familiar rune glowed on the side of the tub. A basic spell kept the water warm inside it. Remus discarded our bags on the dresser and immediately began to undress. Like me, he was casting an approving glance at our surroundings. None of the furniture spelled luxury, but it was sturdy and clean. Above all, it beat sleeping on the floor of a cave in the middle of a cursed forest.

I was halfway through removing my clothes when Remus gently batted my hand away so that he could do it himself. Once more, I melted looking at my beast of a man. He was so big, tall, and muscular, you'd never think he could handle anything or anyone with such care. But above all, it was the constant air of wonder filled with infinite tenderness in his eyes that messed me up.

If he looked at me like this when he hadn't fallen in love with me yet, I could only imagine what it would be like once he did. No one—and especially no man—had ever made me feel so treasured. He stripped me out of my clothes and absentmindedly discarded them onto one of the two chairs by the window. He then picked me up effortlessly and carried me to the tub.

A shiver coursed through me at the intense heat of his bare skin against mine. A part of me mourned the fact that once we were fully bonded, he would likely stop going into heat whenever he was in my presence. I selfishly loved how warm and toasty he felt when I snuggled with him.

He settled me in the water before joining me. It surprised me that we both fit rather comfortably. At a glance, the tub appeared much smaller than it truly was. Remus took his sweet time washing me, just like he had done in the river by the Hunters Lodge. But this time, he didn't keep his touch clinical.

His gaze followed the movement of his hands as they freely roamed over me. They lingered on my breasts, his thumbs tracing the areolas and flicking the nipples until they hardened. My breath felt shallow as I watched him explore every inch of my body. His palms pursued their journey down over my stomach and further south.

To my dismay, he didn't venture towards my throbbing core but went on to wash each of my legs with slow and sensuous movements. My abdominal muscles contracted as he lifted my right foot, forcing me to lean back in the tub. He massaged my foot before gently kissing it. A shiver coursed through me as his lips brushed over the length of my calf, only pausing long enough for him to gently nip at the fleshy part, just below my knee. He continued to move forward, his face partially sinking underwater to pay the same attention to my inner thigh.

He lifted his head to take a breath. A bolt of lust exploded in the pit of my stomach when I locked eyes with him. His sclera was pitch black again, and his golden eyes glowed as he bared his fangs at me. I gasped when the tip of his finger began probing my slit. I'd been so hypnotized by his mesmerizing gaze that I hadn't even noticed the movement of his hands on me.

I inhaled sharply when he inserted a second one, moving them slowly in and out of me while his thumb massaged my clit. He just knelt there, his chin still touching the water while his gaze bore into mine. All I could hear was my labored breathing, the water splashing from his movement, and a low, almost menacing growl vibrating from his chest in a steady flow.

My hands clenched each side of the tub as he accelerated the movement. Pleasure steadily grew inside me. It took me a moment to realize that the water splashing around us wasn't solely due to my man's ministration, but also to my own hips that had begun gyrating as I ground my core against his hand for greater friction.

Intense pleasure struck me like lightning when he crooked his fingers to graze my sweet spot. I emitted a sharp cry, closed my eyes, and threw my head back.

"No!" Remus growled, startling me.

He slipped his free hand behind my nape, forcing me to look

back down at him with an almost savage expression on his face. I gaped at him, stunned.

"I will see your pleasure. It is mine to feast my eyes on," he said menacingly.

Cue exploding ovaries.

I closed my right hand around his wrist still holding my nape. My nails dug into his flesh as I began to crest again. The urge to close my eyes again clawed at me, but I couldn't look away from him. He was both magnificent and terrifying with his fangs bared in a snarling grin.

My orgasm swept me away so abruptly, I likely would have sunk underwater had he not been holding me up. A drawn-out moan followed my blissful shout as my mate rubbed my clit with even more intensity to keep me flying high. It wasn't before I felt the rough texture of his tongue on my nipple that I realized I'd broken eye contact with him. He greedily sucked on my hard little nub while still fucking me with his hand.

His mouth kissed a path back up to my own, and he passionately claimed my lips, swallowing each of my moans. Remus relented at last and lifted his head to study my face with a smug expression. I wanted to smack him, but his arrogance was justified.

He didn't resist when I slightly pushed back on him so that I could return the favor. Once again, his gaze remained locked on my face while I touched every inch of his perfect body. I shamelessly half-washed but mostly groped him. It was surprising how soft and comfortable I felt in his arms considering he was likely the leanest person I had ever seen. Every muscle was well-defined, but not in a disturbingly bulgy fashion.

Every time I would lean forward to kiss or lick his chest or nipples, Remus would cup my nape with his hand, but never in a restraining fashion. He would gently scrape the base of my skull with his nails. For the strangest reason, each motion resonated directly in my clit. Only once I closed my hand around his shaft did he hiss and fist his hand a bit more forcefully in my hair.

He still didn't try to control my movements, but his abdominal muscles constricted, and he clenched his teeth as if in an effort to keep control. I gently stroked him. With each movement of my hand, Remus appeared to straighten more and more in the tub, eventually starting to lean forward. It felt like watching a feline slowly and quietly closing in on an unsuspecting prey before leaping for the kill.

My nipples ached, and my inner walls contracted spasmodically with the thrill of anticipation. I wanted to be caught, subdued, and ravaged by my man.

It happened faster and much sooner than I expected.

He yanked me up with such strength and at such a speed that, for half a beat, I thought I would fly across the room and crash into a wall. But he rose from the water at the same time as he was lifting me, and I found myself slamming against the burning heat of his body. He crushed my lips with an almost savage kiss as he stepped out of the tub.

Water trickled down from us, and I vaguely felt guilty about the mess we were making. But my mate's hands feverishly caressing my body, and his mouth devouring mine wiped out any such thoughts from my mind. I loved the feel of his tongue swirling around mine, his delicious taste, and the hungry way he always kissed me. He claimed my mouth as if he couldn't get enough of me, as if his very survival depended on it.

And I fucking loved it.

Too soon, he broke the kiss. When his hands glided down my back to wrap behind my thighs, I thought it was either to carry me to the bed, or to lift me up and impale me on his cock. It had been straining against my stomach since he'd taken me out of the tub. That thought fanned the flames of lust setting every part of me ablaze. As much as I dreaded his girth, I ached to be filled by him, to be one with my soulmate. The bulge of his knot pressing against my pelvis had me even more impatient to feel him inside me.

A startled cry escaped me, and my stomach flip-flopped like when one experienced a rapid ascent or descent, when Remus lifted me up at dizzying speed. I tried to hang on to his shoulders as the ceiling came rushing towards me, only to end up clenching his hair as my man settled me on his shoulders, facing him. Before I could fully comprehend what was happening, the inferno of his mouth sucked on my clit.

I let out a strangled moan and threw my head back. If not for his left hand on my back, I likely would have toppled over. Remus proceeded to feast on me with a voracious appetite. Each flick of his tongue on my engorged little nub was like a shot of liquid bliss directly in my veins. He dipped it inside me, curving it just the right way to graze my sensitive bundle of nerves, making me beg for more. Voluptuous moans tumbled out of me in an endless string.

My climax didn't build slowly but came at me like a freight train, leaving me disoriented and boneless in my man's arms. I felt myself fall, only to be cradled in his embrace. Still dazed as the tremors of bliss continued to course through me, I vaguely felt Remus sit me in his lap and use a towel to dry me.

My skin erupted in goosebumps, and a delicious shiver ran down my spine as my mate took care of me. His mouth would follow in the wake of wherever the towel touched me. Remus lay me down on the bed to wipe my legs, his short beard tickling my skin as he peppered more kisses their entire length.

Through hooded eyes, I watched him make quick work of drying himself before he tossed the towel in the general direction of the two chairs. My mouth watering, I stared in awe at his godly body as he stood next to the bed, his cock proudly erect. I extended a hand, beckoning him. He climbed onto the bed, and I spread my legs to make room for him as he settled on top of me.

For the next eternity, we exchanged kisses and caresses. A

few times, I thought he would finally take things to the next level, but he always appeared to hesitate before resuming his tender attentions.

At long last, after a deep and passionate kiss, Remus lifted his head to lock eyes with me. My stomach quivered now that the moment had arrived. His golden eyes flicked between mine, searching. I gave him an encouraging smile. The nervous one he responded with surprised me.

He's scared his seed will hurt me.

"It's okay, Remus," I said softly, brushing a few locks of his damp hair from his face. "You're not going to hurt me. To the contrary, you will help make me better until we reach the plateau. I want this with you."

A powerful emotion flitted over his face, and I tightened my embrace around him.

"I want this with you too, my Flame. But what if it was a trick, or some twisted mind game? What if he's wrong? I cannot bear the thought of harming you. Even worse, losing you will kill me."

"You won't lose me, Remus. Doppelgangers cannot lie," I said in a reasonable tone. "And you said it yourself that Lyall really cares about me. He would never tell you to do something that would hurt me."

"I know. You're right," he said in a shaky voice. "It's just..."

He heaved a sigh, defeated. I smiled, my heart swelling with affection for him. I cupped his face with both hands and bore my gaze into his.

"We're Twin Flames, Remus. Fate made us for each other. It only makes sense that your curse would be my salvation until we can get to the cure. This is right. This *feels* right. Be mine and let me be yours."

"My Flame..." he whispered with something akin to adoration.

I drew his face to mine and claimed his lips. He promptly

took charge and deepened the kiss with a hint of desperation. After a few more caresses, Remus positioned the tip of his cock at my opening. He didn't push himself in right away, but locked eyes with me again, his gaze intense.

I loved how he always gave me a chance to back out and made certain I was all in, every step of the way. It only reinforced how safe he made me feel. I smiled and nodded my consent. Worry flicked through his eyes. Even as Remus began penetrating me, he couldn't fully hide the inner turmoil still raging inside him.

However, my gasp of discomfort had him fully refocusing on me. My man was massive. I'd known it would be a tight fit, but I didn't expect it to be this much. I forced myself to relax by concentrating on the warm feel of his soft skin around me, his hands caressing me, and the sweet words of encouragement he whispered between kisses.

With shallow, careful thrusts, Remus gradually gained centimeter after centimeter until my body yielded. I hissed at the slight pain, while my man's chest vibrated with a deep growl. I didn't know whether it had hurt him, but I felt so incredibly full, I didn't doubt his cock was getting squeezed something fierce.

He closed his eyes and rested his forehead against mine. His powerful body slightly trembled on top of me. I wondered if pain, pleasure, the fight to remain still while I adjusted to his girth, or a mix of all of the above caused that reaction. I was taking shallow breaths, assessing the sensation of him deep within. Although it hadn't swelled yet, his knot was perfectly positioned to apply pressure on my G-spot. I slightly moved my pelvis and gasped as an electric jolt of pleasure radiated outward when his knot rubbed me just the right way.

Remus opened his eyes to look at me. I should have been terrified by how his dilated pupils had become, the blackness of his sclera having almost fully swallowed the golden ring of his irises. My toes instantly curled, and my inner walls contracted around his cock with a will of their own.

My mate inhaled sharply through his clenched teeth, and once more closed his eyes tightly shut. This time, I no longer doubted that he was fighting a losing battle against the intense pleasure prodding him to start moving. My own moans rose from my throat as each involuntary spasm sent a flurry of sensations coursing through me, from his knot to the ridges lining his shaft.

My hands glided down his muscular back to settle on his scrumptious behind. I gave each cheek a good squeeze, then pressed them down while lifting my pelvis closer to his. He didn't need me to make my meaning any clearer.

A strangled gasp tore out of me as he carefully started rocking in and out of me. Each movement was driving me insane with the intensity of the pleasure I felt. Sure, being so thoroughly stretched created some discomfort, but that very snugness also multiplied the blissful sensations of his knot and ridges against my sensitive inner walls. The almost feral sounds emanating from my mate added gallons of fuel to the fire growing inside me.

A pool of lava swirled in the pit of my stomach, the searing heat radiating outward throughout my body and to my extremities. Each thrust sent electric tendrils to my nerve endings. Remus quickly picked up the pace, taking me deeper, faster, and harder. And I met him thrust for thrust. Soon, he was pounding into me. The pleasure-pain of his savage possession had me tumbling down an endless vortex of delight I never wanted to emerge from.

Our tongues and our moans mingled as the slapping sound of flesh meeting flesh filled the room. In my arms, Remus's body grew a bit larger. He wasn't doubling in size like when he shifted into his wolf form, but his overall mass noticeably increased as his muscles bulged. His skin was feverish. You'd think he had swallowed the sun.

I was burning both within and without, on the verge of combusting as pleasure almost too much to bear drove me to the edge of madness. Just when I thought my mind would fracture, a bright light exploded before my eyes, and my body seized as a violent orgasm slammed into me. Remus responded to my shout of ecstasy with a feral cry that sounded almost angry. As bliss swept me away, I vaguely felt my mate continue to pound into me, although his movements had become erratic.

Moments later, he lost his battle. Through my voluptuous daze, I heard him emit a savage roar and felt him slam himself in deep. His hot seed erupted in powerful spurts, filling me to the brim. Simultaneously, his knot swelled, locking us together. Before I could even come back down from this mind-blowing orgasm, the strategically placed, increased pressure of his knot on my G-spot sent me over the edge once more.

I couldn't even describe the sound I emitted as I toppled over. It was part throaty moan, part startled cry, and part unintelligible grunt. I was shattered, overwhelmed by too much pleasure while Remus gathered me in his arms, holding me with almost bruising force as if he feared I would attempt to flee.

He rolled onto his back, pulling me on top of him. I could still feel his cock pulsing inside of me. Subtle tremors shook his body while he continued to hold me with near desperation. I was too wrecked to even question his strange reaction. My head resting on his broad chest, I listened to the thundering of his heart as it slowly settled down, lulling me to sleep. Remus was covering my forehead with kisses while whispering words of devotion.

"My Flame, my beautiful mate... Thank you," Remus said, his voice filled with emotion. "I'm never letting you go."

I didn't know why he was thanking me, but right this instant, I didn't really care. He was my soulmate. Whatever the future had in store for me, whether I live or die, right here, right now, I was happy. I was home.

CHAPTER 12
REMUS

F or the tenth time tonight, I woke up with a start. A single glance outside sufficed for me to know I'd only dozed off for a few minutes. Amara was still wrapped around me. But the worry that twisted my insides all the previous times I awakened finally subsided. My Flame remained a bit warm to the touch, but she was no longer burning or shivering even as she was heavily sweating while moaning in pain.

It started about an hour after we made love. No word could describe the terror that engulfed me at that moment. I truly believed my mate was going to die by my fault and my foul seed. To this day, the memory of how a couple of drops of my blood nearly killed Ulric and subjected him to years of debilitating sickness haunted me. It would likely continue to do so until the day I died.

While Amara had also been increasingly feverish, restless, and experiencing clear discomfort during our previous nights together, tonight had been different. She clearly displayed the symptoms of someone who had been poisoned.

To my horror, when her condition first awakened me, my knot had still been too swollen for me to pull out of my woman without causing both of us significant damage. The worst part was that, under normal circumstances, Lycans could will their knot to deflate should they be in danger. But no matter what I tried, my knot refused to release my mate. I kept thinking that if I could pull out and wash out what remained of my seed, it might lessen the risk of her dying from it.

It had been a stupid thought, but in my desperation to save her, I would have done anything.

It didn't help that this was my first time knotting with a woman. The few females I had been with in the past shared my bed more out of thrill-seeking than any actual affection for me. They had been honest about their intentions, and I had accepted those encounters for what they were. But in all those cases, on top of wearing an enchanted condom to avoid any risk of leaking, I had also pulled out before I could climax so that I wouldn't accidentally knot with them.

The memory of that first experience with my Twin Flame set my blood ablaze. How I had longed for this, dreamt for that special and unique moment when two souls also became truly one physically. It exceeded everything I ever hoped for. So when I woke up to find her drenched in sweat, her body alarmingly hot as she moaned and writhed in pain nearly destroyed me.

I cursed myself for not listening to my misgivings and cursed Lyall for tricking me into harming my woman. But then, as my knot refused to set me free, it slowly started sinking in that our inner wolf would always protect its mate. If it didn't release me, it meant that my wolf believed I was doing right by my mate. I studied Amara a bit more closely. And then it struck me that the stench of death that had been growing on her had actually dimmed. With each passing minute, that foul scent steadily decreased. It wasn't a radical drop, but it was significant enough to be noticeable.

I finally realized that her current discomfort was because my venom was attacking the poison slowly killing her. As much as I hated seeing Amara in pain, this unpleasant process benefited her. I just thanked the gods that she remained unconscious through it all. And throughout the night, each time I woke up, the smell of her sickness had weakened further, as did her temperature.

Now, as I watched her peacefully resting in my arms, I'd begrudgingly addressed a silent thank you to Lyall. The mere thought of the handsome doppelganger prodded my jealousy and insecurities. Amara was mine. The cockiness with which he tried to claim my mate angered me more than I could express. And yet, I couldn't blame him for being infatuated with her. Her natural aroma alone was intoxicating. But her personality was beyond addictive.

I gently caressed the bare skin of her shoulder. Another wave of reluctant gratitude swelled within me for Lyall. My mate's skin already looked healthier and less grayish than it had over the past couple of days. However, I wanted to kick myself for not asking him how much of my toxin I should give her. Was there such a thing as too much or not enough? Would there be any outward signs that would tell me she needed another dose?

The second time I awakened, my knot had deflated, allowing me to pull out. Finding out that her body absorbed every last drop of my seed freaked me out. Was that bad? As far as I knew, women didn't absorb all of a male's semen. They had to wash off most of it. Since I'd never spilled inside a female before, I had no idea what normal looked like. Plus, it wasn't the type of question I would have asked Misty as that had never been a remote possibility before Amara.

My head swirling with far too many distressing thoughts, I forced myself to yield to oblivion and fell into a fretful sleep.

By the time morning came at last, I'd finally gotten some restful sleep. Amara's fingers carefully tracing my eyebrows and then the edges of my beard pulled me out of my slumber. A wondrous heat spread through my chest upon finding my mate smiling at me. Her skin looked almost luminous, and her eyes were clear of the gloomy veil that had started to dim their spark.

"Good morning, my Flame," I said, my voice a little thick from lingering sleep. "How are you feeling?"

"Amazingly well," she said with a radiant smile, the sincerity in her voice wiping out the remaining worries that still lurked at the back of my mind. "Had I known getting frisky with my man could be so rejuvenating, I would have jumped you much sooner."

I chuckled and rubbed my nose against hers. "I'm glad to hear it. Feel free to use me whenever you need a little boost," I said teasingly before claiming her mouth.

Passion immediately flared between us, and we both answered its call. We shouldn't have as my knot automatically sprang into action the moment I climaxed. I also worried that a second dose of my seed so early might have adverse effects on her. At the same time, the scent of death was still strong on her despite having dimmed. My venom had much to feast on. Considering its weaker concentration, I wanted to believe that more of it—not less—would prove beneficial to my mate.

Still, I couldn't be mad about bringing my female to completion twice before finding my own release. This would be the last time we spent in any kind of real comfort until we reached our destination. The rest of the journey ahead would be even more arduous than what we had faced thus far. I only hoped that Amara would be able to handle it.

To my pleasant surprise, it took barely half an hour for my knot to deflate this time. Once again, my Flame absorbed everything I had given her. Her shock at not having any mess to clean confirmed that this was not a normal occurrence. I didn't know what to make of it.

In that instant, I would have given anything to be able to further question Lyall about it. He held far more answers than he shared. However, I suspected that, should we meet again, he would be quite stingy with what information he divulged. The phenomenal extent of the powers he displayed led me to believe that he wasn't just some powerful demon or otherworldly creature. While I didn't believe him to be a god, I would bet he was a demigod. In which case, he would be subjected to a series of strict rules called the Covenant, which forbade them to intervene in the life of mortals in a way that might thwart the plans that Fate had in store for them.

By answering too many of my questions, he could influence the choices I made in a completely different way than the ones I would have made given full free agency. But now was not the time to dwell on the doppelganger—or whatever else he might truly be.

We quickly washed and indulged in the hearty breakfast the innkeeper served us. Being familiar with me, he didn't question the extra amount of money I gave him before our departure. He would burn the blankets I slept on to avoid any risk that my sweat during our passionate rumble could have an adverse effect on future patrons, even with them being fully washed.

As per my request the previous evening, he prepared a bag filled with dry breads, cured meats, nuts, and other food that could last for a few days. He threw in a couple of water skins and a bottle of cider to wash down our meals with.

When we exited the inn, Amara frowned upon seeing which horses I was burdening with our meager possessions.

"These are not our horses," she said, confused.

"Good observation," I said with a smile. "We will use the innkeeper's horses all the way to the edge of Storm Hill. They are specially trained to return home on their own. From there, we will climb the mountain until we reach the plateau. There is no easy path for a horse to travel on."

Amara stiffened. "Climb?" she echoed warily.

I nodded. "But do not worry, my Flame. It is not rock climbing, just a non-stop ascension following an uneven path much too narrow for a horse or most standard mounts."

"Oookay," she said carefully. "That's a little reassuring but not fully."

I chuckled and affectionately tapped the tip of her nose with my index finger. "Do not fret. It will not be too hard on you. Once we reach Storm Hill, we'll use the harness so you can ride me."

"Ride you?" she repeated, a mischievous glimmer sparkling in her beautiful eyes. "Then I guess we should've practiced that this morning instead of you doing all the work."

"AMARA!" I exclaimed, heat rushing to my cheeks.

She burst out laughing, the clear, musical sound wrapping around me like a warm blanket. The wretched female enjoyed making me blush. My Flame looked so prim and proper that it always floored me whenever she deliberately made some raunchy innuendo to get a rise out of me. I didn't consider myself prudish, but as I'd never experienced the normal flirting people indulged in from puberty onward, I felt as clumsy as a newborn calf attempting to get on its feet for the first time.

"What?" she asked, opening her eyes wide with the least sincere air of pure innocence. "I cannot walk such a hard path in a timely fashion. I was merely bemoaning the fact that I should have practiced riding a wolf when I had the chance."

I made a face at her, which only made her chuckle some more. By Ferazan! I loved how simply being around her made me happy, even her sweet teasing. And above all, I loved how happiness lit up her face and chased away the dark clouds of the threat looming over her. Whatever it took, I would do everything in my power to make sure they never returned.

"Let's go, you naughty girl," I said with false severity. "We have a long road ahead."

She smiled and placed the sweetest kiss on the corner of my jaw before allowing me to help her onto her horse. We set off at a good pace. A wave of gratitude filled my heart seeing how much better she handled the long ride. Clearly, our coupling improved her health. But how long would it last?

We paused a couple of times along the way before we finally reached the edge of the forest. It opened on a vast clearing with tall grass gradually fading into packed dirt and rocks at the foot of the mountain. Despite being used to harsh travel, even I felt stiff and sore when I jumped off my horse. My poor mate winced a little as I helped her down. Leaning against me, she stretched her legs and her back before allowing me to lead her into the cave that would shelter us that night.

Contrary to the other ones we had slept in, this one offered far more comfort, including a couple of beds with padded cushions which acted as fairly plush mattresses, a proper wooden table and chairs, a fire pit, and basic cookware. While my mate settled inside, I went back out to unload the horses and release them.

They wandered towards the tall grass area to graze and rest. On their own time, they would make the twelve-hour journey back to their owner. The entire forest between the inn and Storm Hill was as safe as the Haunted Woods had been dangerous. Only small game, mostly small herbivores like rabbits dwelled in that area. Therefore, the horses wouldn't meet any danger on their way home. Their reins and saddles were also enchanted so that any potential thief would have a very nasty surprise if they attempted to appropriate them.

Not wanting to go through our food reserves too quickly, I hunted for our evening meal. We ate and called it an early night. Although we indulged in some heavy petting, we didn't make love that night. Not only was the narrow cot not ideal for such activities, but we were also both tired and didn't want to risk overdoing it until we had a better sense of how she responded to my toxins.

The next morning, the horses were long gone when we

stepped outside. Before I shifted into my wolf form, I gave my mate extensive instructions as to how to bind herself to me with the harness I prepared, and how to hang our food and reagents bag in a secure way on me so that it wouldn't bother her.

"What?" I asked when she made a funny face while I finished undressing.

"I don't know. It just feels weird to burden you with all of this, on top of me, and ride you like a horse all the way up that mountain," she said sheepishly. "I feel guilty. You will be exhausted."

I snorted and shook my head. "First off, you weigh three times nothing. Second, my wolf is extremely strong. My stamina, strength, and endurance are at least five times greater than in my human form. You've seen how easily I've carried you in my arms. So carrying you on my back will be no hardship."

She followed my gaze when I glanced at the narrow path ahead. And I gestured at it with my chin.

"This path, though, is not particularly fun. Will I get tired? Absolutely. But it won't be because of your weight or that of the bags. It will be the uneven terrain and the steep incline in some parts. But I'm used to traveling on similar paths. I will be fine," I said in a reassuring tone. "If I get too tired, we'll just pause, and you can scratch my belly to soothe me."

She burst out laughing and shook her head at me. "Fine. But be sure to rest when you need it. I'm starting to know you. Your overprotective side will make you drive yourself to exhaustion just to take care of me."

"Maybe…" I said in a non-committal fashion that made her frown at me.

I kissed her, nipped her bottom lip, and then shifted into my wolf. The swiftness and efficiency with which she put the harness on me and secured both herself and our bags on my back was impressive. In no time, we set off.

The climb wasn't so bad at first, but a couple of hours in, I could feel the strain settling in. It was particularly difficult because we were following an almost vertical rock face where a narrow passage had been carved. It was wide enough for me to be able to stand normally but only left a couple of inches of spare terrain to my right. I thanked the gods that my mate didn't suffer from vertigo. We were literally walking a path less than three feet wide with a jagged stone wall on the left and the void on the right. A single slip would have us plummeting to our deaths.

I only relaxed on the rare occasions that the path cut through the mountain face itself, creating a temporary wall on both sides before opening up again to where we would be fully exposed. Thankfully, although we were climbing fairly high, the temperature remained comfortable in this summer month. No strong winds threatened to destabilize us either.

During the first half of the journey, my mate entertained me with tales of her life, funny anecdotes about her weirdest customers, and random other tidbits I might find entertaining. I hated that I couldn't talk back to her as a wolf. Soon, I hoped we would be fully bonded, and then we would be able to share telepathic conversations.

This leg of our journey was not particularly dangerous—so long as I trod carefully—but was unquestionably the toughest in terms of traveling. We couldn't really stop anywhere to stretch or rest. Under different circumstances, Amara's dismay at finding out that there would be no comfortable place for her to relieve her bladder would have been funny. We waited until we reached one of the narrow passages between two rock faces for her to free herself of the harness so that she could do her business.

Still, her embarrassment at urinating in front of me was hilarious. I made a show of putting my left paw over my snout to cover my eyes. She snorted and muttered something about me being silly. Climbing back on me and securing herself once more with the harness proved far more challenging in the narrow space. She ate as I continued to advance and fed me pieces of cured meat over my shoulder.

"You know, you could stop for a few minutes to eat," she mumbled.

I shook my head and kept going. My poor woman didn't fully understand our current predicament. It dawned on me then that I had failed to fully explain what this first part would be like. As the sun began to set on the horizon, Amara stirred restlessly.

"Are we close to where we will stop for the night?" she asked before yawning and profusely apologizing for it.

I shook my head.

"How long would you say?" she insisted. "An hour?"

I shook my head again.

"Two hours? Three? Four? Five?" she asked when I systematically shook my head after each number she stated. "Nine Hells, are we going to reach it at all tonight?!"

I shook my head.

"What? In the morning then? If you shake your head again I'm going to scream!" she exclaimed.

I glanced at her over my shoulder and made a whining sound.

She stared at me with a crestfallen expression. "Am I to take that as a no?"

I nodded.

A series of swear words tumbled out of her mouth. I made a chuffing sound that we used to express laughter in our wolf form.

"Are we at least going to reach it at some point before the end of day tomorrow?" Amara asked in a defeated tone.

I couldn't be certain. It was likely but not guaranteed. As I couldn't state that clearly, I moved my head from side to side and up and down, forming almost a horizontal eight, or the symbol of infinity.

"Does that mean probably?" she asked, resigned.

I nodded.

She sighed, and I immediately felt guilty for it. I wished I could provide a faster, more comfortable way to get her to our destination. To my shock, she leaned forward and wrapped her arms around my neck. She kissed my nape, rubbed her cheek against it before resting there.

"I'm sorry for putting you through this. I can never thank you enough. You're not just my Twin Flame, you're my guardian angel," she whispered.

My chest constricted when I realized that impatience and annoyance hadn't prompted that sigh, but guilt for inconveniencing me—or so she thought. My mate didn't understand how this hardship was actually the greatest gift anyone had ever given me. I was needed, *truly* needed. My efforts would literally save a life, but not just any life. I'd lived without any real aim or goal, simply going through the motion because I had no other choice. Now, I went to bed every night with hope filling my heart. Every morning, I woke up eager to see her beautiful face again and bask both in her affection and in the addictive way she looked at me as if I was precious.

She may think of me as her guardian angel, but she was my goddess and my salvation. Sad that I couldn't say as much, I emitted a whining sound and gently licked the back of her hand around my neck.

I pursued the journey for many more hours until my body screamed for a pause. At some point, Amara fell asleep. It pleased me as she needed to rest as much as possible. As soon as we reached another narrow passage, I lay down on my belly, careful not to move too suddenly to avoid waking her. I dozed off to enchanting visions of a future where my Flame was chasing after our pups while laughing.

The second day was just as grueling, if not more, but it got increasingly better towards the end as the path grew wider. It allowed me to run instead of the quick walk I'd been forced to stick to on the narrow ledges. Hearing my mate whoop as we reached a plateau cracked me up. The Gods knew I fully shared the sentiment. We made much better time than expected. The hard rock giving way to dirt and then the delightful cushion of grass offered my paws a welcome reprieve.

My heart soared upon seeing the first shrubs. Soon, they turned into bushes, and then into full trees. Their high enough numbers justified calling it a forest, even though they were quite scattered. Our refuge for the night was drawing near. As the sun still had a good hour before starting to set, we would get to enjoy a well-deserved moment of self-care.

It had been a long time since I last came here, but I remembered well the little haven located just past the edge of the rock wall near the large tree with a knot that oddly resembled a face. It wasn't a Warden Tree like could be found on certain blessed lands, or the most famous one named the Watcher who towered near the altar outside the Duskwallow burial grounds. Warden trees were extremely powerful, and each possessed a unique face. They didn't speak with words, and their faces didn't actually move like a human's. But they could express emotions. Woe unto any fool who incurred their wrath but blessed were those to whom they granted their protection.

I ran past the tree, feeling that sudden burst of energy one often got when getting close to home, or whatever destination they were headed to. Amara gasped when I turned the corner of what seemed to be a continuous wall but was in fact an optical illusion hiding the entrance of a cave.

The deceptively narrow entrance gave way to an impressively spacious hideout that was relatively warm in the otherwise cooler air of the mountain at this altitude. Although comfortable enough during the day, it got a little chilly at night.

"By the Gods! Is this what I think it is?" my mate exclaimed as I crossed the large, semi-circular space towards the back.

Some natural light gave us a glimpse of what looked like plumes of vapor near the ground. A slight smell of sulfur—too light to be unpleasant—hinted at what lay ahead. I ran towards it and emitted the chuffing sound that expressed laughter when my woman squealed.

A natural hot spring revealed itself. A large opening in the rock's face acted like a natural window giving a breathtaking view of Storm Hill Valley below. Thankfully, a wide enough platform surrounded the hot spring, making it safe to circle around it. A few rocks and boulders scattered by the edges could be used either to sit or lie on.

As soon as I stopped near the warm water, my mate hastily freed herself from the harness and hopped off my back. To my pleasant surprise, instead of rushing to the water to test it, my mate removed the bags and harness burdening me. This considerate gesture moved me deeply. Too few people had ever voluntarily put my needs first before indulging in theirs.

Only then did she venture near the edge of the spring. I shifted back into my human form as she crouched to dip a hand into the water. Still half morphed, I happily chuckled at the voluptuous moan she emitted upon finding it at a pleasant temperature.

"You're going to have to drag me kicking and screaming out of this hot spring once I get in," she said with a thrilled voice.

"No, my Flame. I suspect it is *you* who will have to drag me out of there," I replied teasingly. "But you get a head start. Hop in. I'll go get some kindling to start a fire for the night and maybe warm a bit of cider."

"Pfft! As if I was going to let you do all the work by yourself," Amara said, sounding almost offended. "Anyway, I need to stretch my legs."

"You should rest," I argued.

The stern glance she cast my way silenced me.

"I wasn't asking for permission," she said in a tone that brooked no argument.

Fuck me, that was incredibly sexy! Once again, the inner

strength lurking beneath my mate's demure and almost timid exterior impressed me. I loved that duality in my woman. A gentle and nurturing touch wrapped an iron will.

I bowed my head in concession. "Consider me duly chastised," I said with exaggerated contrition.

She snorted and shook her head at me while I walked past her, still naked. She slapped my bare behind strong enough for it to sting but nowhere near enough to hurt. I yelped with false outrage, and she giggled before running towards the exit. I chased after her, easily catching up, and scooping her up in my arms. She squealed and laughed some more as I carried her outside while pretending to take bites at her.

By Ferazan, how did she manage to light up my days with even the silliest of things?

"You know, the whole point of me tagging along was to stretch my legs and get some exercise," Amara said in a reproving tone.

I shrugged and gave her a wholly unrepentant smile. "You will in a minute. For now, I need to sate my urge to hold you in my arms. I've been deprived of it for two entire days while you were sitting on my back. Unless you are saying that you've had enough proximity with me and need a break?"

"Nine Hells! You have no shame!" Amara exclaimed when I took on the most piteous sad puppy expression as I asked that last question.

"None whatsoever," I concurred proudly. "But you haven't answered my question."

She playfully elbowed me while making a face. "You know perfectly well that I can never tire of being in your embrace. Stop fishing for compliments."

"I'm not," I said without the slightest sliver of honesty. "I just want to make sure we're on the same page."

"Right. And I'm the Queen of the Ninth Circle," she retorted mockingly.

"Your Highness," I deadpanned.

She bit my cheek then soothed the barely-there sting with a kiss. I tightened my embrace around her and rubbed my temple on her forehead to mark her with my scent. By the Gods, I was falling hard for my woman.

With much reluctance, I set her back on her feet when we reached the sparse forest to grab some kindling. We made quick work of gathering enough wood for the fire. As I bent down to pick up what we had piled up, I saw Amara look at a twig before tossing it as it was too thin to be of significant use.

I couldn't say what came over me, but I shifted into my wolf form and ran after it. I picked it up with my teeth and brought it back to her.

The look on my female's face was beyond hilarious.

"Seriously?!" my Flame exclaimed with a mix of disbelief and confusion.

You didn't need to be a mind reader to guess that she was wondering if this was a natural instinct for Lycans as it was with dogs. Obviously, my people felt no compulsion to go fetch. But being around my mate had awakened a playful side in me that I hadn't expressed in over two decades, since falling out with Ulric.

Tail wagging, I nudged her hand with my snout to make her take the twig. I panted, wagging my tail even more fiercely as I stared at her with an expectant look. Her gaze alternated between the twig and me, as if she couldn't believe what was happening. Then she shrugged and threw it as far as she could. I immediately chased after it again. This time, she burst out laughing.

She took it once I brought it back to her again, shaking her head as if I was a lost cause.

"You silly male," she said affectionately. "Aren't you tired?"

I hopped in circles around her, then pretended to try to nip at her ankles.

"Hey! Cut it out! Nooooo!" she squealed, laughing as she started running away.

I playfully chased after her, pretending that her evasive maneuvers were partially successful. Eventually, she tripped, and I jumped on top of her, pinning her down. I licked her face a few times while she weakly protested between two laughs.

I couldn't say at which point things stopped being a game for me. But one moment I was trying to keep her laughing, the next a powerful hunger took over me. The burning desire to mate with my woman triggered my shapeshifting. Except I didn't fully resume my human form. I still had my tail, a large amount of fur —mainly on my back arms and legs—and I could feel that my face wasn't fully back to its normal self. In that instant, I was half werewolf and half human.

I crushed her lips in a far more brutal kiss than I intended. She stiffened in surprise. To my relief, she didn't push me away but relaxed less than a couple of seconds later. The fervor with which she responded whipped my passion into a frenzy. To my shame, I didn't even fully undress her. In truth, I was surprised her pants didn't get torn to shreds in my impatience to reach my prize. Her underwear didn't enjoy such mercy. With a single swipe of my claws, I sliced it open and barely remembered to retract them before I sank two fingers inside my mate.

Amara moaned against my lips, her nails digging into my back. She lifted her pelvis as if to give better access to my bold probing. In the sudden heat fogging my mind, I took it as an invitation to proceed. A little voice at the back of my head warned that, despite already being wet for me, my mate might not be quite ready to receive me. But I ignored it and focused all my willpower on not ramming myself in as my entire body ached to do.

Still, I didn't claim her in the slow and careful way I normally did with shallow thrusts. She gasped against my lips while I hissed against hers at the burn of her body initially resisting my invasion. I couldn't say whether it was my determined persistence or her body's sudden cooperation that let it yield quickly to my imperious demand.

Once again, my Twin Flame didn't challenge the unbridled way with which I made her mine. The fervor with which she caressed me, and the eagerness of her tongue swirling around mine shouted loudly her consent and enthusiasm. I didn't need further encouragement to unleash my passion on her.

I didn't wait for her to adjust to my girth or even gradually pick up the pace. I immediately began pounding into her, driven insane by pleasure almost too much to bear as her tight sheath squeezed my cock from every side. Every time my knot rubbed against that sensitive bundle of nerves just on the upper side of her inner walls, it sent an electric bolt down the length of my cock and throughout my pelvic area. We were made for each other as both our most erogenous spots were perfectly aligned.

Feeling her tremble beneath me and swallowing each of her voluptuous moans stirred the feral beast lurking deep within. I wanted to wreck her, devour all that she was, mark her irrevocably as mine, and see her falling apart over and over again until her mind broke.

Her body suddenly seized, and she cried out as her climax swept over her. A savage sound tore out of my throat when her inner walls clamped down on my cock. I almost spilled my seed. My claws extruded and dug into the ground as I battled the urge to yield to my own climax. My cock throbbed, and a sharp pain stabbed at my pelvis as I used every ounce of my willpower not to let my knot swell.

On the verge of losing that battle, I pulled out of my mate and flipped her onto her stomach. The sight of the magnificent curves of her round behind had me drooling and my primal instincts surging forth. In a fleeting moment of lucidity, I bemoaned the fact that she wasn't a Lycan. Bathed either by the glow of the moon or the rays of the sun, we would have exchanged mating bites, marking each other as bonded mates.

I grabbed her hips with both hands, lifting her onto her knees, and then slammed myself home. Still half dazed from her recent climax, Amara emitted a strangled cry at my brutal possession, then propped herself on to her forearms. Moments later, she was rocking back and forth, meeting me thrust for thrust as liquid fire spread through my veins, cranking up the heat setting me ablaze a thousandfold.

I leaned forward, hating that she was still wearing her top, depriving me of the skin to skin contact I craved. With a will of their own, my fangs descended further, and I found myself closing them over her nape in a gesture of dominance and possession. Amara released a high-pitched keening sound that might have been the type of whine a wolf or one of my kin would emit in sign of submission. My Flame probably didn't realize she had done it. But even if she did, I doubted it was intentional. Either way, it resonated directly in my cock, and I nearly came undone.

Grinding my teeth, both from the strain of reining myself in and from overwhelming pleasure, I lost myself in my woman. The urge to sink my teeth into her flesh and bind her permanently to me rode me hard. But when that day came—and it would—I would do things right and with her full consent.

But my woman started to tremble. And by the increasingly urgent sound of the voluptuous moans rising from her, I could sense she was getting close to falling apart again. Once she did, I wouldn't be able to resist yielding to my own climax. Knowing all too well what would follow once I did, I pulled out of my woman again, flipped her around, then drew her on top of me as I lay down on my back. I impaled her on my cock in one swift movement. Before I could even thrust more than a couple of times, my woman cried out, swept away by bliss.

Her inner walls clamping down sent a lightning bolt

exploding in my knot. It radiated down to the base of my cock before spreading up the length of my spine. My vision blurred, and I felt as if my very soul was getting knocked out of my body. My seed shot out in powerful spurts of ecstasy that left me reeling. My knot swelled, locking me with my Flame as I tightened my hold around her.

Her face buried in my neck, her body shaking from the spasms of bliss, Amara clung to me with the strength of a drowning woman. Her labored breath fanned my chest as I continued to fill her until I was fully spent.

The Gods smite me, I was crazy for this woman.

We remained in each other's embrace as our heartbeats settled. Amara was lying on me, snuggling, her knees on each side of my legs. I kissed her forehead then carefully rose to my feet. Being still buried balls deep into my mate made things quite awkward, but once standing up, I reveled in the closeness and the way she wrapped her arms and legs around me. The trust with which she abandoned herself to my care moved me to my core.

Chest against chest, I carried her back inside the cave and into the hot spring. Her voluptuous moan as the warm water closed around us had my cock jerk in response. Ferazan take me! It embarrassed me to be so addicted to this woman that any little touch, sound, or even look sufficed to arouse me.

"Hmmm, that feels good!" Amara said in a purring voice. "I can feel the heat seeping all the way into my bones. Until now, I had not fully realized how sore I was."

A wave of guilt crashed over me, and I gave her a sheepish look.

"My apologies, my mate. I never intended on being this rough with you. Sadly, the longer we remain in our wolf form, the more feral we become. I couldn't even fully shift back into my human form."

"Nine Hells! There's no need for you to apologize. In case

you haven't noticed, I was a willing participant," Amara retorted as if I'd said something stupid. "I mean, getting down and dirty with a werewolf is rather hot."

"Lycan! Not werewolf," I exclaimed, outraged.

She chuckled and rubbed her nose against mine. "Sorry, Lycan then. But honestly, right now, you look more like a werewolf than a Lycan. You can't shift back?"

I shook my head. "No, not while knotted. I have to wait until it deflates. I hope you're not too freaked out about my current appearance," I added carefully.

She smiled and caressed my cheek. "Nah, you look a lot more intimidating but in a good way. If I didn't clearly recognize you, it would be different. But these are still your features, my Remus, with just more lupine traits."

The extent of the relief I felt upon hearing those words stunned me. It embarrassed me how much reassurance I constantly needed from my woman.

"Right," I said.

Amara tilted her head to the side, giving me an assessing look. "Can you control your knot? Like could you prevent it from swelling or deflate it at will?"

I shook my head again. "Its responses are pretty much instinctual. I can 'try' to hold it back, but it's pretty much a losing battle. Essentially, my only 'control' over it is stopping myself from ejaculating. The minute I do, the knot kicks in. However, I have absolutely no control over when it deflates. Sometimes, it's faster than other times. Your guess is as good as mine as to why."

"I see," Amara said pensively, a frown creasing her brow. "But what if we'd just finished getting naughty and a threat showed up? We'd both be sitting ducks."

I gave her an indulgent smile. "While I still wouldn't have any control over my knot in such a situation, my self-preservation instincts would kick in and my knot would deflate on its own. It's the only case where it will release our mate before our wolf deems it has done its purpose."

"Its purpose meaning increasing the chances the female will have successfully been impregnated?" she asked, her face unreadable.

I flinched, and my stomach instantly knotted with apprehension. My whole life, I dreamt of having a mate and many pups. Memories of some of the males from the pack sleeping with half a dozen pups dogpiling them haunted me to this day, eliciting a dull ache of longing.

Does she not want kids?

"Yes," I replied carefully, my eyes flicking between hers, searching. "You don't have to worry about getting pregnant, though. The poison currently coursing through your veins makes it impossible."

"I see," Amara replied with that same neutral expression.

"I know we haven't talked about it yet, but do you want to have children?" I asked hesitantly.

An immense wave of relief washed over me when she immediately nodded.

"Definitely. I would like at least two or three. Being an only child sucks," my mate said firmly. "What about you?"

The stupid grin that stretched my lips—which had to be rather scary in my partially shifted form—gave her the answer before I even spoke.

"As a wolf, I would want at least half a dozen pups," I said sheepishly.

She burst out laughing and gave me a look as if I was insane. However, I also noticed that she had not shut down that idea.

"So once I'm healed, we'll be able to have kids?"

I hesitated then shook my head. "We need to be bonded before you can bear my children. As a pureblood human, you are not compatible with me on that front. The mate bond will enable you to conceive and carry a Lycan baby."

"How does the bond work?"

The absence of fear or unease when she asked the question pleased me tremendously.

"The day you're willing to link your life to me permanently, I will give you the bonding bite. We usually do it right here near the shoulder," I said, caressing the spot a few inches from her neck on her right shoulder.

"Will I change?" Amara asked with a slight frown.

I wouldn't say that her reaction expressed worry. However, besides her obvious curiosity about the process and consequences, it struck me that she had likely never considered the possibility that mating with a Lycan might bring radical changes to who she was.

Once more I hesitated. "You won't change externally," I said, choosing my words carefully. "But you will be enhanced with greater strength, increased speed, and heightened regeneration when injured or tired. You will also undergo some minor anatomical changes, especially in the reproductive department. Your glands will produce specific hormones needed for the growth of a healthy pup, and the inner lining of your uterus will thicken and grow more resistant to keep you safe from possible clawing from the little ones as they near the end of gestation."

"Oh wow!" Amara said, seemingly awed. "But does that also mean I will have an increased chance of a multiple pregnancy?"

Again, the apologetic look on my face said it all.

"Sheesh!" Amara whispered.

To my delight, her overly dramatic crestfallen expression hinted that she actually wasn't opposed to the idea.

"So no furry tail for me or wolf ears?" she added teasingly.

"None for you," I replied before kissing the tip of her nose. "Werewolves are the ones who will change you when they pass on the curse."

She tilted her head to the side while her fingers absentmindedly fiddled with the hair mixing with my wolf fur on my nape.

"Is that what you become on the full moon? A werewolf?"

I forced myself to keep a neutral expression. No words could express how much I hated this part of me. I only prayed that my mate would never get to witness it.

"Yes. I do. But it only lasts a few hours, from the moment the moon reaches its full phase until sunrise," I added quickly. "There are plenty of warnings over the days leading up to the full moon, so it's not like it just sneaks up on me. And you have nothing to fear. I will never hurt you, and I am not a threat. Or rather, I take every possible precaution to make sure I am not a danger to anyone in those twenty-four hours."

All tension bled from me when my mate gently smiled in a reassuring fashion. "I know, Remus. I do not fear you. Even though we've only just met, I'm falling hard for you. I can't remember being so in harmony with anyone. Just being with you makes me happy. And no, it's not this whole Twin Flame business talking right now. This is just me, Amara, falling head over heels for the man you are, Remus. So I'll be expecting that bonding bite soon."

Once more, the silliest grin settled on my face while my chest overflowed with affection and a feeling I didn't dare give a name to just yet.

"I share the same sentiments about you, Amara. My physiological reactions to you are only the confirmation of what I feel. With you, everything just feels so natural. I've never been happier than since I've met you," I said, embarrassed by the slight trembling of my voice as I felt nearly choked by emotion.

Amara opened her mouth to ask a question, hesitated, and seemed to change her mind.

"What is it? What were you going to ask?" I inquired, curious.

Her face took on the most adorable air of shyness. "It's just... I don't need to sound pushy."

"Speak, my mate. There's nothing you can't openly discuss

with me, ever. You are my safe haven, and I am yours," I said gently.

She licked her lips nervously, squared her shoulders, and went for it.

"Since we both want the same thing, I was wondering why wait to bond with each other?"

My heart melted when she immediately lowered her eyes, as if worried to read a potential rejection on my face. This silly female didn't understand just how crazy I was for her and how badly I wanted to bind her to me for the rest of our days.

"Believe me, my mate, there's nothing I want more. However, it cannot be done now. In many ways, we are like vampires. Our bonding bite freezes our partner in their current state," I explained. "That's the reason why we do not bond when one of the partners is sick or if they are too young."

"I don't understand," Amara said with a frown. "Lycans are not immortal, right?"

"We're not. Technically, neither are vampires as they can die. They're just long-lived under specific conditions," I corrected gently. "Immortality is for the gods. But Lycans naturally age a lot slower than humans. We have on average three times your lifespan. Bonding further increases that trait as we exchange regeneration fluids and our lifespans become synchronized."

"So if we were to bond now, I would be frozen in this state of sickness?" Amara asked, horrified.

I nodded with a grim expression. "Sadly, yes."

"Ugh, never mind that!" my mate muttered with a shudder, making me chuckle. She then suddenly sobered. "Could I make you sick, too?"

I shook my head. "No, my blood counters your poison. But at the pace we are going, I have faith that we will reach the plateau in four more days. And then, we can heal you."

"I can't wait for this nightmare to be over and for us to start working towards our future," my Flame said wistfully.

I tightened my arms around her, and she tightened hers around my neck. By Ferazan, how I loved belonging to this woman.

"The past few days have been hard on you. And you have no idea how proud you make me, soldiering on the way you have," I said, my voice dripping with admiration and respect. "Despite my seed neutralizing some of the poison, your health continues to falter. So I apologize in advance for the upcoming days. Tonight is a well-deserved reprieve before another grueling round."

"Don't be sorry for this. You are literally saving my life. I should be the one apologizing to you for putting you through all of this. However, if you really want to apologize for something, you can say sorry for getting frisky before we could bring in all the kindling we gathered."

I snorted, my cheeks heating with embarrassment and guilt. "Fact! I'm indeed sorry for that, but I will go fetch it when we're out of the water. After all, I've discovered a new passion for it."

Amara burst out laughing and gave my shoulder a playful tap. "You silly male. You really had me going there for a while. I couldn't decide if you were pulling my leg or genuinely feeling the urge to go fetch."

"The truth lies somewhere between the two," I replied in a mysterious tone before claiming her mouth.

CHAPTER 13
AMARA

After that wonderful 'spa' getaway, we spent another two full days on the path, Remus running with me riding on his back. On the third day, we found a small recess in the rock face of the mountain that would barely qualify as an alcove. It still provided a semblance of shelter while my poor mate indulged in a well-deserved rest.

I felt horrible watching him push himself so hard. It didn't help that he was rationing his food to make sure we would have enough until we reached another plateau where we might find some game to hunt and spare our reserves.

However, I selfishly didn't insist too much on him taking it easy. Mating with him in his partially shifted form had given me a noticeably stronger boost than when I had taken his seed with him in his human form. And yet, I could feel myself fading even quicker every day. I couldn't say if the poison was becoming more aggressive in reaction to that stronger antidote, or if it was just a matter of my system becoming increasingly weak. For this reason, being able to sleep on Remus while he ran all day turned out to be a great blessing.

His determination to see this through moved me beyond

words. He was so wonderful and loving to me. I embarked on this mission without much hope, mostly going through the motions because I didn't believe in just lying down in the face of adversity. But meeting Remus changed everything. I really wanted to live to explore a life with him. Sadly, as we finally entered a proper cave this time for the night, the fear I wouldn't make it steadily grew in my heart.

Already nineteen days had gone by since my meeting with the Weaver, fifteen since the last full moon, and eleven since I'd set off on this journey. By my mate's estimation, we should reach the plateau in a couple more days. That meant that our entire trip to our destination would have taken thirteen days—fourteen if we added the extra delay caused by Lyall kidnapping me.

And that was a problem.

Considering that I traveled on my own horse for the first five days, how long would it take Remus to run back that entire distance on his own? By the time we met with Ranael for my first bite, there would only be about eleven days remaining before the next full moon. According to the Weaver, it would take at least two to five days for his venom to burn the poison coursing through me before I could get his second bite to neutralize it. Assuming the worst-case scenario of five days, that would leave Remus with only six days to get back to one of his safe places before he turns into a werewolf.

Will he be able to get there in such a short time if he's not burdened with me?

But that also raised the question of where I would stay in the meantime. I didn't know what state I would be in after that second bite. All signs indicated that I would likely be a wreck for hours if not days afterwards.

I forced myself to swallow another bite of dry bread and cured meat. Yesterday, I noticed how tasteless food had become for me. Today, I could have sworn I was eating the ashes from a bonfire. My stomach wasn't taking kindly to any food. Drinking cider felt like guzzling vinegar, and even water disagreed with me.

The weight of Remus's gaze on me claimed my attention. Guilt immediately crashed over me upon seeing his distraught expression. Despite his best efforts, my mate couldn't hide his worry for me. But the worst part of it all was knowing beyond any doubt that he was blaming himself for my worsening condition.

Since our wild night by the hot spring, we only made love again once after the second stretch of two-days of non-stop running. Although Remus had once more been partially shifted, the beneficial effects of his seed waned within hours. We hadn't been intimate since, despite having half-decent shelters for each of the following three nights—including tonight—with enough room for us to get frisky.

As much as I would have liked to enjoy more of those moments with my soulmate, I'd been too worn out and feeling too icky to even consider it. Remus hadn't made any overtures in that sense either. It distressed me that his sensitive nose told him exactly what poor state I was in. But I actually feared it was revealing to him that my condition was even worse than I believed.

"Is something wrong, my Flame?" Remus asked in a gentle voice, his underlying worry subtle but audible.

I shook my head. "No, I'm fine. But I was thinking it might be a good idea to show you the magic circle and incantation that will be required to summon Ranael."

My chest constricted at the air of pure sorrow that flitted over my mate's handsome features. I didn't need to go into details for him to read between the lines. By the look on his face, he clearly wanted to give me those generic arguments and platitudes people always spewed whenever they try to convince a dying person that they will somehow make it. Thankfully, he spared me the pain of having a pointless debate about it.

"That could be fun," he said with a smile that didn't quite reach his eyes. "I've dabbled in many things. But summoning will be a new experience. Show me, my Flame."

My heart melted with affection for him. Once again, he was putting my needs first and prioritizing my mental welfare over his own. Tears pricked my eyes at the thought that we might not have much time left together. Fate couldn't be so cruel as to finally put such a wonderful man in my path only to snuff my light out before I could reciprocate the love and care he was showing me.

Over the next hour, Remus displayed a phenomenal level of focus as he practiced drawing the magic circle and memorizing the incantation. It blew me away considering how exhausted he must be after pushing himself almost to his limit running the entire day. By the time we stopped, he had fully mastered it. It gave me a great deal of comfort to know that should I be too incapacitated to perform it myself, he would be able to do it on my behalf.

That night, against all odds, we made love again. When I first initiated it, he seemed hesitant. I didn't have to ask why. But I wanted this intimacy with him. Somewhere, deep down, a little voice was telling me this would likely be our last time.

It wasn't the savage and unbridled coupling that we experienced the last few times since that wild romp by the hot spring. Tonight, despite remaining extensively in his wolf form throughout the day, Remus made love to me in his full human form. It wasn't passionate or lustful but tender and borderline desperate. In truth, it struck me more as a farewell.

By morning, it was clear that his seed had done nothing for me.

I was feverish, groggy, and weak for the remainder of the journey. Although the path once more widened enough for us to find plenty of places to rest, Remus plowed through. He only stopped for me to drink and eat. But in my current state, I could hardly stomach anything. With relentless determination, my mate ran for a day and a half, until we reached our final destination.

We stepped onto the plateau early that afternoon. The timing could not have been more perfect. It provided us with enough time to rest, set up the circle, and prepare our shelter for the night.

The plateau vaguely reminded me of an open outstretched hand, palm facing up, fingers closed together except for the thumb jutting out. The dark stones vaguely reminded me of cooled down lava which had been smoothed and polished by the elements. The surface almost shone under the bright rays of the early afternoon sun. Below, the Storm Hill valley sprawled as far as the eye could see. I couldn't even begin to calculate just how high we were. But it was high enough that the few buildings I could recognize below looked no bigger than a coin.

A shiver coursed through me as I deeply inhaled the crisp but overly thin air of the plateau. I glanced back at the path from whence we arrived. While the plateau lay flat horizontally over a fifty-meter radius, the path itself had been no wider than a couple of meters. No trees or other vegetation adorned that area. Only a small rock face marked the western edge of the mountain, which continued to climb higher. However, there didn't appear to be any practical way to go higher from here.

Remus walked to the rock face towards what appeared to be a shallow nook that could provide a reasonable shelter. In no universe would it qualify as a cave, but it was deep enough to protect us from the elements should it begin to rain, or should strong winds blast our way.

He dropped most of our bags in the nook before donning his clothes. Once done, he came back my way. I had been walking around the plateau looking for the best spot to draw the circle, when I recognized the area where I had done it in the illusion Lyall had cast me into. Had it been his way of telling me this was the best location?

"Here," I said to Remus while pointing at the ground when he stopped next to me. "That's where I will draw the circle."

"I got it," Remus said in an imperious tone.

To my shock, instead of handing me the bag with the salt, candles, and chalk, Remus got to work, drawing the circle perfectly, as I had taught him.

"You don't have to—"

"I don't, but I *want* to," Remus said, interrupting my feeble protest in a firm but gentle fashion. "Right now, what you need to do is rest and save your strength for tonight. You can supervise my work to make sure it is up to your standards."

Once again, tears pricked my eyes at just how thoughtful and protective he was. In that instant, I realized that no one would have brought me here the way he did. They would have bailed along the way or set a much slower pace that would have guaranteed my demise before we ever reached our destination.

I watched as he completed his task flawlessly. He had been attentive during the brief training, but considering nearly forty-eight hours had gone by since then, I would have expected him to forget something or mess up a part of the runic patterns inside the circle.

"You're really good at this," I whispered with awe. "Should you ever wish to reorient your career as a summoner's assistant, you will be quite successful."

He snorted and gave me an amused smile, although I didn't miss the more serious glint in his eyes.

"The only witch I would work for is you. So unless you decide to shift your chandler business to witchcraft, I think I'll stick to my guide career."

He finished positioning the candles around the circle. Once I gave him my approval for a job well done, he carried me back to the nook where he had left the rest of our belongings. He settled on the ground at an angle that allowed him to keep an eye on the circle and sat me across his lap. We cuddled while awaiting nightfall.

"We need to discuss what will happen after," I said softly, my cheek resting on his shoulder.

"After?" he echoed.

I nodded. "There are only ten days left before the full moon. Assuming that the snake tail's venom takes the longest amount of time to neutralize the poison in my veins before I can get the second bite, that would only leave you with five days to reach one of your shelters. Will that be enough time for you?"

To my surprise, Remus smiled reassuringly.

"That's more than enough time. Your number one concern should be about how we will get *you* to a safe place to recover after that second bite," he replied teasingly.

I blinked. "I just assumed I would stay here until I got better, and you would come get me back down to civilization after the full moon."

I felt my cheeks burned with embarrassment at the look he gave me. In truth, I had been too worried about his welfare to focus on my own. Not to mention the fact that, deep down, I didn't really believe I would survive this entire ordeal. It shamed me to feel this way especially now that I had something to live for. But with every passing day, this entire mission struck me as more and more insane and farfetched.

Nobody survived Ranael's poison.

"I would never leave you here. Although this place is technically safe, you will be fighting one of the most virulent poisons in the world. Someone needs to watch over you during that time. I will do so for as long as I can. And it won't be in this unpleasant setting."

"Where will it be?" I asked, confused.

"I have already arranged for a place for you to stay after the second bite. It is not far from here. I only need a little over one day of carrying you to reach that shelter. It belongs to Misty's daughter. She agreed to watch over you when I can't."

"Oh wow! That's wonderful. But I don't recall seeing any dwellings on our way up," I countered.

"Because we didn't encounter one," he replied in an indulgent tone. "You were sleeping when we walked past the passage branching off of the path leading up to this plateau. That other passage takes us down to the valley on the other side of the mountain."

"Okay," I said carefully. "But that doesn't solve the situation for you."

He smiled again. "It will take me less than two days to reach one of my safe houses closest to her home. So that's plenty of time before the full moon."

"Oh! That's great then!" I exclaimed, relieved. "You thought of everything!"

He gave me the most endearing smug smile. "I tried to. That's why I delayed our departure. I had to plan and get everything in place before we left."

The strangest expression settled over his face as he stared at me with an intensity that affected me in a way that I couldn't put into words. Whatever thoughts fueled it, I rather liked it.

"I *will* save you, Amara. We didn't come this far to fail now."

He spoke those words like a pledge.

"If you're trying to make me fall in love with you, you're doing a fantastic job," I said, deeply moved.

"Good. I'm keeping you, Amara. Nothing, not even death, will take you from me. You are my Twin Flame. I refuse to lose you now that I found you."

"As I refuse to lose you," I whispered.

He leaned forward and captured my lips in a kiss filled with hope, devotion, and determination.

We would not be defeated.

CHAPTER 14
AMARA

With much trepidation, I let Remus carry me out of our shelter to the circle in the middle of the plateau. Despite feeling a little weak and weary, I could have walked on my own. But being held in his strong arms, surrounded by his warm body, and listening to the soothing sound of his heartbeat helped lessen my growing panic. Anyway, it could only benefit me to save as much of my energy as possible.

While waiting for nightfall, I forced myself to eat and drink a little. I would need those reserves to help me battle through the venomous bite I was about to request. The little voice at the back of my head was screeching for me to get the hell out of here. Reason told me I should comply, but my stark reality demanded I push forward.

I was dying.

If Ranael didn't kill me, the poison coursing through my veins would do it in the next day or so. I was only grateful that I wasn't on the ground writhing with excruciating pain. According to Remus, the pain manifested itself while I slept. A wave of guilt washed over me at the thought of how, even at night. I'd deprived him of any proper rest by having him worrying over me while I tossed and turned in a feverish delirium.

He settled me down next to the circle then turned me to face him. He opened and closed his mouth a couple of times. No words came out, not that they were needed. His beautiful golden eyes said everything. I gave him a smile meant to be reassuring. The way my lips quivered, I miserably failed at it. I wrapped my arms around his waist, buried my face in his neck, and deeply inhaled his scent.

Remus reciprocated with a bone-crushing hug. I couldn't say how long it lasted. My guess would be close to a minute, but my heart shouted that it had not been anywhere near long enough. With much reluctance, he released me, cupped my face with both hands, and gave me a deep kiss into which he poured all the affection and devotion he felt towards me. I answered in kind.

"I'll be waiting nearby," he said at last, his voice deep with repressed emotion.

"Okay." I whispered, my throat almost too constricted to speak. "It should be over quickly."

The deep pain that flashed over his face clawed at my heart. I flinched inwardly realizing how my words could be interpreted in a more ominous fashion. Before I could find a clever way to amend them, Remus gave my cheek one last caress then walked away to the position near our shelter we agreed he would stand watch from.

I stared at his receding back until he was but a few steps from his destination. Taking a fortifying breath, I stepped into the circle after making sure it had not been disturbed. I got on my knees in the center and began reciting the incantation the Weaver taught me while lighting the candles at each point of the pentagram inside the circle.

"Demon Wolf Ranael, son of Lord Marchosias, hear my cry! Oh fierce warrior from the Underworld, come to me, I summon thee! In my great time of need, I beseech thee, come forth and grant me the blessing of your protection."

I repeated these words, or variations thereof, in a litany. Each time, my voice became steadier and more determined as I shed my fear and embraced the course of action I had embarked on. There would be no turning back. Either this succeeded or failed. But I wouldn't allow the latter outcome to come to pass because I couldn't rein in my emotions. The face of my soulmate floating in front of my mind's eye further strengthened my resolve.

I had almost fallen into a trance when the distant sound of flapping wings finally reached my ears. My heart skipped a beat, but I forced myself to continue to repeat the summons, focusing this time on the protection part of my plea. A shiver ran down my spine when a long stream of fire shot through the sky. Had I not known that Ranael was a demon wolf, I would have assumed a dragon had just breathed fire. I blinked at the brightness it caused in the dark night sky, only otherwise illuminated by the fattening moon in a sea of stars.

Amazed by the majesty of the giant beast, I fell silent as he flew towards me. He was truly magnificent. Nearly the size of a horse, the wolf had the fluffiest and shiniest grayish brown fur with reddish highlights. The fur along his tail gradually faded into scales leading to the snake head. His feathered wings had an impressive span, and a set of horns adorned his forehead. His eyes glowed an angry red that should have terrified me. But it was the intelligence and the endless wisdom that shone within that retained my attention. Still, the hint of madness in his gaze also couldn't be ignored.

He glided down the remaining distance to me before landing with the grace of a cat a couple of meters away from me. Plumes of smoke rose from his snout as he emitted a chuffing sound while advancing the few steps separating us. The corner of his mouth quirked up in a menacing snarl, baring a vicious set of fangs and the terrifying razor-sharp teeth filling his maw. He was visibly struggling to resist the urge to leap and maul me. I didn't know if the magic circle deterred him, or if my protection summons was keeping his rabid side at bay.

"Who dares summon me?" he demanded in an imperious tone.

I shivered, and my skin erupted in goosebumps. For some reason, I had expected him to either take his human form or to speak telepathically to me. After all, Remus couldn't speak while in his wolf form, so I assumed it would be the same with Ranael. And yet, his mouth hadn't moved exactly, at least not the way a human's did to form words. But there was no question I had heard his words through my ears and not inside my head.

His voice was deep, powerful, and like clapping thunder.

Shocked that I could even form words at all, I replied with a steadiness that took even me aback.

"I do, Lord Ranael. I invoke your protection and your aid in my time of need," I said in a firm but deferent voice.

"Protection and aid for what," he asked, his tone just as harsh.

"I am terminally ill."

"Obviously. The stench of death is all over you," he replied in a factual manner.

The dagger claws at the ends of his massive paws appeared to extrude further, cutting effortlessly into the hard rock of the plateau. The thick muscles of his legs and shoulders bulged slightly. I forced myself to ignore what I could only interpret as signs of his control already waning and focused on his face instead. The Weaver warned me there would be little time to conclude our business before his rage took over any rational thought. So I dove right in, skipping any small talk I might have otherwise used to ease him into it.

"I have been told that the venom in your snake tail could counter the poison currently killing me," I said in a controlled voice.

"That is correct. And once it's done eradicating that poison, my venom will kill you," he said, sounding a little irritated as if I was wasting his time with something that should be obvious.

"But it won't kill me if your other venom neutralizes it once I am rid of the poison," I countered.

Ranael visibly recoiling in surprise at that comment left me baffled.

"What other venom?" the demon wolf asked, seeming confused.

"The one from your fangs and saliva," I said in a self-evident fashion.

He snorted and made a jerking motion with his head. I didn't quite know how to interpret it. For some reason, it struck me as hinting at an incredulous laugh.

"The venom from my fangs and saliva will absolutely not neutralize my snake tail venom," Ranael said, sounding amused and like he was questioning my intelligence. "What they will do is liquefy you from the inside out. You could say they are far more potent than even the most virulent acid known to mankind."

"What?! That's not possible!" I exclaimed, feeling my blood drain from my face. "Your bite will neutralize your snake venom. You're a demon wolf. You cannot lie!"

He bared his teeth at me, and an angry growl rose from his throat. In that instant, I didn't doubt that without my protection request, he would have attempted to attack me. As I had never drawn a similar magic circle before, I could only hope that, as claimed by the Weaver, it truly sheltered me from him should he lose control.

Instead of answering me, Ranael suddenly jerked his head to the right in the direction of the semi-cave my mate and I had sheltered in earlier. I followed his gaze only to see him staring at Remus. Partially hidden by the shadows, he was almost invisible.

"Ranael! Focus on me," I commended, stunned by my own boldness.

But when dealing with beings from the netherworld, showing weakness would almost guarantee our demise. To my utter relief, the demon wolf complied and snapped his attention back towards me.

"I do not lie, you foolish woman. As you stated yourself, demon wolves are bound to speak the truth," he hissed.

"But... but the Weaver said that your bite would neutralize the venom!" I exclaimed, utterly distressed.

"That's not what the Weaver said," he replied in a tone that brooked no argument. "You simply misinterpreted her words."

"What?! But..."

My voice trailed off as my brain struggled to make sense of his words. The sincerity in his voice was undeniable. And as we had both stated, he could not lie even if he wanted to.

"Conclude your business, human. I cannot last much longer," he said in a growling tone.

His muscles bulged further, while the reddish glow in his eyes intensified, creating a frightening halo around his massive lupine face. Behind him, his snake tail waved from side to side, the movement almost hypnotic as if it was trying to lull its prey before striking.

"But what did she mean then?" I pressed him. "She said the demon wolf's snake tail would counter the poison in me. And then the bite of..."

I froze, my eyes widening as I stared in disbelief at Ranael.

"The bite of a sick wolf..." I whispered more to myself before glancing at Remus, although I could barely see him in the shadows.

"Yes," Ranael replied. "I am not a *sick* wolf. I am *cursed*. Now hurry!"

Fear finally washed over me when his throat reddened from the fire building in his chest. Teeth bared, wings spread wide, he dug his claws even more deeply into the stone at his feet. Shards of rock flew up where the stone fractured.

"HURRY!" he yelled.

That snapped me out of my frightened daze. Without thinking, I leaned forward and swiped my hand over the edge of the circle making an opening. I had no sooner completed the gesture than the demon wolf's snake tail rushed towards me. Its fangs sank into my throat before I could even blink.

Instantly, the most atrocious pain I ever experienced exploded in my neck, quickly spreading in my face, down my chest, and into each of my limbs. It felt as if my soul was being torn out of my body even as shards of glass ran through my veins, wrecking me from the inside out. I shrieked in agony and collapsed to the ground, shaken by violent spasms.

Through blurred vision, I saw Ranael lunge towards me, his maw wide open. In the next second, he would bite my head off and tear me apart. I welcomed the swift death it would grant me instead of the hell consuming me from within. But before he could grant me that mercy, a blur slammed into him, knocking the demon wolf out of the way.

Ranael opened his mouth wide to spit fire at Remus.

"Nooooooo!" I tried to cry out.

But only a gurgling sound came out as a veil of darkness descended before my eyes. In my last moment of lucidity, I cursed the stupidity of the mission I'd dragged Remus on. I'd killed him alongside me.

CHAPTER 15
REMUS

My heart pounded in my throat as I watched Ranael approach. The feral side of me that had been gradually coming to the fore the closer we got to the full moon was fueling the old anger burning deep within. This creature killed my parents, cursed me, and destroyed the happy life I could have had. However it was fear for my mate that dominated. The prospect that he might also take the life of my soulmate drove me insane. If that happened, it would break me beyond repair.

It took every ounce of my willpower not to run to Amara and shield her with my body when the demon wolf landed in front of her. During my few prior encounters with him, I had been in my wolf form. So although he had been imposing compared to me, I hadn't fully appreciated his size as my own wolf was quite massive. But now, seeing him towering over my kneeling mate, he looked like a giant preparing to devour a child.

Although he appeared to engage in a relatively controlled conversation with my Flame, the dread I felt didn't wane. Judging by his body language, tension was quickly building inside him. Ranael was fighting a losing battle with the rage he'd been cursed with. I silently urged my mate to conclude this

DESTINED TO THE LYCAN

terrible mission quickly. As much as her reaction to his venom terrified me, at least it held a chance of saving her. But if the demon wolf yielded to his rabid instincts, she would never survive his attack.

To my dismay, despite my enhanced hearing, I couldn't hear what they were saying. Then again, wolf shifters didn't normally speak vocally. I presumed he was speaking to her telepathically. My back tensed when only moments into their conversation, Amara recoiled and appeared shocked and then frightened.

What could he have possibly told her to prompt such a reaction? Demon wolves couldn't lie when summoned for protection. What scary truth had he dumped on her? However, his physiological reactions reclaimed my attention. Ranael would soon lose control, as evidenced by the way his claws were digging into the ground, and by how he was bunching up his muscles, ready to leap onto his prey.

"Take the bite and be done before it's too late," I urged in a tense whisper, not that she could hear me from here.

To my shock, Ranael jerked his head towards me as if he had heard my words. I silently kicked myself. As a demigod, his hearing range was far wider and more acute than my own. Our gazes met, and the disturbing connection I had felt the previous times I sought him for revenge came back with a potency that left me reeling. The unholy bond that I shared with that creature struck me hard. As before, I didn't fear for my life where he was concerned. He wouldn't attack me, but my presence might trigger something within him, a helpless fury that he might turn against my woman.

To my relief, the demon wolf returned his attention to my mate when she called to him. They exchanged a couple more words, and then Amara fearfully broke the circle. His snake tail struck with such speed it was literally a blur. With a certainty I couldn't explain, I knew the broken circle, and the taste of her blood on his snake's fangs had shattered what willpower Ranael still possessed.

I didn't recall dashing towards them. I only realized I had been moving when the sound of my clothes tearing reached my ears. In its effort to resist, some of the fabric painfully dug into my skin before snapping as I instinctively shifted into my wolf form. A mere few feet away from him, I completed my metamorphosis, and I rammed into his side, moments before he would have mauled my thrashing mate.

The sound of her agonizing screams tore my very soul to shreds. I wanted to go to her but needed to eliminate the greater threat first.

I jumped back onto my feet, only to be struck by Ranael's massive paw. With a single swipe, he sent me flying a few meters back. I crashed on the hard stones of the plateau, the wind knocked out of me. Dazed, I scrambled back onto my paws only to see his chest glowing red as he prepared to incinerate me.

Waiting until the last second, I rolled out of the way when he opened his maw impossibly wide to spit a powerful stream of fire. The searing pain I expected never came. My brain froze when I realized he had widely and deliberately missed me. Considering his rage had taken over him, I had expected to sustain at least some damage, even though I doubted he would kill me.

The demon wolf threw his head back and emitted a savage cry that sounded more like a dragon's roar than a wolf's howl. Then, with one powerful flap of his massive wings, Ranael flew away.

I didn't spare him another thought and ran to my mate instead, shifting back to my human form in the process. I drew her into my arms, cradling her tightly to constrain the violence of the spasms coursing through her so that she wouldn't further harm herself. Tears pricked my eyes and a wave of helplessness and despair washed over me as I watched her thrashing in my arms. I had known Amara would suffer, but seeing this was destroying me.

A million thoughts swirled in my mind, most of them revolving around how stupid I had been for helping her in this reckless endeavor. Simultaneously, I tried to rationalize how she would have died anyway had we not tried the only option possible. But seeing her foaming at the mouth, her skin ashen, the stench of death growing exponentially, her body burning, and her breathing reduced to a wheezing whistle further seemed to confirm what a fool's errand this had been.

But the Weaver was right about the summoning.

Maybe she was right about this, too.

Still holding my Flame closely against me, I resealed the circle to keep any potential threat at bay. I doubted Ranael would return to finish what he started, but I didn't want to have to worry about him. My mate required all my attention.

And thus began the most nightmarish wait of my life.

Amara burned with an impossibly high fever throughout the night, even as her teeth chattered. Her moans of pain would only be interrupted by an occasional strangled cough. They frightened me the most as she appeared to be choking. The worst moment was when her body suddenly arched violently as if she had received a powerful electric discharge before going limp. I shouted her name, tapping her cheek, fearing she had died on me. After a few seconds that dragged on forever, she abruptly took a wheezing breath before repeating the cycle of moaning and choking.

It was only once the sun was finally up that I took Amara back into the partial cave that served as our shelter. With clouds gathering in the distance, the small space would provide us with some measure of protection. I saved some of the rainwater to replenish our reserves and used some of it to cool my woman and rehydrate her.

It took another entire day before the stench of death finally shifted before totally vanishing. For a few hours, my heart soared, filled with hope as her fever broke, and her breathing stabilized. Although her skin kept a dull and ashen color, my Flame no longer appeared to be in pain. One could have almost believed she was merely sleeping.

Exhausted after more than two days of constant watch, I caught myself dozing off, snapping back awake every other hour only to make sure all was still well with my mate. I hated that I needed to rest, but if I didn't, I would never be able to get her to safety and myself to my safe house before the full moon.

On the morning of the third day after the snake bite, I startled awake to a sour scent that nearly made me panic. And then I saw the first dark vein spreading around her neck near the puncture wound. I cursed inwardly that it should have finally happened in the wee hours of the morning.

I nearly went insane counting every minute of every hour until nightfall. As we had both suspected, my mate was in no condition to perform the summoning herself. Over the past three days, she had occasionally come out of her comatose state but been completely incoherent and barely even aware of what was happening. As much as I wanted to be able to talk to her, I welcomed the fact that she would lose consciousness again so that she wouldn't have to feel the pain of the venom ravaging her.

The sun had barely vanished on the horizon when I raced back to the circle with my mate in my arms. I made sure it was flawless again before calling unto Ranael. Like Amara had done, I recited the summons in a loop. But as the minutes went by with no signs of the demon wolf, a sense of dread took root in the pit of my stomach, growing exponentially over time.

After more than twenty minutes with no result, I stepped out of the circle, leaving my mate within, and called upon him again.

But that also failed.

I swapped places with her and repeated the entire ritual to no avail. What was I doing wrong? I checked the circle. Each rune, each line was perfectly drawn as she had taught me. The candles were lit and positioned correctly. I had memorized the incantation and summoning call. There were no flaws with what I had done. So why was he not answering?

Tears of anger and helplessness pricked my eyes, while an all-consuming rage gradually grew within me. Could Ranael be ignoring the summons because it was me calling upon him? What the fuck was I supposed to do now? There was no time for me to go get Malina—Misty's daughter—and bring her back here to perform the summons in my stead.

I gathered Amara in my arms, and my heart shattered in a thousand pieces as I looked at the network of dark veins spreading up her cheeks, and down her chest. Throwing my head back, I howled at the moon with the full depth of the despair I felt.

And then I heard it.

Wings flapping in the distance. I jerked my head up to look towards the valley from whence Ranael had arrived the previous time, only to realize the sound was actually coming from behind me. I spun around, and my jaw dropped upon seeing a Gharlakan.

The giant flying creature had a somewhat canine body, although the longer legs and arms could have belonged to a werewolf. The face was vaguely shaped like that of a fox, with the same pointy ears and long snout. However the mouth was shaped more like a beak than a maw. It had no eyes, being guided by ultrasound like a bat. Its wings also could have belonged to a bat except for the fact that they were covered in white fur with specks of blue just like the rest of its body. An excessively long and thick tail trailed behind it with long white and dark blue fur fanning at the tip.

What in the world is a Gharlakan doing here?

These creatures did not dwell in these parts. They preferred the cold weather of the northern regions. But no sooner did that question enter my mind than it answered itself.

The creature made a beeline for us, shifting to its human form even as it landed gracefully before me.

"Lyall!" I exclaimed, shock and hope warring in equal measure within me.

"You foolish pup," Lyall snarled angrily. "Ranael will not come for you."

"It's not for me though!" I argued.

"You cannot summon a demon wolf's protection for another," he snapped. "The pledge is only granted to the summoner."

"But she's dying!" I exclaimed. "He *must* come to her! Ranael granted his protection when she first summoned him. He *has* to know his task isn't complete yet."

The angry look Lyall gave me took me aback.

"Ranael *cannot* heal her," Lyall hissed. "He's not coming back specifically *because* he swore to protect her. Any further interaction with her will only speed up her death. He's protecting her from himself."

"You lie! What you say makes no sense!" I shouted angrily. "He has to bite her a second time to neutralize his venom."

"No, he doesn't," Lyall replied through his teeth. "I told you to rethink the Weaver's words. You interpreted them wrong."

I blinked, my mind racing as I replayed the words Amara told me about her meeting with Cliona Nox.

"The Weaver told Amara that she needed to be bitten by his snake tail, and once the black veins appeared, that she needed to be bitten by his teeth," I said, my eyes flicking from side to side as I searched my memory.

"No, Remus. She never said *his* teeth. The Weaver said 'Ranael's tail and a sick wolf's bite.'"

I froze, my blood turning to ice as the meaning of his words sank in. The intensity of his red gaze dared me to argue the truth I didn't want to accept.

"No," I said, subconsciously shaking my head while taking an involuntary step away from him. "What you're saying isn't possible."

"I'm not saying anything," he countered. "You must reach your own conclusions."

"You're implying that it is *my* bite that she needs. *Me*, the *sick* wolf," I hissed. "But that's not possible. My saliva contains the same venom as his snake tail, but a much weaker version. *You* were the one who made me realize it. So me biting her now won't help her."

"That's correct," he said with an unreadable expression.

"So then it cannot be *me*!" I exclaimed.

My blood boiled with rage when he just stood there without speaking a word, staring at me like he wanted to punch the stupid out of me.

"By Ferazan's blood, just fucking speak already!" I shouted. "Enough with your stupid riddles. Amara is dying! We don't have time for your blasted games."

"I have said as much as I can say, you foolish mortal," Lyall replied angrily. "I am bound by the Covenant. You have all the information you need. Figure it out before it's too late."

I opened and closed my mouth, unsure what to say while a wave of despair crashed over me. With this statement about the Covenant, Lyall confirmed my suspicions that he was either a demigod or one of the Ancients—though I believed him to be the former. They were forbidden to meddle with the lives of mortals if it derailed Fate's plans for us. Breaking the Covenant had dire consequences for them.

"I don't know what to do," I said, defeated while tightening my hold around my mate's unconscious form in my arms.

I gazed upon her beautiful face, my heart shattering. She trusted me so blindly, and here I was utterly failing her because I was too dumb to figure it out.

"Then go back to the source," Lyall grumbled.

I jerked my head up to look at him questioningly. "The source?"

"The Weaver. She's the one who told Amara what to do. Maybe ask her to clarify," Lyall said with an unreadable expression.

"The Weaver is much too far!" I exclaimed, looking at him as if he'd lost his mind. "Even if I killed myself running nonstop the fastest I could, it would take me at least three days. And that would be with me running *alone*! With Amara, it would take at least eight to nine days. She will be dead by then. And even if I were to go alone and return with the answer, the full moon would have risen. And anyway, the Weaver never opened her gates for me."

"You had nothing she wanted back then," Lyall countered with a shrug. "Now, you do."

He gestured with his chin at my mate as he spoke that last sentence. My heart leapt. I indeed had something she wanted. The Weaver never helped someone unless there was something in it for her. She wanted my mate's blood once she was cured. Therefore, Cliona would want to help me save her so that she could get her hands on what would have to be one of the rarest serums in the world once she derived it from my woman's blood.

"You make a good point," I said, licking my lips nervously while I still tried to reflect on a solution to the time issue. "But I still will never make it in time to the Weaver's house while carrying my mate."

"I could fly Amara to her home," Lyall suddenly offered with that same expressionless demeanor. "The manor she inherited would be a relatively short run for you from the Weaver's home."

I gaped at him, hope, anger, and deep frustration warring within me in equal measure.

"Why the fuck didn't you offer that sooner?" I demanded.

"And what about the Covenant? Why can you interfere with this but not with the rest? What are you not telling me?"

His anger flared in equal measure to mine, if not more.

"Stop wasting time with your idiotic questions. I tell you what I can when it is appropriate to do so. I may not be allowed to interfere in the fate of mortals, but I have the right to take a dear friend home. You have until the full moon to figure out what to do. After that, Amara will die. And so help me, if you fail her, nothing, not even the Covenant, will spare you from my wrath."

"You're in love with her," I whispered, more to myself than for him.

He bared his fangs at me, his eyes glowing an angry red.

"The question is do *you* love her?" he snarled.

"Yes, I do," I replied with conviction.

He narrowed his eyes at me. "But do you love her *enough*?"

"What?" I asked, confused.

"Do not be late, pup," he simply replied before morphing back into a Gharlakan.

He towered over me by at least ahead as he stood on his hind legs. Their three segments made him look even more like a were-wolf, if not for his pointy face and bat wings. He took my mate from me, the gentle and careful way with which he cradled her in his arms further confirmed the depth of his feelings for my Flame. Whatever happened, he would go out of his way to keep her safe. As soon as he took flight, I shifted into my wolf form. I didn't gather any of our belongings from the shelter, no food, or water.

I just ran.

CHAPTER 16
REMUS

My muscles burned, my legs had turned to lead, and every breath felt like inhaling shards of glass. Every movement awakened a fresh new pain. I couldn't tell how long I had been running. Night gave way to morning and judging by its position in the sky, the sun would set shortly.

A part of me regretted not grabbing some of our rations before beginning my descent. I was beyond parched. You'd think sand coated my tongue and filled my throat. My stomach cramped, but I couldn't tell if hunger or exhaustion caused it. At the same time, another part believed it had been the right choice. Aside from being lighter without that burden, it spurred me into reaching the valley below even sooner so that I could find some prey to sate my hunger and a source of fresh water to quench my thirst.

But every step was becoming harder, my vision blurring as I attempted to plow forward. In my haste, I nearly lost my footing while navigating the narrow path at the edge of the mountain. I yelped and scrambled to get closer to the jagged rock face of the mountain. To my undying sorrow, I had no choice but to slow down a little to avoid falling to my death.

I couldn't recall entering the last narrow passage in the mountain, let alone collapsing in it. By the time I became aware of my surroundings again, night had fallen. I snapped fully awake, realizing I must have passed out from exhaustion. Considering the current darkness, I slept a minimum of two or three hours.

I inwardly cussed myself out for this wasted time as I set off running again. Obviously, I understood that this rest had been needed and that I couldn't dream of reaching the Weaver's house in one piece if I didn't take a moment to recover from time to time. But I wanted to be a lot closer before I indulged.

I resumed my painful journey with renewed vigor. Finally reentering the safe Storm Hill Valley at the foot of the mountain gave me a jolt of energy. I cut through the forest, catching small prey in the process, which I ate whole as a wolf. Since embracing my human form, I had lost all taste for it. But it was faster to eat it raw than to take the time to skin it and cook it a bit. In the end, all that mattered was to get enough sustenance to fuel the rest of the grueling trek ahead.

Although the few creatures I devoured filled the hole gnawing my insides, the thick blood didn't quench my thirst but increased it instead. With less than a kilometer before reaching the Haunted Woods, I headed a bit farther to the east until I spotted the river in the distance. I made a beeline for it, drinking a bit of water before briefly dipping into it. It helped cool my sweaty, achy body as well as slightly reduce the swelling in my paws.

With much reluctance, I stepped out of the water, taking a final sip before resuming my journey. Less than a hundred meters later, the muffled sound of a panicked female voice reached my sensitive ears. At first, I presumed it to be the deceptive calls of an evil wood spirit attempting to lure me, then quickly dismissed that thought. Not only did the mystifiers never bother with me, but I also hadn't entered the Haunted Woods yet.

Although no clear marker indicated its borders, I knew it to still be at least half a kilometer away. Anyway, you could feel the evil in the very air the moment you crossed the threshold into that foul place.

Despite time being of the essence, I went to investigate, running around the bend to see what the source of the commotion could be. Just as I was circling around a giant tree, I spotted a beautiful woman standing by the water. Her single-horse carriage had left the path and ended up toppling over into the river. From where I stood, her horse was still attached to the carriage and was slowly sinking into the water, trapped by the weight of the vehicle and its harness.

On instinct, I ran towards them. Too busy pulling in vain on the harness to try and get her horse back to the shore, the woman didn't hear me approaching at first. Her cries for help and the splashing of the panicked animal further covered the sound of my steps.

Suddenly sensing my presence—unless she caught movement at the edge of her vision—the woman jerked her head in my direction. She gasped, pressed her palms to her chest, and took a couple of backward steps away from me with a frightened expression. Her milky complexion appeared even paler, making her gray eyes stand out as they widened. But her fear quickly gave way to a mix of awe and hope.

"A Lycan…" she whispered under her breath before waving and projecting more loudly. "Please, help me! My horse is drowning!"

I cursed inwardly. Under normal circumstances, I wouldn't have hesitated. But at a glance, I could see it would require a tremendous amount of time and work to get her carriage out of that precarious situation. Beyond the fact that I couldn't afford such a delay, it would further drain more of the limited energy I had left. Truth be told, in my current state, I doubted I was strong enough to pull the carriage out.

I almost kept going. The way she stepped directly in my path and raised her arms as if to block me indicated that she had guessed my intention.

"I beseech you!" she exclaimed pleadingly. "Don't leave me here like this. I will never make it back to the inn or across the woods back to Kairn on foot and on my own. Help me, please!"

Emitting an aggravated growl, I reluctantly slowed down and approached the water. As per my initial assessment from afar, closer inspection confirmed that there would be no easy way to free her carriage. The front wheels were almost fully submerged, and the right back wheel was sinking at an angle in the mud. The horse was also at an angle, its rump mostly poking out of the water while the front of its body had sunk in to the neck. With the carriage gradually sliding further towards the river, sooner than later, it would drag the animal deeply enough that it would drown.

Without my current exhaustion, I would have been able to pull the whole thing out with some effort. But it would never happen now. I could only rescue the horse so that the woman could ride it back to safety.

My decision taken, I partially shifted into my semi-human form so that I could speak to the woman and more easily handle the task of freeing her mount.

"Your carriage is too deep in the mud. I cannot pull it out for you," I said without preamble. "It will take too much time and strength that I don't have. However, I can detach your horse. At least, you will be able to ride back to the inn or forward to the Hunters Lodge on the other side of the Haunted Woods."

"But my carriage is worth a lot, not to mention all my belongings inside!" the woman exclaimed, crestfallen.

The entitlement in her voice pissed me off. Under my current physical and mental state, I had no patience for anyone's demands. Judging by her elegant black riding outfit, with the long skirt, expensive black boots, and tailored vest, she was clearly well off. A bejeweled pin adorned her long blond hair twisted into an elegant bun, with some braids artistically woven in the mix. So what in Ferazan's name was she doing near the Haunted Woods all by herself? I could think of a dozen different answers to that. My guess would be that she'd been warned against such a reckless endeavor, but she stubbornly decided that no one would tell her what to do.

But that was not my problem.

"Your horse is all you get. Take it or leave it," I hissed.

She recoiled and pressed her palm to her chest with a shocked expression laced with outrage. Yeah, that woman was used to people bowing to her every whim and never talking back.

Annoyed when she failed to respond, I shrugged and turned to leave.

"Wait! Please! The horse! I'll take the horse!" she cried out.

Without a word, I approached the water. However, I couldn't help but wonder what could have caused this accident.

"What drove your carriage off the road?" I asked over my shoulder as I entered the water. "What scared your horse enough that it would stray so much from the path and directly into the river?"

The woman waved her hand in a way that expressed confusion. "Honestly, your guess is as good as mine. I didn't see anything. My horse just reared and started running. But one of the wheels had been feeling off for a little bit. I think it might have been coming loose."

I grunted in response. She did strike me as the clueless type who wouldn't see the truth even if it slapped her in the face. However, as I waded in the water towards the horse's rump to sever the breeching, a sense of unease settled in the pit of my stomach. As I reached for the strap around its hindquarters with my left hand, I extruded the claws in my right hand. Once detached, I would be able to steer the horse by its breast collar back to the shore.

But before I could cut the breeching, the feeling of danger struck me hard. Something was definitely off... terribly wrong even. It took me a moment to understand.

All the scents were off.

Actually, it went beyond that. Although I hadn't come close to the woman, I perceived absolutely no scent from her. Not only didn't she seem to possess the natural aroma every living being did, but I also detected no whiff of sweat or fear that normally emanated from someone in this type of predicament. Her horse also didn't smell right. It didn't have the musky odor I usually associated with large mammals like horses, cows, and deer. Instead, I perceived a subtle scent of rot from it.

The only other smells tickling my nose included the water, mud, grass, and an odd fishy smell I couldn't identify.

"Go on, Remus! Free my horse!" the woman exclaimed when I just stood there frozen.

Remus? How the fuck does she know my name?!

My spine stiffened, and I jerked my head towards the woman. Whatever expression she saw on my face prompted her to drop her mask of damsel in distress. Her gray eyes darkened, turning pitch black as an air of pure malice settled on her face.

She raised her hands and gestured while speaking words of power. Simultaneously, I raced out of the water. Just as I was jumping onto the shore, movement at the edge of my vision had me glancing over my shoulder. My blood turned to ice upon seeing three tentacles shooting out of the water. The crescent moon shaped blades at their tips could only belong to a Tentrian. The first one missed its attempt at grabbing my arm, but the other two wrapped around each of my ankles with deadly accuracy.

They yanked me back with brutal force, stopping my leap forward midair. The shore rushed towards me, and I slammed onto the muddy ground, face down. The impact knocked the wind out of me. The tentacles pulled me back, trying to drag me into the water. Despite feeling dazed, I dug my claws into the ground, fighting for purchase. The strength of the aquatic creature dragged me a few centimeters before stopping. My claws felt on the verge of being ripped out of my fingers as the Tentrian continued to pull.

The four-meter-long creature was shaped like a giant eel, with a long dorsal fin and flowy tail. Normally, it would use the blades at the end of its tentacles—or in the two arm-like appendages on each side of its body—to slice the tendons of its victims so they could no longer fight. Then the three tentacles, which shot out from its mouth, would simply reel in its prey into its gaping maw. That it didn't try to cut me indicated it could sense the poison in my blood.

I kicked and wiggled in a vain attempt to free myself of the tentacles' grasp when a shadow appeared over me, accompanied by that subtle smell of rot and sulfur. My eyes widened when I glanced to the side to see the horse standing next to me, its eyes glowing red, dagger teeth filling its mouth, while a black, leathery skin covered its skeletal frame, with some of the bones left exposed. An illusion had hidden the fact that it was a dread horse. The demonic creature reared on its hind legs, intent on crushing me with its front hooves.

I barely had time to roll out of the way before it stomped savagely where my head had previously been. However, doing so forced me to let go of the ground I had been gripping on to with my left hand. The vicious tugging from the Tentrian made me lose my grip with my right hand. I slid back into the water, the rocks mixed into the mud painfully raking my back. As soon as the water submerged me, the Tentrian swam away from the shore and deeper underwater.

It intended to drown me.

My efforts to free myself only had it wrapping its tentacles even more tightly around my ankles, blocking my blood flow.

Soon, my lungs began to burn, my exertion only depleting me even faster of any oxygen.

Understanding I would soon die, I did the only thing I could think of. I stopped fighting the creature's pull, letting it draw me closer to its face. I doubled over, grabbed the tentacle around my right ankle with both hands, and used it to pull myself even closer. Too late, the Tentrian realized my intention. It attempted to release me and flee, but I held on and sank my fangs into the tentacle, releasing as much of my venom as I could.

But my predator—now turned prey—yanked its tentacles so hard that the one I was biting shredded itself over my fangs. Blood spread in the water even as the creature started thrashing from the effect of my poison spreading through it. In my partially shifted form it was even more potent than if I had been fully human, not to mention the additional enhancement from the looming full moon.

Not sparing the Tentrian another thought, I kicked my feet as hard as I could while swimming back to the surface. As soon as I emerged, I took a huge breath, feeling dizzy and my lungs burning. The angry voice of the witch on the shore had me jerking my head in her direction. She was gesturing again, speaking words I didn't understand as she cast another spell. I took a few more breaths before diving down and swimming underwater a short distance away from her but towards the shore.

As soon as I came out of the water, the woman shouted a single command. I nearly jumped out of my skin when a dozen jagged spear-like roots shot out of the ground. A few more centimeters to the right, and one of the spears would have stabbed me in the leg. I leapt over them, shifting into my full wolf form in the process, and began running towards the forest.

It felt like running through a minefield as more of the spiked roots abruptly shot out of the ground directly in my path, forming a deadly obstacle course. A couple of them grazed me, while one of them literally knocked me to my back. Part of the wooden shard embedded itself in my left shoulder.

I glanced behind me at the sound of a quickly approaching gallop. My heart skipped a beat at the sight of the woman riding the dread horse, steam coming out of its nostrils as they quickly closed in on me.

In my peak form, I might have escaped the demonic steed. But in my current condition, I could never outrun them. The sudden shift in the air, the slimy feel to it, and the nauseating magical energy swirling around me marked the beginning of the Haunted Woods. In my haste to flee my pursuers, I had forgotten we were this close to this accursed place.

Without hesitation, I exited the path and ran deep into the forest. I had no idea what that woman was, but if she was human, she would be reluctant to leave the path. But even as that thought crossed my mind, another even more disturbing reared its ugly head. The woman had no scent... just like Lyall. Could it be him? As a doppelganger, he could take whatever appearance he wanted. Had I been wrong to trust him? Had he played me all along to steal my mate and murder me to take me out of the equation?

But why such an elaborate scheme?

As a demigod, he could easily kill me. I hadn't been able to resist his mystifying powers. His illusion had been so powerful, I hadn't even sensed the magic being used against me. If his goal had been to kill me in a way that could look like an accident or a tragedy, he could have simply created the illusion of a straight path ahead as I ran down the mountain but made me jump to my death over its edge.

A look over my shoulder showed the woman far in the distance still on the path. A wave of relief flooded through me. Lyall had no problem walking through the Haunted Woods. This further proved the witch wasn't him. A part of me had known, but it still helped me breathe better to have this confirmation that he had not betrayed me.

But who the fuck is she? And why try to kill me with such a calculated ploy?

I wanted to go back and confront her, but I couldn't risk it, nor did I have the time to spare. Ignoring the now added pain of my bruised ankles and wounded shoulder, I ran the rest of the journey through this cursed land while remaining inside the forest. As was their wont, the mystifiers and other evil spirits avoided me. By the time I reached the other side, I was beyond wiped out.

In that instant, I finally made my peace with the fact that I had overestimated my strength. Far too many hours of traveling remained ahead of me before I could reach the Weaver's estate. I had no choice but to rest if I were to ever complete the journey on time. My chest constricted painfully at the thought that I might fail my woman. Deep inside, I could feel the shift growing. My werewolf was restlessly pacing, eager to take over. The clock was ticking, and not in my favor.

I thought of lying down right where I stood and sleeping until I could go again, but thoughts of the witch made me reconsider. She hadn't attacked me inside the Haunted Woods but in the safe Storm Hill Valley beyond it. If she had been so bold then, what would keep her from doing the same here in the 'safe' Kairn Valley?

I cursed her to the deepest pits of Hell as I turned to run to the Hunters Lodge. With some luck, it would be unoccupied. But even if someone was using it, I could simply stay within the wide area enclosed by the powerful protective wards that would keep anyone with ill intentions at bay. I hated having to make that detour, which added at least ten more minutes to my journey. But ensuring my safety in my time of vulnerability was primordial if I ever wanted to complete my mission.

Grinding my teeth through the throbbing pain in my ankles and shoulder and ignoring the taste of blood in my mouth and wheezing sound of my breathing, I hastened towards the lodge. I didn't need a doctor to know I had undoubtedly popped some blood vessels in my lungs, which would explain the wet sound that accompanied each breath. As soon as I crossed the invisible wall of the protective wards surrounding the large radius around the lodge, I collapsed to the ground. Darkness immediately swallowed me.

∾

The sound of distant voices pulled me out of my slumber. I felt comatose, my eyelids weighing a ton as I tried to pry them open. Soft hands touched my injured legs and shoulder. My instinctive fight or flight instincts died almost instantly. Although my brain was still too foggy to put a name on the presence surrounding me, the scent was familiar... not comforting, but safe. I vaguely recognized a shaman's chant as the pain in my ankles steadily decreased.

"Remus, where is the woman?" an imperious voice demanded once the chanting ended. "What happened to you? Who did this?"

I opened my mouth to answer, but a whiny sound came out instead. Only then did I realize that I was still in my wolf form. Shifting back to my human form was normally effortless and as easy is breathing. But this seemed to drain all the sliver of energy I had managed to regain in however much time I had been unconscious.

"Friend took Amara home," I slurred.

"What friend?" the voice insisted.

After struggling to open my eyes, I found Rolf looming over me, a concerned look on his face.

"I must go to the Weaver," I said, my voice barely more than a whisper.

"What? Why? What happened to you?" Rolf demanded.

"No time," I replied, annoyed, each word demanding a monumental effort. "Beware the... witch in Haun... ted... Woods."

"What witch? Did she do that to you?"

"Must go... to Weaver. Full moon... soon."

"You're in no condition to travel to the Weaver, assuming she'll even see you," Ulric's voice said sternly.

My heart leapt. I couldn't see him from the angle I was lying in. But he hadn't directly spoken to me in years. How sad that it should happen when I was in no condition to engage with him further.

"I must..."

My eyes rolled to the back of my head, and I went limp. As I hovered in a state of semi consciousness, I heard Ulric utter a string of curses. Something was wrong with me. The lack of food and water, and my extreme exhaustion couldn't explain my current physiological reaction. Something was affecting me. Had the Tentrian poisoned me somehow? The blades at the tips of its tentacles possessed a paralytic that further immobilized its prey after it severed their tendons. But I couldn't recall it cutting me at any point.

I bit its tentacle 'tongue' to set myself free.

Could that be the cause? Had I ingested part of its paralytic or some other form of toxin while injecting him with my own?

Multiple voices started arguing, my mind too far gone to make any sense of their words. Then, two strong arms picked me up, wiping out the wandering thoughts from my confused mind. Moments later, I felt myself getting hoisted onto a horse. Behind me, a muscular chest pressed against my back. A wave of emotion crashed over me at the familiar scent of Ulric.

Although he was now a full-grown adult, feeling him like this brought me back to our youth when we were inseparable. We would take turns carrying the other piggyback.

"I missed you, brother," I slurred, then fainted.

I was in and out of consciousness, gently rocked by the movements of the horse while being held steady by Ulric. My throat constricted when I awoke as we were crossing the bridge leading to the south shore and the main road to Willow Grove. Before I could say a word, my childhood friend extended a thick piece of cured meat. I quietly accepted the offering and barely chewed before swallowing, wolfing it down in only a few bites. He then gave me a water skin which I drained in one go.

"Sorry," I said at last. "I didn't mean to drink it all."

He grunted in lieu of a response. Although still feeling a little weary, the unnatural fog that had knocked me out earlier had lifted. I no longer doubted that the Tentrian injected me with some sort of sedative. I glanced at the sky. We'd been riding for hours as the sun was already very low on the horizon and painting the sky with fiery ribbons of blue, purple, and orange.

"Thank you," I said at last, still facing ahead. "I can never repay you enough for this."

"The woman believed in you," Ulric grumbled reluctantly after a moment of silence during which I thought he wouldn't respond. "Save her, and it will be payment enough."

"Whatever it takes, I will," I promised.

He remained quiet for a moment. "I know you will," Ulric eventually said.

A thick silence settled between us as the horse pursued its journey. More than once, I opened my mouth to try and rekindle the conversation, but words failed me. Half an hour later, Ulric slowed down and eventually stopped the horse.

"This is as far as I can take you," he said in a grumpy tone.

In the distance, I could see the gates to the Weaver's domain. Unless you had business with her, it wasn't a good idea to lurk too close to the entrance. The imps guarding the gates were reputed to not only be powerful, but also viciously unforgiving towards trespassers and unwanted visitors.

I turned to look at him over my shoulder. He wouldn't make eye contact, staring at the horse's mane instead.

"Thank you, Ric," I said, using his old pet name. "I know you don't believe it, but I never meant to hurt you. I loved you then, and I love you still. You were more than a friend or a cousin to me. You were my brother. In my heart, you still are and always will be."

He didn't respond, but his eyes glistened, and he blinked to stem the tears that undoubtedly pricked his eyes.

"I miss you. However long it takes, I will pray to get my brother back," I said softly.

Leaning forward, I kissed his cheek. He didn't pull away, content to remain stiff. And that in itself was a huge win. He might not be ready to acknowledge our bond, but he no longer rejected it. I hopped off the horse, a smile on my face as hope blossomed in my heart.

Tonight, I partially regained a brother. And in a few moments, I could only pray that the Weaver would give me back my mate.

I shifted back into my wolf form and glanced one last time at Ulric.

"Safe journey... Brother," Ulric said.

A powerful howl of joy rose from my throat. He snorted, gave me a sad smile, then turned his horse around. I wanted for him to get off the horse so that we could run as brothers in our wolf form as we used to do as pups. But now wasn't the time. Fate willing, we would do so in the near future.

As I ran towards the massive iron gates barring the entrance of the Weaver's home, the old tension returned with a vengeance. I still ached everywhere, but fear that she would once more turn me away twisted my insides, dominating my thoughts.

If I have to climb over the damn walls, I will.

If it came to that, the guardian imps would attack. But I was past caring. Nothing and no one would keep me from facing the

Weaver and getting the answers I needed. If I had to die trying, so be it.

To my shock and utter relief, the gates swung open when I was still a good hundred meters away. I should be elated. For three decades, I dreamt of this day. But now, only a growing panic filled my heart. What if Lyall had been wrong in sending me here? What if I in fact should have stayed on the plateau and continued my efforts to summon Ranael? What if…?

The sight of the humble thatched-roof house—the cliché witch hut—that appeared at the end of the path threw me for a loop. The Weaver had to be extremely wealthy, if only thanks to the insane amounts people were willing to pay someone of her power. But those thoughts, too, I cast aside as I shifted back into my human form to approach the door.

As I reached for the handle, the door opened on its own, startling me. I took a couple of steps inside, transfixed by the ageless woman sitting behind a table facing the entrance. To her right, a few meters back, sat an imposing spinning wheel. A luminous thread, clearly imbued with great magic, hung by the spindle, waiting to be spun.

Cliona Nox was beautiful and yet terrifying. I couldn't say what intimidated me the most between the intense gaze of her purple eyes with the narrow vertical pupils, the unreadable smile that could be interpreted as mocking or flat out threatening, or the insane power that radiated from her.

While I suspected Lyall to be a demigod, there was no question that the Weaver was a goddess. People speculated that she might simply be one of the Ancients. Although it could be possible, I highly doubted it. No mortal or long-lived being could exude this much power passively. She could probably turn me to cinders with a mere thought.

To my dismay, the Weaver raised an eyebrow the moment I walked in, and blatantly ogled me, the corner of her lips quirking with a mix of amusement and approval. My skin instantly heated with embarrassment as I remembered that I was buck naked before her on our first meeting. The fact that her gaze held no lust didn't lessen my mortification. It was like having your blunt grandmother walking in on you while you were in a compromising position.

I meant to apologize for appearing before her in this state of undress. But completely different words spilled out of my mouth.

"Ranael cannot cure her," I blurted out.

The Weaver took on an unimpressed expression. "Hello to you, too, Remus Beltaine. Won't you have a seat?"

She gestured with her hand towards something to my right, her razor-sharp nails gleaming under the lighting—although claws would probably be a more accurate description.

I jumped at the grinding sound coming from behind me and spun around to see a chair I hadn't noticed by the door gliding on the floor. Moved by an invisible hand, it stopped in front of the table, facing Cliona.

Although I could have used the rest, I lifted my chin defiantly and recklessly took on a harsh tone to demand a response.

"I don't want to sit," I said sternly. "I want answers."

All amusement immediately faded from the Weaver, and she gave me a menacing look that almost made me tremble.

"Sit. Down," she commanded through her teeth in the low, almost whispered voice that implied excruciating pain awaited us if we foolishly failed to comply with an order.

I swallowed hard and quietly obeyed. Beyond the fact that I hadn't nearly killed myself running here only to be reduced to cinders by being stubborn over such a simple request, I also realized that pissing off the person whose help I desperately needed wasn't a bright idea. To my shame, I had to admit that getting off my feet in my still weakened state felt rather amazing.

"Good boy," Cliona said, her ageless features softening back to that taunting expression. "I'd offer you some clothes, but as you will be leaving shortly, it would only be a waste of time."

I squirmed in my seat as her purple gaze glided over me. Once more, it was devoid of any lurid undertone. I felt more like a weird animal being ogled at a local freak show fair. The wretched female clearly enjoyed making me uncomfortable.

"You arrived here much faster than anticipated," she continued. "Well done!"

This time, the mix of approval and admiration audible in her voice and expression as she spoke those words touched me. With a certainty I couldn't explain, I believed the Weaver was rather stingy with praise.

"Time is of the essence," I mumbled.

"It is," she acquiesced. "But you must be parched."

Without waiting for my response, she gracefully rose from her seat—which turned out to be a cushioned stool—and walked to the right side of the room, which had an impressive array of potions, herbs, and various paraphernalia anyone versed in the occult would kill for. Her long silver white hair plaited into a single braid gently swayed behind her, the tip almost brushing the wooden floor. She grabbed a pitcher containing a clear liquid with a very pale purplish tinge and poured a generous portion into a tall glass.

"I'm fine," I said nervously.

Yes, I was beyond parched. But I had heard so many disturbing stories about the Weaver. Who knew what type of magic concoction she was serving me?

She returned, her steps completely silent as if she was gliding over the floor rather than actually walking. The only sound audible in the room was the soft rustling of the golden beige fabric of her floor-length dress. It had a slightly medieval flavor to it with the long sleeves, narrow waist, and fluffy fur around the collar and wrists.

Cliona resumed her seat across the table from me and gave the glass a little push in my direction. My stomach knotted when the glass slid on its own the remaining distance in a way that clearly indicated telekinetic energy propelled it forward.

When a couple of seconds passed without me reaching for it, my hostess' expression hardened again.

"It is extremely rude to refuse the hospitality offered," she said in a cold voice that had my anxiety going up another notch.

My tongue burned with the urge to tell her that coercing someone into doing something they didn't want to was even more rude and poor hospitality. But once more, I reminded myself that alienating her would gain me nothing and only further delay obtaining the answers I desperately needed. Although I had just met her for the first time, I could tell there would be no changing her mind. She wouldn't help me until I complied with her demands.

Bracing for what might follow, I reached for the glass and drank.

My eyes nearly popped out of my head as a powerful moan rose from my throat. Whatever this liquid contained, its taste was divine. The glass was at room temperature in my hand, but the concoction I was drinking was perfectly cool and refreshing. Each gulp felt like the lights of the gods themselves were flowing through my veins, soothing each aching muscles, rejuvenating me, and infusing my body with a level of energy I could not recall ever possessing.

Too soon, I emptied the glass. Feeling bereft, I put it down on the table, wishing I could get a second serving. I licked my lips to catch any drop that might linger there. A soft chuckle had me glancing back at the Weaver. My cheeks burned with mortification as I locked eyes with her. I scrunched my face at her smug expression laced with blatant mockery.

"Isn't it better?" she asked, tauntingly.

"Yes, thank you," I mumbled.

To my surprise, instead of launching into some sermon about

being less paranoid, Cliona switched back to the topic that truly mattered to me.

"Little Amara did very well on this mission," the Weaver said pensively. "You both did."

"She's dying!" I exclaimed.

"She is," the Weaver concurred in a factual manner. "And she will."

"WHAT?!" I shouted, leaning forward in shock and disbelief.

"It was always inevitable," she replied with a shrug.

I gaped at her in anger and confusion. "You said she would live once she received the cure!"

"I said she *might* live *if* she receives the cure," Cliona corrected. "But first, she must die and be reborn. No one can survive Ranael's poison. It *always* kills the infected. You better than anyone knows this."

My mind reeled. A part of me had always known my mate wouldn't be able to survive the poison. Everyone had known, which was why the others refused to escort her on that adventure. I had deluded myself into thinking that somehow it would work out because I needed to believe she would be okay, and that I wouldn't lose her. The dark truth that lurked in the back of my head ever since Lyall told me that Ranael couldn't cure Amara attempted to rear its head again. But I silenced it. I didn't want to acknowledge the reality that the Weaver would soon force me to face.

"But how will she be reborn?" I asked.

The disappointed look she gave me struck me hard. She knew exactly what I was doing, but I wasn't ready. I would never be ready for this...

"Amara will be reborn as your perfect mate, of course," she replied with a hint of irritation. "She's your Twin Flame. It is natural that you should bring her back from death."

"*...bring her back from death...*"

I felt myself pale as those words replayed in my mind. For

244

some stupid reason, I'd assumed that the Weaver would teach me some sort of ritual that would enhance my regeneration abilities, and that my bite would kick her heart back into action. But there was only one way for one such as I to bring back someone from death.

"You want my werewolf to bite her?!" I exclaimed, jumping to my feet.

Unfazed, she gave me an almost bored expression. "It's the only way."

"Amara will be cursed! What the hell kind of life would that be for her?! I will never do this to my mate!" I shouted.

The Weaver waved a dismissive hand. "She will not be cursed. Sit down, and I will explain."

"But—"

"Sit down, Remus. You're wasting my time... and my patience," Cliona said sternly, before casting a meaningful glance at the chair.

I let myself drop back into my chair, back painfully stiff with tension as I tried to make sense of her words. How could Amara not be cursed? A werewolf's bite was unforgiving.

"Amara will not be cursed because you will turn her with love," the Weaver explained in that annoyingly slow and over articulated fashion one did with a particularly difficult child.

"But still with a curse!" I challenged.

She shook her head. "The werewolf curse is merely a poison in your veins. A virus if you like. Just like it did with the poison that was killing your mate, Ranael's venom will attack the virus that makes your werewolf rabid whenever the moon rises. Those toxins will fight and neutralize each other but kill her at the same time."

"But if they neutralize each other, how will Amara be reborn?" I argued.

"The venom will only attack the werewolf virus. It will not touch the regeneration part of it. The metamorphosis causes the host's body to create the right antibodies. As she turns, she will produce antibodies that will make her immune to both the were- wolf's rage virus, and Ranael's poison."

I absentmindedly nodded at her words. Not being overly versed in medical sciences, I couldn't really challenge what she said. Based on what vague understanding I had of it all, her state- ments seemed plausible.

"And once you bond with her, you will exchange fluids," the Weaver continued. "Your bite will not affect her, but hers will cure you of the full moon rage and cleanse your blood of Ranael's poison. You will still be able to inject it through your fangs, but it will now be deliberate and by choice, no longer by accident."

I stared at her in shock, robbed of words. Strangely, instead of feeling elated by her words, an irrational anger surged through me.

"You knew all along how to cure me. And yet, you let me spend years in misery. Why wouldn't you see me all these times I came calling at your gates?" I demanded.

She shrugged. "Beyond the fact that I do not *owe* you my assistance, it also wasn't the right time. Your Flame wasn't sick yet."

"Surely, there has been someone else with—"

"No. It wouldn't work with any other as you wouldn't be in love with them," she said, interrupting me.

"Why does that even matter?" I countered.

"Because you must bite her at the height of your rage during the full moon."

My blood turned to ice. While I had realized she wanted me to bite her as a werewolf, I assumed it would be as close as possible to the full moon, but not at its height when I was a mindless beast.

"You can't be serious?! I will have no control at that moment. I will kill her!" I shouted.

"That's the whole point, you silly boy," the Weaver retorted, looking at me as if she was starting to question my intelligence. "You must simply refrain from killing her in a way where her body is so mutilated that no regeneration would be possible, causing her permanent death."

"How will that even be possible!" I exclaimed. "The entire reason why I lock myself up in a cage with powerful wards is specifically because at the height of the full moon I have absolutely no control. I'm feral, a mindless beast with an all-consuming bloodlust. I *will* permanently kill her."

"You won't if you love her enough," Cliona replied dismissively. "It's the only way at this point."

"I can't," I whispered to myself, feeling devastated as a wave of despair engulfed me.

"Then your Flame will die," she replied with a harshness bordering on cruelty. "And I promise you, Lyall will not let you live it down."

I recoiled, stunned by this unexpected comment.

"You know him?" I asked.

"Mmhmm," she replied in a non-committal fashion.

"What is he?" I asked, unable to silence my curiosity.

The strangest emotion flitted on her features before she took a neutral expression.

"Let's just say that he's… a work in progress."

I opened my mouth to pry further, but an irritated gesture from her hand indicated that this topic was closed.

"Against all odds, you got Amara halfway through her healing journey," the Weaver continued. "She blindly trusts you. Maybe you ought to try trusting yourself a bit more."

"But what if I fail?" I insisted, my insides twisting with apprehension.

I couldn't recall the things I did while enraged. I would get the occasional flash, but the true evidence lay in the insane damage I did to my cells while trying to escape my safe houses.

Against the soft flesh of my helpless mate, I would do untold damage.

To my shock, the Weaver smiled with an almost maternal tenderness that left me speechless. Never in a million years would I have believed her able to display such a sweet demeanor.

"You will not fail, Remus. Clearly, you love her enough to keep her safe. I just told you that bonding with her will cure you of the curse that has plagued your entire life. And yet, you hesitate for her sake, putting her welfare before your own. Believe in yourself. You are not a monster."

That last sentence struck me hard. It echoed the words spoken by my soulmate both in reference to Lyall and me.

"Any advice?" I said at last, defeated.

"Saturate yourself with her scent. When the time comes, it will help pierce through the madness," the Weaver explained. "Keep her in a cool environment—borderline cold even—to help slow down the progress of the poison."

The strangest glimmer sparked in her purple eyes. She appeared to hesitate before carefully choosing her words.

"You might want to burn a banishing soy wax candle. You should find some in her workshop in her house. It will help dim your desire to remain in the room longer than necessary. Light it up a few hours before the full moon rises."

For a reason I couldn't explain, maybe due to the intensity of her gaze as she spoke those words, I suspected this task served another agenda or held some sort of hidden message. But I couldn't figure out what. Before I could pry further, Cliona opened a drawer that I didn't realize the table possessed and retrieved a small golden box.

She placed it on top of the table, then took a golden necklace out of that same drawer. It was very simple, with an oval glass or crystal locket. She pulled one of three strands of what resembled blue hair out of the golden box, then placed it inside the clear locket.

"Here, take this and place it around Amara's neck," the Weaver said, while extending the necklace to me.

I instinctively took it and held it in front of me, studying it with a frown. "What's that strand you put inside?"

"It's a Wraith's hair gifted to me by my daughter," the Weaver replied nonchalantly.

"Your daughter is a Wraith?!" I exclaimed, stunned.

She chuckled and stared at me with that unreadable expression I was growing used to.

"She's more what we call a Planewalker."

Once again, I curbed my desire to pry further. I could sense that she would not give me further details. In truth, I suspected Cliona hadn't actually meant to reveal that it came from her daughter.

"What does it do?" I asked instead.

"It warns of any looming danger. Anytime Amara's life is threatened by a nearby enemy, it will emit a blinding light. But your nose remains your best friend. Use it well," the Weaver said in a mysterious tone that had my frown deepening. "I look forward to seeing you both a week after the full moon. Until then, take good care of your Flame."

A clacking sound resonated behind me. I jerked my head around to find the door wide open onto the warm summer night. When I glanced back at the Weaver, I recoiled at finding her no longer sitting behind the table. She was now in front of her spinning wheel, spooling some glowing golden thread.

Having clearly been dismissed, I quietly rose from my chair. With a soft grinding sound, the chair glided back to its previous position against the wall by the entrance. Turning on my heel, I placed the necklace between my teeth, shifted into my wolf form, and ran into the night to my mate's house.

CHAPTER 17
REMUS

It took me far too long to find Amara's house. Although she had told me about its location before when describing the unexpected inheritance she received from her uncle, my mate hadn't gone into the specifics one normally asked when coming to visit. Thankfully, I remembered a few landmarks she mentioned in passing which helped me eventually reach my destination.

I silently thanked the Weaver as I headed towards the bridge leading to the front entrance of the imposing gothic manor. If not for that incredibly revitalizing drink, I would have struggled to complete the journey. But right this instant, I still felt as good as new, like I hadn't half killed myself coming down from the mountain in record time.

A quick glance around the estate brought a few more questions to mind. We were a bit less than three days away from the full moon. I would need to find a safe area to lock myself in after I completed the impossible task awaiting me. As I wouldn't have time to build a proper shelter able to resist the insane power I gained once in my rabid werewolf form, I would have to settle for a restraining circle.

I only used those in case of an emergency. As I wasn't a mage, the basic version I could create as a layman wasn't anywhere near as powerful as those created by a true arcanist, but it would do the deed. With luck, Amara would have some of the reagents that would allow me to draw a more potent version of the circle. If not, I would have to settle for sand or salt.

The three-story mansion was pitched in darkness, except for the top left room which was illuminated. My heart skipped a beat when I spotted a tall silhouette standing at the left window and looking out.

Lyall…

I could almost feel the weight of his stare on me as I approached the residence. Still, it reassured me that he had kept his word by bringing my mate safely back to her house, and that he stayed to watch over her until my arrival.

I swiftly crossed the bridge and shifted into my human form even as I climbed the handful of stairs up the wide porch. I removed the necklace still clutched between my teeth and reached for the door handle with my free hand. A mixed sense of relief and distress struck me at finding it unlocked. As I stepped inside, a deafening silence greeted me, solely disturbed by the steady tick tock of a large floor standing clock.

Strangely, it didn't have the musty scent of abandoned places. For some reason, I had expected it would be the case as my mate had been gone for nearly a month. But a sweet yet subtle aroma of herbs and spices with a hint of fruit permeated the air. It instantly appeased me. It likely stemmed from the candles or potpourri Amara crafted. I couldn't see any candles burning on the ground floor, not that it mattered right this instant.

I made a beeline for the imposing staircase with an intricately carved wooden railing leading up to the second floor. The light under the door at the end of the corridor to my left drew me irresistibly. I thought of knocking but chose to simply open the door instead. I had made no effort to hide my approach, the discreet creaking of the floors further warning them of my imminent arrival.

My gaze zeroed in on the frail creature lying in the oversized bed propped against the back wall on the right side of the room. I paid no attention to Lyall, who was now leaning against the windowsill facing the bed, and hastened to my woman's side. My heart constricted in my chest as I examined the ravage the demon wolf's venom was doing to her.

I sat at the edge of the bed and caressed Amara's cheek. It burnt with an intense fever. Her previously beautiful brown skin had taken an even grayer shade than when I last held her on the plateau at the top of the Storm Hill mountain. Black veins now crawled even higher up her cheeks, some having reached her temples. They had also spread far and wide on her arms and legs. My Flame was breathing painfully, her body shaken by small tremors. Feeling helpless to relieve her pain, I leaned forward and kissed her lips.

Despite knowing it wouldn't do anything for her right now, I placed the necklace around her neck, carefully adjusting the locket on her chest. Behind me, Lyall moved, reclaiming my attention.

"Interesting gift the Weaver gave you," he said in a tone that sounded slightly sarcastic. "It might prove useful when the time comes."

"So you know what she expects me to do?" I asked with an accusatory edge in my tone.

"Of course," he replied with a shrug. "I hinted as much to you to the extent I could."

The frustrated sound that vibrated through my chest expressed the annoyance I felt having to deal with these half-truths and mind games both Lyall and the Weaver had been subjecting us to. I understood the restrictions they faced, but it didn't make it any less aggravating. Instead of making the detour to Cliona's domain, I could have come directly to Amara's house.

But then I wouldn't have the necklace or been so completely rejuvenated by her drink.

I heaved a sigh, realizing the futility of bemoaning what was and what could or should have been. In the end, everything had a purpose, as intended by Fate.

I glanced at my mate's face—beautiful still even in that terrible state—before refocusing on the doppelganger.

"My task is impossible," I said, sounding defeated. "I love Amara with everything that I am. But once the full moon rises, I stop being Remus. The feral beast that I become has no reason, love, or empathy. It just wants to destroy anything in its path."

"Then you will have to love her more," Lyall replied dismissively.

I snorted and gave him an incredulous look. "If that was all it took, then I wouldn't be dreading the inevitable outcome."

I pressed my lips together as I weighed the thought that had been playing in a loop at the back of my head ever since the Weaver confirmed what I had to do. Lyall raised an inquisitive eyebrow when I gave him an assessing look.

"You love Amara, too," I mused aloud. "More than once, you've done what you could to protect her. So I ask you to do so one more time. Whatever it takes, do not let me kill her. And if it comes to that, kill me first."

Lyall recoiled, and his eyes widened in shock.

"Promise to kill me if needed," I insisted when he failed to respond.

His face closed off as my demand snapped him out of his shock. To my dismay, he shook his head as he once more leaned back against the windowsill.

"I can't," he said as a sole response.

"But you love her!" I exclaimed with outrage. "And don't

give me some nonsense about the Covenant. Surely it cannot forbid you from protecting someone you love!"

A strange expression flitted over his face before he shook his head again.

"The Covenant applies to any mortal who isn't my mate or my offspring," Lyall explained. He hesitated, as if choosing his words carefully. "I can only kill you if you become a threat to me."

"Then see that I become one," I snapped in a commanding tone.

The same strange expression crossed his handsome face before it shifted into something more taunting as he tilted his head to the side.

"Are you so eager to die, pup?"

I repressed the urge to smack him. As aggravating and obnoxious as he could be, I was beginning to suspect Lyall used sarcasm and provocation as a defense mechanism to hide his softer or vulnerable emotions.

"No, but I'm eager to see her live, no matter the cost to me," I replied in a factual manner.

This time, his eyes filled with an unmistakable sadness that he failed to suppress. He glanced at Amara with an air of deep longing before turning his back on me. He stared outside the window, his hands clenching the frame. In that instant, I realized he needed a moment to compose himself. I kept quiet, wondering what thought had provoked such a strong reaction from him.

"Amara wants to live *with* you, not *without* you," Lyall said at last, his voice low and slightly belligerent. "So see that you succeed. I do not wish to explain to her why you had to be put down."

Despite the anger and resentment audible in his voice, my chest warmed for him with a wave of sympathy mixed with guilt. I could never be sorry that Amara was my Twin Flame, but I empathized with the deep sense of loss he had to feel right now. My mate's words also came back to the fore. She was right about him not being a monster. Otherwise, he would have gotten rid of his competition while she was incapacitated and focused solely on his desires instead of putting hers first.

"If I'm to have a chance to succeed, I need to find a safe place to retreat to," I replied in a soft voice. "Ideally, it would be a place of power to enhance the weaker magic of the wards I can set. But an enclosed space with strong walls might also work."

Lyall looked at me over his shoulder with a neutral expression.

"You can try in her workshop," he said. "The magic there isn't very potent, but it would be better than nothing. Alternatively, there are a few fairy circles in the nearby woods, but it will be trickier to get you there once you're mindless."

"Her workshop!" I exclaimed. "The Weaver mentioned that I should get banishing soy candles there to help appease me that night."

"Come then. I'll show you where it is," Lyall offered in a mysterious fashion.

Something in the way he spoke those words struck me as odd. But before I could try to pry further, he grabbed a folded piece of fabric sitting on top of the dresser to his right, framed by the two large windows of the room, and tossed it at me. I instinctively caught it and glanced at it to realize it was a pair of pants.

"First, put these on," Lyall grumbled. "I do not care to stare at your cock all day."

I snorted and complied. As a Lycan, nudity was something we often didn't even pay attention to. But had our roles been reversed, I would also not care to see the man who 'stole' my female from me strutting his assets to my face around the clock.

As I finished buttoning the trousers, Lyall headed out of the room. I followed in his wake as he led me down the first set of stairs to the main floor and turned around to cross the corridor running its entire length. We walked past the living area and formal dining room to the left, and he opened the second door on the right. It revealed a large space—which I suspected previously served as a guest room—but now served as Amara's workshop.

Rows upon rows of shelves occupied the entire back wall. They were neatly organized with sections dedicated to candles, perfumes, soaps, potpourri, and scented oils. On each side of the door, long counters with cupboards contained the various ingredients and reagents used to craft her goods. Some were visible through the glass doors of the cupboards. She had placed her worktable on the left side, propped against the side wall. The wide window above it gave a breathtaking view of the backyard, which had to be a delightful scenery to gaze upon while working.

A large cauldron and a firepit occupied the center of the room. It explained why stone pavers covered the floor of this room instead of the hardwood found everywhere else. A wistful smile settled on my lips as I pictured her hunched over the table as she worked, casting the occasional glance out the window at our pups running around the garden while I hunted.

My gaze roamed over the various ingredients on display. As I inventoried the reagents she possessed, my mind bubbled with the various rare ones that I could acquire for her in remote places few dared to venture into or whose existence they weren't even aware of. As a former outcast—and later on a guide—I had explored far and wide and entered places wiser folks would have avoided. Bursting with excitement, I made my way towards the opposite side of the room where she had grouped her candles based on purpose, from advanced witchcraft to scented and decorative.

Halfway through the room, I froze, a familiar scent I hadn't fully acknowledged, slapping my nostrils with force. It was subtle but undeniable. I sniffed the air, my spine stiffening as I recognized why it had drawn my attention despite the countless aromas in the room, from the herbs, spices, and other fragrant sources.

I jerked my head towards Lyall, a shocked expression on my face. Nonchalantly leaning against the door frame, he was observing me with an intensity I was increasingly growing familiar with.

"Do you smell that?" I asked.

He held my gaze unwaveringly. For half a beat, I thought he wouldn't answer. Then he shook his head.

"No, I don't. What do you smell?" he asked in a neutral tone.

"It's the same scent as Amara's sickness, but it's... I don't know... purer?"

He nodded slowly, his eyes locked with mine, the vertical slit of his pupils appearing even narrower.

"But you knew that, didn't you?" I asked, my anger flaring.

"No, I didn't. But I suspected you might find something here the moment you said the Weaver sent you to fetch something in the workshop. She never speaks pointlessly. Every sentence has a purpose," he said with a shrug.

I growled in frustration then shifted my focus back to the scent. It appeared to emanate from under the cauldron. I moved it out of the way and examined the fire pit beneath but found nothing unusual. As the scent was undeniably stronger the closer I got to the floor, it could only mean that the source lay hidden underneath it. However, try as I might, I failed to find any switch, recess, or lever that would reveal the secret cache.

Seeing the doppelganger idly standing by observing me pissed me off to no end. Was he truly not assisting me because of the Covenant, or did he just enjoy watching me run around like an idiot to no avail?

"Is this damn thing poisoning her again?" I asked, suddenly struck by that frightening thought. "Is it poisoning *us*?"

"You placed the Weaver's necklace around Amara's neck. The Wraith's lock didn't glow. Therefore, she's not in any danger right now. If my suspicions around the source are correct, then it is currently harmless to anyone."

I emitted another frustrated sound before resuming my search. As I doubted Amara would be aware of its existence, I speculated that the switch would be located in a place she was unlikely to frequently interact with. Glancing around the room, I spotted four potential areas, three of which were the vacant spaces beneath the shelves on the right side of the door. They were just high enough to store a pair of shoes.

But the fourth spot called to me the most. It was a heavy piece of furniture, shaped almost like a giant cradle on four legs at each extremity. It appeared to be made of bronze or copper. Either way, it was the type of thing you would hate having to move around, and definitely not something Amara would be able to lift on her own. It contained what resembled various sculpted molds and casings, some made of wood, others out of metal, to give her candles those stunning, unique shapes. Along the edge of the cradle, a single bar on the front and sides allowed her to hang ornate chains and woven strings, which would likely be used on the still warm wax to apply elegant patterns.

Those chains and strings created a curtain that hid a far more accessible space beneath. I headed straight for it and carefully pushed the chains and strings to the side. There was nothing there, the stone pavers on the floor as unremarkable as the others that covered the remainder of the room. Still, I leaned forward to run my hand over the back wall in case there was something I couldn't see from this angle. But as soon as my hand rested on the floor for support, my overly sensitive ears picked up a subtle grinding sound.

I leaned back to look at the floor. None of the tiles seemed loose, the grout filling the gaps seamlessly around each paver. I pressed again, the sound weaker or stronger depending on where

I applied pressure. The tile still didn't move but seemed to be spread over at least six pavers. After a few more attempts, I realized that the sound varied from one time to the next when I pushed again on a given area. It took me a moment to understand that I had to press each stone in a specific sequence.

It made sense as, if a single pressure had been required to activate the switch, it could have accidentally revealed the secret cache simply by moving a piece of furniture. But the sequence demanded a deliberate and calculated effort. Without my enhanced hearing, I would never have noticed this. And even then, not knowing there might be a hidden mechanism, had I simply stepped on it, I wouldn't have paid it much attention and assumed the floor had shifted over time, like the squeaking sounds from the hardwood floors and stairs.

It took me only a few attempts to figure out the combination, the sound steadily increasing from one pressure to the next until a grinding sound in my back startled me. I spun around to see a small section of pavers lowering into the floor next to the fire pit. I hastened there, and my jaw dropped upon seeing a bouquet of reddish flowers. At first, I thought they were Gloriosa flowers, also commonly referred to as Flame Lilies. They were as beautiful as they were lethal. However, their swirling stems and flowy leaves marked them as a different species of plants.

"What the fuck is that?" I asked.

Lyall casually approached, looked inside the small secret nook, then crouched before it to reach for the flowers. On instinct, I grabbed his wrist to stop him while giving him a 'What do you think you're doing?' look. He seemed taken aback by my protective gesture before smirking again in that obnoxious fashion of his.

"Careful, pup. Or I may think you're starting to care about me," he said tauntingly before freeing his wrist from my grasp. "Like I said, if my suspicions were right, then the source was currently harmless. And my suspicions *were* right."

He gathered the flowers then stood back up while admiring them. To my dismay, he lifted them to his nose before deeply inhaling their perfume. He glanced at me and chuckled at my flabbergasted expression.

"These flowers are called Lover's Blight. They're the netherworld's version of the Flame Lilies," he explained casually. "And they are indeed what caused Amara's sickness."

"So why are you saying they're harmless right now," I asked, my voice thick with tension.

"Because they only become lethal once they are burnt," he said, glancing at the fire pit. "Great heat causes a chemical reaction within them, which then releases an odorless toxic fume. Otherwise, they're just pretty decorative plants that you can safely breathe in."

"So the fumes would be released every time Amara melted wax in her cauldron," I whispered in shocked understanding. "But who would do this? And why?"

He stared at me without answering. I clamped down on the urge to claw his pretty face off and returned my attention to the flowers. I frowned as another thought crossed my mind.

"If the flowers must be heated or burnt to release the fumes, these ones should be shriveled up. But they look fresh," I challenged.

"Quite fresh," he concurred. "Whoever is doing this still has access to the house and replaced the flowers in her absence. My guess is that they were brought here three or four days ago, right before I arrived with Amara."

"If you suspected all this, why didn't you search the house?" I spat angrily.

He gave me a bored and annoyed look that pissed me off further.

"How many times will I have to remind you that I am bound by the Covenant? For what it's worth, although I suspected these would be inside the house, I thought they would be in the kitchen or by the hearth in her bedroom. Putting it here instead was clever and diabolical."

I mumbled a series of curses at that wretched Covenant and their stupid mind games.

Lyall chuckled. "For what it's worth, we're just as frustrated to have anything or anyone dictate what we can and cannot do."

I grunted in agreement before glaring at the flowers still in his hand.

"So how do I destroy these wretched things without causing further harm, since they can't be burnt?"

He shrugged. "You could feed them to the horse. Like I said, they're entirely safe until exposed to great heat."

"That's a great idea," I said, relieved it wouldn't involve some convoluted ritual as I already had my hands beyond full.

"I can take care of it for you if you wish," Lyall offered, throwing me for a loop.

"That... that would be kind of you," I said, surprised.

He gave me a stiff nod then walked out of the room quietly. I stared at the open door, listening to the soft shuffle of his feet slowly fading while trying to make sense of that strange male and the surreal situation I had found myself in. Shaking my head, I made sure there was nothing left in the secret cache before using the hidden switches to close it again.

Browsing through the inventory of candles, I quickly found the banishment soy candles the Weaver suggested I used. However, as I turned back to reexamine the room, it became clear that I could never use the workshop as my safe holding cell. Even if I moved the cauldron and drew the magic circle in a wide radius around the fire pit, I still ran too great a risk of trashing the place during my madness or even just trying to get into the circle.

With the three candles tucked under my arm, I exited the workshop and opened the door we had walked past on our way here. As I had hoped, it revealed another staircase leading to the basement. To my dismay, it wasn't the dark and damp place I expected to walk into, but a properly isolated and illuminated space that had been divided into what could eventually serve as additional guest rooms—although they currently stood empty. One of the rooms was used as food storage and larder.

It was a thick metal door at the back that rekindled a glimmer of hope. It wasn't locked, although a heavy key hung on a nail nearby. Surprisingly, the door didn't squeak and whine as I thought it would but quietly opened on its well-oiled hinges. My heart soared when I stepped into what must have been an old cellar. It sat empty with thick brick walls, an elevated arched window with decorative forged iron bars. Cool, not quite damp, it would be perfect for my purpose.

I placed the candles on the floor and raced back to the workshop, which contained everything I needed to set up the wards, including reagents that would enhance its magic. I made a mental note of all that I plundered so that I could replace them once this ordeal was over. Without delay, I returned to the cellar and drew the circle, runes, and the wards that would keep me trapped until I regained control of my mind and senses.

The beauty of this circle was that I could freely enter, whatever state I found myself in. But I couldn't leave so long as it detected that I was feral or enraged. The challenge was to enter it after the full moon had arisen. Normally, I would enter the circle or my safe location at least a couple of hours before it did The thought of what could happen that night twisted my innards. The only things that gave me hope were the Weaver's confidence in my ability to pull this off, and having Lyall as a backup.

Although the doppelganger hadn't promised to take me out if I became a real threat to my mate, I knew at a visceral level that he wouldn't sit idle while Amara was being slaughtered. After giving one last look at my work, I exited the room, feeling satisfied, and headed back to my Flame's bedroom.

I found an appropriate position for each of the three candles, snuffed out the fire in the hearth, opened the windows, and stripped Amara out of the thick nightgown she'd been wearing. As it wasn't the outfit she'd initially worn when Lyall took her from me to fly her home, I tried to silence the instinctive jealousy I felt at the thought he had seen her naked while changing her clothes.

In a way I couldn't explain, I genuinely believed he wouldn't have taken advantage, done it in an inappropriate fashion, or acted with questionable motives. Amara and I traveled up the mountain for a few days without access to a body of water to bathe in. Then we slept outside for a few more days while she was drenched in sweat from her extreme fever. Putting her in bed as is would have been worse.

I carried her to the adjoining bathroom and gave her a bath, using colder than lukewarm water. Seeing the full extent to which the venom was spreading broke my heart. How would she survive two more days of this? I carefully dried her body then dressed her in a much lighter nightgown. Hearing her distressed moans as I cared for her tore me apart. Surely there was something I could do to alleviate some of her pain? That she remained unconscious didn't mean she didn't feel all of this as indicated by her tense features and the sounds she emitted.

Moments after I brought my mate back to her bed, Lyall's footsteps resounded loudly in the hallway. I realized he was making sure I was aware of his imminent arrival. Once more, such considerate behavior clashed with the cold and heartless image he initially projected and that was standard for members of his species. As if to further fuel my confusion, he knocked and waited for me to bid him come in before entering.

His eyes didn't have the same intense red as was the norm for him. They had taken a much paler hue that was edging towards purple.

"Nice work you did downstairs," he said the minute he walked in.

For some dumb reason, that compliment from him touched a sensitive cord deep within that hungered for some form of paternal approval. It was all the crazier that I considered Lyall as I would any other male within my age range. Then again, as a demigod, chances were he had already lived a few hundred years by now.

"Thank you," I said, feeling shy. "I want to further reinforce the door in the morning, just in case my wards don't hold as well as I hope."

He nodded before glancing at my mate, the cold hearth, and the open window. Although he didn't comment or look at me strangely, I felt the irrational need to justify my actions.

"The Weaver recommended I keep her cool as much as possible."

Once more, he didn't respond and merely tilted his head to the side as he silently observed me.

I shifted on my feet, looking for my words. "Thank you for everything you've done to help me with Amara. We never would have made it without you."

He clenched his teeth and grunted in response. I couldn't tell which emotion dominated on his face between sadness, anger, and resignation. They shone through despite his great effort at plastering a neutral expression on his face.

"I just wish—"

My voice trailed off as a thought suddenly struck me. I looked at my woman before staring back at Lyall.

"I would have one more favor to ask of you," I said in a hopeful voice that piqued his curiosity, although he observed me with a guarded expression. "As you can see, Amara is semi-conscious and in pain. Would it be possible for you to pull her into a happy illusion? The one you trapped me in was so realistic. If you could do something similar, but without her getting chased by something evil, I would be eternally in your debt."

Lyall gaped at me, visibly stunned by my request. In that

instant, I realized that thought never even crossed his mind. To my delight, he didn't say a word and merely nodded. Seconds later, the lightning shaped streaks under his skin glowed lightly, and my mate went silent. All tension drained from her beautiful face. If not for the dark veins and the grayish hue to her skin, you would think she was peacefully sleeping.

CHAPTER 18
AMARA

My eyes fluttered as I felt myself floating on a cloud. I couldn't recall the last time I wasn't in deep pain or agony. For what seemed like an eternity, my world had been nothing but an endless torture with my body burning as if I had been cast into hellfire. I blinked at the bright light blinding me before realizing the cloud was in fact the most divine mattress I had ever lain on.

I stretched, emitting the least ladylike grunt, then let my limbs fall back down on the heavenly cushion feeling almost too groggy to get up. Still lying down, I peered at my surroundings, stunned to find myself in a magnificent room. It looked like an ancient Roman palace with insanely high ceilings, sculpted columns, and countless tall windows with long, sheer, white curtains. Straight ahead, at least ten meters away from the bed, a giant set of French doors stood open onto what seemed to be a massive terrace or balcony.

I slipped out of bed, the beige stone tiles feeling lukewarm beneath my bare feet. The long flowy white dress I was wearing gently caressed my skin with each step as I headed towards the balcony. Only then did I realize this had to be some sort of palace in the sky or at least located very high in the mountain as I could see an endless valley sprawling far below.

But it was Lyall, leaning against the railing and looking down at the valley, who claimed my attention. As with my previous encounters with him, he was bare chested with a white skirt draped around his waist. This time, it fell to his ankles unlike the knee length one he wore the first time we met. He turned around as I approached and smiled at me with a deep affection laced with sadness that turned me upside down.

"Lyall," I said as I closed the distance between us.

"Hello, Amara. It is good to see you awake," he said in a gentle voice.

"Where are we?" I asked, glancing around us at the imposing temple-like palace, and breathtaking landscape surrounding us.

"This is my home in Nephilim Valley," he said wistfully. "I have not been here in far too long."

I slightly recoiled. "Nephilim? Are you an angel?"

He snorted and shook his head with an amused expression. "No one would *ever* call me an angel. I'm a doppelganger."

I huffed. "You're much more than that, and we both know it."

He smiled, his expression softening. Although he didn't answer, I took it as confirmation and chose not to press him further. We were all entitled to our secrets.

I walked up to the railing made of intricately carved stones and leaned forward to glance at the valley at an insane distance below. It looked as if a village had been established down there. To the left and right, other impressive mansions protruded from the mountain face.

"I always understood that Nephilims were angels, or rather the hybrid children of humans and angels. Is that why they named this place like this?"

"You could say that. Not all Nephilims have wings. Originally, they moved into the valley while their parents settled in these mountains so that they could be close to their offspring. But now, you have a great variety of people living here. You have angels, demons, fallen, cambions, and even grim reapers."

"Wow! That is quite the eclectic society!" I said, impressed before a disturbing thought entered my mind. "How am I here? Did I die?"

He rested his elbow on the railing as he leaned against it and looked at me with a strange expression.

"No, Amara. You're not dead yet."

"But I'm dying," I insisted.

"Yes, you are," he said in a sympathetic tone. "It is inevitable."

My shoulders slumped, and a wave of sorrow washed over me. Long before I embarked on this journey, I had made my peace with the fact that I wouldn't survive it. Meeting Remus changed everything. I didn't fear dying. I just dreaded what it would do to him to be once again left behind while someone he cared about died to the Cursed Demon Wolf's venom.

"So this is an illusion?" I asked with sudden understanding.

He nodded. "The pup suggested I take you here so that you wouldn't suffer unnecessarily in the real world."

My heart melted with love for my mate. Once again, he was proving that he would do anything to make me happy or make my life easier. I stared at Lyall with a pleading look.

"Please, look after Remus for me when I die. He will be devastated."

All softness vanished from his face, tension and a hint of anger brewing under the surface.

"He's still fighting to save you," he grumbled.

I blinked in confusion. "Fighting? But you said—"

"I will let him explain everything to you. I *hate* your mate. Every fiber of my being wants to kill him," he said angrily, taking me aback. "If not for you, I probably would have. For all that, he has earned my respect."

I stared at him for a few moments. It took everything in my power not to challenge his words. Despite what he said, I knew at a visceral level that he didn't actually hate Remus. I just felt guilty to be the cause of the sadness he felt.

"Remus is a good man," I said softly.

He made an indistinct sound that could be both an angry growl and a grunt of assent.

"He would gladly die to save you, thus why he has earned my respect," Lyall said reluctantly.

But my mind remained stuck on the first half of that statement. "Don't let him die!" I exclaimed. "Whatever mad plan he's putting together, please protect him. I don't want to live without him."

I flinched inwardly even as the words left my mouth. As much as I meant them, I could have been more sensitive in my wording not to further twist the knife in the wound.

"I'm well aware of that," he said in a clipped tone, although I didn't miss the pain in his eyes.

He turned his back to me and rested both hands on the railing, his claws extruding as they sank into the stone.

"You know, I would have died for you, too, Amara," he said bitterly as he stared in the distance. "I could have offered you a much easier and far-less-painful path than the one you are treading."

"I know, Lyall," I said in an appeasing tone. "But we both would have regretted it later. You have a good heart. Somewhere out there, your soulmate will find you and will see what a wonderful male you are."

He jerked his head to the left to glare at me over his shoulder. "Really? *You* see my *good heart,* and yet you don't want me. So why would that hypothetical soulmate?"

"Because she will be destined to you!" I countered in a soft but firm voice. "I belong to another. It is how Fate intended things to be."

"Why did the Weaver send you to me only to take you away?" he asked angrily, his eyes going out of focus. "Is that her way of punishing me?"

"No, Lyall. She's not punishing you. She blessed me and Remus by putting you in our path," I said with fervor. "Your good deeds will be rewarded. Karma will repay you a thousandfold."

With a will of its own, my right hand settled on his cheek in a comforting gesture. Lyall turned to face me and pressed his hand to the back of mine, leaning into my touch. My heart shattered as he closed his eyes, his face taking on an air of deep pain and sorrow. It lasted but a few moments. He released me and took a couple of steps back, his face suddenly devoid of any emotion. I almost wondered if I had imagined this brief display of intense vulnerability.

"I will bring your mate to you," he said in a conversational tone before waving at our mesmerizing surroundings. "You have free rein here. Whatever you imagine or desire will happen. If you want to have wings and fly, visit an exotic place, or enjoy a feast fit for a king, you only have to wish it. Fear not, I will not spy on you."

Before I could respond, Lyall vanished. Half a beat later, Remus appeared in his stead, looking utterly confused.

"Amara!" he exclaimed the moment he noticed me.

I threw myself into his arms. He effortlessly picked me up and spun us around as we kissed. When he stopped twirling, he didn't put me down but kept me in his arms, my feet dangling above the floor. Arms wrapped around his neck, I feasted my eyes on his beautiful face.

"By Ferazan, this feels so real!" he whispered to himself.

"It's an illusion by Lyall," I explained softly.

His eyes widened in shock, then his face took on an air of disbelief laced with gratitude.

"What do you know... That doppelganger never ceases to

amaze me. He brought you here so that you wouldn't feel pain. I was sleeping next to you when I got pulled here. I thought this was just a much nicer dream. Seems like I will have to thank him for yet another thing."

"Yet another thing?" I echoed with curiosity.

"Mmhmm. I have a lot to update you on," he said with a grim expression.

He took my hand and led me to one of the three sets of comfortable couches on the immense terrace. He sat down then pulled me into his lap. I snuggled against him, my fingers absentmindedly playing with the short hair on his chest.

He launched into a detailed recounting of everything that happened after Ranael's snake tail bit me. The way he's been killing himself trying to run back freaked me out, but I nearly lost my mind upon hearing about his encounter with the witch.

"By the Gods! Why would she attack you?! Who was she?" I exclaimed.

"I don't know," Remus replied with frustration. "Although I have my suspicions. She was tall, slender, with very pale skin, and long blonde hair."

"Any particular feature, like a scar or birthmark?" I asked, disappointed when he shook his head with an apologetic look. "Sadly, I meet a lot of people in my trade. Pale, slender women with blonde hair are a dime a dozen when it comes to witches and arcanists, especially necromancers. I have encountered tons of them since moving to Willow Grove."

He nodded with a grim expression. "I figured as much. But I wonder if she could be the person attempting to poison you. It seems awfully convenient that such an unprecedented attack should occur right when I was racing back to Willow Grove to get the final instructions to cure you."

I pursed my lips, unconvinced. "That seems like a stretch and overly elaborate just to get rid of me. I am no one."

"Well someone disagrees enough with that statement that

they built a secret cache in your workshop. They regularly snuck inside your house to place a fresh supply of Lover's Blight in it so that its toxic fumes would slowly kill you every time you used your cauldron."

That left me speechless. Who could possibly hate me and my family so much? As far back as I dug into our family's history, we never made enemies. Sure, we had some of the usual neighborly spat, but nothing that would trigger the type of vendetta to kill my father and now me. Not to mention the remote possibility that my uncle, too, fell victim to that witch.

"Do not fret, my Flame," Remus said reassuringly as I remained stunned. "We have removed all of the Lover's Blight from your house. I inspected every room to make sure there weren't any other stashes elsewhere. Lyall is in the house, so no one can sneak in unnoticed. I have sent a raven to Misty. She will have one of our shamans come to the house to set the same types of protective wards erected around the Hunters Lodge. No one with ill intentions will ever be able to enter your house again."

"Thank you," I whispered with sincere gratitude.

He resumed his accounting of events. Learning of the unexpected assistance that Ulric offered him knocked the wind out of me. Although I had sensed that a deep hurt fueled Ulric's brutal comments about Remus and his efforts to undermine him, I never expected this sudden turnaround. He hadn't struck me as malicious, as he had been honest saying that he didn't believe Remus would force himself on me once we were alone. But I thought his resentment was running too deep to allow him this act of kindness. I wanted to believe this would mark the beginning of the rekindling of their past near brotherhood.

"You seem unsurprised," Remus said with a frown in light of my stoicism after he revealed what the Weaver told him about how to cure me.

I gave him a sheepish smile. "I found out seconds before Ranael's snake tail bit me. Frankly, it embarrasses me that I didn't figure it out sooner. The worst part of it all is that when you first mentioned that you were a sick wolf, I remembered the Weaver mentioning that. But I dismissed that thought before it could fully form because I didn't think you had the type of virulent venom that I would require. I never truly analyzed it like that, but I think my subconscious did. I just hate putting you in that position."

"You can't blame yourself for that, my mate. I should have figured it out as well, not to mention that Lyall had also alluded to the fact that we were misinterpreting the Weaver's words when he first abducted you."

"We were both silly. But at least now we know what to do."

"The other good news is that, according to the Weaver, bonding with you after you are healed will heal me as well."

I startled myself with the high-pitched squeal that tore out of me. "I KNEW IT!! I knew the Weaver would help cure you! I can't believe that it will come from me. But it's only right as my cure will also come from you. We were truly fated."

To my shock, instead of rejoicing with me, Remus appeared distraught.

"What's wrong? Is there a potential complication?" I asked warily.

"It's just that... I'm scared, Amara. You know that I love you and would never hurt you, right?" he asked, his eyes flicking between mine.

"Yes, I know that," I said in all sincerity.

"But my werewolf—"

"Don't, Remus," I said sternly, interrupting him. "I trust you. I fully trust you. We haven't come this far to fail now. Do not feed the beast by wallowing in uncertainty. Manifest the positive outcome we both want and deserve. No one could have gotten me through this but you. And I have complete faith that you will bring me back from the other side. It is fated."

"My love," Remus whispered before capturing my lips in a passionate kiss.

We remained for a while in each other's embrace, just savoring this moment of peace and intimacy. Although Lyall had given me free rein to manipulate this dream world and travel wherever my imagination wished, Remus and I decided to pass on that offer. Instead, we focused on each other and the future we wanted for ourselves. Now was not the time to be distracted by pretty places. All that mattered to me was to infuse myself with my beloved mate's presence.

CHAPTER 19
LYALL

I flew in circles over Amara's house for hours. Although I doubted any danger would come to Amara and the pup, I stupidly felt duty bound to remain here until she was cured. Every time I would zoom past her bedroom, the urge to go inside and slaughter her pet swelled within me. Fate had it wrong. Amara should be mine.

The taste of her memories never faded from my tongue. I wanted to bite her again to bask in the perfection that she was. How could a mere mortal possess such a beautiful soul? My chest ached remembering how she caressed my cheek on my balcony. I could still feel this softness of her palm on me. The tenderness in her eyes as she gazed upon me stabbed at the deep longing that tore me apart for her.

If not for that wretched wolf, she would have fallen in love with me.

Once again, I fought the urge to yield to my base instincts and slit his throat. Yes, Amara would be devastated by his death, but I could easily fill her mind with happiness. In fact, I could kill him and take over his appearance. She would be none the wiser. Before, I couldn't fool her since I had never tasted his blood. But now, I knew every single memory he shared with her, everything that he was, even down to his scent.

She would never know, and she would be mine…

I completed another circle around the house and hovered in front of her window. The usurper was cuddling against my female peacefully sleeping while enjoying the paradise I had created for her. It should be me showing her the wonders of both the human realm and the netherworld.

I landed on the windowsill and seriously weighed the pros and cons. A few weeks ago, I wouldn't even be debating. The wretch would be long dead. But Amara's blood changed something in me. She had awakened what she would describe as a softer side that I deemed a shameful weakness. I didn't want to admire the selfless devotion he showed her. I didn't want to hold myself back to honor her personal desires.

My whole life, I always indulged in whatever I fancied. If I wanted to kill, I did. If wreaking havoc, causing chaos, and spreading fear and terror was my latest form of entertainment, I would dive headfirst into it until I got bored or a new interest claimed my attention.

And this was the main reason I was now holding myself back.

Was Amara just the latest fleeting passion burning within me? Would I tire of playing house with her in a few weeks or months? The nagging voice at the back of my head swore that this was different. I would love her always. Moreover, I could give her the type of life the pup never could.

But what if the voice is wrong?

The old me wouldn't have cared. Whatever happened, happened. And if she got hurt in the process, oh well, such was life. But I couldn't bear the thought that I would be the cause of any sorrow or distress Amara could feel. To add insult to injury, her words still echoed deeply in my mind. As much as I wanted her to be mine, Fate had decided otherwise. Creating an illusion where she would happily share her life with me would only be poisoned in the long term. I wanted her to love me for me, not because I made her believe she did.

We both deserved better.

And as much as I resented the Lycan, I didn't truly want to harm him. In a different world and a different time, I might have wanted a friendship with him. He showed me the type of trust no one had ever given me before. He left in my care the one thing he valued more than his own life. And then thanked me with a genuine gratitude that still rankled.

Nine Hells, how I hate him!

Ignoring the mocking voice at the back of my head calling me a liar, I flew back to the entrance of the house. Less than thirty minutes remained before the moon would reach its full phase and the shitshow would begin. With heavy steps, I climbed the stairs to the second floor. I entered the room and went directly to Remus. Silencing the less-than-charitable thoughts crossing my mind, I picked him up and carried him to another room at the opposite end of the hallway.

Saying that I didn't consider tossing him over the railing or letting him tumble down the stairs would be a lie. Obviously, Amara wouldn't have approved. But there was no crime in entertaining the idea. I dropped him unceremoniously onto the bed then walked out of the room, closing the door behind me. Whatever my feelings about the situation, letting him awaken in his werewolf form next to Amara held too high a risk that he might instinctively kill her before he could at least try to get his feral nature under control.

As I approached Amara's bedroom, all thoughts of the Lycan vanished from my mind as I felt a foreign presence seconds before I even entered her room. My heart skipped a beat when I saw Pharos standing by the bed. Ominous with his black wings, dark hood which partially covered his face, and the bones of his ribs protruding through the skin, the Angel of Death was looming over my woman.

"Why are you here?!" I demanded angrily as I marched towards the bed.

He lifted his head and gave me an amused smile. His red eyes sparkled with mischief as he raised an eyebrow in a way that implied I'd asked a silly question. As all the other Reapers, be they Angels of Death like him, or Grims like our brother Haroth, Pharos's eyes were a little sunken, the skin around his eyes receding to leave the bones exposed, not to mention the three bone spikes that jutted out of his chin.

He was as handsome as he was scary.

"Hello to you, too, little brother," Pharos responded mockingly. "And you know perfectly well why I'm here. Amara will be dead in the next few minutes."

"It may be so, but you can't take her!" I exclaimed, outraged. "She is to be reborn!"

He gave me the obnoxiously soft and appeasing smile he normally reserved to the dying to comfort them before he escorted them to the other side.

"Yes, Lyall. She is *hopefully* to be reborn. Whether or not it occurs, it won't be right away," he explained in a gentle voice. "It takes a few days for the mutation to be completed. Amara's soul must go to a safe place in the meantime."

"The dead don't return once they've crossed over!" I argued angrily.

He gave me an indulgent smile as he nodded. "If they go to the afterlife, then yes, you would be correct. But Amara is going to Erebus. It is not limbo, but just an in between for people in special circumstances. Charon will find a nice place for her to wait out her rebirth."

I scrunched my face, fighting the urge to argue some more. In a way, the aggravation I felt stemmed more from the fact that I knew better but had allowed panic to cloud my judgment. Hell's breath, how pathetic I had become over a woman who didn't even want me... Charon, the Ferryman of the dead, would indeed find a beautiful place for her soul to wait until her body was ready for her return. I still hated the thought that she would be taken to a place where I couldn't follow or rescue her from.

"Fine," I grumbled at last.

Pharos chuckled in a way that immediately had my hackles up.

"What's so funny?" I asked with irritation.

"It is good to see you finally care about someone else more than yourself," he said softly.

I bared my fangs at him, which only made his smile broaden, pissing me off further.

"For all the good it did me," I growled bitterly.

My brother shook his head at me as if I was a lost cause.

"It did, you fool! It did you an incredible favor," Pharos countered.

"How?" I challenged angrily. "By making me ache for what I can't have?"

"By saving your life," Pharos said, his voice and face hardening.

I recoiled, shocked by his statement. While Reapers and Angels of Death were not bound by truth like doppelgangers and demon wolves, Pharos had never been one to lie or prone to exaggeration. He always meant what he said. And this time again, I didn't doubt that he did.

"You were going down a dark path, Lyall," he continued mercilessly. "Remember that I can see everyone's life thread. You, little brother, were headed towards an early demise. Amara gave you the opportunity to choose a different path. Luckily for you, you did. Your lifeline is no longer stunted."

To say that these words struck me hard would be the understatement of the millennium. I could be arrogant and cocky to the point of sometimes thinking myself invincible. As so few things can harm me, I often acted recklessly. My own mortality was never something I even contemplated.

"Maybe that would have been a blessing," I surprised myself muttering. "What's the point of an empty life once you've tasted happiness? There's a reason she doesn't want to live if he doesn't."

"I want to smack you so hard right now," Pharos said with an irritation that stunned me. "Stop being a spoiled brat. You have no idea how many wonderful paths have opened up for you in the past few weeks. And one of them holds your happily ever after. But you must stay the course. Mother gave you exactly what you needed by sending Amara your way."

"But stay the course for how long?" I demanded, annoyed with how whiny I sounded as I asked the question.

"However long it takes," he said with a shrug.

"I already waited two hundred and fifty years! How much longer must I wait?!" I exclaimed.

My brother rolled his eyes, the effect made even more uncanny in his partially skeletal face.

"I already waited two hundred and fifty years!" he repeated in an obnoxiously entitled voice. "So fucking what? You call Remus a pup but seem to forget that so are you. Remember that I am three times your age. I was trapped in the pure hell of Cornelius's mind for double your lifespan before Mother freed me. And you have the nerve to complain about being lonely while enjoying your freedom?"

I scrunched my face, properly chastised.

"Get over yourself and count your blessings," he concluded sternly.

I muttered an apology—another rare occurrence for me. Of all my siblings—and I had far too many to count all sired by different fathers—Pharos was one of the few I had the closest relationship with. Ranael used to be my conscience until he was taken from me.

Pharos placed a hand on my shoulder and gave it a comforting squeeze.

"Take heart, Brother. Mother killed two birds with one stone. There was no one better than you to help save Amara. By saving her, you bring our brother Ranael closer to his own freedom. Mother took a big leap of faith in you. And you came through for all of us including our brother. I'm proud of you."

'I'm proud of you...'

Those were not words spoken often about me, if ever. I huffed and shrugged to hide how deeply his words touched me. Not fooled in the least, my brother's smile broadened, which further annoyed me.

I was looking for an appropriate snarky remark when I felt a ripple at the back of my head. It took me a second to realize that Remus had escaped my illusion. Normally, it would be nearly impossible for pretty much anyone, even demigods like me. But there was one of very few things that trumped my powers.

I glanced out the window at the full moon. At the same time a terrifying howl rose a far-too-short distance away.

"You have one of the most important decisions of your life to make, my brother," Pharos said in a soft voice. "Stay the course."

He gave my shoulder a gentle squeeze then walked to a dark corner of the room, his gait so fluid he appeared to glide over the wooden floors, as Mother often did when she moved from her spinning wheel to her table. He then faded into the shadows, making him completely invisible. Although I couldn't see him, our blood bond allowed me to continue to sense his presence. He would remain a silent observer until the time came to reap Amara's soul.

My back stiffened upon hearing the crashing sound of a door slamming open. I silently moved to the opposite corner of the room, closer to the head of the bed, and partially morphed to also blend with the shadows.

My chest constricted as I gazed upon Amara's peaceful face. Even with the dark veins marring her body and the now ashen color of her skin, she remained breathtakingly beautiful. I couldn't do much against what would happen next, but I could spare her the pain of death. By keeping her in the current illusion, she wouldn't suffer through her passing.

My pulse picked up, and my spine tensed as the thumping sound of clawed paws grew nearer. A menacing growl resonated right outside the room before the door burst open. It took everything in me not to lunge at the creature that stepped in.

Standing on two legs, claws extruded, vicious fangs bared, the werewolf stood in the doorway, white foam clinging to the corner of its maw. Unlike when a Lycan partially shifted, the werewolf didn't have a recognizable human face. He fully had a wolf head with a much larger jaw, crazy glowing red eyes, and elongated arms. The only thing he still had in common with the pup, was the color of the short fur covering his body, and his long fluffy tail

Aside from that, Remus was nowhere to be found in this beast.

CHAPTER 20
REMUS

I fell out of a place I didn't quite understand and back into my body. Pain engulfed me as I evolved from my weak form into an apex predator. I welcomed it, embraced it. Soon, it would allow me to sate the endless hunger in bloodlust that whipped my blood.

Even before I finished shifting, the sound of my bones cracking and reshaping themselves still popping in my ears, I limped towards the door, my gait straightening as I completed my transformation. All thoughts of running wild and hunting the countless prey begging to be savaged by me ended the moment I opened the flimsy door that sought to keep me imprisoned in this room.

The most irresistible scent lured me to a room just a few steps away. A hunger like no other immediately twisted my insides. Saliva flooded my mouth, and blood pumped in my veins as anticipation increased my heart rate.

I reached for the door handle. My need for violence felt cheated when I found it unlocked. That didn't stop me from slamming it open. It smashed against the wall with a cracking sound as some of the wood splintered under the strength of the impact.

It pleased me.

I almost used my claws on it to shred it to pieces, but the irresistible aroma of my sleeping prey beckoned me. Although glad for this easy meal laid before me, I once more felt cheated, but this time out of the thrill of the hunt, the intoxicating scent of fear, and the blissful screams of terror and pain as I decimated my prey.

However, the stench of death lingering over the female almost stopped me in my tracks. Her meat was foul, poisoned, and decaying. Surprisingly, it didn't repulse me the way it normally should have. The poison coursing through her was familiar to me. It was mine, but not quite.

Nevertheless, the female's underlying scent still made my mouth water, and my innards knot. But it wasn't hunger that triggered that reaction. Something about her didn't make me want to feed or maim... I wanted to claim her.

But why?

The female was a weak and helpless creature, visibly at death's door. Killing her would be a mercy. Killing her would grant me the pleasure of the destruction I craved. And yet, my skin was heating in an unnatural fashion, while my blood boiled, and my cock swelled, gradually growing erect.

Surely, the sickness coursing through her was messing with my head.

In one powerful jump, I leapt onto the bed, landing on my hind legs at her feet. I dropped to my knees, my hands on each side of her calves. A wave of fury swelled through me when the impact didn't wake her, even if the mattress shook under my sudden weight. The wretched female was denying me the terror that was rightfully mine before I ended her life.

But that scent...

I yanked the thin blanket covering her and sniffed her legs up to her crotch. Blood rushed to my cock, and it hardened painfully as a powerful need set my loins ablaze. With a single swipe of my claws, I ripped her flimsy dress to shreds, scratching her skin in the process. A few beads of blood seeped out of a shallow cut right above her navel. A painful growl rumbled out of my throat as another wave of burning need twisted my insides.

On instinct, I licked the blood and nearly spilled my seed. I released a powerful howl then rubbed my snout all over her skin as I inhaled her scent, heedless of the stench of death that failed to hide her more alluring aroma. I lingered for a brief instant between her breasts where it was a little stronger before sniffing a path up to her neck.

A flurry of nonsensical images began flashing before my eyes. The female was smiling at me with a tender expression. In the next image, she was kissing me. I could almost taste her on my tongue. Then she was naked, her back arched, and her face dissolved in an air of pure bliss as she cried out in ecstasy. The woman curled up against my wolf's flank, rubbing her face against my fur. And then she was laughing while throwing a stick.

I shook my head, infuriated by what had to be some kind of mind trick. My prey was creating some sort of distraction while pretending to be asleep. I slammed both my hands on the mattress on each side of her head to wake her. She remained still. Anger surged within me to be thus ignored. I grabbed her shoulders with both hands, my claws sinking into her flesh as I shook her.

No reaction.

However, the smell of her blood called to me. I leaned forward to lick it. But movement at the edge of my vision had me jerking my head to the left. The sight of her palpitating artery whipped the burning need in my loins into a frenzy. Her scent—

more potent in the crook of her neck—wiped out what control I had remaining.

The savage side lurking at the edge of my consciousness took over. I only realized that I had bitten her when the divine taste of blood exploded on my taste buds—tainted though it was. Any rational thought fled my mind as I surrendered to my feral side. I emitted an enraged growl, furious to have been denied her terror. But I would punish her by tearing her apart. Opening my mouth wide, I lunged to rip her throat out, but a blinding light shot out from her chest.

I howled in pain and jumped backwards off the bed, away from the unnatural light stabbing my eyes. Arm raised before my face as protection, I blinked and tried to assess the source of the threat.

To my shock a tall silhouette approached the bed from the right. I couldn't clearly see who it belonged to under the glaring light. Then it suddenly faded to a weak glow on the woman's chest. Only then did I realize it emanated from a golden necklace I had previously ignored. But that, too, I dismissed from my thoughts. The male held my entire focus.

Where did he come from? There were no other entrances into this space. Had he been here the whole time? If so, how had I not noticed?

He doesn't have a scent...

That sudden realization took me aback. Everything had a scent.

In the split second that it took me to register all of this information, the male sat on the bed next to the female. He tilted his head as he examined the mangled wound my first bite had left on the fleshy part of the woman's shoulder, just above her left clavicle. Seeming completely unfazed and unbothered by my presence, he glanced back at me with an unimpressed expression.

"Tsk, tsk. So messy! That's no way to treat a lady," he said in a conversational tone.

His lack of fear in my presence infuriated me. But seeing him lean forward and kiss the woman's lips shattered something inside me. A single word exploded in my mind.

"MINE!"

Blind fury swept over me. I lunged at the male, who moved away at an impossible speed, sending me crashing against the headboard of the bed. He was but a couple of meters to my right. I leapt forward and swiped my claws at him, but once more, he moved at such dizzying speed that it almost looked as if he had vanished and reappeared near the window. He raised a taunting eyebrow and smirked provocatively.

I roared with rage and jumped towards him, hoping to pin him down on the floor before feasting on his face to wipe that mocking grin off. This time, he didn't just dodge my attack, he twirled out of the way towards the door. I crashed hard into the dresser, my teeth rattling in my head as I slumped to the floor. Pain radiated in my right shoulder, which had connected solidly against the corner of the dresser. I jumped back to my feet only to find the male leaning against the door frame, legs and arms crossed.

"Did that hurt, pup? Such unnecessary violence," he said with the most disingenuous air of sympathy laced with a hint of disapproval. "You need to rein in that temper, or Amara will choose *me* over a mindless animal like *you*."

Amara!

I knew that name. It awakened a powerful longing and a rabid possessiveness. Enraged, I swiped at the dresser, tearing off part of the wood, and sending the lamp sitting on top flying towards the foul male. He effortlessly sidestepped it, then swiftly backed away when I started running towards him. A buzzing sound resonated behind him as he appeared to be yanked backwards out of the room. Only once he turned the corner did I realize a pair of bug wings hung from his back.

I didn't have time to try and make sense of how these

appendages suddenly appeared on him. Instead, I burst out into the corridor to find him only a couple of meters away from me. My mouth watered at the thought of his blood pouring down my throat and of the sound of his bones shattering between my teeth while he screeched for a mercy that would never come. To my dismay, just when I would have caught him, the stripes beneath his blue skin glowed brightly, blinding me. The next second, he had vanished, replaced by a giant bat that flew to the end of the hallway. If not for him turning back into his oddly painted human form, I wouldn't have believed it was truly him who had morphed into a different shape.

This time, he leaned against the railing of the stairs, crossed his legs again, then began to pick at some non-existent dirt under his nails.

"Fight me, you coward!" I growled, my words barely intelligible to my own ears.

I couldn't recall ever having to use speech with prey. But then, I couldn't recall ever being able to indulge in the hunt. What vague memory I had of my past awakenings involved some sort of cage that prevented me from answering the call of the moon.

But this taunting, I knew with certainty that I'd never experienced it before.

"You're not worth my time," he replied dismissively. "I've squashed bigger beasts than you without breaking a sweat."

You will pay dearly for this disrespect.

Snarling, fangs bared, I dropped to all fours and ran towards him. His relaxed stance as he calmly watched me approach had a red haze of rage descending before my eyes.

"You know, maybe I will kill you after all and turn your pelt into a decorative carpet," he said pensively as he watched me barreling down towards him.

Moments before I would reach him, he threw his legs over

the railing of the staircase and casually slid down the length of the railing to the ground floor.

I growled in frustration before racing down the stairs after him.

"Yes, I'll make love to Amara on your pelt in front of a fire," he taunted, his elbow resting on the railing at the base of the stairs.

Images of him rutting over my woman had me foaming at the mouth. I emitted a savage roar and swiped at the male's face, who was still casually leaning against the ramp. To my dismay, my claws passed through a mirage that vanished into smoke. Then I saw the bat again, flying half the length of the corridor before turning right into an open door.

My heart soared, realizing the foolish male would soon run out of place to flee. He should have exited the house instead of seeking refuge in its bowels. A single thought dominated my mind: catching and eviscerating my prey. I would bathe in his blood and feast on his heart.

The coward continued to flee, leading me to the lowest level of the house. I couldn't even enjoy the thrill of the chase. He had me too enraged, and the absence of the scent of fear deprived me of that extra jolt of adrenaline. The wretch had no scent *at all*. He didn't scream, only mocked and laughed at me.

A triumphant roar bellowed out of me when the fool ran the full length of the lower floor into a dark room at the end. There would be no exit, no escape for him. Now came the time for retribution.

I ran on all fours to the entrance of the room, then rose to my hind legs as I filled the doorframe. The male stood with his back to the wall, a defiant glimmer in his red eyes. Only then did it finally register that he wasn't some powerful sorcerer with glowing runes on his body. He was something else, as per his red eyes and vertical pupils. But whatever he was, his death would come at my hands.

"I will feast on your innards!" I hissed before dashing forward.

The male remained still instead of trying to run away. A sense of doom crashed over me when he gave me an eager, almost victorious smile. Something was wrong, but I was already mid-leap.

Then I felt it.

A tingling sensation washed over me as I crossed a field of magic. A few feet before I would land half-on top of my prey, I crashed into an invisible wall, then fell down onto the stone floor with a loud thud. Half-dazed, I shook my head and jumped back onto my feet only to see the dreaded familiar circle illuminate around me as magical symbols came to life.

"No, Remus. You won't," the male said, sounding almost bored. "Enjoy your time out, pup."

Without another word, he casually strutted out of the room, circling around the magical cage that kept me trapped. I screamed, howled, and trashed pointlessly against it. I knew this magic. I couldn't remember when or how, but I'd been confined by it before. No matter how viciously I battered the invisible wall, it wouldn't yield.

I was trapped.

~

I stirred, feeling like death warmed over, lying on the cold hard floor, my cheek pressed against the unyielding stone. Every muscle felt sore, and my fingertips ached as if someone had attempted to rip my nails out. My eyelids fluttered as I grog- gily pushed myself up. As the fog clouding my mind lifted, I glanced around the room.

My magic circle!

I couldn't remember the event of the previous night. But I

shouted with joy upon realizing that some way, somehow, I had found my way back into the restraining circle. I jumped to my feet only for my joy to instantly shatter. The taste of iron lingered on my tongue, and streaks of blood had dried around my claws and fingers.

Human blood.

Amara's blood.

"My Flame," I whispered, horrified.

I darted out of the room, the wards letting me through as I no longer represented a threat. I raced up the stairs, nearly losing my footing in my haste to reach my woman. I shouted her name, fear twisting my insides upon seeing the damage my werewolf's claws had left on the railing of the stairs leading to the second floor. I irrupted into Amara's room, further distraught by the destruction of her dresser before my gaze finally landed on my woman.

A choked sound of relief escaped me when I found her lying peacefully in the bed. She was wearing a different nightgown than the last one I had put on her. That one now lay in a shredded pile next to the dresser. I snorted with conflicting emotions upon seeing a neatly folded pair of pants on top of it.

I addressed a silent thank you to Lyall as I approached Amara. My chest constricted upon finding her skin completely cold. She wasn't breathing and had no pulse.

My mate was dead.

But more importantly, she was still whole. The vicious scar of my bite on her neck had been properly cleansed. I didn't have to ask who had done it. Even the sheets had been changed so that she wouldn't lie on blood-stained blankets.

Once more, I silently thanked the doppelganger. I had no memory of what transpired last night, but the traces of claws on the dresser and my Flame's lacerated nightgown hinted about how savage I had become. I didn't know how Lyall managed to get me in my cage while ensuring that I didn't maim Amara to the point that rebirth wouldn't be possible. But I was grateful to be alive.

I gently kissed my mate's cold lips, fetched the pants and put them on, then began the long wait until her rebirth.

CHAPTER 21
AMARA

I emerged from the most wonderful slumber of my life. An unusual energy coursed through me. I felt strong, incredibly rested, and rejuvenated. The intense brightness that stabbed at my eyes forced me to blink a few times before they adjusted. Although I'd lived in this house for well over a month before I set off on this most improbable adventure, it felt as if I was seeing it for the first time.

The world looked brighter, the colors more vivid with shades I never noticed before. Every detail stood out even more to me, from the patterns of the wood on the floor, to the delicate texture of the plaster on the molding around the corners of the ceiling. The acuity of my hearing also blew me away like picking up the gentle rustling for the sheer curtains swaying to the barely noticeable draft seeping in through the window and the quickly approaching footsteps outside the room, muffled though the sound was.

But the biggest difference had to be how I could now detect the subtle nuances of every scent. And right now, the most beloved of all scents wafted to me through the closed door, revealing the identity of the newcomer before he even entered the room.

After a discreet knock, the door opened on Remus. The wave of emotion that crashed over me got my throat too constricted to speak.

"My Flame!" Remus whispered.

His face constricted in a way that made it hard to tell whether he wanted to smile or cry. But in a couple of long strides, Remus rushed to my side and pulled me into his embrace. He crushed my lips with a desperate kiss into which he poured all the love, distress, sorrow, hope, and joy he had endured over the past few weeks.

I held him tightly, responding in kind with all the love and devotion he inspired me. Right here, right now, in this man's arms, I felt home. He broke the kiss, and I buried my face in his neck, inhaling his scent deeply. Nine Hells! He was so intoxicating. It went beyond the pleasant spicy aroma. It was the emotion that smelling him invoked in me, the way one felt when being wrapped in a warm blanket, devouring a cinnamon roll freshly out of the oven, or coming home during a winter storm to a hot cup of cocoa. Remus embodied warmth, comfort, safety, and love.

He gently leaned back to be able to look at me, tenderness with a hint of worry on his handsome face.

"How do you feel?" he asked.

"Amazing!" I said with enthusiasm before suddenly feeling self-conscious. "How do I look?"

"Breathtaking, as always," Remus replied, the sincerity undeniable in his voice.

While reassured, I couldn't resist hopping off the bed to go to the standing mirror in the corner of the room. A mere glimpse in the mirror confirmed the truth of his words. I *did* look breathtaking, even though I technically remained 'identical' to the original Amara. However, there was something more to me now.

My skin had reclaimed its dark complexion without the gray undertone that had tainted it in the last stages of my illness. It had a mesmerizing glow, as if sun-kissed with golden highlights. A silver ring now surrounded my irises, giving me an other-worldly look. My breasts seemed a bit fuller, but definitely perkier as they stood proudly under the thin fabric of my night-gown. My waist looked narrower and my hips rounder, blessing me with the perfect hourglass figure that would have any woman drooling with envy. Although my body remained utterly femi-nine, the muscles of my arms and legs were a lot more defined and hinted at far greater power than my otherwise delicate appearance would suggest.

I brushed my curly hair back—which was longer and fuller than before—to expose my ears. I didn't know how I felt about finding them still almost entirely human. Upon closer inspection, one could see that the rounded tip was slightly pointier than before. However, it remained subtle enough that no one would suspect that I was now a werewolf. Thankfully, my transforma-tion didn't make me hairy. I wouldn't have been too keen on that part.

"I do look good," I said timidly.

"More than good, my love," Remus said tenderly, wrapping his arms around me, his broad chest pressing against my back. "Over the next few days, we'll have to teach you how to use your new talents."

"Actually, we should start now. I feel incredibly restless, like I'm bursting at the seams."

Remus laughed.

"Our pups are like that, always overflowing with energy and running all over creation. It gets exhausting just looking at them."

"I can imagine," I said with a chuckle before freeing myself from his embrace to face him. "If they feel anything like what I'm feeling right now, they must be wild."

He chuckled. "They can be. But we should feed you first. You've been sick for days and haven't eaten or drunk anything in forever. You must be famished!"

I paused to assess myself for a moment, then almost immediately shook my head. Sure, I wouldn't mind a bite, but I couldn't say I was hungry.

"Honestly, what I really need right now is to move. I'm feeling so incredibly antsy, I might start climbing the walls," I said sheepishly before realizing I was shifting restlessly on my feet. "It seems like being reborn reset the hunger meter."

Remus hesitated for another second before bowing his head in concession.

"Alright, my Flame. Let's go burn that excess energy of yours," he said with indulgence.

I squealed, and all but raced him down the stairs before shooting outside. In passing, I absentmindedly noticed that the dresser in my room had been replaced, and that parts of the door frame and staircase's railing seemed to be made of newer wood. I could imagine what might have caused the need to make these changes, but there would be time later to discuss it. For now, I wanted to embrace this new body and how it would allow me to experience the world in a completely different way.

I almost leapt down the stairs of the front porch and took a few steps forward then stopped on the pavement leading to the bridge. Arms spread wide, my face lifted towards the warm caress of the late morning sun, I inhaled deeply. It felt like breathing life itself into my lungs, saturating every cell in my body with an energy that borderline the divine. Even the cold stones beneath my bare feet seemed to want to communicate with me. For the first time in my life, I sensed a form of communion with the natural world around me in a way that transcended the physical realm.

Then, for no apparent reason, I started running towards the woods surrounding the estate. I should be wincing at every step as my bare feet pounded the ground covered in grass, fallen branches, and rocks. Yet it felt like running in the most comfortable hiking shoes. The short skirt of my light nightgown whipped around my thighs as I ran like the wind.

Footsteps behind me quickly caught up as Remus ran by my side, also barefoot, wearing nothing more than a pair of pants. The air of pure joy on his face reflected the one that filled my heart to bursting. I was healed, free, and sharing a unique experience as I embraced my awakening to my new true self.

Trees flew by us at dizzying speed as we raced through the forest. Before long, my mate's attitude changed in a subtle fashion. It took me a moment to realize that he was no longer running alongside me but was actually chasing me. I immediately joined the game, loving the fact that I was now his prey. A very willing prey who wanted to be caught, but that he needed to earn.

Something shifted inside of me. Adrenaline pumping, I redoubled the speed at which I ran, weaving around the trees, random mounds, and boulders in our path to make it harder for him. To my shock, claws jutted out of my toes and fingertips. They dug into the ground, propelling me further with each step. A small voice at the back of my head screamed that I was moving too fast, and that I would soon end up crashing into a tree or otherwise hurting myself. But I couldn't stop. My body seemed to know instinctively what to do.

More than once, Remus almost caught me, his hand brushing against my hip or arm. Each time, it gave me an instant burst of energy that had me dashing ahead even faster. To my shock, as he was closing in on me too fast for me to have a chance of circling around a massive tree, I caught myself leaping onto it instead. The claws from my hands clung to the bark, but I didn't hang in there. Instead I used the sole of my feet to kick myself off the trunk, and backflipped over Remus half a beat before he would have nabbed me.

I twisted my body midair so that I would face the ground and landed on my hands. I pushed forward to go into a run on all fours. However, my movements were awkward, and I found myself flopping on my belly. My body knew that I could do it but was simply doing it wrong. Sadly, I didn't know how to fix it yet.

Before I could get back to my feet to resume my escape, my mate's warm body settled on top of me, pinning me to the ground. I tried to knock him off, but his teeth closing on my nape felt like lightning struck my spine. It hadn't actually done so or caused any pain, but my body immediately went limp with an all-consuming need to submit to my alpha's dominance. A whining whimper rose from my throat with a will of its own. It felt odd, but I understood that some wolf traits were now an integral part of me and we're instinctively kicking in.

Remus flipped me onto my back. His pitch-black sclera, his golden eyes glowing in an exotic fashion, and his fangs bared in a menacing snarl had a bolt of lust exploding in my core. Something primal snapped inside of me. I grabbed his face with both hands and crushed his lips with mine. Remus emitted another growl, this time deeper, hungrier, that resonated directly in my clit.

The scent of his arousal struck me with force, acting like a potent aphrodisiac that had moisture instantly pooling between my thighs. I couldn't tell if my strong reaction was due to the novelty of me now being able to perceive it. Either way, it had my inner walls palpitating with the need to be filled.

Remus broke the kiss, his fangs softly grazing my skin on a path down to my neck. His hands boldly caressed my body. As his lips wandered towards my chest, my mate emitted a frustrated growl. The sound of my nightgown ripping under a decisive swipe from his claws made me realize the fabric obstructing his exploration of me had prompted this destructive response.

Far from upsetting me, it heightened my own arousal. There

was something incredibly erotic about the almost feral way my man was acting. This hint of danger, of being at the mercy of the wild beast who would have given his life for me was the biggest turn on.

I arched my back and moaned as his mouth closed around my left nipple. This new body's sensitivity was off the charts, each touch and sensation enhanced a thousandfold. The rough texture of Remus's tongue on my taut little bud made my toes curl. I sank my fingers into his silky mane and lifted my chest for greater contact as he licked and sucked on my nipple.

His left hand glided down my waist and over my pelvis before slipping between my thighs. I spread my legs to give him better access. My underwear met the same fate as my nightgown. But all I cared about were his thick fingers teasing my slit and my clit before sinking inside of me. My inner walls instantly contracted around them, greedily drawing them in deeper to fill the endless void that screamed for him.

The scent of my own arousal, combined with his, further fanned the fire burning in the pit of my stomach in a vicious cycle that grew exponentially in intensity. I ground my sex against his hand, seeking greater contact as he crooked his fingers and began to expertly rub on my sensitive bundle of nerves with each motion.

My climax came hard and fast. I shouted my mate's name as waves of pleasure crashed over me. A strangled moan escaped me when the searing heat of his mouth settled on my clit. It shouldn't have been possible, but the inferno raging inside me burnt even more fiercely. I crested higher until a second orgasm slammed into me before I ever recovered from the first one.

My entire body thrummed with bliss as my mate continued to devour me, his free hand caressing me as I slowly came back to reality. He kissed his way back up, reclaiming my mouth with a possessiveness that had me tingling in all the right places. I spread my legs wider, making my desires clear.

He didn't resist.

Remus settled between my thighs and pushed himself in. The first thrust made it clear that my rebirth had reset *everything*. I almost growled in frustration as my body resisted him. Protective as always, my mate began inserting himself with slow and careful movements. But I wanted him to throw all caution to the wind and unleash his beast on me.

I sank my claws into his back. For a brief instant, I feared I might have broken skin, which had not been my intention. Thankfully, the absence of the smell of blood reassured me. However, it had the intended effect. Remus growled against my lips and started thrusting into me a bit more forcefully until my body yielded.

We both hissed at the burn of his sudden invasion yet welcomed the pleasure-pain it gave us. Remus didn't pause to let me adjust to his girth and pursued his rocking motion, his speed gradually picking up. To my dismay, as soon as I started gyrating beneath him, wanting more, my man suddenly pulled out and flipped me onto my stomach.

I instantly propped myself up on all fours. The pool of lava swirling in the pit of my stomach erupted in powerful streams of liquid flames that flooded my veins. My burning anticipation was quickly sated as my mate rammed himself in with one powerful movement. A blissful growl vibrated in my throat as I began to rock back and forth, meeting him thrust for thrust. That same primal instinct resurfaced as Remus started taking me deeper and harder.

I tumbled down a vortex of bliss, each stroke of his cock, each caress of his knot against my sensitive spot, setting off electric sparks on my nerve endings. His claws pricking my skin as he firmly gripped my hips had my own claws extruding further, digging into the ground. The light breeze caressed our feverish bodies while carrying the sound of our voluptuous moans and growls.

As pleasure built towards yet another apogee, something shifted inside me. An odd pressure in the lower half of my face finally took on its full meaning when a sharp sting stabbed my gums before a pair of fangs descended. My spine appeared to expand, and my muscles tensed. But Remus's fingers rubbing my clit just as his cock was striking my sweet spot at the perfect angle thwarted whatever phenomenon had attempted to take place.

I threw my head back and cried out as ecstasy swept me away for the third time. The sound that came out of me was a strange mix between a shout and a howl. Remus emitted a savage roar, his grip tightening painfully on my hips. At first, I thought he had also surrendered to bliss, but he continued to pump in and out of me, his movements erratic until he got his emotions under control again.

This time, as soon as I regained my own composure, the 'phenomenon' that had begun to manifest itself before I tumbled over the edge came back with a vengeance. My fangs ached, my skin burned, and something in my throat swelled. It felt like having some sort of glands. But my muscles also joined the fray as a surge of energy coursed through them.

I suddenly pulled away from Remus, mid-thrust. He appeared stunned when I turned around, still kneeling, and bared my fangs at him with a menacing growl. His stupor gave way to an air of pure lust that had my nipples harden painfully while more moisture trickled down my inner thighs. I lunged at him, pinning him to the ground on his back. He didn't resist or fight back, his lips stretching into a feral smile, exposing the sharp tips of his intimidating set of double fangs.

Still driven by instinct, I rested both my palms on his broad chest, my claws pricking his skin, and I impaled myself on his cock in one swift movement. He threw his head back, his face dissolved in an air of pure bliss as he growled with pleasure. My mouth watered, and the aching sensation in my fangs went up another notch as I stared at his exposed throat.

I began to ride him with unbridled abandon. By the gods was he beautiful and all mine. The world around us ceased to exist. All that mattered was the perfect man beneath me, his hands on my hips holding me as if he feared I would disappear, his cock filling me to the brim as he thrusted upward in counterpoint to my own movements, the sound of our voices mingling in a voluptuous chant, and the infinite love that burned in his eyes locked with mine.

A tingling sensation at the back of my head nearly broke the lustful trance that had engulfed me. I almost cast it out to refocus on the intense pleasure building within me. But it persisted, needling me like a gnat buzzing in my ear. Only once I granted it my attention did a doorway I never expected opened. It wasn't something to which I could give a physical description. It felt like a new channel of communication or level of consciousness had been established.

And then I heard his beloved voice in my mind.

"Bond with me, my Flame," Remus said telepathically.

My eyes widened, and the aching in my fangs intensified exponentially to almost painful levels. My glands swelled even more. And a cool liquid dripped from the tips of my fangs. I didn't know how to reciprocate but never got a chance to.

Before I could respond, my mate slipped his right hand between my legs and rubbed my clit with his thumb. My spine seized, and my orgasm crash into me with the violence of a tsunami. I didn't cry out. I roared, and guided by instinct, I darted forward, burying my fangs into his neck. Through my voluptuous haze, I heard Remus roar even more savagely than I did at the same time his seed exploded inside me, filling me to the brim. Simultaneously, my own glands deflated as my essence flowed through my fangs into him.

Still flying high on the wings of ecstasy, I vaguely felt him yank my head back, removing my fangs from his neck. Then the sting of his bite in my own neck quickly faded, replaced by liquid bliss flooding my veins. It triggered another climax that left me wrecked and boneless as I collapsed onto his chest, destroyed.

"I love you, my Flame," Remus whispered, his arms tightly wrapped around me. "Welcome back."

Head resting on his chest, I smiled and tightened my embrace. "I love you, too, Remus. Thank you for bringing me back and for never giving up on me."

We remained in each other's embrace, locked together by his knot, and linked for eternity, body and soul by our bond. With Fate, the Gods, and nature as our witnesses, we were one.

EPILOGUE
AMARA

In the week that followed my rebirth and bonding with my soulmate, Remus and I divided our time between marathon-length sessions of love making, him watching me gorge on obscene amounts of food—as my body apparently needed the fuel to finalize the changes it was undergoing—and then training my new abilities.

At first, we believed I would only have a werewolf form, which looked semi-human. To our mutual delight, we discovered that I actually also had a full wolf form. I still struggled with both of them, mostly when it came to running on all fours. My stupid brain kept wanting to keep my hind legs much too straight in that position. It had me traipsing around with my butt sticking up in the air. Remus systematically teased me by saying I only had to ask if I wanted a spanking, there was no need to flaunt my rear end like that.

He would then take off running before I could get my hands on him to give him a spanking of his own. The wretch was much too fast for me. Not only was he stronger, but he also mastered his body in all its forms. Still, I was steadily catching up and didn't doubt that it was only a matter of time before we were evenly matched.

However, with my still stunted shapeshifting abilities, we both believed it wiser to ride our horses all the way back to the Weaver's house. For a reason I couldn't explain, a sudden wave of apprehension settled over me as her gates quietly opened upon our approach. I wanted to believe it was merely the guardian imps sitting on the pillars of the gates who unnerved me. Their owlish eyes glowed yellow as they watched us enter, the weight of their stares lingering as we rode up the path to the humble hut the Weaver lived in.

We dismounted our horses—Remus rushing to my side to help me down in the most adorable display of chivalry—then walked up to the door, hand in hand. It parted before us, once more revealing the Weaver already sitting behind the table directly in front of it, clearly expecting us. A mysterious smile stretched her lips while her purple eyes sparked with either a mischievous glimmer, or a taunting one. Then again, with her, it was likely a mix of both.

I gasped when the grinding sound of chairs gliding towards her table startled me. I had expected the one to the left of the door as she had then the same thing when I first came to see her. But I had not expected the presence of the second chair hidden behind the open door, which also slid over the wooden floors to stop right across the table from her, next to the first chair.

I scrunched my face at her when her taunting smirk broadened, confirming she was enjoying messing with her guests... or at least with me. We both took our seats in front of her.

"Cute ears, Amara," the Weaver said in an amused voice.

My cheeks immediately heated. As part of my shifting troubles, I would occasionally end up stuck with my ears remaining pointy instead of resuming their normal rounded human shape. After trying for nearly half an hour of shifting in and out of my wolf and werewolf forms and back to human in between to no avail, I finally gave up. I had hoped that my hair would cover them enough that she wouldn't notice. But obviously, you couldn't hide anything from Cliona Nox.

"But I'm surprised that you both came riding horses," she continued with the same shit-eating grin.

"I'm still clumsy with shifting and running as a wolf," I muttered, embarrassed.

"You're learning very quickly, my love," Remus interjected with a protectiveness that had me melting from within.

I gave him a grateful smile, which he returned with a tender one.

The Weaver chuckled. "Yes, shapeshifting abilities can take a while to master. But I see that you two are bonded. Well done," she said, gesturing with her chin at the bite mark on my shoulder, barely visible at the edge of my collar.

"Yes we are, thank you," I said timidly. "As you can guess, we are here for me to repay my debt, but also to ask about Remus."

She tilted her head to the side and raised an inquisitive eyebrow.

"What about Remus?" she asked.

I shifted in my seat and licked my lips nervously. "It's about the venom in his blood."

"You already took care of that with the bonding bite," she said with a dismissive gesture then shifted her attention to my mate. "Your fluids are now safe for others, unless you make it otherwise."

"Excuse me?" Remus asked, his confusion reflecting mine.

"The same way you can inject venom through your fangs, you can flood your bloodstream with it as a defense mechanism. This way, you will continue to benefit from the protection it afforded you when you explore dangerous places as it naturally repels potential predators."

"That's... that's fantastic," Remus said, stunned.

The Weaver nodded. "However, beware. The antibodies Amara gave you will neutralize the venom within a few hours, less even based on the amount you flooded yourself with."

"Duly noted," he replied with a serious expression.

"What about the full moon?" I insisted nervously. "Will it still affect him... and me for that matter?"

She smiled. "You are both werewolves. The urge to shift will remain once the full moon rises. That will not change. I cannot say whether you will be able to resist it. Only time will tell. I can only say that it will be extremely difficult. That said, neither of you will be mindless, rabid beasts. You will retain control of your mental faculties, which is all that matters."

My sigh of relief died in my throat, and my chest constricted seeing Remus blink rapidly to stem the tears that clearly pricked his eyes. In that instant, I realized that the curse that had plagued his entire life had finally been lifted. For the first time, he was no longer a freak, a threat, the boogeyman that mothers warned their children against.

I reached for his hand and gave it a gentle squeeze. He glanced at it before peering back up at me. The depth of gratitude and adoration in his eyes wrecked me.

"Thank you, my Flame," he whispered.

I gave him a shaky smile, overwhelmed by emotion. "No, my love. It is I who thanks you. None of this would be happening had you not agreed to embark on this journey with me and see it through to the bitter end."

He leaned forward and kissed me. It was brief but expressed everything that could never be put into words. He pressed his forehead against mine, and I silently thanked the gods, and all the people who contributed in even the smallest capacity in making this happen. To think it all began with a suggestion from the adorable Ronika to seek the Weaver. I couldn't wait to go tell her the good news.

A clicking sound snapped us out of this moment of tenderness. Embarrassed, we jerked our heads towards the Weaver to see her removing a strange stylus from an intricately sculpted jewelry box. It was made of wood, adorned with gold and precious gems. The stylus itself also appeared to be made of gold. From the same box, Cliona retrieved a glass ampule with a head that looked like it could fit perfectly into the hollow end of the stylus.

She extended a hand towards me. Immediately understanding her unspoken request, I placed my left hand in hers. A shiver coursed through me at the incredible softness and warmth of her palm against my skin. For a reason I couldn't explain, I had expected her touch to be cold and unpleasant, as if the slightest contact with her would drain the very life force out of you. Instead, it made me long to be drawn into her embrace, which would likely feel like being wrapped in the divine light of the gods.

Although she kept her eyes on my arm, the smug smile on the Weaver's sensuous lips and her discreet chuckle seemed to imply she knew exactly what thoughts were crossing my mind. My cheeks heated, but I kept quiet. Cliona turned my hand around, palm facing up, and the inner side of my wrist exposed. She ran her finger along the barely visible vein in my wrist. My jaw dropped as it immediately protruded. A cool sensation spread over a small radius around the vein. I suspected she had also disinfected the area with her touch.

Cliona deftly stuck the pointy edge of the stylus in my vein. To my pleasant surprise, it didn't hurt, the pricking sensation almost nonexistent. She placed the glass ampule at the end of the stylus, and it immediately started to fill with my blood. I stared in fascination as the patterns engraved on the golden stylus suddenly lit up, revealing a series of magical runes. To my shock, they shifted, forming new runes a few times while my blood in the ampule appeared illuminated from within. By the time the runes faded, my blood had turned into a clear liquid.

A wave of unease twisted my insides as I watched the Weaver remove the ampule from the stylus and hold it before her eyes with a triumphant expression. The vertical slits of her pupils dilated, almost swallowing her purple irises. Her gaze suddenly flicked towards me, her pupils narrowing back to their normal size. She tilted her head, an almost predatory expression descending over her features as she lowered her hand and placed the ampule inside the box without ever looking away from me.

"Do not fear, little Amara. I pledged that no harm would ever come to you from this, and that I'll only use it to do good. That has not and never will change," she said in a soft voice, although I didn't miss the underlying hint of hardness.

"I didn't mean to offend you," I said, apologetically.

Her face softened, and she gave me a stiff nod. "Only a fool would not worry about giving a part of them that could be used in a devastating way against them, especially by one such as I. But our affair is concluded."

"Thank you for saving our lives," I said sheepishly.

"No, child. Thank *you* for saving many more lives than you realize," she said in a mysterious tone.

My tongue burned with the urge to pry further as to who she was referring to. However, Remus addressed the Weaver, reminding me of the last important topic I had forgotten to bring up.

"Before we go, I found the Lover's Blight that was hidden in Amara's workshop. But we have no clue who was bringing it there, how to find them, or how vulnerable my mate might be to another similar attack," he said in a concerned voice.

The Weaver smiled and absentmindedly ran her hand over her single long braid.

"You met the would-be assassin outside the Haunted Woods," she said, matter-of-factly.

"So it was her!" Remus exclaimed, anger seeping into his voice.

"Mmhmm," Cliona said with a mysterious expression. "She wanted to stop you from saving Amara."

"But why?" I exclaimed, baffled.

"And where can I find her?" Remus demanded.

"To prevent you from giving me this serum," the Weaver said to me with a shrug while waving at the ampule in the box. She then turned her attention to my mate. "As for you, you don't get to find her."

"WHAT?! But—"

"No, Remus Beltaine!" Cliona said in an imperious tone that made me want to wither in my chair. "Your part in this story is done. The witch is no longer your concern. You had one chance to defeat her in the forest. As it was extremely slim, you made the right choice by leaving. Now, it falls onto another to make her pay for her many crimes."

"But she threatened my mate!" he exclaimed, outraged. "I will not sit by idle fearing the day she will strike again!"

She made a disdainful gesture. "The threat to your mate has passed. Killing Amara before her rebirth would have prevented me from securing this serum. Had Amara's father survived, the Wheels of Fate would have likely caused him to provide this serum instead. The witch has no quarrel with you or your bloodline, Amara. You were just a casualty in a greater war. Your part is done."

"So we'll never see her again?" I asked, shaken and furious at the callousness with which this stranger had destroyed our innocent lives.

Cliona shook her head. "She's already shifted her focus to another in a vain effort to prevent the inevitable."

"Just promise me that you won't let her get away with this," I said with a hardness that took even me aback.

I had never been the vindictive type. But this woman caused too much harm to simply get away with it and not face the retribution she deserved. The malicious, almost evil expression that settled over the Weaver's face sent a cold shiver running down my spine. In that instant, I almost felt a sliver of pity for the witch.

Almost...

"Have no fear, child," the Weaver said in a chilling voice full of the most lethal promises. "She will pay a thousandfold. Even Death will feel sorry for her."

I swallowed hard, glad that I hadn't gotten myself on her enemies' list.

"Thank you, Weaver. Thanks for everything," I said, rising from my chair.

"Yes, thank you," Remus echoed.

Her face took on an extremely soft expression that I never thought possible from such an intimidating female. It was almost maternal.

"You may call me Cliona," she said with a strange expression, leaving me speechless. "Be happy, Amara. Take good care of your mate."

Something about her troubled me. I couldn't quite put my finger on what. I gave her a smile, slipped my hand into Remus's, and turned to leave. As the door opened before us, I froze, and turned to look at her, shocked by my sudden realization.

"Your eyes," I whispered, stunned. "They're just like his!"

"Like whose?" she asked, her face suddenly closed off.

"Lyall," I replied, studying her reaction.

Remus recoiled and looked at me with confusion.

"No, my love," he said softly, a hint of concern in his voice. "Lyall has red sclera with no irises. The only thing they have in common is the vertical pupils."

I placed my hand on his shoulder in an appeasing gesture while shaking my head, my gaze still locked with the Weaver's.

"That's the way they look by default," I conceded. "But when he's happy, when he shows his more vulnerable side, they change to look exactly like hers, with the white sclera, purple irises, and vertical pupils."

The strangest expression crossed Cliona's face.

"Lyall showed you his true self?"

Although she worded it as a question, it was more of a statement to herself, as if she was trying to digest information she never expected.

"I believe so," I said carefully. "He was beautiful, with a divine aura and ethereal wings… or at least luminous forms behind him that reminded me of wings."

"The silly boy truly loves you that he should reveal himself to this extent," she said pensively.

"So you do know him! Is he your sibling?" I asked.

She burst out laughing, her wistful expression fading to be replaced by her usual mocking demeanor. "My sibling? Oh, how you flatter me child! No, Lyall isn't my brother."

"Do you know of his whereabouts?" Remus asked. "We haven't seen or heard from him since the night of the full moon. I just want to make sure that he's well and unharmed."

Cliona looked at my mate as if she was seeing him for the first time. "You truly are unique, Remus Beltaine. Whatever resentment you may bear Ranael, he has passed on to you his protective and kind heart. Most other males would wish ill on one who coveted their female."

"We owe him a lot. Without him, we likely wouldn't be here," Remus said.

She smiled. "No, Remus. Without him, you would both be dead," she said with an unnerving finality. "But yes, Lyall is fine. There was no point for him to linger and torture himself staring at what he can't have. But don't be sad for him. You helped him make the right choices." She glanced at a bare section of the wall behind the spinning wheel and appeared to examine something before returning her attention to us. "Thanks to you, the path to his happiness now lies before him."

I blinked in confusion before looking at the wall. Like on my previous visit, it was completely bare. But this confirmed that she could see something there that remained invisible to our eyes.

"Safe journey to you both, and enjoy your new extended life Amara," the Weaver said.

With this, she turned her back to us, and the stool she was sitting on glided silently back to her spinning wheel. I shook my head, unsure as to what feelings I felt towards Cliona. She stirred within me a mix of fear, awe, respect, but also an inexplicable affection.

Remus gently tugged on my hand, snapping me out of my wandering thoughts. Hand in hand, we walked out of the room towards freedom and a new life filled with possibilities.

~

REMUS

Heart pounding, I pushed open the heavy doors into the Howl Inn. The boisterous voices inside turned quiet the moment they saw me standing there with my mate by my side. More than eight weeks had gone by since I walked out of here with Amara on our way to what was deemed not only impossible but flat out suicidal.

Although we were returning victorious, the whole way here,

I dreaded the type of welcome we would receive. After years of being treated as a pariah, I had made my peace with the fact that I would never really be welcomed. But now that I had a mate, things weren't the same. I didn't care about disrespect towards me, but I wouldn't tolerate anyone treating my soulmate the way they had treated me.

Granted, her poison had never been a threat to others, but they could be mean to her simply because of her association with me. My back tensed as we entered the room, every eye leveled on us. To my surprise, they were curious, not hostile as had previously been the norm.

"Remus!" Misty exclaimed, rushing from behind her counter towards us.

We smiled, her infectious joy spreading to us. She drew us both into her embrace, kissing our cheeks in turn, before giving each of us a separate bone crushing hug. Amara giggled at the excessive demonstration of affection from the older woman.

She held my mate by her shoulders, examining her from head to toe before leaning in and taking a good whiff. Under different circumstances, this would have been deemed an extremely rude behavior. But throughout the room, everyone else was doing the same but in a more subtle fashion.

"I knew you would come back! I knew you would beat this," Misty said, her voice suddenly thick with emotion. "There's no more sickness in you! There's no more sickness in either of you!"

As one, everyone started muttering their shock and disbelief.

"Yes, Misty. We're both cured," I said, stunned that I could still speak without my voice cracking.

"And the full moon will no longer turn him rabid," Amara said proudly, slipping an arm around my waist as she leaned against me.

The mutterings went up another notch as the same incredulous expression could be seen on every face.

"All thanks to you, my love," I said, the adoration I felt for her audible in my voice.

Then I turned to the crowd, my eyes locking with the man who had been my brother for many years before things turned sour.

"And to you, Ulric. I wouldn't have made it back in time without your help. I am forever in your debt," I said.

A strange emotion crossed his features before he lifted his chin with a smug expression.

"The pack always stands for its members," he said matter-of-factly.

"Hear, hear!" everyone replied in unison.

I froze, too stunned for words. His gentle, almost apologetic smile snapped me out of my daze. I blinked back the tears pricking my eyes. With that single sentence, he had reclaimed me as a full member of the pack, no longer the pariah. As the future leader of the pack, his word weighed heavily. But more importantly, the others loudly express their agreement with his statement.

Too quickly...

Normally, someone would have questioned, challenged, or balked at his claim. No one did. In that instant, I realized that Ulric had likely started paving the way for my return the same day he escorted me back to the Weaver.

"Come then," Rolf said in a semi-grumpy tone, gesturing for us to sit at their table. "Introduce your bonded mate to the rest of the pack and then share the tale of that wild adventure you embarked on."

"At least, that will be one wild story likely to hold more truth than the tall tales Ludvic loves to shove down our throats at every turn," Ulric said mockingly, looking at an older member of the pack, well-known for his over exaggerations.

His protests drowned under the deluge of friendly jeers and teasing from the others.

I exchanged a glance with my mate, my heart filling with love for the woman who had given me everything.

"I love you, my Flame," I whispered telepathically.

"I love you, too, Remus," she replied.

Hand in hand, we rejoined our pack.

THE END.

CLIONA NOX

AEGARIM

ARRAPHILON

RANAEL

GHARLAKAN

TENTRIAN

LOVERS' BLIGHT

I Married A Naga
I Married A Birdman
I Married A Minotaur
I Married Wonjin
I Married A Merman
I Married A Dragon
I Married A Beast
I Married Krogal
I Married A Dryad
I Married An Incubus
I Married A Mothman
I Married A Catman
I Married Amreth
I Married Kayog

THE MIST
The Mistwalker
The Nightmare
The Mistwalker: A Graphic Novel

DARK TALES
Bluebeard's Curse
The Hunchback

THE SHADOW REALMS
Destined to the Wraith
Destined to the Reaper
Destined to the Lycan
Destined to the Doppelganger

VALOS OF SONHADRA
Unfrozen
Iced

BLOOD MAIDENS OF KARTHIA
Claiming Thalia

EMPATHS OF LYRIA
An Alien For Christmas

OTHER
True As Steel
Alien Awakening
Heart of Stone
Oops! I Summoned a Liderc

ABOUT REGINE

USA Today bestselling author Regine Abel is a fantasy, paranormal and sci-fi junkie. Anything with a bit of magic, a touch of the unusual, and a lot of romance will have her jumping for joy. She loves creating hot alien warriors and no-nonsense, kick-ass heroines that evolve in fantastic new worlds while embarking on action-packed adventures filled with mystery and the twists you never saw coming.

Before devoting herself as a full-time writer, Regine had surrendered to her other passions: music and video games! After a decade working as a Sound Engineer in movie dubbing and live concerts, Regine became a professional Game Designer and Creative Director, a career that has led her from her home in Canada to the US and various countries in Europe and Asia.

Facebook
https://www.facebook.com/regine.abel.author/

Website
https://regineabel.com

Regine's Rebels Reader Group

https://www.facebook.com/groups/ReginesRebels/

Newsletter

http://smarturl.it/RA_Newsletter

Goodreads

http://smarturl.it/RA_Goodreads

Bookbub

https://www.bookbub.com/profile/regine-abel

Amazon

http://smarturl.it/AuthorAMS